THE CRUSADERS
ISLE OF THE FALLEN

THE CRUSADERS
ISLE OF THE FALLEN

NICHOLAS MORROW

TATE PUBLISHING
AND ENTERPRISES, LLC

The Crusaders: Isle of the Fallen
Copyright © 2015 by Nicholas Morrow. All rights reserved.

No part of this publication may be reproduced, stored in a retrieval system or transmitted in any way by any means, electronic, mechanical, photocopy, recording or otherwise without the prior permission of the author except as provided by USA copyright law.

This novel is a work of fiction. Names, descriptions, entities, and incidents included in the story are products of the author's imagination. Any resemblance to actual persons, events, and entities is entirely coincidental.

The opinions expressed by the author are not necessarily those of Tate Publishing, LLC.

Published by Tate Publishing & Enterprises, LLC
127 E. Trade Center Terrace | Mustang, Oklahoma 73064 USA
1.888.361.9473 | www.tatepublishing.com

Tate Publishing is committed to excellence in the publishing industry. The company reflects the philosophy established by the founders, based on Psalm 68:11,

"The Lord gave the word and great was the company of those who published it."

Book design copyright © 2015 by Tate Publishing, LLC. All rights reserved.
Cover design by Gian Philipp Rufin
Interior design by Manolito Bastasa

Published in the United States of America

ISBN: 978-1-68028-367-9
Fiction / Action & Adventure
15.01.08

Contents

1. Fallout 9
2. Capture 21
3. The Fallen Ones 28
4. Escape 39
5. Exiles 54
6. The Phoenix 63
7. Sever 73
8. Brotherhood 85
9. War 94
10. Celebration 102
11. Recruitment 112
12. Crusade 126
13. Community 150
14. Underground 163
15. Crusade II 181
16. Union 194
17. Duty 210
18. Splinter Cell 232
19. Indoctrination 246
20. Executioners 251
21. Sin 256
22. Inequity 262
23. Truth 268
24. Reformation 282

It's never too late to get to where you're going

—JR

1

Fallout

"Terra! Terra! If you're going to zone out, at least make it seem like you're paying attention you backwater, ingrate!"

How many times had he called me that by now? Just by that day's count, it would have to at least been ten. Maybe eleven. I separated my face from Christian's shoulder after I had given him a nice pool of drool dripping down his sleeve. As I looked around the seating area, everyone had their eyes centered on me, trying their best not to erupt with laughter. Well everyone aside from Captain Stagg over there that is. His face was stone-cold as his eyes attempted to pierce into my very soul trying to deflate it. I bowed my head to apologize, and my necklace of the cross slipped forward dangling in front of my face.

"Forgive me, Captain," I started off saying, "But with all due respect, this is the seventh mission trip for our unit. We all know the protocol by now." I began to wave my hands and nod my head back and forth to emphasize how mundane these briefings had become. "We're heading to a primitive world devoid of the guidance of the Word of our Lord. It's our mission to enlighten them about the truth of all the worlds: There's only one God, and you either adhere to His mercy through servitude or death. We've given that ultimatum so many times it should just be a business card at this point, sir."

I leaned back against the shaking, metal interior of our room and raised up one finger so that the whole team could see. "All we need is one thing," I said.

I got up from my seat and drew my sword, a rapier that had been a memento of my father and thrust its point into the floor as I said, "At the end of the day, we all know that the righteous Word of God will be spread not by the silver of our tongues, but by the crimson of our blades anyway. So it's pointless to go over all of these scenarios regarding how to interact with an indigenous population."

Captain Stagg, a man twice my size, age, and experience as a Crusader shook his head before he spoke, "And this is why you're known only as Terra, the Executioner. You and your affiliation for spilling blood…"

"Hey I learned my impulsivity of killing natives from you, sir," I said with an obvious tone of disrespect as I thought about Kita, my departed friend.

We could all see the pale complexion of his face shift to a bright-red-like texture as he took a step forward toward me. "You and your attitude, Terra—"

"Has saved my life on numerous occasions, Captain," interjected Christian. "Of course, I'll try to exert the most peaceful measures that I can, but, just as my brother said, we'll not be afraid to resort to force if need be. We're going here to help liberate their lives from the dark shackles that bind them, but I have no intention of letting any of my vassals serve as a sacrifice to ensure that these heathens know the truth."

"And that's why he's our king," said Reginald. "He always knows just the magic words to say to make men die for his cause and women die to sleep with him. All hail, Christian!"

There was nothing but silence as we waited for Reginald's tan face to turn white out of shear embarrassment. We tried to hold our tongues, but after a few moments, the whole team broke out into a fit of laughter. Those guys were certainly something else. Here we were moments away from executing the mission that would determine the course of the rest of our lives, and we were giggling away like schoolgirls. I wanted to say that it sickened me, but I too was among them laughing away at Reginald's jest. They were a stupid lot, but they were our stupid lot. They were the family that Christian and I had not had since we lost his father so many years ago.

Their official titles were Crusaders, members of a religious militia that traveled from world to world spreading the Word of God by force if necessary. Well, technically, none of us were Crusaders yet. We were more so cadets or recruits than actual Crusaders at that point. Our unit was filled with war orphans and unwanted misfits that had been recruited by the Crusaders since they were children, and Christian and I were among the newest batch of recruits five years ago. All of us had joined for one reason or another. Some wanted the prestige of being a part of such a noble group. Others wanted the accolades that came with the title, and of course there were a few that just wanted the free meal ticket. Christian and I though were different in that regard. I sat back down and looked down while gazing at the clouds underneath the transparent floor. Looking down at the world below from the confines of that airship, made me feel like I could relate to how God felt. As a boy, I had always wondered why such a supposed benevolent being allowed me to experience such hardships and tragedies in my life, but as I looked down upon the world we would soon be traversing into, I could understand why. From up there, the people looked like specks of dust that we quickly passed over as we circled through the skies. I had never once considered the plights of insects that suffered around me, so why should a being that could look down upon us like that do the same?

No, I knew I shouldn't think like that anymore, or rather I knew that Christian would have a fit if he caught me thinking like that again. According to Christian, the teachings of the Crusaders were supposed to show me how merciful our God was. My suffering all happened for a reason that he was sure made the world a better place in some way was the main point that he always tried to drive into my psyche. With all of his hard work though, all he had managed to do was plant the seeds of his lessons in my mind. No matter how much nourishment he tried to give though, those seeds never took full root. After being in the Order of Crusaders for five years, I certainly believed in the teachings, but I was not nearly as passionate about them as Christian was. Christian tapped me on the shoulder and asked, "So how many people from Earth have been able to soar through the skies like this?"

He knew the answer to that, but he always liked to remind me anyway. Out of all the people that had been recruited by the Crusaders, he and I were the first recruits from Earth, a backwater or primitive world as our superiors referred to it. I never truly was able to wrap my head around the entire concept, but aside from Earth, there were countless worlds parallel to it. The concept was different from being able to see other planets, but was as far as I could get. The science of the matter didn't appeal to me. All I needed to know was that only by using these airships held by the Order, we could travel to other worlds to go on these mission trips.

Jumping between parallel worlds, riding in a flying ship, training to be Crusaders were all beyond the wildest dreams I could ever conjure up in my mind. The simple fact of the matter was that we were in a position that no other person from Earth had been in before, and we were about to reach even higher plateaus soon. I raked my fingers against the ebony tint of my skin as I exhaled a nervous sigh. I may have not been the most devout amongst our unit, but I still wanted to do well on the mission. The magnitude of our mission was finally starting to hit me. It was finally starting to hit all of us as our ship stopped moving and just hovered over a large island.

Whatever anxiety or apprehension we had suddenly was magnified as we got a good look at the island below us. Every airship had the luxury of being installed with a solid glass floor which allowed for any Crusader to feel like God as they scoffed at the heathens below them. This time around, it felt as if that world was scoffing at us though. It was much bigger than we had imagined. Though Earth was labeled a C class world, it was one of the few that actually had multiple geographical areas. Most worlds outside of Earth were the size of a small country and only consisted of one consisted climate year round. As we all just looked down at the world below us, I could hear the nervous tap of someone's foot as his nerves were getting the best of him.

For the last five years, we had trained for that final test, the test that would promote us to the rank of official Crusaders. All of our dreams were anchored down below on that island, and we all had the means to go forth and claim them, but it was still nerve-racking to realize this moment was finally upon us all.

I looked over to Sariah and her younger sister Rebecca. They had a calm demeanor on their faces that made me even more restless. The two of them were always the energy of our group. Whether it was from their hilarious stories to their exuberant personality, I was always glad to have those two around. Seeing that expressionless look on their faces was almost heartbreaking. The normal pristine glow in their eyes that glittered like the stars themselves had all but died leaving nothing but a cold stare I thought that only the dead could exude. They weren't the only ones though. All the laughter we shared not too long ago had faded away like the last bit of sunlight before a sunset leaving nothing but a cold darkness lingering in the room. Dreams had a way of rising up people's hopes until they are just in arm's reach before they were suddenly yanked away leaving our hands grasping nothing but air. We all had experienced that feeling more than once in our lifetime, so we were afraid of it happening again. It was our fear though that made Christian greater than any of us. As we sat there allowing our fears to weigh us down, Christian stood up in the middle of our group.

Christian was by far not the biggest amongst us. He stood around six-foot one at best. He was also not the strongest or loudest among us either. He was the best-looking I'll give him that one. Him and his stupid long blond hair was apparently a rarity in other worlds. Aside from his pretty boy visage, Christian was above all else a natural-born leader. He looked around at all nine of us. Each of us had our eyes fixated on every subtle movement of his body. We were his vassals, his knights that were the embodiment of his will. Not all of us had committed to his ideals when we first met him, but we all were sworn to him now.

Christian spun around so he could look at all of us and said, "Everyone, from the bottom of my heart, I thank you for the kindness and loyalty that you've shown my brother and I over the last few years. You've been there for us just as we've been there for you, and now the time has come to put the bonds that we've forged to the test. This whole mission is not simply about us passing or failing a test, but it's about us coming together to pass the Word along to another group of people that are in dire need of it! We must not forget our purpose here, and we must not forgo our duty because of the fear that holds us down. You may call me your king, but after this mission we'll all be Crusaders, sworn vassals to the Word, and thus we shall all be equal. I look forward to the day when we all can put on the sigil of the cross upon our breasts, and I look forward to the day when we can look back at this moment and say we showed no fear, no hesitation, and no qualms as we descended down to take our destiny with our own two hands! We are Crusaders, my brothers and sisters!"

His speech had instilled courage into every part of my body as we all stood up giving him a round of applause. He truly was a natural-born leader, and it was my job to make sure he was protected down on that island. We all began the last-minute preparations we needed to do. I tightened my belt and ensured that the sheath for both my rapiers was secured. As I buttoned the sleeves of my black tunic, I looked over to Reginald, who was wearing his tunic unbuttoned. His lack of discipline when it came to his uniform had always bothered me. The uniform of a Crusader was widely recognized as our holy symbol. It was a vestige that symbolized our status and purpose and should be maintained with the utmost detail. Being from a world where most of my race was forced to wear rags, I found the elegant style of the Crusaders to be mesmerizing. The uniform incorporated a black standing collar that was a part of a black tunic with gold trim and maroon cuffs. The black pants were straight leg and tucked into black knee-high boots. I double-checked the gold buttons on the front of my tunic and stood up. We were all ready to go, but I truly hated the next part. From the meeting room, we followed Captain Stagg into the drop hangar.

Apparently being a Crusader was all about style and entry. In order to promote the idea that we were heavenly messengers, we would always descend onto any new world from pods that were dropped from the airship and landed in the ground. The pods were tall enough for one person to stand in. Aside from that though, the cylinder-shaped container offered no other room. Before I entered the pod, the scene to my left caught my attention. Rebecca was tugging on the sleeve of Dom making it look like she was begging for his attention. The shine had returned to her eyes as it often did around Dom, which was good, but I found her performance a discomforting one. Ever since that one night together, she had begun to cling to him like a parasite. Dom never did once feign his emotions for her or rather lack of them. He slapped her hand away from him and crawled into his own respective pod. It was against the Creed of the Order for any Crusader or recruit to engage into any sort of intercourse outside of marriage once he had taken his oath and even then the Order strongly suggested the union should be a chaste one, but it was a brittle rule that seemed to be broken at every turn. One would have imagined that Dom and her would have broken it for a special reason, but he merely wished to pursue the desires of his flesh and the moment he did, he tossed her by the wayside. When the incident occurred, Dom was the most known man in the Order amongst the recruits for the way he used her. There was hardly a single man that did not praise him for his actions. As I learned repeatedly, the Crusaders were great orators at speaking the truth but not the greatest practitioners at upholding it on their end.

I wished she would understand that she meant nothing to him aside from a quick meal, but her heart was too smitten with the very existence of him to let her see such simple truths. It always amazed me at how selfish people could be. I climbed into my pod and shut the latch. The small window on the metal casing allowed me to see the disappointment on her face as she sulked away into her own pod. The darkness of the room disappeared as red flashing lights along with a wailing siren filled the room. I closed my eyes as I heard the countdown over the speaker from the pilot.

"5…4…3…2…1…Commence Fallout!"

When I opened my eyes once more, all I could see was the image of our ship getting smaller and smaller as we plummeted toward the ground. The entire pod was shaking as if an earthquake had been sealed inside its metal walls. It was a rough ride, but one I had grown accustomed to. After a few moments I could see the other casing of pods falling next to mine. We were always dropped in two casings, long poles that held five pods each. For a split second, I could see Christian's smiling face in the other casing, but that peaceful sight vanished once a ball of fire emerged from below us and exploded against the side of his group's casing. I pressed my face against the window so I could get a better look and saw nothing but smoke along with tiny pieces of debris falling. I couldn't even think for long because another loud explosion was heard as a sudden wave made my entire pod shake even more than before. I figured that my casing must have been hit as well. The clear image I could see before vanished as I was thrown back against the wall of my pod as it began to tumble through the air. I gripped onto the handle of the latch and held on for dear life until my descent finally stopped with a loud crash.

I crawled out of the pod as quickly as possible and immediately puked on the sand of the beach. With my insides now before me, I turned my head away in slight shame and crawled forward a few more feet. The whole world spun around me as a ringing kept persisting in my head. As I tried to stand, the rocking motions of my sight caused me to continuously slip in the sand. I rolled over to my back and looked at the bloody laceration on my hand. The pain from the cut stung immensely, but that pain paled in comparison to the sight I soon saw. In the sky above me, seven fiery lights descended down upon the island far away from my position. Almost in unison, there was a resounding boom as the sounds of the crash landings resonated all over the island. I knew those lights were the pods, and suddenly the realization hit me—I was stranded from my team in a strange world, in an apparent hostile environment. As I lay in the sand, I looked for any sign that the airship was coming back for us, but there was no trace of it in the sky. I scanned over the rest of my body to see if I had sustained any other injuries aside from my hand. There were some cuts and bruises but nothing to be concerned about. Slowly, I got back onto my feet as I tried my best not to place any pressure on my hand.

It looked like I had crashed-landed on the coast of the island not too far out from the jungle. I walked back over to my pod to assess the damage of the crash, but I was stopped before I reached it by a scream I knew without a doubt was Rebecca. I turned to my left and saw that there was smoke in the distance further down the beach. I tried to run toward it, but my body had not yet shaken off the aftereffects of the crash, so I stumbled through the sand for a moment before I transitioned into a full sprint. The closer I got to the smoke, the more debris I saw littered all over the beach from the explosion of our casing. I moved around the shards of metal as best I could until I finally reached the crash site of another pod. I saw Rebecca near another pod struggling to pull something out. As I got closer to the scene, I saw that Sariah was trapped underneath some debris from her pod. I rushed over to them and things were worse than I had thought. Both of them had sustained far worse injuries in comparison to my own. Rebecca's uniform had several tears revealing multiple deep lacerations in her arms and legs, but most notably was a large piece of metal protruding from her side. Blood was soaking through the fabric of her uniform as she ignored her own wounds to save her sister. Tears streamed from Rebecca's eyes as she pulled her sister's hand while enduring the pain of the piece of metal lodged within her side.

Her focus was so into saving her sister she didn't even notice me until I had walked up to the pod and dug my hands underneath its hull. My fingers shifted through the sand until I could get a firm hold of the pod and began to lift it as high as I could. I could feel my legs shaking as the pod didn't even move an inch, but I continued until finally I was able to lift it slightly off the ground. The biceps of my arms tightened every inch the hull was lifted off the ground. The metal dug into my palms until trickles of blood could be seen dripping down my wrists. Once I felt the weight of the pod placed further on me, I looked to Rebecca and yelled, "Hurry get her out while I can still hold on!"

Her reaction was quick and greatly appreciated as she pulled Sariah out before my arms gave way. Sariah was not even conscious and Rebecca continued to bleed out without any concern. I looked toward the jungle that covered the majority of the island and could see several clouds of smoke. The rest of my team had been scattered throughout the island and judging from those two over there, the others may have been in even worse shape. I knew I couldn't dwell on that though. I had to start looking for Christian.

The natives of that island should never have possessed the power to launch an aerial attack, and there was no way they should have seen our ship or thought we were a hostile presence. That was a class D–ranked world, so at best the inhabitants of it should have just known how to begin to forge steel weapons. They were supposed to have been even more primitive than the people of Earth! Whatever was going on needed to be ascertained before we made anymore moves, so I had to find Christian before he tried to do anything rash without me there to back him up.

As I began to head toward the jungle, Rebecca called out to me, "Where are you going, Terra? Sariah is hurt! I need you!"

I took another step forward trying my best to disregard her plea. Unlike the others, I cared nothing for the plight of these lesser beings of various worlds. All I cared about was protecting Christian. I came to the Crusaders in order to protect my brother and that was all. I did not care about the conditions of other worlds. I did not care about spreading the Word. I did not care about anything aside from my own desires, and my strongest desire at that time was to see my brother safe and sound. The fate of those two should not have bothered me, but I found that I had grown attached to the members of my team as of late. It was an annoying attachment that I wish would be severed because at that point it was hampering my more-important task at hand. I reluctantly returned to the two of them and examined over Sariah's body. It did not look good. Rebecca and Sariah both were women with small frames that could incur any manner of injury. They always acted as the medics of the team, and in combat situations, they acted from long-range support. They had not trained their bodies for this kind of injury. Rebecca was beginning to look pale in the face from a lack of blood no doubt, and Sariah had suffered a broken leg. Sariah would be fine in given time, but Rebecca was in far more serious danger, and Christian would not forgive me if I had allowed one of his vassals to die on my watch.

So at that moment, I rearranged my priorities. Before finding Christian came the well-being of those two. I had nothing but the most utmost respect for the medical skills of both sisters, but at that time, I decided to go against their usual methods and use my own. Rebecca was still zeroed in on her sister so she didn't even notice me sneak behind her and knock her out with a well-placed strike to her neck.

Now all I had to do was to start a fire and close the wounds. Starting the fire was hardly a problem with all the smoldering debris lying around, fixing the wounds was a whole other challenge. The palms of my hands had the crimson stain of Rebecca's blood on them as I pulled out the piece of metal. I heated the metal of my rapier as quickly as I could and placed it on the wound to seal the gash. Thankfully I had done a good job of knocking her out because she didn't even scream during the process, and in a few moments all I could do had been completed. I sat back on the sand and wiped the sweat from my brow. In one day I had managed to save two white people from certain death. I wondered if my father would have looked down on me for my actions to save the same race that had condemned us to a life of slavery. Either way it didn't matter. I was no longer the ignorant boy that knew nothing of the world. I was no longer the property of another simply because of my skin. I was no longer a stain upon a society that hated me—I was Terra and I was a Crusader.

2

Capture

1855, Southern Mississippi

The first six years of my childhood were not what most people expected, especially those who know me best. I can't blame them. I, too, would doubt that a boy and his father avoided slavery by living in an abandoned log cabin in the middle of the woods. Looking back, I'm still amazed at how far I have come from those days with Father. Father…well, he was an interesting man to say the least. When it came to his paternal duties, he was certainly no Abraham. He always told me that love was just an anchor that dragged people down, but duty was a raft that one could keep floating on. He never said much more to me than he ever needed to. If anything, he was more of a teacher than a father. The skills he taught me ranged from reading and writing to fighting. Thinking back on it, it was quite strange for a man to teach his six-year-old son how to defend himself with a forgotten practice like swordsmanship. At the time though, I was naïve enough to think of his lessons as nothing more than a game, but the results I gained suggested otherwise. He would give me a sturdy wooden stick and tell me to pretend it was a real sword. He told me I had a natural gift of wielding a blade, which had been long forgotten by the people of our world.

Aside from honing my swordsmanship, he ensured that I was much smarter than many of the others that shared our skin color. It took some time to understand why, but Father always told me that all others like us were nothing but simple animals destined to be subjugated. While his words did indeed turn out to be true, they were far too vague for me to understand back then.

As for my mother, she died when I was being brought into this world. My father never spoke of her to me, but I frequently heard him late at night saying a woman's name in his sleep. I never could make out the name, but his tone was one of profound remorse. The only thing I knew about her was that she gave me my name, Terra. Father often laughed when he told me this, as if it was some kind of joke, but I never did learn why.

There was nothing else particularly interesting about him. He kept to himself and usually partook in activities such as reading and drawing. We didn't have a loving father-son relationship like Christian and his dad, but I didn't mind because he always took care of me. Back then, my life was happy and simple.

The only rule I had to abide by was to never, under any circumstances, leave the forest without him. I didn't think much of it for years. I just obeyed his command, but my curiosity grew over time. I wanted to know what kind of world was behind those trees.

I knew very little about the outside world, and what I did know was filtered greatly from my father's point of view. Father told me that the people beyond the woods were always fighting over nothing important. His infamous words were always that, "they bicker like newborn dogs blindly fighting for their mother's milk." Still, I wanted to meet them despite my father's warnings. Playing by myself got boring after a couple of years. My heart yearned for change and I couldn't contain it any longer.

When the day finally came when I had decided to leave, I slowly climbed out of my window and proceeded toward the woods. My heart was on fire as I glanced around my shoulder every few seconds or so trying to see if I was being pursued. Tons of thoughts about what the world past these trees would be like danced around within my mind. I heard stories, so many stories about the heroes of other worlds from Father, but I never once thought about what the people from my own were like. I pictured that all the children would look exactly like me, and the adults would be just like Father.

I was so foolish back then.

I wish that I would have just known what I was about to experience. My father did the right thing by trying to keep us isolated from the world, but I never imagined anything like I was about to see. My mind was just so occupied with all of the ridiculous things I would be able to do soon.

I never pondered why my father kept us isolated.

I really should have.

All I did was keep running toward my dark future like a fool. It didn't take me long to figure out my crucial error: I had never been farther than the pond near our cabin. Once I ran past the pond, I didn't take the time to realize my error. By the time I finally did take notice, I was completely lost. My exuberant curiosity soon turned into a vexing anxiety. I frantically looked around in all directions trying to locate my original path. Nothing was there to be found. I wandered around through the forest for about an hour before sleep began to overtake me. I found the nearest tree, sat down and, leaned my head up against its cold bark.

I awoke to the laughter of children. It was a completely foreign sound to me. Neither my father nor I had ever made such happy sounds in our lives. I peered through a gap in a nearby bush to see what was going on. That was the first time I ever saw another human being aside from my father. They were different from me. That's the first thing that came into my mind when I saw them. Their clothes were much nicer than mine: no dirt, no grime, and no stains. The most perplexing thing about them was their skin. I had never seen or heard of anyone with skin that fair before. It was as if I was looking at a cloud in human form. It was weird but they didn't seem bad whatsoever. They were playing a strange game that involved running and touching someone and then that person would go and touch someone else and the cycle would continue onward. I didn't understand the fun of such a game, but I didn't let it bother me.

After they were done, they began making that laughing sound once more. They all looked so happy laughing that I soon found myself trying to mimic those same sounds. I had never truly understood what it meant to have friends, but back then all I wanted was not to be alone any longer. When they left, I decided to follow them without them seeing me. I kept close to the bushes despite all of the scrapes and cuts I got from the thorns. When they finally stopped, I looked like a horrid mess with leaves and dirt all over my clothing and countless tears in them as well. All the same though, I still had a big smile on my face. I didn't have to follow for much longer long until I reached my very first village. I climbed to the top of a tree that overlooked the village. It was nothing like I had expected.

There were people walking around everywhere, and all of them looked different from me. I didn't see a single one that resembled me in the slightest. It was an unexpected sight but far from a disappointing one. I watched them for a while and tried to take in as much as I could about their society. For all of Father's warnings, they seemed like quite the docile bunch, but I soon learned how naïve my eyes truly were in those times.

When I had finally had enough of just watching them, I decided to join in. I climbed out of the tree and ran into the village. The moment I entered, I could feel the eyes of everyone looking at me. All of my anticipation to enter was suddenly cut down by their harsh glances. I found it hard to breathe when I was amongst them. I tried to run from that particular area and just go to another, but the looks seemed to constantly follow me no matter where I went. But the looks were nothing compared to the words that soon followed. After I had been running for a few minutes, hunger began to take me. I went to a fruit stand to grab an apple. Right as my tiny fingers enclosed around its crimson surface, the vendor picked up a stone and threw it at me. The stone left a purple bruise on my arm that stung when I touched it.

Tears welled up in my eyes as I looked upon the man who exuded nothing but hate toward me. He was a fat man with a round belly that jiggled slightly as he yelled out, "What do you think you're doing you, dang monkey? What in the world made a worthless piece of garbage like you think you could take out food? I should shoot you where you stand, monkey, but I might upset your master. Where's your master anyway?"

I was at a loss for words. I didn't understand what he was talking about. I just looked at him still somewhat frightened.

"So you don't plan to answer me, huh? I'll get you to talk," he said as he walked over toward me.

He picked up more stones and threw one after another at me. I ran away from him as he continued to try and hit me. When I thought I was safe, I was wrong. Some of the other villagers picked up on the vendor's actions and started to throw stones at me as well. There was nowhere I was able to run without getting hit. As I fled for safety, there was a sight that made me stop cold in my tracks. Hanging in the middle of the town was the lifeless body of a black man strung up in front of a crowd. When I say "body," I use the term very loosely because it could have been debated that all that was left was a sack of tortured meat. As a boy, my eyes were not yet ready to bear witness to such a horrid sight. For a moment, I didn't feel the pain of the stones being hurled at me, all I saw was the body of that man placed on display as some kind of warning that I should never harbor the delusion that I was the same as these people.

Father had taught me much about God at an early age. His faith in God seemed to be one of the few things he cared for and I could tell he wished to imbue that faith onto me. I thought back to the words of spoken in Galatians 3:28, "There is neither Jew nor Greek, there is neither bond nor free, there is neither male nor female: for ye are all one in Christ Jesus."

As I looked upon that corpse of that tortured soul, I questioned every lesson that Father taught me of the Word. Men were supposed to be created equal and yet...

Time seemed to return to me as I felt the jarring blows of more stones striking my body. With tears streaming down my face, I resumed my escape from the hypocrites that chased me. As I continued running, I lost my place and tripped. In order to lessen the damage from the stones, I curled up into a ball and trembled as they continued to pelt me. With the sting of every stone that bruised my skin, my feelings of sadness turned into hatred for them. I didn't understand why that was happening to me. I only wanted to see the village. I screamed for them to stop over and over again, but they never let up. In fact, I think the stones were thrown harder as my pleas increased. The barrage of stones ceased though as I heard a booming voice ringing from the crowd.

"What do you, people, think you're doing to my property? Should I just go around randomly throwing rocks at your horses and homes? Get out of here before I'm further angered."

I uncurled myself from my defensive position and looked at the man who saved me. He held out his hand and pulled me up. He looked like them. I could feel my anger contorting my face as I gritted my teeth at him like an animal backed into a corner. I instinctively pulled away, picked one of the stones that they threw at me, and threw it at him. It hit him dead in the face.

But all he did was smile at me and say, "I suppose it makes sense that you would react in that way, but don't worry I'm not here to hurt you. I want to help you. Why don't you let me take you home so there won't be another incident like this?"

I trusted his words for some reason and nodded my head. I led him all the way back to our home.

As I emerged from the woods near my home, Father came rushing toward me and embraced me in his arms. This was the first time he had ever shown this much affection in my life. It was an odd feeling, but one that I began to enjoy as I wrapped my arms around him. He looked at my injuries with concern and held me even closer to him. It was the first good feeling I had all day. Suddenly, the look of happiness faded from my father's face as he saw the man that I had led there. He looked around frantically for something, but it seemed that it wasn't around him. The man laughed as he pulled out a revolver from behind him. I didn't understand what was going on.

My father held me closer saying in a hushed tone, "Remember that this isn't your fault, Terra." He looked at the man and sighed. "Looks like this little façade is over. I knew this day would come…just as she said."

The next thing I knew the man hit my father and I. Father fell to the ground instantly. The man then went inside our house and shortly after, I saw flames beginning to consume the structure. He walked out from the burning house with a smile on his face. Nothing made sense to me at that time. I didn't understand how that day went from me looking forward to finally getting out from the woods to me watching our house burn to the ground. I understand now, of course. The man was nothing but a slaver looking for new and mainly free merchandise. He found me and got me to lead him to my father. I gave him an easy two-for-one deal. He then burnt our house just for the fun of it. Despite what Father had said to me, this was my fault. The bondage we were to suffer through for the next six years would be my entire fault. It was because of my actions that we were sent down a path of turmoil and hardship.

3
The Fallen Ones

Night had taken the sky and still Rebecca and Sariah slept like babes. It was no surprise given the manner of their injuries, but still it had been over twelve hours already. I wondered what would have befallen the two of them if I had not come by when I did. Rebecca would have most likely bled out, and Sariah would have been crushed under the debris. They were truly fortunate. I could only hope that the others had managed to land safely. Christian, Reginald, Coleman, Dom, Jon, Marco, Tennaz, and Captain Stagg; I truly worried for the fates of all of my comrades, aside from Stagg that is. I took hold of a nearby stick and began to poke the firewood in the fire. Smoke slipped into my lungs and made me cough as I looked out to the horizon of the black sea before me. When sitting on a beach like that, it was hard to imagine that beyond that dark horizon was a plethora of worlds that had yet to be discovered. Such thoughts truly had a way of making you seem much smaller in the big picture, but I tried to not let them weigh me down. As I continued to look out toward the horizon, I heard footsteps trying their best to conceal their presence. There was only one person.

    I placed my hand on the hilt of my rapier, and before the attacker could sneak up on me, I quickly turned around with my blade drawn. I had expected some sort of native or perhaps one of the people that shot my team down from the sky but instead it was…another Crusader. It was a tall, lanky man wearing our uniform or what I thought to be our uniform. The color had long faded and the design was slightly different from others with the color scheme being more of a red-and-gold combo rather than a gold and black. His loose, straggly hair that covered most of his face implied that he had been most likely trapped on that island for quite some time, or perhaps he was some kind of prisoner. Either way, I didn't have the time to find any answers because the man quickly attacked me. His weapon was naught but a crudely made spear from wood and a sharpened stone that could hardly be used as a sufficient letter opener. I dodged the first thrust that made my way and before my attacker could make another move, I used the base of my handle to shatter the bones in his hand.

The screams of my attacker were more annoying than the wails of newborn baby torn away from his mother's bosom. I wished nothing more than to rip his tongue out to put an end to his screams, but I needed to find out what I could before I ended him. I pushed him down to the ground as I held the tip of my blade to his throat. That quickly made him cease his wailing. I held my blade steady against his neck as I asked, "Who are you and why do you have that uniform? Answer quickly or I swear that hand won't be the only thing that's broken on your body!"

I waited for him to give an explanation, but he held his tongue. I believe that he didn't think I was serious about my threat. If only he had the chance to talk to the other natives of various worlds that had ignored my threats, then I'm sure that the defiant look in his eyes would have quickly diminished. In fact from the uniform he wore, he should have either been a Crusader or have encountered one. Either way, he should have known to fear our organization then. We were not the garden variety missionaries that had only cared for peaceful resolutions that many people envisioned. We were just as bad as the ones that were prominent in my home world that came to America under the pretense of love but left behind plagues and blood. I was determined to make sure he understood those facts soon enough though. I placed the tip of my blade over the kindling fire and waited until I saw the heat transfer. I then hovered the tip of my blade over the eye of the attacker and watched as the glowing tip from my blade illuminated the fear in the pupils of his eyes. His lips finally parted as words flowed freely out begging for his life.

He said, "You can't do this! You're a man of God. Such means are barbaric!"

I made a motion pointing to his broken hand as I said, "I did not earn the title of Executioner for my civilized demeanor! Now I have a few questions that I want you to answer for me. Do that and I'll make sure you don't lose any other body parts. So what exactly is this island? This is supposed to be a primitive world with no means of power to resist us. How in the world was my team shot down from the sky?"

"This is the Isle of the Fallen. It's unlike any other world that you have encountered in your time. So all that training that they imparted you with in Olympus holds no merit here. Even the strongest among your kind have fallen prey to the men of this isle. You and your team should just get used to the idea that you're going to die here you worthless piece of—"

I decided to slit his throat before he angered me any further.

"Are you sure that was the best course of action, Terra?" asked Sariah groggily.

I looked over to her and saw her laying on her side near the fire. Rebecca was still out cold, but the glow of the fire showed the pale texture that had once consumed Sariah's face was all but gone. Her rosy cheeks had retained their color and her auburn air hung loosely over her shoulder making her look like a fiery goddess as she sat next to the fire pit.

I turned away from her and began to pat down the man I just slew as I responded to Sariah, "Well looks like I don't even get a thank you for going through all that trouble to save your life. As for him, you know I can't stand his type. We'll get intel from some other source."

"That's not a reassuring notion, Terra, when we don't even know what's going on here. We were attacked there's no doubt about that, so I find it surprising that you just killed a viable source of information!" she yelled.

"You heard him as well as I did. He said we are on the Isle of the Fallen. If that's true, then we have all the intel we need unless all the stories that Clay told you about this place were false. We both know where we are and the kind of place that this is."

"Clay died for knowing that information, so we both know that his stories were true, but I still refuse to believe that we're there of all places, Terra. It makes no sense. That guy was just trying to mess with your mind."

"Through countless times reaping the consequences of ignoring your warnings over the years, I know it's not best to question your intuition, Sariah. You're practically a walking oracle these days, but still we have to keep what he said in mind."

"I know you have little faith in the Order, but you could at least trust that our superiors wouldn't send us to our deaths like that couldn't you?"

"I don't know," I replied as I stopped searching the man. My fingers curled as they dug into the sand as painful memories flooded back into my mind. Sariah could see my frustration and called my name but I cut her off. "It would not be the first time that the Order sent you and me to our deaths through a mission. Rehabilitation, the process of reeducating Crusaders that lost their way about the amazing Word of God by force if necessary. That was what they called it. Compared to some of the missions we were sent on during that time, this place looks like a cakewalk. The only thing that we know for sure is that our mission was to bring the Word to the citizens of this primitive world and then establish a church here. This was by no means going to be a short mission, so we packed supplies for the long haul, but those supplies—"

"Are likely scattered throughout the jungle now because of the crashes right?"

"That would be my guess," I replied. "At first light, I'm heading into the jungle to procure any sort of food and scout out the area. We all know the contingency plan should we get separated from the group, so we have about a week until we need to meet up."

"Christian always said in cases like these to take a few days to secure food and shelter and then scout out the area. We were supposed to meet at the highest point of whatever terrain we are around. It was a very sound idea that I never expected to actually use."

"Crusaders get separated from each other all the time during a mission. It just so happens we're the first that it has happened to in the initial drop phase. We'll survive as along as we can keep our heads."

"That's rich coming from the guy that has an impulsive streak to cut down anything that rubs him the wrong way. So you're not the best model of self-control, Terra."

I playfully threw the sand I clutched in her direction. I then gave her a wicked smirk toward her and said, "I didn't mind you rubbing me the wrong way. Actually you rubbed me the right way on numerous occasions."

"You're disgusting you know that? I can't see what I saw in you. I can't see what any woman does either, but if they all knew how you really were then—"

"They would slap me and then end up sleeping with me again and again just like you do. How long has it been…hmmm about a week right?" I asked grinning constantly.

"I can't remember. I guess our last encounter was not that memorable, but I do remember what I had for breakfast that week every day."

I could see the sly smile on her face, but I ignored her last statement and said, "Now if you're finished, I suggest you get some rest for the morning."

"I hope that not all people from Earth are like you, Terra. If so, then it's a truly wretched world."

"The funny thing is I'm actually one of the better ones. Trust me," I assured her.

The following morning, I left before either of the girls had woken up. Despite their injuries, I knew that they could handle themselves if they were attacked. That's what I told myself when I left, but after I entered the jungle I knew I was lying to myself. The moment I stepped into the thick greenery of the jungle, I couldn't help but be reminded of the woods that were near my first home. Granted the isle's jungle was much more exotic, but it had the same feel to it. Both places felt isolated and cut off from society.

The chorus of the animal life was all around me as I heard all manners of sounds from tweeting birds to howling monkeys, to roaring lions and even foreign sounds I did not recognize. In fact, the diverse chorus was a bit too strange. Never before had I encountered so many different types of animals all in one location, and I had hardly been there that long. I laughed to myself as I realized that I must have crashed into the remains of Noah's Ark or something.

I had perhaps only traversed a hundred yards into the interior of the jungle and already I discovered so much, but the animals paled in comparison to the food sources around there. Nearly every plant, tree, or bush had some viable form of food growing from it. Many of which I had learned about during my training to become a Crusader. One fruit caught my eye though. I bent down and swatted away some vines that my leg had become entangled in as I took a closer look at an ivory bush. There was a crescent-shaped fruit that could have only been the Charlatalian melon. A sacred fruit known only to grow in the confines of the gardens of Olympus.

I plucked the fruit from the bush and rubbed my fingers across its coarse exterior. The Charlatalian melon was similar in regards to a coconut. Once you could get past the hard shelling, inside was a nutritious liquid that we had to drink every day during our training. The taste alone was enough to make a man want to kill himself, but I could not argue with the results. The juice of the fruit had some kind of restoring qualities that helped cure any ailment and when mixed with and grinded into a paste it served as a great ointment as well. Seeing that fruit reminded of all the training that we had to undergo to get to this horrid situation. I couldn't pinpoint if the memories I had were more joyous or melancholy because there was such a wide array of memories those last five years. The training given to us by the Order was brutal, but it helped me develop a sense of community among my team that I had never before had in my life.

    I gathered as many as I could carry and began to head back down to the beach. As I stepped out from behind the wild scenery and into the sandy landscape of the beach, I saw a group of men surrounding Rebecca and Sariah. Like the man that I had killed before, they all wore the uniform of a Crusader except it had really faded out. These men though were much more groomed than my last attacker and from the looks of it they were more heavily armed as well. I counted around half a dozen men all with steel longswords brandished and ready to cut us down. As I approached them, I held my hands in the air which made me drop all of the melons that I had gathered, but I figured that was the least of my concerns. I found this whole situation to be a little humorous. Here we were the ones coming to this world to save these people and now that was the third time that we had been attacked by the ingrates of the island. Well if that place truly was the Isle of the Fallen, then I could understand why all of that happened to us, but still it was an unsettling thought. Once the men thought that I was close enough, they stopped my progress and placed a blade under Sariah's chin.

    I continued to hold my hands in the air and said, "My comrades and I mean you no harm. We're simple missionaries here to spread the Word of our Lord God. There's no need for any violent action to be taken here, Sirs."

    Despite my formal address, they still kept their blades at the throats of my comrades and kept their eyes pinpointed at me.

Finally the one with his blade at Sariah's neck spoke and said, "That's funny considering we found the body of one of our men here not too long ago. That's a funny way to show you come in peace."

Sariah gave me a nasty look indicating that she *told me so*. I rolled my eyes at her and continued talking to the man and said, "He came out of nowhere and attacked us. I have two feeble women to look after, Sir. I had no choice but to resort to such vile means. While it pains me to take a life, it could not be helped and I have prayed every day since that day for my Lord's forgiveness on the matter."

I thought that perhaps the whole praying bit was a bit too much. It had only been less than a day. Even Rebecca now was giving me an addled look that made me want to kill both of those girls. I continued to ignore them as I pressed on in my discourse, "I'm glad that you've come here though. My friends are injured and are in need of medical attention. If you could provide us aid, then that would be greatly appreciated, Sir."

I hated speaking in such a way to others. It reminded me of my days when I was trapped being nothing but a slave during my childhood. I thought once I was free I would never have to return to those old habits of mine, but the attitude drilled into me as a child was always going to be lurking deep inside my heart. It may not have been my normal personality, but it was an effective mask that allowed me to maneuver situations well. My only concern at that time was seeing if my mask would indeed deliver us from the predicament that we were in.

The man in the lead motioned his men to lower their arms, and the blades were removed from the girls' necks. Right when I was about to express my thanks, the man spoke quickly, "Don't get me wrong though, we don't trust you or your team, but my king was very clear in his instructions to bring you alive. So if you don't wish for any problems I suggest that you just come along with me."

I expected as much. If those men had some sort of affiliation with the Crusaders, then they were not ones to just slaughter anyone in sight. It would be a direct violation of our Creed, a creed I hardly ever followed, but it was nice knowing that some fools were bound by the letters printed in our holy book. I followed the men without another word said between us. They placed a couple guards around the three of us to limit communication. It was a basic practice implemented by the Crusaders. If we were to ever capture a group of enemies, we were to separate them at all cost to prevent any sort of planning taking place. It was certainly strange seeing myself as the target of such principle tactics we had used, but at least I knew that guaranteed our safety for the time being. The men blindfolded us and led us through the jungle to where their camp was. I tried my best to memorize what direction we were heading in, but we took so many twists and turns, I couldn't keep track. Most likely that too was a maneuver to make sure we had no idea where we were going. Our blind trek came to an end abruptly as the blindfold was lifted from my eyes.

My vision was blurry for a second due to the fact that a piece of the cloth from the fold got in my eye. I went to rub it out, but that only made my eye more irritated. After I felt a tear streaming down my face, my vision returned. Everything slowly came into picture all around me. We had stepped out from the jungle into a large clearing that was manmade judging from the amount of open space. I heard the flow of a nearby stream, which indicated why that location was chosen for their camp. Their hideout was apparently some sort of ruined temple lodged within the base of the mountain I had spotted overhead earlier. The plant life had practically grown over every inch of that temple giving it an unhabituated look, but strolling around the temple grounds were men and women alike wearing the skins of animals to cover themselves. I shot a glance to Sariah to see what she thought, but her eyes were fixated on the grand scope of the temple. Despite the moss growing over every inch of the structure, it was obviously once a masterpiece that was hardly rivaled. Decrepit statues of the Virgin Mary and King David were lined up next to the entrance of the temple. Hanging above them was an image of the Last Supper chiseled into the stone above the main door.

Wherever that place was, it was not the class D world that we were led to believe. That place, no most likely that whole isle, had already been touched by the hands of the Crusaders. The only question was why were we sent there in the first place then to liberate a people that had already been supposedly liberated?

I found myself blurting out the question that was burning on all of our minds, "Who are you, people?"

Emerging from the open door of the temple right on cue was a white man of smaller stature than me. From the entourage of uniformed Crusaders behind him though, I knew must have been the king earlier referred to. As we all looked on at him, my escorts kicked the back on my knees, causing me to fall to the ground. They did the same thing to Rebecca and Sariah, too. As I tried to get back up, a blade was held at my neck as one of my captors said, "Show your respect to our king and kneel, you self-righteous scum." Being forced to kneel like some sort of dog made me rake my fingers against the dirt until my nails had turned brown. Being forced to submit in the presence of a greater man was not a foreign action for me, but I had promised to never do it again. I saw the people that were walking around barefoot on the temple grounds kneel as well.

In an eerie unison tone, they all began to chant, "Hail to the Father. Hail to the Father."

Whatever the previous Crusader group had tried to do to that place had obviously failed. Those people were likened to a cult or something which was an idea that didn't sit too well with me. I looked upon the little man that they called Father standing under the visage of Jesus himself. He had a pair I'll give him that for taking such a title. He wore a long white robe over his Crusader uniform and a held a scepter that looked to be carved from a nearby tree. His face had been powered white; his lips covered with red lipstick, and he wore a crown of thorns upon his head. He seemed to be in his midforties, but despite that fact his hair was snow white. Most likely he had it colored to give off a holier presence. In all honesty, the man looked like a clown in my eyes. I had a moment of weakness where I couldn't contain my laughter and a chuckle slipped out. Almost immediately afterward, one of the guards quickly hit me with the hilt of his sword. It was a well-placed blow that would have knocked out any other man, but I was stronger than that. I shook off the blow and continued to look at the clown ahead of me as he walked down the temple stairs.

As I looked on at that man, I mumbled under my breath who did he think he was? Either he magically heard my question, or he had practiced his welcoming speech beforehand as he said in a booming tone, "Welcome, hypocrites, to Ataxia, the village of the Fallen, the home of the Exiled Crusaders."

I sighed as my head dropped. It was true then. We were indeed trapped on the Isle of the Fallen.

4

Escape

1855, Southern Mississippi

Capture seemed to be a natural occurrence in my life. It has happened so many times that I fear that my life is somewhat cliché, but each capture made me who I am. Each time I was forced to bend the knee toward another man, I gained new strength from the ordeal. For that reason I will never forget the first time I was captured.

There was a time that looking back now, I suppose I hated myself. I hated my lack of power and strength, and I hated my foolish naiveté that made my father and me slaves. After the slaver captured us, we were taken back to town and offered up for sale. Frightened doesn't begin to explain how I felt at that time. All I can precisely recall are the drops of sweat that kept dripping from my face. The entire time I never looked up at the crowd bidding for my life. All I did was focus on the drops of sweat or perhaps in fact they were tears. It had been a couple hours since they had separated me from my father and chained me up with those other animals.

Animals…yes that was how I thought of them. I hated them just as much as I did the whites that attacked me. I hated them for making my life the hell that it had become. *If only they were like me, then we would not be in this situation,* I thought. Such hatred I can articulate into words now, but back then as a boy I had no definition for my feelings. I only knew that looking at them disgusted me. Perhaps in my short time among the whites, I had been taught to hate my own kind. I hated that man that I saw hanging in the town for not being strong enough to fight back and I hated myself for going down that same path.

As I stood on that stage looking over the crowd, I struggled frantically to find him but the chains that were bound to me were too strong for me to do anything. I didn't quite understand what was going on, but I knew it would be nothing I'd like.

We were all herded over onto a platform and displayed to everyone. I saw all sorts of men that kept looking at us and whispering into the ears of the others there. When I was first bound up with the other slaves, I was glad to see others that looked like me, but I was soon able to tell after a little while that they were far different from me. I tried to talk to them, but they either paid me no attention or looked at me as if I was some sort of plague. I hated being around all of them. I hated being in that whole situation. I didn't understand how in the world things turned out that way. The tears continued to run down my face, and I could hear the chuckles of those in front of me. I just cried even more when I heard them, but I kept my head down. Perhaps I was foolish enough to believe that if I never saw the men buying me then it would all just be a dream and would vanish once I lifted my head. I soon heard my chains being unfastened from behind. I thought that Father had finally come to save me. I turned around with the biggest smile on my face to only see the man that put me in those chains to begin with.

When he saw my smile, he quickly struck me down with the back of his ring-covered hand. Blood trickled down my face as I was dragged to the center of the platform. I lifted my head up and looked at all of the men bidding on me. I was spun around multiple times reinforcing the fact that I was on display. During this time, the other men yelled out various numbers while this was happening until all was silent. I heard a "going once, twice, sold!"

I saw the man pointing toward someone in the crowd. I turned and looked in that direction and saw my future owner for the next six years of my life. Even to this day that hideous face of his still haunts my dreams. In retrospect, he was actually quite the handsome man, but when I looked at him it was like his inner evil contorted my view of him. I never could see him for his fleshly appearance, but I saw the dark spirit within him. When his hands reached for me, I saw talons in the place of fingers and horns in the place of ears. I was so sacred that I can say without any shame that I soiled myself right there on the spot. Once I was in the clutches of the reincarnation of Satan, I was chained once again and thrown into the back of a wagon with several other slaves. Among the slaves stuffed into the wagon was my father toward the back. I quickly crawled over to him and lay down in his lap as more tears came rushing out. He didn't say anything. All he did was stroke my head and hold me close.

I was stuck in that wagon for three days with Father and the others. At times, it seemed unbearable. But I was able to get through it since he was with me. We soon reached some remote town in Alabama where half of the slaves were traded to another wagon. I was so scared that Father and I would be separated again, but at least one good thing happened for us. From there, I believe that we continued to travel for a few weeks until we reached the southern edge of Mississippi once more. During our travels together, Father tried his best to explain the situation we were in. I understood the gist of it all, but I was still perplexed as to why we were the ones to be slaves. My father and I had done nothing wrong our whole lives, so why must we get punished so severely like the others?

He told me that he honestly didn't have an answer. After he said this, he gazed out at the sky in somewhat of a daze. The hypocritical tendencies of this world made no sense to him. When we finally arrived at the plantation, Father informed me of what I needed to expect. I knew about the grueling labor and the inhumane treatment that I would receive, but knowing and experiencing are two different things. I learned that the hard way. We arrived at the plantation by midday. The humidity along with the natural season made it feel like I was walking into an oven. As we were all hauled off of the wagon, I was able to see some other slaves that were already working in the fields. At first glance, the work they were doing didn't seem half as bad as Father made it out to be. All I saw was them going around the fields and harvesting the various plants growing there. I would do the same kinds of stuff back at home, and I actually enjoyed it. On top of that, there were at least twenty or thirty of them working together. I was sure it couldn't be that hard.

A brief smile came to me as I thought this wouldn't be all that bad. My reassuring thoughts quickly died after I saw one of the workers collapse from fatigue. A man resembling the one that had captured us rushed over to the fallen worker. He suddenly began yelling at the man and kicked him a few times telling him to get up. After his abuse was over, the worker tried to get up, but his knees wobbled as he tried to stand, and he fell over again. The man yelling at him quickly pulled out a whip and started to lash the exhausted man while screaming obscenities at him. The scene seemed so pointless that I didn't know what to think. As the man was being brutally beaten, not a single one of the others helped him. I didn't understand why he was left all alone to suffer. I tried to run over to help him, but the chains shackled around my feet made me fall.

Father came to get me, but I still tried to go help the man. He soon got up though, and went back to work as if nothing happened. He didn't seem angered by the torture he had endured; he just looked as if he had no soul left within him. I didn't know which I was more terrified of: being whipped or having that soulless expression plastered on my face. I soon got back in line with the other new slaves and followed the man who brought us there to the front of the house. He grabbed the majority and pulled

them into the fields. Father was among them. I trie
but I was held back by another one of the men who
there. He took several others and me inside the manor on the
plantation. When it came to shelter, I had known nothing but
our shack in the woods, so I was enamored by the size and structure of the plantation house. However, my newfound joy quickly
dwindled as I was hit for staring too long at the house. I, along
with the other weaker-looking slaves was taken to the manor to
serve out our sentence for the crime of being born.

For the next seven months, Father and I lived two different lives. He worked in the fields as I worked in the house. Our
labor differed greatly because of our age and body size. He did
every possible thing out in the fields. I would see him through
the window sometimes having a hard time with the whole thing,
but Father was smarter than the other slaves. He figured out the
rounds of our owner as well as his men. He was able to take a little break every now and then without getting caught. He could
handle most of the work at first, but I could see that it was beginning to take its toll after the first few months.

As for me, I was subjugated to do simple things around the
house, but even the slightest mistake caused whippings by the
owner's wife. She hated the fact that "things like us" were inside
her precious house. She wasn't much different from her husband.
She was a cruel and bitter woman who didn't even treat her children very well. She had several children whose faces all came
back blank to me, but there was one I could never forget, Jasmon.
She was a girl my age that I had been assigned to clean for. I
could not say if I thought she was cute or not; it's hard to recall
my feelings for girls at that age, but I do know that I became
infatuated with her to a small degree. It was her kindness toward
me I believe what drew me to her. Unlike her father and mother,
she treated me with decency and I loved her for that. It was a silly
relationship where I would stare at her as she never spoke to me.
I translated her silence toward me as a kindness in opposition to
the vocal cruelty her parents expressed daily.

One day, out of the blue, she asked me to play with her though; the game we played I do not recall, but I remember clearly that in the game I was her servant while a stuffed rabbit played the coveted role of her husband. As we played that game day after day, I finally asked why I could not be the husband instead of that rabbit. Her answer was surprisingly cute and innocent for the harm that it caused me.

"Because God doesn't allow for races to mix, silly. Everyone knows that much."

Those were her cute and innocent words that she said to me with a smile. God, God had forbid me of having happiness just as He had failed to come to the aid of Father and me. I did not know enough about the Bible to challenge her word, so since she read it more than I did, I had to assume what she said was correct. From that day on, I kept my distance from her, an absence she seemed to not mind in the slightest. Aside from Father, I knew that I was all alone in the world. There was no hope for any sort of relationship other than a piece of property among the whites, and Father and I were black sheep among black men, so there was no room for us there either.

Though I shared no particular love for the others trapped with us, I hoped we could perhaps help one another survive the endless torment, but that was out of the question. We really didn't get along with the other slaves. They called us traitors for being so well-adapted with the "white man's language." They even believed we were spies. We didn't care much for their opinion, though. All we needed was each other, and that's how it continued for the next few months. With each crack of dawn, we cursed our existence, and with the rising of the moon, we wished for our salvation. I longed for the days of freedom, alone in the woods, watching Father cut wood.

No matter how much I loved being with Father, I still couldn't stand the life we were living. I grew tired of having to sleep in the corners of those small cabins, shivering in the cold. I used to look forward to seeing the rising sun, but that soon turned into another painful reminder of the life I was forced to live. Over time, the owner's wife also grew colder. She became unbearable after she received news that her eldest son died during a raid on an Indian settlement. I would often hear her crying for hours at night. She blamed us for the death of her son and prayed to God smite the colored fiends that took her son away. The way she spoke to Him at night though made me think he was some kind of executioner instead of this loving Father.

I was always confused about how those people always spoke of the will of God, and yet I remember passages of treating those around you fairly and with love. I was but a boy, but the reminder of how confusing people were caused me to draw further away from the Word that my Father taught me. There was a time after I discovered their love for God that I began to have hope that perhaps they would be nicer one day. It did not take much time for me to quickly realize that was not going to happen within my brief, tortured lifespan.

As opposed to living with love like I had been taught, day after day they sowed more pain into our lives until it became commonplace. All the house slaves were on their toes whenever she came around. We all knew that the slightest mistake would bring calamity upon us all. One time somebody forget to lock the door and then the owner's wife had him killed, and from what I heard from Father, being around the owner wasn't any better at times.

Once I got to the point where I feared for my life on a daily basis, I knew that we needed to get out of there somehow. I told Father of my desire to leave, but he wanted nothing to do with it. He said that we would be hunted down until we died. He said he didn't want that type of life for me where I was always running and looking over my shoulder. A life where I could never be happy, yet I couldn't stand my current one. I would have much rather have taken my chances on the run than stay there. I followed Father's directives for another month or so before I had reached my limit. I figured that if Father was too scared to leave, then I'd leave him behind, and that was exactly what I did. One night after Father and the others slept, I made a mad dash for freedom. I quickly hopped over the fence and kept running.

I had made a couple of preparations before I left. I destroyed the lock to the kennel where they kept all of the pursuit dogs, so I knew that would buy some time, but besides that I did nothing else of significant importance. Owner ruled on fear alone, so he figured that he didn't need to keep many sentries to watch us if we decided to escape, but looking back on it all, it was strange that there was literally no one else out that night aside from me. Escaping was almost too easy.

I had no idea where I was going, but for a time period that did not matter. I remembered how free I felt running through the woods when I first left home and tried to feel that feeling once more. Sadly, my heart was weighed down with far too much fear in order for me to be happy in my escape. I had never been anywhere near the woods of Mississippi, so this land was completely foreign to me. I needed to find some sort of path quickly before daybreak came. I rushed through bushes and leapt over any log that blocked my path as my footsteps left a path of crunched leaves on the ground.

I feared for daylight because I knew when it's burning rays came overhead, the owner would begin his search for me. But my travels through the woods weren't as easy as I had hoped. Everything in the woods looked the same to me, and I really couldn't distinguish north from south. I soon came to the conclusion that I was finished at this rate.

A couple hours after sunrise, I soon collapsed from fatigue. I lay there in a puddle as I thought how foolish I was for leaving. It was only a matter of time before they realized that I was gone and began their search for me. I fell asleep even though I knew that I might awake back at the plantation as a dead man. I welcomed the notion of falling asleep never to return to that nightmare.

A gentle tapping kept bothering me as I slowly awoke from my slumber. For someone on the run, I was always surprised at how calmly I awoke that day. My initial premonition was that they had finally found me and that my time was up. I glanced up to see the outline of a shadowy figure being obscured by the sunlight. Once I was no longer blinded, I got my first glance on the person whose actions would shape the outcome of my life from that day on. When I saw him, I sensed that he was different from the others that looked like him. I could see it in his eyes. He smiled. At that moment, I knew that any doubts I might have had about him were assuaged. He came over to me and handed me an apple.

"Here, take this. You look hungry," he said.

He tossed me the apple. I just looked at it and then back at him. He smiled again at me. I took a deep bite into the apple. It was probably the best thing I had eaten in months. I consumed the entire thing in no time at all. After I was done ravaging the fruit, the blond-haired boy began to laugh.

"Well, I'm glad that you liked it. Hey, if you're still hungry, I have more food at my place. It's not too far from here," he said.

I nodded and he smiled, saying, "Great. Let's get going then. By the way, my name's Christian. What's yours?"

I just stared at him with a blank look on my face. It took me a while to finally answer his question.

Since Father and I never were too keen on speaking to one another, the first few years of my life I didn't speak often, so I stuttered a bit as I responded to his question, "Terra."

"Terra, huh?" He stroked his chin as if my name was some kind of revelation. "My father once told me that Terra meant son of the Earth," he said as he tucked his hands into his pocket.

"What you mean?"

"Beats me. My dad always says the most random things that are supposed to have deeper meaning or something. I don't know."

He looked into my eyes for the longest time and then gave a big smile just as the sun began to shine on him again, making it look as if he was glowing.

He threw his arm around my shoulder and said. "I think that name will suit you just fine in your life."

I was addled to say the least. There was certainly something strange…no special about Christian that I could just feel as he spoke to me. It was a sensation that would stick by my side for the rest of my days. Because of this initial encounter, I have to admit that I was enamored with him as a young boy. I wanted to know exactly what made him so special. After a moment, I finally was able to come to my senses, and I asked him if I could stay at his place for a time. It was a blunt request to be sure, but I was now well aware of my current situation. I was a runaway slave that had no clue where I was running to. Even at that age, I knew that was a poor combination indeed. When he heard my request, he didn't even seem to care about my reasoning for it. If anything, it seemed that nothing would have pleased him more than to allow me to stay there. He motioned me to follow him, and thus I did so with no questions asked about where we were going. I could just feel that this was right. It made no sense at all, and it didn't seem plausible, but I trusted his word.

I followed Christian back to his home. It was a rather large farmhouse on a medium-sized chunk of land. It was considerably smaller than my owner's land, but I didn't see a single slave there. His father wasn't home at the time, but Christian showed me around to every speck of his land. I still couldn't believe that he offered to take me, an unknown runaway, into his home. During our time together, Christian never talked down to me, and he continued to feed me apples. The initial apple he gave me was the first I had ever had, and I decided that it was my favorite food.

Christian told me a lot about his family and how he and his father had traveled to exciting places I had never heard of before: Zanzibar, Seneca, and Olympus, and they all seemed like amazing places that I wished to go to someday. His life seemed like the complete opposite to mine entirely. It was filled with all sorts of happiness and excitement, but I wasn't jealous of him. On the contrary, I was more captivated by his tales and persona.

I believe that I was with him for hours that day just listening to his tales. Though I only spent a short time with him, he made me feel as if I wasn't different from everyone else in the world. What was even better was the fact that I didn't have to wonder why he was helping me. I could see the sincerity in his eyes. Every word he said was without a doubt the truth. It was nice to be able to not have to question anyone's motives for helping me. He made me feel like my life was actually worth something. For the first time in a while, I was happy. However, he finally decided to ask about me, and I was hoping it never came to that.

"So I take it you're a runaway, right?"

I really wanted to lie to him, but when I tried something inside of me wouldn't allow it.

"Yes."

"Are you all alone, or did you run with someone else?"

"I come on my own."

"Really? How about your parents?"

That was such a hard question. I didn't know how to answer, so I just said what I felt.

"I…I…he held me back. I better on my own. He too scared to run away with me," I said as I lowered my head.

"So you left him behind without telling him anything."

"It for best."

"No, I'm sure that he's worried about you," he said as he placed his hand on my shoulder.

I felt terrible at that moment. I had never given Father's thoughts any consideration. I was only thinking of myself the entire time. I imagined how lonely he must have been during my time away. Father had always told me that the cruelest punishment a person can suffer is exile from the things that he loves. He said it as if something was constantly tearing away at your heart and pulling you back, but you cannot move. The thought of him bearing that pain due to my absence caused me to see the error of my ways fairly quickly.

"I…I…have to go back. He need me."

"Knowing that nothing but pain awaits your return, you'll still journey back there?" Christian asked. "The power of the bonds of man is truly a powerful thing indeed, just as my father said. I only hope someday that I, too, will possess a bond like the one you have with your father. Thank you, Terra. You've given me something that I was searching for a long time. I am in your debt."

"What?" I asked casually as I continued to focus on my thoughts of my father.

"It's nothing. I'll tell you when you're older," he said with a silly grin.

"Right," I replied, confused by his cryptic demeanor now.

Christian showed me the path I would need to take in order to return to the plantation. I just wish I had been prepared for what awaited.

I was able to return to the plantation by nightfall. I should have noticed that something was amiss; it was far too quiet for a plantation that just had one of its slaves escape, but I was still too young to take note of such things. I tried to slip back into the shack where all of us slept, but when I did, I noticed that no one was there. There were scattered things all over the floor as if there was some kind of fight in there. I had even spotted a couple blotches of blood on the wall. Even though I was young, I knew something was up.

I left the shack and went around to the back of the plantation manor because I could hear various sounds coming from there. A sense of anxiety pervaded my very being. Something was making me feel uneasy. It was like a foreboding premonition that kept on bugging me. I hastened my pace and began to run to the back of the manor. When I finally made it there, the sight I beheld was too much to bear.

There, on top of a platform before everyone, was my father stripped naked with a rope around his neck. He was so battered that he couldn't even hold himself up. The rope around his neck was tied to a banister above him that kept him somewhat upright. Anyone could tell that he had been beaten severely as of late. The image of my father reminded me of the dead body I saw hanging in that village. The comparison between the two was so uncanny that I nearly fainted when I took it all in. So many gashes were on his body, it was repulsive. I knew that he was barely conscious from his beatings. It was horrible to see. There was even a pool of blood slowly forming around him as he stood there. I immediately knew the cause of all of his pain. I knew it was my fault. I never would have thought that the owner would punish Father for me running away, but now it makes perfect sense. When I arrived, all turned their attention toward me. The crowd of black figures that were crowded together began to part like the Red Sea as I slowly approached the battered body of my father. The owner, who was in the middle of whipping Father still, began to laugh hysterically as he walked toward me. We met in the middle of the black sea of people surrounding us. The way the fires burned allowed me to only see the white pupils of everyone focused solely on the owner and me. He reeked of whiskey, a smell I had become quite familiar with as of late. He hit me with the back of his hand and knocked me to the ground. The soil was wet, but not from rain. Father's own blood had seeped into the soil giving it a clayish tint. As I tried to get up, the owner put his foot on my head, which kept me down.

As he drove my face further into the earth, he began to speak, "Well, look who's finally returned and not a moment too soon. You have arrived just in time for all of the festivities."

He took off his muddy boot soaked in Father's blood. I looked up to see his battered body not too far from me. That sight was one that would be burned into my mind for the entirety of my life. I screamed out toward him to see if he was still alive.

"Father!" I cried out.

The owner kicked me a couple of more times.

The impact of his boot striking my gut continuously knocked the wind out of me, and just as I began to squeal like a frightened pig, he let up a little saying, "For a monkey, you've got yourself a pretty decent Pap o'er there, lad. When I asked about your vanishing act, he didn't say a word. He kept silent even when I threatened to kill some of the others. It was interesting to see the stone-cold look on his face as I killed a couple of the other slaves."

Suddenly his mocking demeanor turned into one of rage.

"Do you know how much money I lost by killing those stupid monkeys?" he asked as he grabbed a handful of my uncouth hair. "I figured that you and your Pap owed me a fortune, but the moment I even mentioned the thought of killing you as compensation, your docile old man snapped and attack me. Dang monkey!"

I could see that the owner had multiple bruises and a bad limp. He spat toward my father's frail hanging body.

"Stop it!" I pleaded.

"Don't worry about him, lad, he'll be okay, but it's all up to you," he said, lessening the pressure on my head.

"What?"

"Well, here's how I look at things, kid," he began. "I decided it would be far too much fuss and hassle to have to hunt you down and make you pay for your crimes, so I went with a more immediate solution after your dear ole dad here volunteered to take your punishment for you."

The horror of his words rang in my ear. I knew that he had taken the beating for me, but I never would have guessed that he volunteered to do it. Tears streamed down my face as the truth of my selfish actions came into the light.

"Let him go! He been hurt enough already!" I protested.

"I have a deal for you, monkey. Now, I'm a man, who believes a great deal in luck, so why don't we make a deal? In that revolver there's one bullet. If you can shoot the rope that's tied around your dear daddy, then I'll let him live and set both of you free. No strings attached. If you happen to miss though, everything returns to how it used to be. Sounds fair enough to me."

Everything inside of me dropped that second. The mere prospect of being able to save Father and leave that life behind was amazing, but at the same time, hearing the terms of that psycho's sick game almost took my breath away.

I knew that if I made the slightest mistake I might just end up killing Father myself. Such an idea was far too cruel, but I couldn't think of another way out of it. It felt like the walls were closing in on me. I curse myself to this day for not just shooting the owner with the bullet, but I ended up going along with the owner's sick game like the fool I was.

I took the gun and focused in on my father who was barely clinging to life. I could easily see the rope that was slightly hanging him at the moment. I aimed at the rope knowing that freedom was in my grasp. My heartbeat was out of control. During the whole time I aimed at Father, I couldn't stop myself from crying. I never wanted any of this to happen because of my selfishness.

I hated myself for all of the fun I had been having with Christian all day while Father suffered at my expense, but I was determined not to let my selfish decisions be the end of the man that raised me. Images of Father and I going to Christian's home ran through my mind. It sounded like the perfect story.

Suddenly something happened. I felt as if someone's hand was guiding me as I aimed for the rope. I smiled as I lined up my target and finally pulled the trigger. As soon as the bullet left the barrel, I knew that I had made the shot, but fate had different plans. The moment I fired the bullet was when Father suddenly awoke. He jerked his head up high from the shock of the sound and ruined my shot. From his sudden movement, he made the rope go up higher and his head was right where I had been aiming. The bullet stayed true to its course, and I killed Father that night.

5
Exiles

The tragedy of my father haunted me for the rest of my days. I made a promise that in order to make up for his death that I would never be in bondage to another man again. Sariah knew this just as she had become privy to much knowledge about me as of late, so that was why she had such a nervous look in her eye the past week as we were held captive. She knew how adamant I was about that promise and I suppose that she began to fear for her own safety because there was no telling what I would do in her mind. Rebecca had been taken from us by the clown in white they called Father, and ever since the two of them had been reunited, Sariah had the vexing habit of constantly worrying over her sister.

Due to the elongated time period she was gone, I could only assume that she was being tortured for intelligence because she was the youngest, being the tender age of 16. It was due to her age that would have made one assume her ties to the Crusaders were not as strong. Pumping information from her would have been the logical choice that I would have resorted to in their shoes. Their decision in that case was wrong. Out of all of us, my loyalty to the Order was the shakiest, and I would have gladly sung like a bird if asked to as long as I did not endanger Christian or the others, and for the most part Sariah shared my sentiments in this as well. Rebecca had joined the Order mainly because her sister had been recruited, and she wished for nothing more than to reunite with her. She saw the Crusaders and Sariah as one in the same. Betraying them would mean betraying her sister in Rebecca's eyes, so I doubted they would get anything useful. On the other hand though, she lacked the natural resolve and fortitude to undergo torture, so whether she would talk or not was up in the air. I couldn't mention my thoughts to Sariah though, whether she knew about her sister's predicament or not, I believe she was more worried about me doing something that could put her in danger.

"Terra," she said. "Terra, what do you have planned?"

"What do you mean?"

"I know…I know how much you hate being imprisoned, so I'm begging you to not do anything rash since they have Rebecca," she pleaded.

"I swear, you people, think I'm some kind of bloodthirsty beast or something. I don't plan to do anything until we find out more about this place."

"Well, we already know that this is the Isle of the Fallen, though it's different from what I imagined."

"Yes, I suppose it is."

> Thou shall not kill
> Thou shall not steal
> Thou shall not covet
> Thou shall not lie
> Thou shall honor ones parents
> Thou shall not perform adultery in or out of wedlock
> Thou shall only have one God

Those were the tenements etched into the minds of every upcoming Crusader. They were basic principles of life that we had to adhere to in order to be who we were. Becoming a Crusader was not a choice, but a destiny. We were hand-selected as children to become Crusaders and spread the Word to these primitive lands. Once we were chosen, we were remade into a new human being stronger in both body and mind than all others. In order to spread the Word, we must have the power to protect and the intelligence to imbue it upon others. We were able to become living examples of its truths by showing the lesser beings of those primitive worlds that if they adhered to our tenements then they too would be allowed to possess our power.

As with any society, there were times that the rules that served as the cornerstone for it were challenged and broken.

Many a time a Crusader was sent to a hostile land and forced to kill.

Many a time a Crusader had to steal food to survive or steal a relic in order to destroy a group's faith.

Many a time a Crusader had to lie in order to do his job or maybe because being a scion of truth was too hard every waking second.

Many a time a Crusader coveted the power and freedom of those we were sent to convert.

Many a time has the hunger of our flesh taken over and we have broken the promise of purity. I myself was guilty of that on more than one occasion.

Such breaches in discipline were not tolerated at all within the ranks of the recruits. For every rule I had broken that was discovered, I had forty lashings. In fact, I believe that I have more scars on my back from my punishment as a recruit than from my time as a slave. We were instructed to maintain our purity at all costs and normally that would keep us in check, but there were always those that didn't fear the pain of discipline. They feared the loss of their humanity far more than the loss of some decreed morals by a third party they had never seen. When the rise of this disobedience became more prevalent, that's when I first heard of the Isle of the Fallen and the Exiled Crusaders. A small, isolated world that was meant to serve as an exile for all Crusaders that failed to embody the tenements vested upon them. We had all heard stories of the dark nature of the isle that caused a man to lose his mind the moment he sets foot on the beach. Those stories had been passed around long before my time. The whole entire thing seemed to be more of a charade to scare us than a real punishment, but it seemed like we were all gravely mistaken. Sariah and I had heard of the isle before from our previous captain Clay. Night after night, he would tell us of a time when he crash-landed on the Isle of the Fallen and of the hospitality of their people. For the most point, he avoided telling us any detailed account of his time there, but he surely let us know that it existed. I thought of asking Sariah if he had told her anything more due to the fact that she had known him longer, but any mention of Clay's name to her would be sure to sully her demeanor.

The number of worlds out there is truly endless thus the number of recruits for the Crusaders was endless as well. I could not say how many of us there were but from what I had been told, there were a rough 30 percent that had fallen into the ranks of the Exiled Crusaders either officially or secretly. I myself had only met a handful in my time. Sariah used to be among their ranks before she was transformed into an executioner for the Order alongside myself. I wondered if she feared that these people would look upon her as a traitor. Actually, I truly wondered if the people of this isle even knew about other Exiled Crusaders roaming around. The ones that were caught were sent to the island, but there were certainly others they evaded detection from what I heard.

They were not some sort of malicious group and from Clay's time around them years ago, the Exiled Crusaders were very similar to the Order except for the fact they didn't want to be held down by the tenements. That was the only real difference. Though one would never come out and say it, the Exiled Crusaders believed in the idea that since they were bearers of the truth then they were allowed to be absolved for whatever sins they committed. The Order would tell all of the new recruits that anyone that fell into the grasp of the Exiled Crusaders would be cut off from the grace of God, so the idea of exile for breaking the tenements was a sound plan that kept many desires at bay.

I knew I was not the most righteous of Crusaders. I left that title for Christian, but I had not fallen into such depravity that I deserved to be exiled. In fact, my entire team was perhaps one of the best aside from a few miscues that were commonplace. I refused to believe that we had been sentenced to that isle. But no matter how much I fought against the notion, all I had to do was look at the evidence around me. I was trapped on a primitive world that was supposed to have no offensive capabilities to challenge us, yet our casings were blown out of the sky; the inhabitants all wore faded versions of our uniforms; the religious relics scattered all over the place indicated those that lived there possessed the Christian faith, and looking at Sariah was a grim reminder of the multitude of tenements I had broken with her alone. All the evidence pointed to my exile from the Crusaders. I had thought the Order had forgiven us for our supposed sins we committed years ago that had been washed away from the reeducation, but it seemed as though their trust had a limit we had broken.

With all of this truly settling in, the weight of despair rested itself against my heart. I leaned my head against the pole Sariah and I had been tied to the last week and let out a sigh that caused Sariah to laugh, saying, "I suppose that you've just figured out the predicament we're in."

I laughed as well as I agreed with her, "Yeah, we may have just become exiles without even knowing it. Well at least we're given a wonderful room to stay at during our vacation."

"Always the coy one," she said. "This is serious, Terra. Think about the others we have no idea what's going on with them. And we all know how obsessed you are with your brother."

"I hate to break this to you, Sariah, but we don't have the luxury to worry about them. We're in a bind ourselves…did I really just say that while tied up?"

"Yeah you kinda just did there," she said as she shook her head. "Wow."

"I'll say."

We laughed together, forgetting all about our situation for the time being. That's what was great about Sariah. Whenever she was around, she had a way of making me smile somehow. That power was a much-needed remedy at that time. I couldn't speak for her, but the last couple years in the Order I was able to remain sane solely because of her presence in my life. Even though I did not blame myself entirely for what happened on Lactia, I knew I was a small piece of the machine of sorrow that ruined the lives of so many people I had grown to trust. With Sariah being the only one left from that time, she could share the pain I had to endure. Though I never came to her for comfort directly, there was an understood bond between us that had been forged on the private tears we had shed over the years. What started as a bond forged from sadness transformed to one where the sight of her smile and sound of her life filled me with life. Our laughter was interrupted when the clown came in with the tail of his white robes dragging behind him. I was disappointed that he didn't have a choir singing as he came into our humble little tent, but I suppose not everyone was perfect. He had a stern look on his face that made it look like he tried way too hard to look scary, but that time I was able to keep my chuckles under control. Behind him was a man around my age wearing the same uniform we had except his sleeves had been cut to show off the definition in his arms and the top portion of his uniform was unbuttoned, showing off quite the forest of hair on his chest. His brown hair was kept at buzz and his hand stayed on the hilt of his short sword the entire time. He worried me.

The clown pointed his scepter in my direction as he said, "My name is simply Father. I'm the king of this village. I see that you all find your situation humorous. I found that the other one among was much smarter to fear us."

Once her sister was mentioned, Sariah jerked at the ropes that bound us and yelled, "Where's my sister! I swear if you hurt her I'll make sure that this whole village burns!"

The man that worried me walked up to Sariah and gave her this hard look that even made me pull back. His face was constructed in such a way that it looked like he was angry all the time no matter what could possibly be on his mind. In one quick strike, he silenced Sariah by delivering a blow to her face.

"Lucas," the clown called out, "that's enough. We need her to be able to speak."

Lucas nodded his head and walked back behind the clown acting as a very dangerous shadow that could be set loose at any time. I needed to proceed with caution, so I made the first move and said, "So I take you guys are exiles too. We were sent to this isle on the pretense of liberation, but we can see that was a falsity. The reality is that we've been abandoned now just like you, so why are we being treated like invaders?"

"We know exactly why you have come to our land. We're all once Crusaders and recognize an airship and a casing a mile away. I was hoping that attack we made would be the end of you'll but it seems I was naïve. Rest assured though that you will be doing no sort of liberation on this land. All those that come here have been exiled by the High Order of the Crusaders. You all are no different from dirt to them," said the clown.

"Then why are you treating us the same way?" I asked. "You shot us down and now we're your prisoners. What could you possibly want?"

"Abandoned or not, there are always those that wish to defy their fate and *liberate* this land as a show of good faith to the High Order. You're here to ascertain your motives."

"My motive is to ensure my team survives. I'm its king! And it's my fault we were exiled here. All I want is to survive and not ruin their lives further because of my selfishness."

The clown gave me an addled look as he studied my face and then asked, "You're the king for your group? The king, as in the leader of a particular unit, whose goal is to spread the Word? I find it hard to believe that you are kingly material."

"Don't you dare insult my king, you swine!" yelled Sariah. "He's a greater man than you'll ever be in your life no matter how many fools call you Father!"

And once again I found a reason to want to kiss that woman. She became perfectly aligned with my thought process instantly. The clown had made a flaw when it mentioned that he ruled only one random village of the isle. That meant that the isle basically separated into regions where power was divided, which could mean that my team had fallen into the regions of differing powers outside of his scope of view. As far as he knew, we were all that was left of my team and I was the king not Christian. Until we figured out if we could trust that man or not, we had to make sure he didn't discover the existence of the rest of our team. Despite his get-up that man was exiled for a reason, so I knew not to take him lightly.

I continued to press our act onward saying, "I'm guilty of committing an adulterous relationship of fornication with both of the women that were with me. And as their king…I'm proud of what I did!"

I couldn't see Sariah, but I knew she was shocked to hear me take that angle instead of being apologetic for my transgression. I continued my speech, "I'm tired of the stifling ways of the Crusaders! We're men, and men and women are meant to love and feel the passion of our love. Why are we given these passions if they're to be banned by some clandestine group of elders shrouded in holy light? I regret that my actions caused my women pain, but I'll never regret the passion that we all shared over and over and over again."

That last bit may have been a bit too much, but I was dealing with men who I was sure have wanted the feel of a woman many a night before being exiled. This was not some confession toward the pope of a world, this was an interrogation between two exiles and thus I had to take a different approach whether I meant what I said or not. I could feel the heat of Sariah's nostrils fuming on the back of my neck when I mentioned that I had been with

Rebecca as well. That of course was a lie, but it sounded like a much better reason to be exiled in my opinion. I didn't even have to worry about Rebecca because no matter what answer she gave it was mine that would hold the most weight. If anything, she would be expected to lie about the incident between us.

"You're certainly a different sort of king. A man that we could find common ground with. So tell me then king of adultery, how many of you came to this isle?" asked the clown.

"Five. Including myself, there was five of us, so two of my men are unaccounted for. If you could help me find them, then I would be in your debt," I said.

I couldn't tell him that there were only three of us. It would have been far too convenient to believe and besides if he did indeed allow me to look for them, it would give us a perfect chance to find the others. I could only hope that he bought my story and didn't question it any further. If there was ever a time I was glad to be a Negro, it was then. Despite meeting people from differing worlds, my race still came with certain preconceived notions. One of which was that all of those that shared my skin ran rampant with adulterous hearts.

The one he called Lucas came forward and said, "If there were only five then why did we shoot down two casings?"

The clown nodded his head in agreement as if the idea had never occurred to him. That instant let me know for sure that Lucas was the more dangerous one between the two.

"One casing was simply filled with supplies for the Crusade. I'm sure that if you search the island, then you will find the burnt remains of our supplies," I said.

The clown looked at the two of us again and said, "You may be cleared of such suspicion on one condition. We have a trial by fire that all those that claim to be kings who have fallen from grace must endure. If you wish your people to walk among my children, then you too must do this."

"Trust me I know a little something of walking through a fire unscathed," I said.

6

The Phoenix

1861, Southern Mississippi

It's funny, really. It's not often that I take the time to dwell into the past discretions of my childhood. If I could, I would have preferred to omit these incommodious memories from my mind, but no matter how much I wish, such things are unfeasible. Those were such dark and hard times for me. I felt as though there was a hole where my heart had once resided. I remember how much I hated the world at that particular time following Father's death. I would lie awake and ponder why fate permitted such tragic sorrows to befall me. My father often told me how I was supposed to be something "special," but my faith on that notion dwindled with each passing day. I ran away because I thought that a "special child" such as myself should never go through the tribulations of slavery. Such horrid conditions were more befitting of those monkeys that were supposedly my "brothers" than me. Thanks to my father, my logic and intellectual skills far surpassed theirs. Talking down to their remedial level of intellect was perhaps the most trying task I had to endeavor.

All their minds were ever fixated upon was survival along with the embarrassing history of our primal ancestors. It's disgraceful to think that I hailed from the same race. Thankfully, I didn't have to put up with this deplorable lifestyle for long. When I came to twelve years of age, I was sent to work and harvest in the fields for the very first time. During my six years in that wretched place, most of my time was spent caged up within the confines of the manor. I had heard the ominous tales of the dreaded fieldwork, but I was sure that anything was better than the inside of that manor.

I was certainly a fool to believe that.

Sure, I got whipped a couple of times when I was in the house, but that was nothing compared to being branded for just dropping a simple bundle of wheat. Life outside of the manor was a living hell to put it in the simplest terms. Each day out there became worse than the one before it, and being out there all alone was the salt poured into my gaping wound. Even though I despised the lowly monkeys I was forced to work with, I would have gladly accepted the company of one of them to ease my suffering. But as time went on, I began to adjust to the mundane yet painful routine of the fields. After a day's excruciating work was fulfilled, the monkeys and I went over to the pig's trough, and to make matters worse, they were actually grateful for it! I still can't wrap my mind around the concept of being content with eating from the same place as pigs. We were being looked upon as even worse than them, so I never ate with them. Although I'm sure if I even tried to, they would not permit me.

After that *one night* occurred, they all stayed a fairly good distance away from me. My existence had become completely ignored for I was nothing but an enigma to them. It was probably for the best, though. I doubt that I could have handled hearing all of their talk about the ongoing war. Their eyes would radiantly shine with inundating hope whenever word of the war was brought up. How sad. I pitied them for such naïve fantasies. The only occasion I ever felt any semblance of joy back then was during my visits to my father's grave.

My last visit was particularly memorable.

That day was so perfect: there was not a single roaming cloud in the boundless azure sky, spring's copious effects had just begun to nestle within the land, and the weather was neither too hot nor cold. It was at a perfect balance. It was just one of those days where it seemed that nothing could go wrong and that the world was just a beautiful place, but I knew all those thoughts were nothing but futile contemplations. I stood that day atop a hill looking at my father's tearstained tombstone, a lone rock indicating his tragic death, knowing that I was responsible for him being there.

The perfect ambience of that day just further exacerbated my rage and misery. He was all that I had in the world at that time, and now he was gone. I would have much rather been whipped a thousand times by the hardest, sturdiest rod than to have to look down upon his grave. Though I despised my fellow slaves, I was yearning for at least one person to show an ounce of compassion to my dejected soul, but such is the nature of the world. I learned that at an early age in my life, but it still hurts just as much. I don't believe that I moved for hours that day; there was just something in me that made me stay. Whatever that feeling was, it was powerful enough to inundate my fear of being whipped that day for being late.

It was then when my soul was in the very depths of despair that I met her. I never knew when she showed up, but when I felt her warm hand rest on my shoulder. I looked up and saw her cloaked figure. Draped in a black robe and hood that obscured her face like some sort of black phantom, she stood beside me looking at the grave. At that moment, my dark despair was lifted a tad for some odd reason I couldn't explain it back then. She never once looked at me when she spoke, but her words still held an obvious compassion to them.

"Your father was a good man, Terra," she said.

Her voice was angelic and sweet, like she was an angel sent to comfort me.

"You knew him?" I asked.

She removed her hand from my shoulder and bent down to my eye level. As I stared into the dark void of her hood, I felt a chill seeping out from it as if she was some kind of being devoid of life. I froze as I continued to stare into the abyss of her hood and she pointed her finger at me saying, "Yes, and he told me quite a bit about his pride and joy in this world: you."

"I'm no blessing. I'm just a curse upon all who come to me," I said as I knocked her hand away.

"Yes, I heard of your particular tragedy. You should not hold such guilt within your soul at such a young age."

"Then what do you think I should do? Just forget he ever lived and go on with my life?"

"You should do as he wanted you to do and live a full and happy life. Remember, you're something special, Terra."

"Yeah…I've been told." I replied in a sour tone.

"From this point on, I'll be your guardian."

I've learned over the years that conversational skills have never been her strong point, but to just come out of the blue and say that certainly woke me up from my daze of self-loathing misery.

"What?"

"Your father asked me to look over you if he ever passed from this life."

I snapped at her, "I ain't need ya help! I can take care of me!"

"I gave him my word that you'd be looked after whether you want me to or not."

"Just go away."

"There's so much hatred in your heart, Terra. You remind me of myself in a way. It's a shame that you didn't take more after her though. She truly was an angel."

"Some angel. Father's still dead and I'm still alone," I said with little regard to her actual meaning to her previous statement.

Tears finally began to stream down my face and roll over my cheeks as they splattered on the rock of Father's grave. Within the depths of my sorrow, she embraced me within her arms. My head rested right upon her chest where I could hear the sound of her beating heart. Such an embrace reminded me of Father, which made me wrap my arms around her as I buried my face in her cloak.

"One day you'll walk the same path as your father and myself, the path of an exile, Terra, and until then I shall look over you and protect you from harm."

As my tears finally came to an end, I found myself drained of all my energy. My grip on her loosened and as I fell back to the ground slowly losing consciousness I heard her say, "Always stay close to that boy Christian."

I awoke at dusk in the same place I was before, and yet there was no sign of the mysterious woman or the blade she carried. I realized that it all must have been a dream, and I cursed myself for letting such idle fantasies enter my mind. I was nothing but a stone wall when it came to accepting the help of others, and it needed to stay that way.

I didn't look back at the grave. I just continued walking. On my way back to the plantation, night began to slowly take the sky, and with each rising inch of the moon meant my fears would soon be realized for I was already hours late. During my sprinting trek back, a howling cry caught my ear. Huddled in the corner of a nearby bush, I spotted a wounded, shivering fox. I thought back then that this was a perfect opportunity for me to obtain some well-needed food since my owner fed me "so well." As I approached the animal creeping upon death's door, it tried in vain to flee from me, but the gash in its side prevented such actions. It was all too easy; my mouth watered with the thought of actually having a decent meal for the first time in ages, but as I reached for the helpless prey, I felt an irritating prick upon my hand. I looked down and saw that a baby fox had bitten my hand and then retreated back to its apparent mother. I drew my fist ready to retaliate out of anger, but the cub showed no fear. It didn't hesitate to protect the most important thing in its life as I did. I could see the determination to allow nothing bad to fall upon its mother.

I felt ashamed that a mere animal of basic instinct that lacked even an ounce of my superior logic did a better job of protecting its parent. I left the scene and continued to traverse back to the plantation. As if the day wasn't bad enough, it started to rain, and by the time I returned to the plantation, I was completely soaked and tired.

Waiting by the entrance to my lonely shack was my oh-so-munificent owner who seemed delighted to see me. I came over to him with my head down and tried to ignore him, but he stepped between the door and me. Without warning, he gave me his backhand, and I dropped to the ground. The natural power behind his strike was enough to bring me to the ground, but it was the studded rings around his fingers that caused my face to swell. I felt the blood trickle down from my cheek right as I heard him crack his whip. The storm had just really picked up. Lightning flashed through the sky as Owner raised his whip ready to unleash his righteous judgment upon my back. As I lay in the mud facedown, I felt the cold sting of the whip. He probably went at it for a good ten minutes or so. I don't remember much because I passed out sometime through the process. I awoke the next morning in a pool of blood from my midnight lashing. I could barely move for the pain was so severe. I wanted to continue to lay there in the pool of my blood and sorrow, but the longer I stayed there the more I thought of Father and the way he died.

I had finally reached my limit. I wasn't like all of those other slaves that could put up with the inauspicious conditions being thrown at us. The next morning, I didn't go out to the fields. Instead, I went to the woods surrounding the seventy-five-acre plantation and grabbed a large rock and returned to my cabin. For the next few hours, I waited for my master to take notice of my absence. I could hear him yelling for me as I sat in the corner of the shack. My hands trembled for a bit as I heard his footsteps approaching my door, but when I heard the knob turn, I found my resolve to do it. Right as he opened the door, I charged him with the rock, which I had put in a leather bag I stole from the house.

I swung it up against the side of his head, and he dropped in a second. I stood there amazed at what I had just done and how simple the entire transgression had been. A month or two ago, I would have never attempted such a stunt, but there was something powerful driving me that day. All I wanted was to put an end to the miserable existence that I had called a life for the past six years, and I was willing to do anything to do it. A wicked smile came across my face as I remembered the shock on his face when I attacked him, but I had no time to congratulate myself for my deed was far from done.

It took me the rest of the day, but when night came, all my preparations had been made. I took a seat right in front of my bound owner and sipped some of his best wine as I waited for him to wake. The taste was bitter since I had yet to develop a taste for fine wines. Still, it was a sweet taste to have a drink in honor of my owner's suffering. I felt so powerful having him in such a state in his own manor, his supposed safe haven. Perhaps it was another hour or so before he came to. I can't blame him, really. His head was still swollen from the impact of my blow. He frantically looked around, screaming and cursing. To be honest, I don't even remember what he said, nor did I care. Just seeing him so helpless, struggling for freedom and trying to call for help, amused me. All were in vain. I had taken all of the necessary precautions to ensure my plan fell through to the letter.

As for the other slaves, I had set them free. With the owner being so tightly restrained, no one would pursue them. Once they found out about my plan, they all took for the hills. Also, this fool of an owner was a notorious cheapskate, so he started trying to run the plantation on his own with help from his family, meaning he had no hired hands for backup.

By now his temper began to really flare-up. His face had turned red as his veins popped out from his neck. Spit was slung all over the floor as he jerked back and forth with his mouth yelling more obscenities my way. I laughed the entire time until I heard footsteps coming down the hall. He then laughed and said I was done for and to pray to God that I die quickly just as my father did. I walked over behind one of his couches and pulled the pistol he had stowed under it. I found that thing years ago, and I knew it would come in handy, but it still plagues me to why he would be so stupid to leave something like that around his house in the first place. Was he wishing that somebody would kill him?

I butted him with the pistol right against his head to shut him up and I continued to wait for my anticipated guests, his wife and two kids. They didn't even have the time to ask the owner what was going on. By the time they had one foot in the door, it was over for them. The look in their eyes as they all realized one by one that they each had been shot was just too great. His wife stretched out her hand before I put another bullet through her right in her forehead. That was one of the few positives of my ordeal with the death of my father. I now never missed a shot when it came to a gun. The owner's cry of agony for the loss of his family was perhaps the most euphonious sound that ever crossed my ears. He jerked and jerked around thinking that he could save them.

How foolish.

They were nothing more than just corpses at that point just like Father was. Through his sobs and cries, I heard him curse me so many times. I loved every second of it. I didn't even have to rant on to why I did this. He knew why, and now he knew exactly how I felt years ago.

"God will make you burn, boy! God will send you to an eternal dangation for all eternity!" he screamed out. The very mention of God only further angered as I released an impulsive bullet into his kneecap.

"And do you think that you won't?" I asked. "It always amazed how you Christians could so blatantly mistreat others and then go to church the next day professing to love your neighbor. There was once a time when I wanted to be like you all and follow your God, but if this is how your God reacts to the misery of others, then I'll go on without him," I said.

He began to start screaming at me again, but suddenly he just stopped. I suppose that he finally figured out that the floor was soaked in something other than his loved ones' blood. He stared hard at it and realized that the whole room had been drenched in lamp oil. I laughed when I saw his wide eyes look at me and beg for forgiveness. I learned that day just how pathetic some people are. I thought back to how powerless that baby fox was, yet it still fought with pride to protect its mother. As I looked at Owner beg for mercy, I didn't know if I was happy or just disgusted with him. But that feeling only lasted a moment before I realized I was just ecstatic to be in this situation. I continued to laugh even as I pushed over the candle I lit behind me and ignited the room. The inferno roared as the entire house caught fire, and it took no time for my former owner to catch fire as well. His screams almost made me cry for joy. My plan was complete.

There was only one thing left to do. I closed my eyes embracing the closing flames around me as I waited for my own blazing demise.

As I began to feel the clothes of my back heat up to a painful degree, I felt my body move. I opened my eyes, and it seemed like I was flying through the house. I looked up and saw that I was within the arms of the cloaked woman from before. She raced through the flames and made it outside without seemingly getting a single burn. I tried to run back into the flames when she put me down, but she grabbed me and punched me in the gut. I was out in an instant.

The next thing I knew, I was in a warm bed with the rays of the sun beaming down upon my face. I looked to my left and saw

Christian holding my hand smiling at me. His smile was so pure and warm. I couldn't help but smile back. He patted my leg.

"Good morning, Terra."

"Ay…Christian," I moaned as the burns from the fire left my back searing with pain.

"It seems as though fate intended for us to become a part of the other's life, doesn't it?"

"Huh?"

"Well last time I checked, you're a runaway with nowhere left to return because of an unforeseen fire that caused the deaths of your owners. I spoke to my father about you staying with us."

I had never trusted any other soul aside from my father in six years until that moment. All of my hate and anger inexplicably melted away just like that, for I believed him. I believed that I had finally been given a new home.

"Sounds good. I'm going to bed," I responded, drearily.

"I suppose that means that from this moment on, we might as well be brothers," he said as he tightened his grip around my hand.

"Brothers huh…I like the sound of that," I said, drifting back into sleep.

7

Sever

There was still no sign of Rebecca yet. I could tell that Sariah was starting to get worried, but she tried her best not to let it show. Normally, I would let her handle her own issues, but since I was now playing a charade as her king I had to keep up my image. It was hard though considering that I had my own troubles to worry about. This trial by fire that the clown spoke of was truly a clandestine event. The two of us had been blindfolded and led into another tent where they returned my two rapiers. I was able to hear a great amount of commotion outside, but the voices had clamored into one giant mesh of sound, so I couldn't make out what they were so excited about. There were four sentries, men clad with bronze armor and a spear guarding us, so we had no choice but to wait until it was time to commence this trial.

I noticed that one of the guards had his eyes fixated upon Sariah as he scanned her from head to toe. I could feel the heat in my chest flaring up. I knew I wanted to kill him for giving off such a look toward her, a look that I myself had given her numerous occasions. Such a lecherous look would have cost me another forty lashing back at home, but there on that isle, giving off such looks were commonplace. Everything about that island represented freedom from the ridged ways of the Crusaders. As we were blindfolded, the smell of tobacco and ale pervaded the very air around us. I could even hear the echoing sounds of two people completing an act of fornication right as the man's wife walked in. It sounded like such an awful event, but everyone else in the tent that could hear it was just busy laughing. Maybe it was a play of some sort going on then because I could not imagine that a group of people found adultery to be a humorous endeavor.

    I took out my cross-shaped necklace and rubbed its ridged points with my fingers as I prayed for Christian's safety. Once my prayer had finished, I heard the veil of the tent opening as someone came in. The guards around me welcomed Lucas, the man that followed the clown, into the tent. I heard him tell the guards to grab me. The moment the directive left his lips though, I heard Sariah stand up and begin to ask where they were taking me. I told her to stay where she was and allowed for the guards to lead me out of the tent. Because of the blindfold, I had to rely on the guidance of who I perceived to be Lucas pulling at my arm roughly. The force of his pull made me stumble a couple of times before I yanked myself free of his grip. I was not going to be tugged around like some sort of animal. It was not long after I had freed myself that my blindfold was removed which revealed to me I was in a circular dirt field with high walls surrounding me. I lowered my head and sighed as I noticed the stadium-like arrangement for the crowd all around me. I should have known that a world like that would have at least one gladiator pit somewhere.

    Captain Stagg had told us in our training that one day we would most likely find ourselves in one since the primitives were obsessed with these things, but it still was a bother to find myself doing it. In comparison to the one I read about in Rome, this arena was like a child's playpen. The walls were short enough that I could climb over them if I got a head start running, but I could see that the top of the wall had been covered with barbed wire. I looked ahead and saw that the clown and Lucas had their own special pulpit to watch the match. Standing alongside them was

Rebecca and surprisingly there was not a scratch on her. It looked like my whole premonition on torture was off base there.

Still, seeing her with the clown could not mean anything but trouble for me especially since she may have accidentally blown my cover story for being the king. No, I quickly dismissed that to be the case, but she may have been there as a sign of the power that the clown had over me. Either way, I cringed as I watched his disgusting fingers wrap around her shoulder like a spider about to entangle its prey. The clown stood up and directed his hands like some sort of conductor to silence the crowd. Once there nothing but silence, the clown spoke, "Welcome, my children, to another great day where we can offer up our praise to God for allowing us to enjoy the simple pleasures we're about to witness. As most of you know, we have another batch of Crusaders exiled from their home because they wished to do nothing but follow the instincts that our Lord had imbued upon us. As per tradition, I'm more than happy to allow them to become my children, but as you all know, we must test their conviction to our cause!" He threw his hands up and the crowd went insane: men were spilling ale everywhere and women began to flash their chests to…well I don't know if there was a point but they did it. The clown calmed the crowd down once more and continued to speak, "As you all know there's only one way for a king and his followers to join our ranks. He must be willing to sever the sacred bonds to the tenements that have bound his soul to the Crusaders since he was a child. It's now time for the Festival of Severing, my children! And the first event is the Ritual of Blood! Bring forth the challenger!"

The clown sat back down as Lucas began to whisper in his ear and they both shared a laugh. The crowd continued to let out their excitement as they waited for whoever I was supposed to fight. Looking at the crowd, losing all sense of themselves, was a sight to see. It was almost impossible to believe that every single one of them had been a Crusader or recruit at some time in their lives. They were more likened to a tribe of primitives than the refined organization I was a part of. Did people really become this depraved once separated from God. If so, I understood the point of exile now as a punishment. Their intensity picked up as a man wearing a tattered version of my own uniform came forward with a katana in hand. My heart dropped and I looked over to the clown once I saw who the man was. I took a few steps forward and was face to face with one of my squad mates, Dom Paris. The way he looked at me indicated that he knew that this was going to happen beforehand. I don't know for how many days he had known, but I could see it in his eyes that he had found the resolve to fight me. I suppose him finding that resolve wasn't too hard considering that he was still furious about the whole Rebecca incident in Fiore during my executioner days.

I could see the scar that Sariah had left upon him where his eye used to be even though it had healed well over the past two years. His head had been shaved and I could see signs of torture as well at certain places over his tanned body. I thought back to the words of the clown regarding the whole severing idea. Whatever his goal was, he intended me to break one of the most sacred of tenements of the Crusaders and kill Dom, who was supposed to be one of my subjects at that time. The bond between a king and his vassals was not one that was taken likely in the Crusaders, so to just order a king to kill one of his own was beyond low.

"So what's the confused look on your face, Your Highness?" asked Dom, starkly.

I could see his hand shaking as if he had a nervous breakdown, and most likely it was due to the harsh torture his body had been through. Overall his body didn't look well in the slightest.

"Dom, what have they done to you? Are you all right?" I asked.

"Wow, Terra, my king is actually concerned about little ole me? This is such a wonderful surprise. It's not every day that a king would concern himself with the well-being of his vassals," he said as he let off a strange laugh.

The longer we stood there together, the more I began to suspect that his mind was not there any longer. Had he suffered through the process of reeducation as Sariah and I had? If so, I feared there was no hope for him. I doubted the exiled Crusaders were as gentle as the Order was. As I looked upon the wounds on his body, a powerful fear crept into my heart.

"Dom," I cried out, "What did you tell them about us?" I realized that with Dom's anger toward me and Sariah, his loyalty was shakier than my own.

"I told them nothing. I told them nothing as they cut into my body and burned me and drowned me and hit me again and again and again! I told them nothing for Christian! But things changed when I heard that you were my king now, Terra!" he cried out.

I didn't have the time or patience to deal with Dom and his misplaced anger issues, so I moved on to what was important.

"Dom, have you made contact with any of the others? If not, have you heard anything?"

"Why would you care about the others? You're king now of your own little band. You don't need us."

The way he kept saying king bothered me, so I took another step closer to him and grabbed him by the collar asking, "Dom, if you know anything about Christian and the others then please tell me!"

The roars of the crowd were just loud enough to keep our conversation a secret between the two of us, but still I had difficulty hearing him at times.

He pushed me off of him, "I've heard nothing from him. The only thing I heard about was your selfish ambitions and how you got us exiled here! You're such a hypocrite. You condemned me for sleeping with Rebecca, yet you did the same thing with her sister and still think I'm trash but you're holy. Sariah took my eye and justified it saying how, as a leader of the unit, she was entitled to serve the king's justice. The same justice that remained elusive for her when rumors of your *closeness* together were brought up."

I thought back to when I first told Sariah of the relationship that Dom and her sister had and never before had I seen her face turn such a shade of red from the boiling fury in her heart. Sariah knew full well the punishment that her sister could face if news of her relationship with Dom were to spread to the higher members of the Order. The entire scene with that occurred in Fiore was one I wished to forget. He had always blamed me for the loss of his eye because I felt the need to inform Sariah. The Dent sisters were always seen as an enjoyable pair that would never result to such violent means for any reason, so it was the assumption by many and mainly Dom that I urged Sariah into her rage.

"Dom, this has nothing to do with us! We need to find Christian! So why don't you get your act together and we can get out of this mess!"

"Why? So you can live out in the jungle with the Dent sisters to yourself? I heard how you were with Rebecca too and that's why we were exiled! They told me everything you said! It makes sense though. You had Sariah come after me so you could have Rebecca to yourself. I always suspected that was the case. I may not have cared about her, but she was still mine, Terra! It was my choice to do away with her, not yours! You've always had the bad habit of stealing from others, Terra. If you had the stones to steal Rebecca, then I know you have the stones to steal the title of king from Christian."

I couldn't believe what I was hearing. That kid was so inundated by his anger and whatever they had told him that he was not thinking clearly. I had told him time and time again that I had no interest in Sariah's sister, but after the actions I took to bring down the wrath of Sariah upon him, I knew he had no desire to believe my word. And now that petty dispute between the two of us was making him doubt my loyalty toward Christian as well. I had made it very clear in the past that I never wished to be a king and that the entire title was the worst thing ever.

"Dom, listen to me. Forget about all of that and help me figure out how to get us out of this. They want us to kill each other," I pleaded.

"I know. Here on the Isle of the Fallen, there's a rule that if a king gets his vassals exiled because of his action then they have a right to challenge him for revenge. I'll kill you to end your ridiculous ambition of being king and rip away your claim on those sisters! If I kill you, then they will be free from whatever charms you try to place on them!"

"You're not serious are you? You want to fight me over that?"

"I'm sure that I could find plenty of reasons to fight you, Terra, but for now all I need is that taking your life will spare mine. So if I have to go through you to do it then so be it! After all we're exiles now, so I have no loyalty to you or Christian that I have to fulfill."

That last part really struck a nerve.

"So you're saying that you'd turn on your own king if it benefited you now, Dom?"

"By this point, Terra, I'd gladly gut the man if it meant I wouldn't be branded as an outcast among these people."

I drew my rapier and pointed it his way, "As the right hand of our king, Dom, I sentence you to death for the act of breaking your sworn oath to your king. May the Lord forgive your filthy soul."

"You self-righteous prick! How dare you call me filthy after all of the tenements you've broken! You parade around exalting the name of the Lord and of Christian, but you never take their commands seriously and go about doing as you like. People like you need to be killed."

The only reaction that his declaration produced was a chuckle from me. That was how all of the students of the Order were. Those types of actions were always looked down upon as being trivial and just altogether nonsense. You can preach all day about how you feel, but only your actions could carry the weight of your convictions. That's what made the Crusaders a force to be reckoned with. We exuded the truth of the Word through our actions rather than our words.

Some would call such an attitude as a blatant display of how egotistical we all were. When it came to our ego, to put it mildly we all thought they were the best and most aptly skilled warriors among all the worlds and to be honest we most likely were.

As such, there were few things that I learned to respect during my time training, and the abilities of my fellow recruits were one of them. Aside from Christian and myself, Dom was perhaps one of the best to have learned alongside me when it came to swordsmanship. He was young, the same age as Rebecca, so he was still a little raw in some areas but the kid was a natural.

I knew how serious to take this threat. We both took up our stances and waited for the first one to make a move. It was one of the first lessons that we had both learned. Stagg's words echoed in my mind. *Rushing into a fight does nothing but improve your chances to fall.*

We slowly began to pace around one another. I only had one of my two swords drawn at that time. It was not a form of disrespect to Dom, but merely a way to gauge to see if I needed to try my best to win. I had no idea if the people watching in the stands could very well be my enemy tomorrow, so I had to try my best to win without showing them my potential.

As we continued to pace around one another, I took note of the terrain. The dirt was dry and allowed for no loose footing, so any chance of me slipping and him getting lucky was out of the question. The crowd though was something to be concerned about. They had already begun to throw rotten fruits at us because we were taking our time as any true warrior would. In fact, hadn't most of them been trained as a Crusader in some capacity? If that was the case, then why were they such a bloodthirsty lot? Had the training and education they received from the Order dissipated the moment they set foot on that island? Just looking at Dom only further exacerbated my cause for concern. He was normally one to be chill in any given circumstance. To see him so worked up after only spending a week on the island was certainly concerning. I wondered that if the longer we were all there then would we all start to feel those affects as well.

But thoughts such as that were pointless at that time. Dom was the only concern on my mind. Without a moment's hesitation, I took off toward Dom.

He and I had spent a fair bit of time together in the past, but all of those memories meant nothing. Not only did he turn his sword against me for the insignificant feelings toward a woman, but he turned his back on Christian, and for that I had to see him die. My blade felt heavier than usual. Despite my resolve to end that kid's life, it was hard to just turn my steel on one that I had called friend. I felt the weight of my blade slow down my movements. I tried to bury my emotions, but I kept seeing images of us laughing together with Christian and the others. He was a friend despite all that had happened between us. Dom must have seen the weakness that exuded from my body as he took a firm step forward and slashed his sword toward my head.

I quickly took a defensive stance and was able to just barely block his incoming attack. I was able to push him back which left him off balance for a moment. I looked closely at how his feet staggered backward. I knew if I attacked at that moment, then that fight would be over. Stagg had always said that I fought like a street urchin that did not know how to dance with a blade. I was one that would never be able to read my opponent's movements let along coordinate my own for an effective strike. I laughed at how little faith he placed in my skills. With one powerful swing of my blade, I went for Dom's head.

To be honest, I had expected better of Dom. With victory in hand, a smirk emerged on my face but a little too soon because Dom quickly countered by pulling out a dagger from his side and blocked my deathblow. With me now off balance, Dom showed why he was called the Dancing Blade among the other recruits. He gracefully executed a series of quick slashes at me that would only be described as art. Using only his crude, chipped dagger and his katana, Dom was able to perform a flurry of attacks that seemed to come from every direction. Due to me being off balanced, I suffered a deep laceration in both of my legs that slowed down my footwork as I did my best to block off Dom's attacks. The cuts burned as I still attempted to rely on my legs to move about with the level of finesse I was accustomed to, but the more I used them the more the pain insisted that I just stop.

The first initial attacks I was able to block with just one blade, but as the intensity of Dom's attacks increased, I decided to turn the tables and draw my other blade. I was disgusted in myself for having to resort to my trump card so early on in the fight, but my fears about Dom had proved to be true. He was far better than he used to be with the blade and from his flurry of attacks along with my hesitating blade, I could see that I was outclassed in this fight.

My only option was to attempt to turn the tables by using both of my blades because if this continued any longer I would soon be joining Father in the grave. As I reached down to draw my second blade, Dom tossed both of his weapons in the air and with his bare hands dealt me a vicious series of fierce blows across my body. The attack made me stagger back and this left me open for Dom to follow up his punches with a sweeping kick that knocked me to the ground.

As the impact from my fall knocked the wind out of me, I realized my mistake. Time and time again, Dom had seen me battle with two blades, so it was only natural that he was waiting for me to draw my other blade. I looked up and saw that Dom was charging toward me with his dagger and katana once again in hand. I tried to get up but, the blows that Dom had dealt had broken at least a couple of my ribs which hampered my movement. I tried to work through the pain, but Dom quickly tossed his dagger right at my chest in order to end that fight. The blade sunk deep into my hand as I caught the blade in midair. I tried my best not to scream as blood gushed forth from my wound and dripped onto my chest. If I had caught that dagger any later, then I would be a dead man. It had been aimed directly at my heart. Typical, only a student of the Order would have such pinpoint accuracy.

I dropped his danger and winced as I slowly drew my second blade at that time. Pain had a way of dissipating even the cloudiest of dreams. My memories with Dom as my comrade had long ago faded away the moment he turned his back on his king and my brother. I was a fool to allow any sentiment that I had for the kid stifle in my mind. He charged at me with his katana raised in the air and attempted a downward strike. I blocked the attack easily with my blades and then dealt him a kick in the chest to push him back. I could still feel the burning sensation of my wounds as I made even the slightest moves, but I stomached the pain. As he stumbled onto his back, I stopped and waited for him to get up. I had no intention of having a misplaced step by a child assure my victory, but then I thought for a moment he was no longer a Crusader. He was a mutt that turned his back on his master, thus he deserved no mercy or respect from me. I then leapt on his body driving both of my blades into his chest before he could get up.

I looked into his tear-filled eyes as blood began to leak from his mouth as I said, "Now you die, you disgrace among our kind. May your soul never find the peace it seeks, you traitor." With those last words hanging in his ears, I saw the light fade from Dom's eyes and his head fall back into the ground. Almost simultaneously, the crowd erupted with cheers. Cheers? They cheered the life of a boy that had been slain because of his own foolish pride like it was the greatest thing ever. Despite it being my hands that robbed Dom's body of life, I took no joy in the deed as they did. How could those that had been raised to be righteous from their youth revel at such a sight? It was then I knew I was truly on the Isle of the Fallen. And it was then I decided that I wanted to kill them all right there. Forget about salvation or any sort of brotherhood with those mongrels. People that blatantly spit on the word as they did should not be tolerated. I picked at random a man that was stuffing his face while laughing at the body of my former comrade and I decided he would die first. I grabbed Dom's dagger ready to let it fly when I noticed that Lucas had a bow and arrow in hand ready to fly if I made my vengeful choice.

I knew what he was telling me. I could not act in such an impulsive way which would result in the deaths of the two girls. I looked over to the pulpit where Rebecca stood with Lucas and the clown, and saw a tear stream from her eye to the ground. I knew full well that she had feelings for Dom when he took her into his bed, and I knew that she would most likely hate me for what I did. I knew as Dom's body lay there in the dirt that I had now crushed his heart twice in order to further my own desires. Even though I had denied the fact that I informed Sariah of their relationship out of a sense of righteousness, I had in fact only done so to get her to further open up to me. If I had been in his shoes, then I would have done the same thing. He was the sacrifice for my pleasure and my beliefs in the way I lived, and I didn't care at all. I was alive and well and he was dead. It was that simple. If he had done things according to how I told him, then he would be standing by my side ready to help Christian.

Despite how I felt no guilt for my actions, I could not ignore the crowd cheering the words that meant that I had broken one of the sacred tenements of the Crusaders. I had severed myself from the Order by killing Dom. I was now officially an exile.

8
Brotherhood

Dom had always said he could never understand the bond that Christian and I had. He knew we came from the same world and that I was adopted into his family but that was it. The Crusaders forbid all recruits from sharing their past experiences with others once they joined the ranks. The best way to be purified from the world was to forget it ever existed, so I never blamed Dom for his ignorance. In order to understand my loyalty to Christian, it goes much further back than his family adopting me. Much further back indeed.

In a town miles away from Vicksburg, Mississippi, 1863

I was fourteen at the time. The last two years of my life were the best to date by far. I had been living with Christian's family as one of their own for a while now, so I had finally begun to get used to the whole crazy notion. Just as my father had, they taught me the skills necessary to survive in the world, so I proud in the fact that my speech had improved during that time, but as I've learned many times in this life of mine, things are never as good as they seem. So far, our land had not been affected by the war aside from the economic issues that happened from the lack of trades, so we mainly just kept up with it from the papers. I, for one, never gave the thing another thought nor did I ever imagine I would become involved in such a trivial affair. Sure that whole concept of all of my "brothers and sisters" being freed sounded nice in theory, but it was obvious that it would take years for "them" to attain equality with the whites. It might be easier if everyone was more like Christian's family. They were just too naïve to understand…the fools, but they weren't alone in their foolishness. Maybe I was the real fool. I believed that happiness would continue to coincide with me forever at that point in my life. I should have known better. I should have known that they would have come one day seeing how the war was going.

That fateful day, a Confederate unit marched into town. It was a branch of Lieutenant General John Pemberton's forces under the command of that horrid Captain Hannon. He was nothing but a run-of-the-mill planter that was given his title because of so many deaths that had occurred in the higher ranks, but that run-of-the-mill farmer was the man that destroyed my peaceful existence with Christian's family. I was a well-trusted member of the family, so when one of our neighbors came by informing us of some kind of commotion involving some soldiers. Christian's father decided to send me down alone to assess the situation. I was quite surprised by the request at first, but it soon made sense to me when I remembered that Christian was off doing errands. Besides, I didn't think it was anything to get excited about. I figured that some drunken Confederate was probably going off about how they were beginning to lose the war. I went to check it out all the same though. When I left our farmhouse on the outskirts of the woods, I began to head toward town.

The walk to town was never long. It usually took me about twenty minutes depending on the weather, and that day was a perfect one. Our plantation was well situated on the outskirts of the nearby woods so whenever autumn came through, the fields were always covered with the colors of the season as the leaves littered the ground. I found myself enjoying many morning walks back in those days since the beauty of the day seemed to reflect on how perfect my life was.

Despite the beautiful weather of the day, I still didn't want to go into town. I didn't mind the task. I just never liked going to town because I'd always have to wear those darn clothes: leather shoes, those all white shirts I'd have to keep super clean, and the worse were the trousers and the suspenders. I never did like the whole proper attire they dressed me in, but I didn't want to cause any trouble for them, so I went along with it. My trip into town was further aggravated by the absence of my usual apple. Every time I would go into town, I would grab an apple from one of the trees from our neighbor's property along the path. Those apples were the most prized possession of our neighbor Mrs. Dend and it was a household rule to never take one of her apples. Christian's dad told me not to, but I felt like I just had to. I always felt so much better afterward. I soon got over it though and continued on with my soon-to-be eventful day.

When I entered the town, I could immediately see that something was going on for all of the shops were abandoned, and hardly anyone was in the streets. I looked around a good long while for any sign of life in the area before I decided to capitalize on my situation. I picked up an abandoned duffel bag and visited the various empty shops and "borrowed" a couple of their possessions from each store and food stand. After my little shopping spree, I headed down to the town square where it looked like all of the commotion was going on. As I got closer, I saw that what seemed as a peaceful gathering from afar was in fact a full-out riot of some kind. I heard men yelling in the middle of the circle the crowd had made. I wanted to go into the crowd to get a better look, but someone grabbed me by the arm when I tried. I looked behind me and Christian was holding my arm and had raised his finger over his lips to order my silence. He quickly looked around and pulled me into one of the back-alleys.

"What in the world are you doing here, brother?" he asked.

"Your father." I began to say but he gave me a displeased and annoyed look.

"I mean our father sent me here to find out what the commotion is," I corrected myself.

Christian poked his head around the corner and looked at the exuberant crowd.

"We need to get you out of here as soon as possible. It's not safe." he said.

"What do you mean?" I asked.

"Come I'll tell you on the way."

Christian yanked on my arm, but I pulled away.

"Why don't you just tell me now huh? What's the big deal here?"

He looked around. He knew very well that once I became stubborn on a matter back then that I wouldn't budge an inch in my decision.

"A group of soldiers have come in."

"I know that," I said, rolling my eyes.

His hand wrapped tightly around my wrist as his voice took a firmer tone saying, "Well did you know that they've come here threatening to recruit a few of us in order to sure up their numbers at Vicksburg? A few have already joined voluntarily, but others have been forced at gunpoint. That's what the crowd is about. A few of your less-devoted "fans" have told the soldiers that you're here in order to save their own children from having to join. A couple of men have gone out looking for you. We need to get back to the house before that happens."

"I'm not a coward, Christian! If they want me, I'll fight them myself!"

"You truly are foolish," he said as his hand slipped away from me. "Don't be stupid. Just trust me. I'll protect you no matter what happens. Remember, we made each other a promise. That's why we have these necklaces."

I just nodded my head and followed him back home. The trip didn't take nearly as long because we sprinted there the whole way. When we ran through the door, Christian's father could tell something was wrong. He had the same worried look on his face that Christian would get. It was funny how much they looked alike even for a father and son. In just five years from then, Christian would become the spitting image of his old man in almost every way except his father had long hair. He came over to us and heard the whole situation. The first thing he did was hugged me and told me how sorry he was for sending me there.

A hug from my own father was certainly a rare occasion, but Christian's father more than made up for it with all the hugs he gave me. He then told us to hide in the cellar and wait for him to go and get us. I never wanted to go there. I pleaded to let me help him, but Christian, always being the obedient one, told me not to. I calmed down and followed him to our cellar. The cellar was a well-hidden facility underneath a carpet in the middle of the living room. Not much was kept down there save a bed and some water. Though we were under the house, we could hear what was going on up top for the most part.

I could never understand Christian sometimes. It didn't take long for the men who were looking for me to arrive at the house. While I tried my best to listen in on what was going on, Christian just lay back on the bed and tried to sleep. I wish I could have had his whole "everything is going to be all right" demeanor when it came to these things. He always kept a cool, level head no matter what happened. I think that man could have slept straight through a hurricane while on a boat if he wished to. I hated him for it back then though. It always seemed like he didn't really care.

There didn't seem like much was going on at first. I could only hear Christian's father being formal to the soldiers. My name did come up quite often though. After a while, I began to hear footsteps all through the house. They were looking for me. It never occurred to me at that time that if they found me that I would be going off to war to become a weapon or a sacrifice for some man who wouldn't even bother to remember my name. The only thing I thought about was being torn away from another family because of the color of my skin. I cringed at the thought that such an ill fate was truly possible in this world. It was at least two hours after they arrived I heard Christian's dad ask if they were done. They were getting really frustrated. I could tell just by the impatience in their footsteps. A smile came upon my face when I thought they were leaving.

Suddenly, I heard a crash followed by the shouts of an angry soldier, "Look, we ain't leaving this here place of yours empty-handed! If you ain't got no monkey here, then we'll be takin' yere other boy wit us then."

The mere thought of having Christian taken from him sent his father into a rage I've never heard before.

He began yelling how that would never happen, and they would have to take each of us over his dead body. I think a tear rolled down my cheek when I heard him say that, but I wish he hadn't. I recall one of them shouting the order to take him outside. I heard some struggling, but eventually they won. After I was positive they had left, I grabbed Christian and told him what was going on. He still didn't seem worried, but I could see that he wanted to see what was going on now. We came out of the cellar and went into the living room to see what was going on through the window. There were around seven soldiers outside around Christian's father. One of them had a rifle to Christian's father's head and two others had lit torches in hand.

We both knew what they were trying to do. Captain Hannon, the leader of the men cried out, "Hey, monkey, I know that you're in there. If you come out, I won't have to kill this nice man that tried to help you. A bullet to the face is much a messy way to die, don't you agree? You wouldn't want his blood on your hands now, would you? So just come out, or we'll torch the place after we kill him!"

Even though I knew how this world still deemed someone like me as nothing more than a tool, I still couldn't believe this was happening. My whole life was about to be taken away from me again. I looked at Christian; he had a grim look on his face. I laughed a bit when I realized how meaningless my life was. It was either going to be his father or me. I would make the same choice. I found the resolve in me to stand up and accept my fate once more. They saw me through the window. I began to walk toward the door but Christian tackled me.

He shook me by the collar as he said, "What are you thinking? We made a promise. I just told you that! There's no way they're going to take you away from me!"

I was utterly speechless. I had no idea what to do or what to say. An endless stream of tears ran down my face as I saw a stupid little smile form on his. I wanted nothing more in the world than to just stay there, but despite my own desires, I realized that there was still a cruel reality waiting for the two of us. Christian rose up his head and looked out to see them. He could see that they were about to set the house on fire. Despite what we wanted to think, we knew there was no good way out of this. It angered me so much. The mere concept that I was being hunted for no other reason than my skin color was infuriating. My eyes glanced down to my arms and focused in on their dark complexion. It was because of that simple difference: the same difference between a white shirt and a black one was why my world was being taken away. A color! A stupid, stupid color!

I looked over to Christian one more time. I had never seen him look so down; I hated seeing that. Christian sighed and then grabbed my hand. I had no idea what he was doing, but he gave me that look saying that "everything would be okay."

Yeah I was a sucker for that sort of thing. No matter what the situation would have been back then, if Christian asked me to have faith in him, I would. That's just how we always were for a while. He let go of my hand and put his hands behind his head as we walked outside together. A couple of the soldiers lowered their weapons when we came outside, but Hannon's men still had a gun on Christian's father. Christian took another couple steps in front of me. I never expected this next part.

"Hey, how 'bout we make a deal?" shouted Christian as we emerged from the house.

The soldier gave Christian an addled yet interested look. He motioned for Christian to go on.

Christian continued on saying, "If you tell your men to forget everything that happened here today, both my brother and I will join your forces."

My head turned around on a quick swivel. I wanted to punch him for suggesting such a ludicrous plan, but I kept my mouth shut. I just looked back at them to see their reaction. They were just as stunned as I was by his proposal. They never would have thought that he would volunteer to join the forces that held his father at gunpoint. The worst part about it was the fact that in all my years with Christian he had never told a lie. He always said it was one of his ten principles of life, so I knew that this was no sort of ploy on his part. All of the men turned toward their leader waiting for his answer. He looked up at our home and then back at Christian and then toward his father and smiled. Christian's father raised his head so his eyes met Christian's. I saw him try to mouth off something, but I couldn't catch all of it. I turned to Christian and saw his eyes watering.

My mind was in far too much of a daze to see who exactly said it, but one of the soldiers said, "Sure you can join us, kid, but first I have to take care of something."

I looked up to see Hannon walking over to the soldier over Christian's dad. He took away the rifle, took aim and fired a shot right into his face. I didn't think; I didn't cry; all I did was react. The other soldiers were just as surprised, so my move was much easier.

As I sprinted past them, I quickly stole a bowie knife from the hip of one of the men. I continued my straight-line dash toward their leader and went for the kill, but I was tackled by one of the others seconds before I got to my target. I squirmed and struggled, but they would not let me free. My anger further rose as the man who took away my life stood over me.

"According to the law, that man was illegally harboring a runaway slave. The price for such an offense is death. All I did was follow the law. Men, raid the place and take whatever you need!" ordered Hannon.

Instantly, the soldiers turned into wild scavengers as they rushed inside our home. Christian just stood there as they knocked him down and ran by. Hannon looked at Christian with a disgusting smile as he said, "I'm sure you don't mind this. We're your only family now, so we might as well share everything."

I struggled even more to get free, but Hannon knocked me out by hitting me with the blunt end of his rifle in the face. I was out cold. Christian told me the next day that they burned down our house afterward.

That was the beginning of the next two years of our lives as Confederate soldiers. Christian told me not to act up because he didn't want me to get hurt. I didn't want to agree, but I did in the end after much arguing. He promised me that we would leave when the time was right, and when we could find a home of some sort. I was okay with that because I promised myself I would kill Captain Hannon, so I was okay with staying for the time being as I plotted my next move.

9
War

Two years. I fought for two long painful years in that accursed military, but despite my bitterness, my experiences weren't all for naught. It was with them that I learned my three cardinal rules: do whatever it takes to survive, pledge my life to Christian, and never allow someone weaker than I suffer unless it's by my own hand. With those three philosophies etched into my heart, I miraculously survived battle after battle on the front lines alongside Christian without ever taking a bullet. Actually, I don't believe either of us was ever injured in our time fighting, but we were not oblivious to our supposed "luck" as the others called it; in fact, I for one began to revel in our immortality on the battlefield. As I would charge into battle along with the others, I would feel the bullets graze past me and kill those who were merely a couple inches next to me. So many cries of anguish rang through my ears as my unwanted comrades fell before me, but their deaths meant nothing to me. In fact, their deaths and my uncanny survival put a pleasant smile on my face each and every night. The only lives that mattered were my own, Christian's, and Captain Hannon's. I did whatever I could each battle to ensure their survival at all costs.

When we were first forced to fight for them, I thought that Christian would be a burden because of his disdain for hurting others, but his resolve to live and continue fighting was equal to my own to protect him. He…he wanted to make sure he did something important. I could tell from the way he fought. Christian was the only one I could trust on the battlefield. There were countless times I would hear the bodies of my attackers from behind falling seconds before they killed me. Every save was due to Christian. To be honest, our skills were uncanny: I don't remember a single one of my shots that I fired ever missing when it came to Christian. We were both perfect shots when it came to helping each other. I saved him just as many times as he saved me.

I actually believe that it was our time together back then that made our bond so strong for all of those years. We both knew that all we had was each other. I was looked at as the immortal slave and he was looked upon as the immortal slave keeper. It was so much fun to go into the taverns after a battle and witness all of other soldiers' jealousy. I couldn't really blame them, though. We were still just children on the battlefield and we were showing them up in every way. It was sad to see the kind of men that claimed to be the protectors of their so-called great new nation. Most of these *noble gents* fighting for equality with the North would constantly harass the waitresses and cause nothing but trouble. They believed that they deserved whatever they wanted. It was humorous to see the scenes that would occur with Christian and the others. Usually it would be the same old story. A waitress would turn one of the drunken soldiers down, but then she would go talk with Christian even though he was about five or six years her junior. After that, a fight would normally happen in which I would have to do the fighting.

The challenges would always vary from fights to drinking contests and so forth. It was a good workout to say the least, but it was little weird as well. There was Christian and I, two sixteen-year-old boys that turned from sheltered children into top soldiers in two years. I often pondered how such a thing was possible, but I realized that it wasn't worth the time to figure out.

I wasn't the only one that thought of our questionable abilities that emerged. The others hated the fact that their worthless friends and family died while we two nobodies continued to survive. At the end of the day though, they came to respect us despite their hatred. Even Hannon acknowledged our strength and importance to the unit after some time: for the first few months there, we were kept under constant watch and usually confined, but later on we were given free reign. It was a huge mistake on his part, but I made sure that he wouldn't regret it until the very end.

Our two-year service began at Vicksburg, the last stronghold of the Mississippi River. If we were to fail there, then the fighting strength of the South would severely be hampered, and the war would shift back into the North's favor. Captain Hannon was extremely fervent about not losing this location to the North. He would always tell all of the soldiers that their dreams lied here in Vicksburg and that in order to preserve them we must fight. It was a ridiculous motto, but it somehow inspired the other soldiers. I think that even Christian was somewhat moved by the ideology. Whatever the other soldiers' reason to fight though was sure didn't help them during the Vicksburg battle.

It was only two months after Christian and I had been *recruited* that we were thrown into the fires of battle. We marched for five days toward Vicksburg to rendezvous with Lieutenant General Pemberton's men, but during that march the others constantly messed with Christian and me. They would always say that we were going to be put on the front lines and told us how painful death is. I had never actually thought about death before, so many dark questions seemed to hang around the concept, and I didn't want to know any part of it.

Everyone else could tell how anxious I was becoming over the last couple of days. Before I had even stepped on the battlefield, I was losing the battle of my nerves. My fear consumed my every waking moment, which caused me to be nothing but a burden to the others around me. As time went on, I even heard talk in the camp about them *taking care of me*. I don't blame them though; I couldn't help myself. All the horrid tales of war pervaded my mind. When I slept, I saw blood and heard the screams of others. For four straight days I had these dreams, but Christian soon came to my aid.

Christian was never the sort of person that gave long speeches to make someone feel better. He would usually just say a sentence or two then I would feel better, but this time was different. It was the night before we would reach Vicksburg. He just came over to me and without even saying why, he was there telling me a random story. Every time I tried to say something he gave me *that look,* a simple glare with his head tilted to the side, and simply continued his tale. It's funny that I don't even remember what he said, but it did help me significantly. I soon calmed down and went to sleep without a hitch. My goal was to simply keep going on day after day and not worry about the day before. I wish that idea had gone like I had planned.

Finally, the next day came and thus the battle would soon begin. I had heard most of the current situation from Christian. We were heading into a battle in our favor completely. Apparently, General Grant has tried to take Vicksburg by attacking upriver four times and each of them was a failure. Not only that but our forces far outnumbered Grant's forces, which made things easier as well.

Maybe it was bad luck because the moment I stepped foot in that place, bad news came. When we arrived, it was obvious that something was amidst for the whole town was bustling with soldiers moving from place to place shouting orders to set up artillery and get all of the bases secure. The quiet town I heard about had transformed into an all-out stage for battle.

A few things had changed since Christian had gotten his information on the situation at Vicksburg. The great General Grant had acquired some friends. By merging his forces with the Army of the Gulf's forces, the Union had started to gain hard-fought victories at Port Gibson, Raymond, and later on at

Champion Hill. With Pemberton's forces now stretched out, this made an opportunity to attack our current location, Vicksburg, and General Grant took full advantage of that by surrounding the city. Luckily, we just so happened to pass through one of the few spots where his men had not settled on our way here. Back then, all of this just meant that I was about get in the biggest fight of my life.

May 22, 1863 is when everything began. Christian and I had not been given explicit orders since we were just young meat ready to be disposed of at any time, so we didn't know of the amazing battle plan going into the fight. We were just put into a unit with other kids about our age ready to die for no good reason. No one knew what to do. They gave us guns and then we were supposed to go off and die like good boys and hope we take a few of them with us. We were all placed in the front lines in the city streets waiting for the Union to make the first move.

It was a hot summer day made even worse by the fact that our uniforms, though tattered and worn, were burning us up inside of them. We all sweated like pigs, waiting to be slaughtered. The eerie calm before a battle had to have been the most aggravating feeling in my life. The whole lot of us was lined up in a trench waiting for something, anything to occur. The boy next to me kept crossing his heart and praying for a quick deliverance from this world. On any other day, I would have certainly made fun of his convictions, but at that moment in the trench, I found myself just as afraid.

My rifle trembled in my hands as I waited for anything to happen. It was mind-numbing knowing that at any moment from that point on, you could die. Well my anxious fright ended after several sudden rounds of artillery shells were fired from the Union. Buildings crumbled around us and the debris sent flying acted as indirect fire from them. I initially ducked and put my hands over my head. I kept my eyes closed as if all of this was going to be a bad dream and that I'd wake up soon. My pleasant notions were broken when I felt something heavy and wet fall on me. I opened my eyes and saw the bloody body of the guy who was a few feet from me. That's when I really began to freak out. The sounds from the constant barrages followed by the screams from my fellow soldiers were too much for me to handle. Everything started spinning, but I calmed down after Christian grabbed my arm. It was as if his simple touch brought me back into reality. Once I could see clearly again, I could tell that everything was nothing but pure chaos now. Our lines were scattered and now Grant's men had begun to attack. My first instinct was to run, but Christian looked me in the eye.

"Are you with me?" he asked.

With no thought, I answered, "Till the end."

We gave each other a nod and ran into battle.

We were only taught how to fire the rifle and reload from the others, but we had been hunting before, so we knew how to use a gun. Bullets flew past us as we shot our rifles and the explosions around us added to the effect. It wasn't long before I noticed that tons of other small units had joined our charged. For a brief moment, I thought that this was actually fun, but the feeling died when I fired my rifle, and a man dropped dead in front of me.

Everything around me froze. It had been years since I had killed another man, but the feeling of overwhelming guilt was still with me. I dropped my gun and fell to my knees. I was frozen. Soldier upon soldier ran past me and died as I stood helpless and scared. I saw one of the Union soldiers charge at me and take out his bowie knife. I looked up and saw not the eyes of a soldier but the eyes of a grief-stricken man. I could see it in his eyes. I had killed his friend and he wanted revenge. I closed my eyes and waited for it to happen, but when I heard him scream, I opened my eyes. I saw Christian laying on top of him. Christian had tackled him and used his own bowie knife against him by stabbing him in the back. With the man's blood on his face, he looked at me and held out his hand. I remembered then that I had to continue to do whatever was necessary to protect Christian. I picked up my rifle and rejoined to battle.

I never got over the feeling of blood on my hands, but by the end of the day, Grant's men retreated and Christian and I were still standing. I killed seven men that day. I still remember their faces. That month continued to be the same as we continued to fight for Vicksburg. I progressed as a soldier, but I never was proud of the fact that I was becoming a better killer. As long as Christian survived, I was able to stomach all of that though. All of our efforts turned out to be for naught though. We surrendered Vicksburg on July 4th 1863. Luckily my unit led by Captain Hannon knew that it would be best to pull out early, so we avoided capture. Back then I didn't know whether he was just clever or a coward. Now I believe the latter.

The next two years were similar to Vicksburg. We would roam around from battle to battle to battle and then pull out when it looked we were about to lose. It happened often as the Union began to gain momentum and decimate the Confederate forces.

Over time my guilt over killing lessened drastically, and I had no quarry with taking another's life. I began to view the lives of others as insignificant things that I need not be bothered with. As time went on, Christian and I realized that Hannon was slowly losing his mind from all of the defeats. It became obvious that the North would win the war, but he wouldn't believe it. Once Christian saw this, he came to me one night and said it was time to leave. I still don't know what made Christian want to stay there with Hannon as long as we did for we had ample opportunities, but we stayed true to our team.

Our group was in Missouri at the time trying to make an impossible trek to the east coast to aid in those battles. Christian said that he had made plans in the last town we were in and that we were leaving tonight. It was the best news of my life at the time. Since everyone was asleep, he began to make his way to the woods. I told him that I would catch up soon. I snuck over to Hannon's tent and pulled out my bowie knife while he slept. He looked so peaceful and innocent; his peaceful slumber only made my next move all the sweeter. I placed my hand over his mouth and suddenly stabbed him in the leg. My hand muffled his scream. I laughed, and I looked into his frightened eyes.

"Two years ago," I started off as I dangled the knife above his eye, "you murdered my father. Do you remember? You said he was a criminal and deserved to die. I have fought in this war since then because of you, and now I'm paying you back for all of the blood you made me spill."

I stabbed him a little above the heart, so he would eventually bleed in a slow painful death. Despite how used I had become to killing, Hannon's death was the first in which I felt good about. I felt nothing but joy as I left him to rot in his tent as I headed toward the other men sleeping. While I looked over my sleeping comrades, I thought back to how they burned our home and helped kill Christian's father. With those memories driving my actions, I stabbed each and every one of them in the heart. After my ties had been severed to the army, I left and joined Christian in the woods.

10
Celebration

As I lay in my bed, I could still hear the commotion outside. For three days and nights straight, these people had partied celebrating my victory over Dom. Apparently watching people fight in that arena was a favored pastime of theirs, which was not surprising considering we had been taught to fight since we were children. Still it was Sunday, the day that was to be dedicated to honoring our Lord and those people were still out parading the streets with booze in hand not giving a dang about our Lord. I had only been there a little over a week by that point and the outside visage of that little village didn't fit the truth it exuded. I remember seeing all the statues of great men of God, the Original Crusaders, such as David, Solomon, Paul, and Peter littering the courtyard, yet those same statues that they were supposed to pay reverence to in more cases acted as a clothes rack for people to throw their attire upon as they went streaking through the streets. Their debauchery had no limits indeed.

There was a tray of stale bread still laid out next to me that I had refused to touch days ago. I had not eaten in days, and I did not possess the appetite to. Dom needed to die there was no question about that, but it didn't help the way I felt about now officially becoming an Exile in my own mind. Sariah tried to soothe my pain by saying that no one would ever know back home and

I was just defending myself, but it didn't matter what the Order thought back home. All that mattered was what Christian and I thought of myself, and I knew Christian would not be very forgiving about killing one of our own.

I continued to dwell on such thoughts until Sariah and Rebecca came into my room. As it turned out, the Clown had begun to fancy Rebecca, so that was why she wasn't around us when we were first captured. I had no clue to if he had touched her though as she did not speak much about the subject. I was pretty sure that man had at least thirty years on her when it came to age, so I was certainly appalled to see that him drooling over her. Still I was glad to see she was unharmed. I would have hated to bring Christian back two bodies of our comrades because of my failure to protect them. As they strolled into my room, I noticed that their uniforms had been replaced with identical long skirts, leather sandals, and nothing to cover their chest except a bikini made from the fur of some slain animal. Their midsection was blatantly exposed as the light from the sun made their skin glow slightly.

Despite their ravishing appearance, I scoffed at them, "I see that you, guys, are going about celebrating Dom's death is style."

Normally Sariah was the one to slap me, but Rebecca picked up her sister's slack in that case as she struck my face with enough force that if I was white it would have left a mark, "How dare you accuse us of anything when you were the one to kill him! We're just doing what you should be doing and mingling with the people of this village, so that they won't see us as an enemy," she said.

Following Dom's death, I began to see the clarity of our position and illuminated the girls at that moment, "Rebecca, we don't even know if we're enemies to these people or not. We were exiled to this land without our knowledge and have no idea where the rest of our team is. I would have loved to find Christian by now, but with these injuries I'm stuck here for a while longer. Besides for all we know, they're all dead and even if they weren't we have no idea what we're to do here."

Sariah quickly entered the conversation, "We're exiles here now, Terra. We have no mission to liberate these people and frankly I don't see any other option besides assimilating with them. They know the Word just as well as we do and choose to ignore it. We can't change people that is that lost."

"So you're suggesting that instead of saving them we just join in on their fun?"

"No, I'm just saying we should try to understand their culture more and—"

"The only thing I need to understand is that these people don't share the same convictions or faith as I do, so I should not waste my time on them. Why should I lower myself to their level in order to understand their plight or their suffering? The Word is a gift that you should be able to acknowledge for yourself, and if not then I'll not bother with you. We only exist to help those who are willing to be helped. It's that simple."

Rebecca slapped me again, "It's that attitude that makes people hate the Order! I thought you of all people would've been against such a mindset. It's because of that ridged mindset why these people have fallen so low. Besides, have you ever given any thought to maybe we're not 100 percent right on everything. Maybe they can offer us some insight that we have failed to see."

"The only insight they can offer is how to behave like animals, but I can see you take this seriously, Rebecca," I said as I got up from the bed. The cover around my body fell to the ground showing that I was recovering from my injuries but slowly. Not one of my scars had yet to heal and the medicine they had been giving me left me feeling constantly sleepy. "As the acting king until we find Christian, then I suppose it's up to me to ensure you don't give into that weak mind of yours and end up like Dom. Come. We shall go and partake in these festivities so I can show you what an abomination these Fallen ones have become."

I saw Rebecca's hand shaking as if she wanted to slap me again before she stormed out of the tent where I was recovering.

I looked over to Sariah as she spoke to me, "Why are so adamant about the Word now? I know you've always wavered in your faith, but you seem to be on fire at this point."

I rubbed my hand over my recently shaved head and sighed, "We're in trouble, Sariah, and we need all the help from God that we can get."

"So serving God is a last result for you when you need His help then?"

When she voiced my actions in that kind of light, even I felt guilty, but I tried to shake her off by saying, "No, I always serve Him. I've just done it in my own way, but I decided to try something different."

"Sounds like that's an excuse to make you feel better."

I ignored her last statement as we walked of the tent together, and I left my shirt and jacket to my uniform inside at the behest of the girls. In order to fit in with such a primitive bunch, I had to walk the temple grounds without any sort of shirt. Of all of all the tendencies on the Isle, that was the one I had the least problem with. As we walked to the center of the temple grounds, we passed by a grand number of women that didn't have the same modesty as the Dent sisters and walked the grounds with nothing covering their tops aside from paint.

The temple grounds in general were fairly easy to navigate. Aside from the crumbling temple that was built into the face of the mountain, there really was nothing else but tents and shacks made of timber along with the remnants of the debris from whatever buildings used to stand on other grounds. As we walked to the center, many of my thoughts of their worldly nature were confirmed as I saw on multiple occasions couples disregarding their chaste vows in plain sight without a care in the world. In fact, they looked on at us as we were the freaks because we were not partaking in the same passionate actions as they were. The temple square was indicated by the towering statues of David, Moses, Elijah, and Solomon acting as a symbolic pillar for each corner. As we proceeded into the square, we saw all manners of attractions. In a line that encased the entire square, tent after tent had some sort of spectacular performance going on that had attracted quite the crowd.

But what truly caught my eye were a man and a woman kneeling before the statue of Solomon praying. I left the girls and approached the couple wanting to congratulate them for being the only people with some decency of these fools. They are modestly dressed and had no kind of crazy paint going on, so I assumed they were pretty normal.

As I approached I asked, "What is it that you two pray for?"

My approach came as a surprise as they were so shocked they nearly fell on their faces, but they answered all the same in a meek tone though, "We pray for Solomon to give us the wisdom to change our fortunes soon."

"A noble prayer," I said, "what have you brought then as a sacrifice for this prayer?"

They seemed addled by my question.

"I mean what did you bring forth to tithe? Forgive me. I forgot every world is different."

The two of them laughed as the woman answered this time, "Tithe, sacrifice. We haven't done that since we left the Order. We simply came to ask him to make our hands lucky tonight in a game of dice."

"You mean you asked one of the wisest kings in history to help you gamble and offer nothing in return as a show of thanks?"

"Why would we do something silly like that? We have better things to do with our money. Maybe if we had a little bit more we would tithe to Solomon again but not right now," said the man. And with that they walked away to try their hand at a game of dice.

Before I could further reflect on the incident that had just occurred, Lucas came up to me and bowed to the statue.

"Are you asking for Solomon to guide the dice as well?" I asked.

Lucas paid me no attention as he continued to pray.

"Hey," I repeated, "I asked you a question."

Lucas got up and walked over so that we were only inches apart. He wore his uniform open exposing his chest and from the red lip marks scattered all over his body, I could see that he was quite the popular man.

He smirked as he said, "I was praying that Solomon could do the impossible and drill some wisdom past that iron wall you erected to keep yourself away from us. I prayed to him so that maybe you can stop treating us like some sort of plague that if you touch us you'll be cursed."

"I never said anything like that."

He raised his finger up to my face and said, "I can see it with your eyes, Terra. I can see it all with your eyes. Look around you. All the lights, the music, the half-naked girls, all the festivities were done for you. We did this to welcome you to the Isle, but you look at us as if we're a pestilence polluting the very soil you walk on and the air you breathe."

"That's because you people are! Your very existence addles my mind. We were all trained to be Crusaders, the symbol of righteousness for all the worlds to aspire to. We alone have the truth of the worlds in our hands and yet you spit on it for this life of debauchery."

"What you look upon as debauchery I look upon as freedom. This is no celebration for you killing a boy before his time. No, this night is a celebration for you gaining the freedom from the supposed truth that has anchored you down all your life. Truth is nothing but a construct of reality for whoever holds the rulebook, Terra. And the Crusaders are a prime example of that."

"You call this freedom? This island is nothing but a prison for us all! It's a way of showing you the foolishness of your ways."

"Really? We're sent here not because of our foolishness, but because we asked why the sky was blue."

"The sky was blue?"

"Yes, the Order of the Crusaders were like parents that always told their children how the world worked, but the one time we ask why the sky was blue they throw us out the house and lock the door. While they think they are punishing us, they are really setting us free from the bonds that forbade us from living like ourselves and not the porcelain dolls that they had constructed. Can you honestly say you agree with everything the Crusaders have told you?"

I had to pause before I gave him a response. It was an unintentional pause, but it was enough to prove his point. I had indeed had my own doubts about the Order many times especially considering what I went through during reeducation.

"That's right," he said, "you spent so much time looking down upon the rest of us from your high perch that you never bothered to notice the strings attached to your arms and legs that were making you dance like a fool."

In a sudden fit of rage, I pushed him down and stood over his body screaming, "You think you know everything? You know nothing of me and my life. I was born into darkness and the Crusaders saved me from that hell and showed me the light. They showed me—"

"That you actually mattered in the world! They showed you that not everything about your life had to be full of sadness and grief. They gave you a purpose, right?"

"How did you know that?" I asked as I backed off of him.

"Because you and I are the same. I too was saved from the Crusaders and shown a light I thought never existed," he said. "I was born in the darkness and the Crusaders showed me the first light I saw. Thus they were the light for me and I never questioned their ways. But such obedience only breeds ignorance and traps us within the ideal world that they have created."

He understood then. That after being exposed to a place like Earth that if the alternative was the Crusaders then I'd gladly do all that they asked of me. But if he knew that…if he knew what lied out in the worlds past the protection that the Crusaders offered, then why did he leave? His words from earlier hung in my ear when he spoke of how the Crusaders were the first light for him just as they were for me. I was trapped in a world full of darkness where as a boy I was forced to kill in order to survive. The Order took me from that darkness and showed me the light, but didn't mean they were the only light. That's the conclusion that he must have reached. I just knew that had to be it.

"Why then? You speak of all this talk of freedom and righteousness, but why did I have to kill Dom to achieve it?"

I helped him up to his feet and we began to walk toward the center of the grounds were the festivities were ongoing.

"Blood is the key to all freedoms."

"Blood? What do you mean?"

"Just as Jesus shed his blood for our sins in order to free us from the shackles of hell, so must we take the blood of a comrade to free us from the shackles of the Crusaders. The blood of Christ had no magical properties to it, but it served as a symbol to remember his sacrifice and keep us on a righteous path. The blood of our comrades shall do the same. Every king will never forget the blood he spilled to set him and his people free. That blood will serve as the foundation for the freedom that we all live for now. I've never forgotten my comrade just as you shall never forget Dom now. No matter what ill feelings you two bore toward one another, he'll be forever etched in your mind."

"You were a king?"

"Yes, the notion surprises many people. But I'm no more a king than you are, Terra. Like you, I wore a false crown for my own personal reasons."

We both stopped in front of a group of women that began to dance around us like we were a part of their elaborate act in a show. The long veils that hung from their arms flew freely around us obscuring my vision for a second as we continued to talk.

"How did you know?"

"I had captured Dom long before we got a hold of you, and thus I knew all about your team from him. That's why I find you so interesting, Terra. I've heard of your trials with the Order as an Executioner and how you still serve them like a dog. But I've also heard of your exploits with women along with your violent and impulsive nature. You live a life of sin and impurity and yet you stand strong by the ideals of the Crusaders. All Crusaders and recruits alike are meant to forgo having casual relationships aside from marriage, unless you understand a vital truth."

"And what is that?"

"That we're humans and should be allowed to live like them!" He proceeded to slapping one of the dancer's butt and pulling her into his arms before they shared a passionate kiss. Once they were done, he released her from his grasp and placed his hands on my shoulders saying, "I don't even know her name, yet I was able to assert the human passion that the Order wished to subdue."

I looked around at the ongoing merriment and saw the blissful expressions on all of their faces. They were truly happy. Despite being exiled, they were happy. I saw Sariah and Rebecca in the crowd with the same smiles on their faces dancing with a couple of guys. Whether they were happy or not though, I had to find Christian before we decided on anything, but in order to do that I needed their help. The wounds that Dom gave me prevented from going forth into the jungle blindly, so I needed them. If I were to reject their ideals, then I was sure they would shun me. I needed to be a part of their society to function. I needed to be a part of their society to live on in that world. The Order always preached against the idea of blending in with a society in order to convert them, but in that case I saw no other option.

I grabbed a nearby girl that just happened to walk by and kissed her. I felt nothing for the girl and I can't even remember her face, but I remember the smile and the shine in Lucas's eyes as he embraced me saying, "Welcome to the island, Terra."

The rest of the night I joined in seamlessly into the festivities as if I had been a member of that society my entire life. Lucas was sincere in his words to have me join them because he treated the girls and me as if we were members of his own team the entire night. At first, it was hard to throw myself into such a lifestyle due to my mind worrying about Christian, but as the night went along, I found myself caring less and less about Christian and more and more about the activity in front of me whether it was a drink, a game, or a woman. I dove head first into the culture of that village, and I didn't know if I was going to drown in it or find some way to float back up to the top.

11

Recruitment

Lucas's words held merit to them, but the one thing that he could never understand is that while the Crusaders did save me from Earth, I did not go join their ranks because they asked me to. I joined their ranks because he wished me to join their ranks. Everything that I have done has been for Christian. Even Dom's death will do nothing but benefit Christian in the long run just as me falling in place with the rest of the people of the island will as well. Nothing has changed since those days. Everything that I am and everything that I do is all for Christian at the end of the day.

Oregon 1865

The music of the morning tribal dance jarred me away from my sleep as I rubbed the crust from my eyes. The scratches on my back from the previous night still stung as I swung my legs out from the mat that the Karuk Indians called a bed. My awakening caused enough of a stir to wake up Kita as her slender fingers grabbed my hand preventing me from getting up. Even though it was morning, the way that I felt about her the previous night had not changed at all. It was hard to look her in the eye knowing such thoughts, so I put on a smile and told her I was going out for some air. Whatever words she said to me didn't reach my ears as I hurried to lace my pants and quietly snuck out from her tent. The dry grass of the plains pricked at my bare feet as I hurried back to my own tent without a soul seeing me. The first rays of the sun had barely began to shine on the horizon, so moving about was an easy task. I entered my tent from behind and quickly crawled underneath the blanket of bear fur that Kita had made for me. Its warm embrace made me wonder if that was what the embrace of a mother felt like. I began to drift back off into sleep, but my brother decided that would be a horrible idea.

As I was just falling back asleep, Christian busted into my tent unannounced of course. Yes, he certainly would find some way to liven up my day. He could never do things the easy way.

"Come on, Terra, it's about time you got up already. It's half past noon," Christian said.

He was always one of those people who believed in Benjamin Franklin's quote, "All mankind is divided into three classes: those that are immovable, those that are moveable and those who move." I wanted to be the immovable one in this case, but I ended up being the one who is moveable. I don't know why he was so obsessed with that man, but after a while I just stopped caring.

"Why should I be getting up?" I asked.

"Because it's our turn to catch the morning game," he reminded me with that chiding voice of his.

Reluctantly, I threw the blanket off me and inadvertently revealed my bare backside along with my markings from the previous night with Kita.

"Those are quite the scratches you got there, brother. What kind of beast gave you those?" he asked.

I laughed as I got back on my feet and grabbed my spear and a beaver-skin vest and put on a pair of moccasins. "It was a wild animal that took all night to subdue, brother. I'll tell you about it later," I said.

"Well just make sure that the chief doesn't find out about your late-night hunting. I'm sure he would've your head for it," Christian warned with a smile on his face. We left my tent and headed off north into the plains with the tribal music fading away as we jogged toward the horizon.

I woke up that day with high hopes for the future: the war was over, I was a sixteen-year-old kid that was on the road with my brother, and I was a free man again. It was June 27, 1865, if I remember correctly. Over the last couple months, Christian and I had found refuge within an Indian settlement in Oregon that treated us with great kindness. It had been a hard transition going from the life of a soldier to a simple hunter among the same people once referred to as savages, but it was a peaceful life that I got used to very quickly. Even from our remote location, news of the end of that accursed war had finally made its way over to the western frontier, and to my joy, I heard that the South had indeed lost the war.

As we stalked through the plains that summer morning, I was able to get a good view of the ocean as we proceeded to higher elevation along the rolling plains. The camp had been on the constant move as we searched for a place to settle and build a community, so with every day we ventured further west with the Karuks. I stopped as I took a good look at the shimmering ocean on the horizon. It had been my first time setting my eyes on that boundless sea. The smell of the sea was an intoxicating one that just screamed of freedom. I had heard many tales of brave men venturing out into the sea with no goal in mind but just as a means to escape the world. While looking at that pristine beauty, I couldn't help but agree.

As I was gawking at the sea, Christian had stopped as well to look up in the sky as if God himself was speaking to him. I went over to place my hand on Christian to shake him out of whatever trance he was in, but I stopped when he asked me, "Have you ever just wanted to leave this world and go somewhere else, brother?"

His inquiry caught me off guard as I chuckled, saying, "Well considering how I was sold into slavery, killed my own father, conscripted into service, and now living on the run then yeah I can honestly say that thought has passed through my mind many a day."

"Father used to tell me stories of how there were wondrous worlds out there much different from the one we reside in. Worlds where you could truly be free and happy," he said while still looking up.

"Yeah my old man told me the same thing. It seems that they meant to give us some sort of false hope. This is the world that we have been tethered to and we must just live with its rules."

"But what if there was…" he stopped and shook his head. "You're right. We must just do our best with the hand we have been dealt. Here, how about we spilt up to cover more ground. It's already been quite some time. I suppose they'll be expecting us to return soon," he said.

I agreed and the two of us went our separate ways. I stalked through the grassy plains for another solid hour before I realized that the hunting goddess that Kita was so fond of was not with me that day. I was about to head back when I heard something rustling through the grass. I raised my spear waiting for some manner of beast to pounce on me, but only Kita came stumbling forward laughing.

She had followed me? I can honestly say I was neither thrilled or the least bit excited to see her, but I had to continue smiling as if I was.

"What are you doing out here?" I asked.

She had listened to what I said the other night and didn't have any paint ruining the beauty of her face. She circled around me before planting a kiss on my lips saying, "I'm just hunting my prey just as you are."

She began to slip off her nightgown revealing her bare body before me and said, "I can't stop thinking about our night together and how we both gave each other our purity."

I wanted her gone. The other night had just been a moment of lust that I let get the better of me. I had thought that I cared about her before that night, but the moment that we finished our hunt, I realized that I wanted nothing to do with her. All the feelings that I thought I had were just a simple desire that I wanted fulfilled. She didn't understand that.

I turned my back on her. "Go back to the camp, Kita. I need to hunt. We can talk later."

Her arms wrapped around my body as she whispered in my ear, "Or we can talk about it now."

She pushed me down to the ground and began to unlace my pants. Christian had spoken to me many a time regarding my lustful habits. He told me that I should aim to be celibate once you get the taste of lust into your flesh, it's a hard one to ignore. Those were the words that Christian left with me as I promised him I would not give myself to a woman before marriage. I never realized how hard such a promise would be to keep, but what he said was right. Once you get a taste of the flesh, you always want it.

It was with that realization I gave into Kita's advances and was ready to break my word to Christian once more. She crawled over my body and I saw her lips move, yet I could hear no sound aside from the booming crash that resounded from the distance.

We both looked over toward the direction of the sound to see the source of it and saw a large cloud of dirt and smoke erupt in the air not too far from our location. Upon another look though, we both realized that the crash had occurred right at the camp. The look of passion in Kita's eye faded into one of rage that I had only seen before she planned to go into battle. While I may have held little respect and admiration for Kita as a woman, I had nothing but the sincerest regards for her combat prowess. Without even asking for my help or lacing my pants back up, she ran over toward the smoke to be joined back with the rest of her kin no doubt.

I wondered if Christian had heard the crash or if he was there already. He always had a curious spirit that could get him into trouble, so I began to rush over to ensure that would not be the case. I moved as fast as my legs could carry me as I ran to the camp. The grass parted before me with every long stride I made. A flock of birds flew overhead away from the campsite which was never a good sign, so I quickened my pace further. By the time I reached the camp, sweat dripped from nearly every inch of my body and catching my breath was more difficult than catching a wild pig on the loose. I could hear much commotion as I took cover behind one of the tents to check on the situation.

If I had known all I did now, I would have handled things differently, but that was the case with all primitive worlds. No one ever knows the best way to handle the Crusaders once they drop down. By the time I arrived, everything was occurring in typical fashion for how the Order liked to do things. The whole tribe had gathered around seven Crusaders, the typical number for any squad, and listened in while the king of their group spoke, "Once again, I shall beseech you all to forgo your worship of these pagan gods and come and acknowledge the one true god of all worlds. There's still time for you all to accept his wondrous mercy and grace."

In typical fashion as well, with every group of primitives, there was one who was always vividly against the Crusaders' words and it was Kita in that case. As the daughter of the chief, she had the authority to speak for her old man while he was away negotiating with neighboring tribes, and she had every intention of utilizing that great power.

She pointed her finger at the king of the group and said, "We've seen what the work of your one true god pertains. All you that worship him have done is slaughter our people and drive us from our lands! Is it not in your covenant to decree thou shall not kill? And yet our blood is drenched all over the frontier. Didn't you guys say thou shall not lie and yet you have broken all the treaties you have promised us? Was it not you people that said thou shall not steal nor covet and yet your desire for our land made you steal it from us! From what I see, you people are nothing but hypocrites! And if your god allows such blatant disregard for his laws, then I want no part of serving him."

I could only smile at the truth of her words. Far too long have white people claimed to serve the interest of God and yet turned a blind eye to the sins that they have wrought. My owner claimed to be a devote Christian that went to church every Sunday morning, yet treated us like dirt that very same night. Those people had no regard for God and I found myself liking Kita even more after she called them out on it. I walked out from behind the tent expecting to see the Crusaders running with their tails between their legs at the truth of her words, but instead I just saw the shadow of tragedy lurking over my life once more. Without giving her another chance to speak, one of the Crusaders drew his sword and slit her throat in one clean slash.

She didn't even know what had happened as her eyes were still filled with fury when her body fell to the ground. Whatever fury that she did have left though was transferred over to me as I grabbed hold of my spear and chucked it at one of the Crusaders. My aim was true and impaled the man with a clean strike. As he fell to the ground, I rushed over and took Kita's place as a shield for the tribe. The majority of the men had gone out hunting as well, so I was all they had. All that was left were mainly women, old men, and children with tears in their eyes over the death of Kita. I glanced down at her lifeless body and the pool of blood surrounding it. I thought of how Father died and then how Christian's dad died as well. All three of them had that same pool of blood spilling from their wounds to indicate that they were gone and would never come back onto my life. I grabbed the blade that had killed Kita from the man's body. I felt it was only fitting for me have it at that point. The blade I held also had the hilt fashioned into the shape of a lion's head with a slender silver blade protruding from its mouth. The blade felt right in my hand. When I looked at the Crusaders they had all had an empty look on their faces.

I overheard one of them say, "Captain Morgan…that, that primitive just killed Dylan."

The one referred to as Captain Morgan was the king of the unit and as he stepped forward, he drew a blade of his own and said, "Well, boy, it seems as though you have some grit to you. But I suggest that you back down quickly. My man killed the girl and now you have killed him. We're even. So let us continue peaceful talks shall we?"

"Peaceful talks? You white people don't know the first meaning of peaceful talks. You are all the same. You wear a grand mask promoting peace and righteousness, but in all truth you look down upon all those that don't share your skin," I said finally able to speak the truth of my mind.

Captain Morgan took another glance at me as if I was some kind of monster and said, "Well, if you have no intention of being peaceful then I suppose we shall have to implement other means to assure you how wrong you are in your pagan worship."

He pointed his sword, a matching copy of the one in my hand, toward the sky and as I looked up I saw one of the flying airships that the Crusaders were famous for in other worlds. Because I had yet to know anything of their Order yet, the sight of the airship made myself along with the other natives freeze. I didn't know if that was some sort of demon or angel hovering above us. The others began to chat in their native tongue revering it, but it was too late as the ship began to rain down fire upon us like it was God smiting us for our sins. The balls of fire rained upon us with extreme prejudice as no one was safe from the explosions aside from the Crusaders.

The fires from their attack were slowly spreading across the camp as everyone began to frantically run for their lives. I stood my ground frozen in awe at the power of the ship had continued to rain fire down all around me.

It was chaos as flames had practically encircled us. The fire had spread quickly throughout the camp. The smell of burning wood and flesh pervaded the air around us to the point where breathing any more in made me cough. The scent of burning flesh became stronger and stronger as a screaming woman engulfed with fire as if it were a living coat came running by me. Her screaming came to a stop as her body just continued to burn at my feet. The smell of her flesh burning almost made me want to thrust that blade into myself. After the war and burning my own owner alive, I was what anyone could call a veteran when it came to dealing with the smell of burning flesh, but it was different that time. All the times beforehand I was able to prepare myself for what was to come, but the suddenness of this attack…it threw me off and I was frozen because of it.

As I looked down upon the charred remains of the woman and children, my heart began to feel heavy. With the flames acting as a prison that we could not escape from, Captain Morgan raised his blade once more and yelled out, "By the power of God, I plead for these heathens to be saved by your divine mercy!"

He swung down his blade and in complete resonation with his swing, the airship began to pour out concentrated bubbles of water large enough to put out all the flames around us. As the water hit the ground it exploded in every direction drenching the majority of us and washing the blood away from Kita's corpse. And just like that the flames had been put out just as quickly as they had fallen to us. There was nothing but silence for a moment as I'm sure Captain Morgan and his men waited for the Karuk to bow down to their floating god. But I knew the truth. No god would ever act on the commands of a single man. I looked up at the airship still ignorant of what it was, but positive that it was no heavenly deity come to deliver us. Even though I knew it was no god, the problem still remained that it had the power of one. I was afraid to stand up to those people out of fear of more fire raining down upon me.

Captain Morgan could sense my fear as I held tightly onto my blade with both hands. My hands were shaking not from the cold that being drenched brought with it but from the uncertainty of what I needed to do. While I stood there shaking like a girl, the Karuks began worshiping the airship once more. I wanted to hate them for their weakness. The Karuks had always been such a proud tribe that would never adhere to the will of the US, but all that resolve had melted away from the fires of that ship. I wanted to hate them, but I could not. Even I had the shadows of fear creeping through my body as I stood before Captain Morgan.

"So, boy, I suggest you follow the leads of those others and bow down," said Captain Morgan.

He was right and I knew that. What was I to do before such great power, so I bent down and began to pray, but as I opened up my mouth, I saw Kita's face staring at me. She had been the very embodiment of pride and honor, and she died with that pride still intact. I told myself that I would never allow myself to become subject to the whims of another man after I killed Hannon, and I had every intention of following through on that promise. I silently thanked Kita for giving me my resolve once more as I slashed at Captain Morgan's knees. My attack had caught him off guard as he expected my fear from the airship to paralyze any thoughts of action. As he fell to the ground like a tree that had just been cut down, I pounced on him and drove the blade through his chest.

I could hear the silence return to the camp as everyone had fixed their eyes upon me and the blood upon my hands. Before I could even think, I reached to each side and upholstered the two flintlock pistols I had stolen from Hannon. The Karuks had always hated the fact that I held onto those relics of the war, but I was glad to have them at my side at that time. I rose up and took aim at the closest Crusader I could see and fired one bullet into his chest. I turned to the next one and fired the other bullet into his. The smell of gunpowder from the pistols lingered in the air as I threw down the empty guns and picked up the sword I used to kill Captain Morgan. Never again would I be subject to the whims of man. Never again would I do anything against my own will. I charged forward at the three remaining men, fully expecting to die either by their hand or from fire from above. I ran past Kita without looking down and told her I would see her soon and pressed onward. The three men screamed as they vowed to avenge their comrades, but before they could take another step an arrow was shot through the chest of one of them. Their screams ceased as the other two turned around, but another arrow was loosed into another man.

All there was left of the Crusaders then was one man. He turned to see Christian behind him with another arrow pointed at his face. I was overjoyed to see my brother, but that feeling quickly dissipated as the arrow he was holding back was fired in my direction just barely grazing past my face.

I froze in shock as I watched Christian scream at me, "Silence, Terra! You have no idea the severity of your actions here." He bowed down to the last Crusader and humbly said, "Forgive me, oh great warrior of God, for my sins. I could only see your back, so I took your men for bandits. I repent a thousand times for my grave error, righteous one. As for my brother, please forgive him. He knows nothing of your Order, but if he did his face would be facing the dirt as well," he said.

Christian's words were like a hammer striking a piece glass as my world crumbled around me. Not only had he never spoken to me with such a disrespectful tone before, but for him to bow down to the men that killed Kita was beyond me entirely. Had his pride vanished entirely? No, Christian was not that kind of man. There had to be some reason for him to throw away his pride so easily. I knew I could never judge Christian so harshly since I respected him more than any other man, so I stood there and waited to see that whole thing play out. The Crusader seemed just as perplexed about Christian's demeanor than I was. He took a long look at him before he asked, "How is it that you're familiar with my Order, boy?"

Christian still kept his face toward the ground as if he was in reverence of that man and responded, "Because my father was a member of your Order. Richard J. Black was his name, Sir."

"Turncoat Black? You're the son of Turncoat Black?" asked the man in shock.

"Terra, throw me that blade you carry," commanded Christian.

I followed his orders thinking that he was about to cut that man down, so I did so with a smile on my face knowing that my faith in my brother was about to pay dividends. I tossed the blade gingerly through the air and Christian flawlessly caught it by its handle. I saw the man's head turn to Christian quickly as if he was waiting for something to happen but nothing did. Christian just held the blade for a moment before he handed it to him as a peace offering.

Suddenly, the man began to burst out in laughter, "Only the son of that fool would willingly give me a weapon knowing full well I could kill you. Then that must make that dark lad over there the son of Vincenzo Morris, Turncoat Black's accomplice."

I had no idea what that man was talking about, but the one thing I knew was that my father he spoke of…

"Yes," said Christian, "that boy is indeed the son of Vincenzo Morris just as I am the son of Richard Black. Both of which are deceased."

My father…Christian knew who my father was? I didn't even know the name of Father, yet Christian was able to recite it like a bird singing a tune. It flowed straight off his lips with no hesitation, so I knew he wasn't lying. My father and Christian's father had worked together with those monsters? I didn't want to believe it, but I thought back to all the stories Father told me of different worlds and how he was so much more educated than the regular people of our race. I couldn't believe that it may have been true, but my biggest frustration was with Christian for keeping all that from me. I wanted to say something anything really, but I couldn't move a muscle. As I stood there frozen, the man asked Christian, "So what is it that you want then, son of Richard Black?"

Christian stood up and impaled the blade I gave in the charred soil proclaiming, "I wish that my brother and I be allowed the join the ranks of the Crusaders and bring honor back to our fathers' disgraced names. And before you say 'no,' I must remind you, Sir, that you're now severely shorthanded in your unit and may need the extra bodies."

The Crusader looked around at the fallen bodies of his comrades and said, "Well you two have both displayed a raw talent for killing that needs to be refined, and having two individuals on a class D world know so much about the Order could be problematic. Besides, I need to return with something since this mission was a huge failure. Okay, boy. I'm sure I'll get hell from the Order, but I'll bring you back and allow for them to decide your fate."

"Come on, Terra," said Christian, "we have to leave soon."

I was stunned. I didn't know how things could have turned out that way. I saw the Crusader wave his hands in the air and then the airship shot down three pods with cables attached to the top. The Crusader wasted no time getting in his, but I just looked at the one meant for me as Christian walked over my way.

"Come on," he said.

I was tired of him acting like nothing was wrong with this picture. I grabbed him by the arm and tried to pull him away from this whole scene but he wouldn't move an inch. I tugged at him a little harder and still there was nothing. He really had no intention of moving. I walked around to look him in the eye, but saw nothing but emptiness in him like his soul had just been stolen.

"You're dead serious about leaving," I said. I grabbed him by his shoulders and began to scream in his face, "You can't leave. You can't leave! We came here to get away so we could be safe from people like that, not join them. He's no different than Hannon!"

He threw my hands off him and said, "We came here so you could find a safe place to live! But we don't have to run any more. I've been assured that while it may be hard, you'll not be forced back into slavery, and you can make a life for you where you can live as an equal among others, Terra." He turned away from me and continued to speak, "I'm sorry it had to come to this, but there are things out there bigger than this world and I intend to help as much as I can as my father did before me. You've given me the motivation to do so, my brother," he said with a tear rolling down his cheek.

I wanted to be there for him, but I couldn't. Whatever those Crusaders were, I knew that they thought they were making the world a better place, something that Christian could relate with. I could just feel that he was meant to join their little Order. As for me, I was meant to never be tied down by the whims of another man again. Those people looked like some sort of military force, so I wanted nothing to do with the idea of joining another army, so I slowly backed away from Christian. I wanted to be with him, but I promised myself that I would never again be a slave to anyone. It was only a matter of time before they too like all the others began to simply use me as some sort of tool. So I ran.

I turned my back on Christian and I ran away as fast as I could, weaving through the charred remains of the campsite. I didn't need to hear the ship flying away to know that Christian was gone. I could feel it in the very depths of my heart that he had left me. Once that feeling sank in and I knew that I was truly all alone in the world, I fell to my knees and began to crawl through the grass with tears streaming down my face.

12
Crusade

The warmth I felt when I crushed the crystal had vanished as I felt the gust of the wind around me as I plummeted from the sky like a shooting star. I had long envied birds for their gift of flight, as I longed for the freedom that was woven within their wings. That freedom had finally been granted to me. I opened my eyes and looked at the world below me. The setting sun casted an auburn glow upon the sea below me as I drew closer and closer to its rocking waves. I held my breath as my body crashed through the watery surface of the first world aside from Earth that I found myself on. As I sank deeper into its depths, the stinging sensation all over my body from my impact prevented me from immediately swimming upward. I struggled through the pain and began to kick my feet as I soon broke the surface of the water. Water dripped from my head into my eyes blurring my vision, yet I was still able to see the grand scene before me. My body rocked back in forth as I floated in the water and before my eyes was the image of a grand city built along the coast of shore. Standing in the background of the beach was a walled city overlooking a small pier like a giant's shadow. Sharing the water with me was an arrangement of ships raining cannon fire down upon the sturdy wall of the city. Flames danced atop of the wood shacks of the pier as the shells from the artillery crashed down upon them.

It was just as Zion had told me: I was truly falling into the midst of a full-fledged battle. I knew I had to hurry because there was no telling if Christian was in the thick of battle or captured. Zion had been very vague when she spoke of the danger that he was in, but either way as long as he lived then I knew I had to do everything in my power to save him. I wasted no time and swam to the shore of the beach. The water was warm because of all the blood that had seeped into its depths. I kept my eyes pointed forward as I tried my best to avoid the bodies and debris that floated in the water with me.

I dragged myself from the water and crawled onto the beach exhausted from my swim. The destruction that had befallen the pier was even worse up close as I could feel the heat from the flames even from the shore. I got onto my feet and froze as I looked upon the horror of war once more. Bodies had been strewn along the beach, indicating the tides of battle had begun there. I never wanted to see the signs of battle ever again, but it was just as she said. I had to let go of my fears in order to strive forward. I had lost my shoes in the water during my swim to the shore, so the soles of my feet made their imprints in the wet sand as I walked further up the shore. I took a look behind me and noticed how my footprints had been left in the sand. Normally I would never pay attention to such a thing, but I knew those were the imprints of my first few steps onto a world other than Earth. Not too long ago, prior to my arrival, I had been in the safety of my cabin in the woods, but due to the intervention of one woman I had traversed the very boundaries of space.

Looking at those shallow indentations in the sand made me think back to my meeting with the hooded woman, Zion, before she sent me on my journey.

Several hours earlier...

I closed my journal. It had been the only thing that had kept me sane the last two months since Christian left. It had been an important gift Kita had left for me just prior to her death. She had intended for us to record the journey of our lives together.

It pains me to no end that we were not even able to record one line together due to her bloody departure. The exterior was crisp and blackened as it was the only possession of mine that survived the fire two months ago. As I placed the journal into my back pocket, I dragged my feet over to my drawer near my bedside while trying to avoid the mound of clothes and trash that blanketed my floors. I reached into the drawer and pulled out Captain Hannon's twin flintlock pistols. I had always promised myself to never resort to using that kind of weapon again after the war, but I knew in my case I may have no choice. Besides, I had begun to notice that I had a bad habit of breaking promises I made to myself. The iron had rusted quite a bit since the last time I used it, but as long as it could fire in a straight line, I figured it would get the job done.

I looked over to the drawer where I had stored my journal and wondered if those words I placed within it would be my last? When I looked upon my hands, they would not stop from shaking. Those very same hands had gotten me through battle after battle, yet they shook like a child's trembling in fear as I questioned my resolve. I looked over to the door of my cabin as the truth of the matter began to hit me. I was truly about to leave this world for good. As I walked to the door, my feet stepped upon the surface of the bear skin rug that had been at the mantle of my home for the past few months since I left the Karuk tribe. When I looked upon the fierce expression on the bear's lifeless face, I could not help but be reminded of the Karuks. Before the incident with the Crusaders, they were a proud people that revered their gods. They were warriors whom I could call family. Christian and I had joined their tribe because we felt a sort of kindred spirit between the three of us, but that spirit had burned in the heat of the Crusaders' fire that rained from the sky.

Following that event, their pride had all but vanished as they adopted the religion of the white man. All of the text and artifacts that they had once held as sacred relics of their ancestors were burned to ashes. In the midst of their weakness, I left them.

I could not stand to be by their side any longer especially with the memory of Kita always lingering in my mind. The daughter of their chief had been slain like cattle, and yet they honored the god of the men that did the deed. I cut my ties with them and set off on my own and had lived a life of solitude in the woods for the last two months. Life alone had been a new experience for me as I had always shared my home with some sort of soul, whether it was by choice or not. It was a dreadful life in all honesty. The tranquility of the wood might have appeased some of the older veterans that survived the war, but the constant silence did nothing but remind me of the eerie silence before a battle ensued. The woods were truly chilling to me, and I was happy for the chance to leave them behind.

She had come to me the night before offering me the chance that I had wished I had taken months ago. To finally see Christian once more.

It had been some time since I had seen the hooded woman, yet I still remembered my last meeting with her. Not only had she told me that she knew my father, but she mentioned in passing that she may have known my mother. Those two factors led me to the conclusion that she must have some way for me to be with Christian once more. That is why when she came to me with promises that she could help me undo my past regrets, I knew that she meant me seeing Christian. I left the cabin and just as I had thought was the hooded woman waiting for me on the stump of my steps. She never turned her head my way yet she still said, "I see that you're packing light, Terra. That's good because you won't need anything aside from what you're wearing for where you're going."

"And just where is that exactly?" I asked.

She got up from the stump and stretched her arms as she said, "Before I tell you that, I believe that you should know just who you're about to be dealing with."

"Those people called Crusaders you mean. They seemed to know about both my father and Christian's as well. The thought has dwelled on my mind for quite some time now. If you have answers that can quell my concerns then, please tell me."

"I suggest that you sit then because this shall be a long tale. There was a time, Terra, where the Crusaders and your father were one in the same. In fact, Christian's father, your father, and myself were all once members of the Crusaders once upon a time," she said.

The very idea of my docile father commanding flames to rain down upon a lot of innocent wretches for defying him angered the lingering memory that I had of him. I could never picture him among those pompous fools that placed their own views of the world above the views of others. But with the mysterious nature that Father always exuded along with all of his stories about other worlds and his skill with an outdated weapon like a sword all led me to take the woman's words as the truth.

"Despite how much I wish you're jesting, I know you speak the truth. Tell me then what is the whole story between the three of you."

She wasted no time in telling me the full story and once it was done, all I could think about was how much I owed my father for the sacrifices he made for me. The lives of my mother and father were nothing short of an epic tragedy that even Shakespeare would weep for. I had considered myself alone ever since Father died. Despite the kindness that Christian and his family showed me, I knew that I was nothing but a mutt that they saved. After hearing that story, I felt like I had found a small piece of myself that had always been missing. It was a great feeling, but there still was more I needed to know.

"So I know why Christian had to leave, but why are you helping me find him? If anything, it sounds like you allowing me to make contact with the Crusaders would go against everything that my father sacrificed."

"As you have witnessed firsthand, the Crusaders are a force that tries their absolute hardest to spread the Word and will resort to force very easily if needed. Christian is now among those ranks and he has been sent to another world to carry out that mission, but if things are the same as they were when I last checked on him, then his life is in grave danger. I promised your fathers that I would keep you both safe, but there's no way that I can interfere in an area with so many Crusaders aiming for my head," she said. "Besides, the two of you are nearly grown men and are capable of making your own choices when it comes to you lives. I'm not here to tell you whether the choices that your fathers made were right or not. As you now know, I have no right to make any judgments on those two men. If you wish to save him then save him, but in doing so you'll be ensnared within the clutches of the Crusaders for all time. Once they learn you're alive, they may just kill you on the spot."

After seeing what those men did to the Karuk, there was no doubt in my mind that this group should be feared, yet I knew that I had to go save Christian if he was truly in danger. We had sworn to one another that we would always have one another's backs but I betrayed that promise when I ran away from his request to join him. Now that I knew the truth I knew that it was impossible for the two of us not to have been drawn to one another. Our fates were tied to each other. Even if I would be killed, I knew that I owed him far too much to leave him alone with an ominous force hanging over his head at all times.

"After everything that I've been through, I'm sure that a pretentious religious group will be the least of my worries. All I need to know is that I need to help Christian, so how do I get to him?" I asked.

"This," she said as she tossed me a small crystal. "Crush this in your hand and it will transport you over to the world Christian is. But keep in mind that the journey is a one-way trip, so if you need to leave that place you can only do it with the help of the Crusaders."

"I'll worry about that when the time comes then. One thing at a time," I said as I looked at the crystal in my hand.

"Are you doubting that such a small thing can really take you to a whole other world?"

"After the whole raining fire incident, there's not much else that can truly surprise me in the world. Well I better get going then. I'd hate to keep Christian waiting any longer for me."

"Before you break that crystal, let me tell a few things you need to do the moment you arrive."

Her words of advice were the next thing that ran through my mind. I looked around the beach and the first task she had instructed me to do was easy to complete.

"When you get a chance, take a uniform off of a dead Crusader and use that to move freely through the city without standing out too much."

With the remnants of the battle scattered all over the beach, it was not hard to quickly find a uniform that was my size and put it on. Once the torn and bloodstained uniform had been placed firmly on my body, I took a step forward when the putrid smell of death began to hang over my body like a cloud. The body I had taken the uniform had begun to rot but not enough to deter me from wearing the garments of a dead man. There were several holes around the torso section of the uniform indicating that he had been pelted by arrows and led to his death. Zion had told me that the Crusaders were a religious militia of sorts whose main goal was to convert heathen worlds to the Word of Christ mainly by force. I wondered if whoever that guy was felt if it was worth it to get pelted by the steel tips of arrows just to see a naïve native of that world bow to his whims. I turned my head away from his body, so I could focus my mind once more on what really mattered. My eyes keyed in on the wall looming over me. Christian was beyond that wall and I knew that I had to find him.

I had expected to the hear the cries for help of whoever used to reside in the pier, but aside from the crackling of fire, there was not a single sound around the area. I covered my mouth and proceeded through the fiery scene that had engulfed the pier. Fate had been kind to me as most of the fires were beginning to dwindle down leaving naught, but the black ashes from their destruction. I maneuvered through the area with my head tilted upward keeping my eyes on the wall of the city as it came closer and closer to me. After a while, the silence of the area was broken as I heard the shouts of men not too far ahead of me. I crouched down and used the debris of a fallen building as cover as I looked upon the scene. There were a total of five men not too far ahead of me, near the gates leading into the city. Two of which wore the same uniform as me indicating they must have been Crusaders while the other three men had the dark complexion similar to an Indian as they wore lightly plated armor similar to what the Greeks and the Romans had worn in my world. The two Crusaders were tied together and from the look of their faces, they were prisoners of war that had incurred the wrath of their captors.

While I wanted no part in whatever was going on, I knew that I had little to no chance of sneaking past those soldiers in order to get to the gate. Zion had warned me beforehand and instructed me to avoid any sign of conflict. Even I was a little disappointed in myself that it only took me a couple hours to go head and break one of the promises I had made to her. With the element of surprise on my side, I knew that three to one were still favorable odds. My hands went to my rapiers and stopped as I curled my fingers around the hilts. I never would had described myself as the sentimental type, but having the same blades that my father used when he was a Crusader was something that managed to put a smile on my face even during that instant. I thought back to how according to Zion that the last time that those blades had been used was during Father's escape. Never would I have imagined that Father did so much for me.

The Crusaders were a much more complex organization than I had originally thought. My initial impression was that they were just nothing but loudmouth priests that decided to carry around swords to invoke their religious stance. I could not have been further from the truth. They were many things: a secret society, an army, a relief force, the shadow of kings. They were a massive group with their own creed and beliefs, and my father had been recruited by their scouts when he was a young boy and raised among a multitude of others like him. While Zion said that she barely had any knowledge of my father and his past as a child, she said that practically all Crusaders share the same story. They were children orphaned by either war or a Crusader attack and due to their young, malleable minds they were taken into the ranks of the Crusaders to be integrated within their forces. She assumed that my father was no different in those regards, but what made him different was that he met my mother.

The Crusaders stood upon the highest moral platform that was possible, so they expected all of their members to follow the laws of their creed. One of those laws was that all Crusaders were to remain pure and never engage in any sort of relationship unless married. She did not know all of the details, but apparently that rule was a hard one to follow for Father. Mother and he had a strong connection to one another that the simple ink words written to paper could not prevent. At first their relationship was nothing but innocent acts that the Crusader would never catch word of, but the day came when Mother discovered she was with child and that news spread quickly through their ranks. She was detained and sentenced to be burned as a heretic for spitting on the laws that they held as sacred. Father was safe though. No one knew that the child would be his, so he could have sat back and did nothing, and that was exactly what he intended to do. Even with my time with Father, I knew he was not the noble sort. He was a good man, but in the face of those circumstances he faded into the shadows and turned his back on Mother in her time of need.

The Crusaders were cruel indeed. Instead of allowing mother a painless death, they made her suffer for her transgressions against them and made her to go through the pain of bringing me into the world alone. She nearly died during the process, but she lived on to see my face and hear my cry as she cried as well alongside me in a filthy cell meant only for vile criminals. Zion said that the real pain was not birthing me, but knowing that she could never be with me. Mother cried endlessly up until the day she was burned at the stake for her transgressions against the Order of God. Father was among the crowd as he stood there and watched his love burn. But the burning he saw was not of her charred flesh but rather the burning rage in her eyes as she stared him down for leaving her there to die. With my mother's final words she screamed out to, "Save Terra!"

I looked back down at my blades and realized that I had inherited the blades of a coward, but I fully intended to use them in order to save Christian and bring perhaps a slight bit of honor back to my legacy. I emerged from behind the debris and shot two of the men with my pistols and before the third one could react, I slipped behind him and slit his throat with my new blades. The two Crusaders I had just saved began to laugh at the slain bodies. They went on and on about how they deserved a much more painful death for not accepting the Word. I looked upon the three new additions I sent to the gates of heaven or hell and thought back to the ignorance of the Crusaders that came to Earth. Did those three really deserve to die? Perhaps I should have killed the Crusaders and asked the other three for help with Christian. Those questions were hardly able to take root in my mind as the two men I cut loose embraced me like I was their brother.

I pushed them off of me and sheathed my swords. They both bowed their heads and thanked me for my help as they introduced themselves one at a time.

"Reginald Gonzales of the 186th cadet squad!" he said as he saluted me by placing his hands together as if he was prayer. Reginald was a man I would come to spend a lot of time with in the future, but back then I thought nothing of either of them. Reginald was shorter than myself with a thick beard engulfing his face. He looked to be of Hispanic descent, but since we were all from different worlds it's hard to say what he truly was.

"Jonathan Rampersad of the 186th as well," he said but in a much more relaxed tone. Between the two of them, Jon was certainly the more relaxed one. He shared a similar skin tone to the natives of that world but the uniform of the Crusaders made him seem to be completely different from the others. The two of them both had a longsword sheathed on their backs along with the markings of war upon their bodies. Both of their fingernails had the remnants of dried blood coating the surface. Their uniforms were not in favorable shape at all, and from the bags under their eyes, I could tell that they had been fighting nonstop for days on end.

Jon came forward and asked me, "What squad do you belong to?"

I recited back an answer word for word as Zion had told me to, "I, Terra Morris, have no squad anymore. These blasted heathens wiped us all out so now I'm nothing but a wandering blade hell-bent on enforcing the retribution of Father God."

"It seems as though we're cut from a similar cloth because of this battle. Well thank the heavens that we slayed plenty of Gays this day before we move out," Jon said.

Gays? The word was a foreign one to me, but I assumed that the people of that city were most likely called that due to the name of their city. While I did not know the name of the city, I figured it must have been Fagapolis or Fagcrin. Something of that nature I supposed.

I stepped a little bit closer to the gate and asked, "So shall we enter the city now, my brothers?" It truly felt strange to call another person brother aside from Christian.

Reginald laughed as he said, "Sure, as long as the airship decided to crash-land in there and then picks us up. Maybe you didn't hear but we have received orders to return to the far side beach. The plan worked perfectly and now we have a devoted follower of the Word sitting upon the throne in the place of that gay, repulsive uncle of his." There was a strong hint of disgust in Reginald's voice as he mentioned the old ruler. "It's a shame though that it cost so many of us to do it."

He looked past me and stared as the scattered remains of people he may or may have not been close with, but I know that gaze for I have held the same gaze in my own eyes as well at times when I fought in the war. Jon came from behind him and placed his hand on his shoulder.

"It's okay, Reginald," he said. "We can put this awful crusade behind us now."

The crusade was over? If that was the case, then I had no idea what sort of danger that Christian was in. I looked back over to the gates leading into the city. I just had some sort of gut-feeling that Christian was still in there. I quickly asked Reginald, "Are there any others still left in the city?"

Their eyes went toward the floor as Jon began to stutter as he spoke, "We didn't want to leave them, but Christian and Tai-lee were just too persistent. They kept insisting that we save her, but the chances of that were zero and—"

I grabbed Jon by the collar of his uniform and lifted him into the air, "Christian is in the city and you left him there? What's his situation?"

"You must've been in one of the more peaceful districts then," said Jon. "We met our goal and killed the king, but once the news of his death spread throughout his faction, they went into a blind fury. Grief dulled all other pain they must have felt as they rampaged through the city causing death and destruction to whomever they could find allied with the new king. Several other squads had made camp at an abandoned church and were the last ones to receive the order to withdraw. But it was too late. The last remnants of the old king's forces surrounded the church. We pleaded with Christian and the others to retreat before we were completely surrounded, but he would not hear our words. Those savages had captured one of our own and he's determined not to leave her behind. They may all be dead by now."

"What kind of soldier leaves his comrades to die like that?" I asked.

When I took another look into Jon's eyes, I saw that he was giving me a cold stare before he said, "If it was not for Christian and him disobeying orders, we wouldn't have been in that situation. Instead of purging the remainder of the Gays like we were ordered. He instructed our groups to help them instead since the battle was over!"

I threw Jon to the ground. His ignorance reminded me of the mindset that the whites had toward anyone that treated blacks as equals because I had heard all I could stomach. That guy was mad at Christian because he was acting out of kindness? It was rare that I would actually inquire into another person's mindset toward something, but there was something different about that guy.

"What kind of war is this where orders are given to execute an entire purge just because they have decided not to accept the Word?" I asked.

"Are you soft in the head, man?" asked Reginald. "This battle has never been for redemption for these heathens. We came into this with the sole purpose of exterminating these abominations. We only save those that are worthy of our Lord's grace. All others we deem as just blight upon this fair universe."

A blight upon the universe? Did the Crusaders truly hate gay people that much? While it was no hidden fact that those that preferred the same sex were generally treated with great disdain in society, I would have expected better from an organization that preached to be the moral apex of the universe. Either way, my greatest concern was that Christian was one his own in that city. I turned my back to the two of them and began to walk toward the gate. The wooden gate with reinforced steel hinges was as long as a building but the bombardment from the ships had left a gaping hole in its side allowing for free entry into the inner city. As I proceeded toward the gaping hole, Reginald called out to me, "Hey, the lower city is practically overrun with the old king's men. If you go in there then you'll surely die.

I shouted back at him, "As Crusaders, is it not our duty to put our lives on the line in order to save others. Who has the right to decide what group of people deserved to be saved and get killed? In my world, anyone that isn't born with white skin is treated on the same level as a mere animal, so why would I pray for others to treat me equally but then turn around and slaughter another group of people because they're different from me. Christian was born in the same world, so he understands that. That's why he helped those people. If anything he's the only one exuding the Creed that we're all taught. And even if you don't agree, he's still our comrade so we should have his back through it all. If we're willing to save the wretches from primitive worlds, then why shouldn't we offer the same loyalty to our own comrades?"

I must have struck a nerve within the two of them because it didn't take much longer for the two of them to join me as we all entered the together.

It was pointless for me to ask for the specific reason behind their change of heart. As a soldier myself, I knew how hard it is to just walk away from a battle whether you like your comrades or not. The guilt of abandoning their kin must have been eating the two of them up from the very core of their beings. It looked like selfishness was a recurring trait within the hearts of all Crusaders. It was not just my father's heart had succumbed to the inner desires of his heart as he fled for safety, but those two had done the same thing has well without a second thought until I intervened. It bothered me to no end that I had to lecture those supposed "righteous people" what the right decision was. Perhaps righteousness was nothing but a naiveté of the actions and they committed on a daily basis. Was that how people like that could so easily claim to be righteous?

A chill ran through my body as I imagined an entire organization with the power to change the entire state of worlds possessing the same blind righteous persona that those two and Father had. They were only able to rectify their ways because of an outside influence calling them out on their foolishness. But who would call out an entire organization with as much power as the Crusaders? If the answer was what I thought it was, then I could do nothing but feel sorry for countless worlds that would be subjected to the righteous fury of the Crusaders as they continued to conquer worlds based solely on the prejudice hating all those that disagreed with their ways. But who was to say that they were right and the rest of the worlds were wrong?

The situation on the other side of the wall was completely different from the pier. The flames of war had not scratched any homes nor were there any bodies laying around in the street to be found. Being inside the city just gave me more reason to doubt the cause of the Crusaders as the architecture of the city was magnificent. I had never seen the pinnacle of human architecture because I had been regulated to plantation life, but I could tell that the scope of that city was far grander than any city made on Earth. I remember the story about the Tower of Babel and thought to myself how every building seemed to be a copy of it as the city towered into the very heavens themselves. I could hear a loud commotion going on further down the street and my prior history when it came to crowds gathering in a town told me to get as far away from that sound as possible.

"That's probably where Christian and the others are being held up," said Jon. "The remaining forces of the old king should not be too great in number but we're still only three. Since you're the one to want to come back here so badly, what's your plan?"

"Scout the area," I said. "I want to know exactly what we're dealing with before we head there to save Christian and the others. Meet back here in half an hour so we can compare info."

I didn't know if I should have been giving such a long time limit, but I could not take any chances when it came to Christian. I just had to hope for the best and pray that he would still be safe after I had found a way to save him. Having the weight of another life upon the shoulders as you planned to save it was a cumbersome burden that I didn't particularly enjoy. My mind flashed back to the tale that Zion told of my father and I could not help but laugh at the idea that I was essentially copying my old man. Just as he had abandoned my mother, I had abandoned Christian when he asked me to join him, but now I was ready to risk my life in order to save him just like my father was willing to risk it all to save me when I was a child.

The image of my mother's passing haunted my father over the next few months. He tried his hardest not to think of me, but my fate was the hottest gossip around the Crusaders at that time. The brass was deciding if it would be better to kill me as well to set another example or if I should just join the ranks of the Crusaders. Around that same time Father had gotten injured in a Crusade to another world, so as he recovered, he was only assigned to guard duty in the cells. It was during that time that he met Zion. She had seen the horrors of the Crusades for too many years and decided to go AWOL to live the life of an exile, but her freedom was a short-lived one as the Crusaders quickly found her once again. Ever since then, she had been regulated to cell life and it was during her jail time she met my mother. Their time together was short, but according to Zion, she had formed a strong bond with her as they both waited for their execution. As fate would have it, the cell that Father had been posted to guard was none other than Zion's and she knew who he was right away from the description that Mother gave of him to her. Zion said that the next few months were amusing to her as she kept tormenting Father for his decision to abandon Mother to her fate as he sat back and retained the benefits of a Crusader. Day in and out she chided him for his betrayal of Mother, but Father never said anything back. He just stood his post and took in all of the scrutiny that Zion had for him. If he had really wanted to, he could have asked for a transfer to another part of the dungeons, but Zion suspected that he wanted for her to keep chiding him. It was when she came upon this revelation that she began to notice the signs of Father's depression. He was becoming thinner by the day; his eyes had bags on top of his bags, and his eyes had a constant glaze to them as if he had been crying for hours.

After she saw this, she stopped chastising him and instead began to recount the stories of the few days that Mother held me in her arms after my birth. As it turns out, Zion had helped birth me into the world and even take care of me for a second while I was a mere baby. While she told stories of how much of a handful that I was for my mother and her, she said that she was able to see my father smile for the first time since she had met him. Suddenly Father ended his silence and began to ask questions about me like how big I was and whose eyes did I have. The two of them grew closer to each other as they both recanted their own insecurities when it came to the Crusaders and how they both expressed an earnest desire to leave the group. Once those words were said though, the idea to save me came into both of their minds. Father saw saving me as a sort of redemption for allowing Mother to die like that. For my own protection, Zion said it would be best if I didn't know the rest of the story between them because it would put the lives of others that helped them at risk. All I needed to know was that as her jailer, he let her escape and in return she helped him rescue me and run away to Earth along with the aid of Christian's father. I was the redemption that Father sought after allowing Mother to perish in the flames of the Crusaders. Now I sought the same sort of redemption with Christian as I wished to rectify my past mistake of allowing him to join the Crusaders alone.

Thirty minutes had passed by quickly as I waited for Jon and Reginald to return. We went into a small alleyway to conceal ourselves and compared the notes that we had. It was just as they had mentioned to me earlier. Christian and whatever forces he had were trapped within a church that was surrounded around a few dozen men that wanted nothing but to spill of the blood of those inside the church. Luckily for us, Christian had seemed to turn that entire church into a fortress as he had archers positioned at every available window which prevented the opposing forces from attacking in earnest. But such a tactic would only last for so long. I knew that I would have to come up with something to help them escape, but such a plan was proving difficult to say the least. Even though the church was abandoned, it still rested on a large plot of land which allowed for the old king's men to surround every possible exit that Christian and them could take to escape from. The overall location was not an opportune one as well as the church itself rested more so in the interior of the city. It was only a matter of time before they would get bored and decide to smoke them out. Once that thought ran through my mind, I devised a plan not only to help Christian but to take out that force once and for all.

I wiped away all of the trash that had cluttered the alleyway where we stood. Sticky and filthy from moving all of the trash, I rinsed my hands off in a nearby puddle. The stains of blood that had been left on my fingers vanished along with the smell of the trash on my hands, but just because there were no signs left on me, I knew that I had still done those actions. I didn't need to see the dried crust of the blood from another man upon my hands to know I killed him. With those thoughts fresh in my mind, I wondered if by saving him would I ever be able to forget that I abandoned him when he asked me to join him as a Crusader. No matter how much a man scrubs, he can never erase the stains of his past deeds from his hands. But saving him would be a good of start as any. The protests from the men surrounding the church were becoming louder as I drew my blade and used the tip to draw on the street. I constructed the best picture of the scenario from the info we had all gathered and showed the layout of the map to Reginald and Jon.

I began my plan by saying, "While it may seem like a disadvantage that the church is on such a large plot of land, it actually works to our advantage."

"How is that?" Jon asked.

I marked where all the main pockets of forces that the old king's men had surrounding the church and further explained, "The fact that they just haven't stormed the church means that Christian must have a considerable amount of forces in that church. Enough forces in fact to be able to take them on in the open field and perhaps take out a large number of their men."

Reginald interrupted me by adding, "By but that same logic applies to Christian as well. He must still have smaller forces for the old king's men or he would have attacked by now."

"Christian is a defensive fighter and tries to only employ tactics that don't cost a lot of men in the process," I said. "The reason he probably has not left yet is because it would cost far too many lives at this time. He's simply waiting for an opportunity to present itself." I drew three x's in the pavement at three different positions behind the enemy forces. "We're that opportunity. Because of the decrepit state of the church, the grass surrounding it has become largely overgrown. If we were to say light that grass on fire, then the enemy forces would have no choice but to proceed closer to the church, which would give Christian the advantage to go on the offensive and strike them down. From there, we could mix in the fighting and take out as many as we can from their back flanks."

I sheathed my sword and looked upon my plan with pride. It was the first time I had constructed a battle plan, but I had seen enough of foolish captains constructing them to get a general idea of how to proceed. My markings in the pavement had the quality of a child's handwriting when playing a game, but it was truly the quality that mattered. I did notice though that Reginald had a constant smirk on his face the whole time I was drawing the pictures.

We split as we quickly got in position around our respective areas. Mine was the closest as I took cover within a collapsed general store not too far from the center of the enemy forces. I had only scouted that area from afar so I had no idea the state the store was in until I entered. The store looked like a wild animal had torn through the place. The surface of the floor had been covered with grains of rice spilling from open bags. The shelves had been knocked over like a row of dominoes causing one to lay on top of the other. Scavengers must have raided the place because nearly every article of food had either been opened up or lay half-eaten upon the ground. I kicked my way through the clutter on the floor until my foot struck something soft and wet. My head glanced down right as a hand shot forth from beneath the junk and grabbed my ankle. Unsheathing my sword, I shook the hand off and was about to impale the body right when a pathetic groan came from the body. Upon further inspection, the hand that had grabbed me was attached to a dainty wrist that looked like the slightest pull would break it. I dug underneath the grains of rice and flour and pulled out the body of a frail girl that looked as though she had not eaten for days. A truly surprising irony considering everything that she was around. I brushed off some of the flour off of her and sat her down. Her eyes had a glazed look to them like she was not there, but after I touched her face, the light came back to them and she began to scream and hit me. I endured her weak blows to my chest but quickly covered her mouth so the enemy would not rush there.

The little brat bit my hand which caused me to let go of her. The moment she was free she said, "I hate all you Crusaders! You told me that being a Crusader meant helping others and improving the state of the worlds, so there would be no more orphans like me, but everything going on here is…is…" Tears began to swell up in her eyes as she ran away. I remember how confused I was during that whole scene until I remembered how Crusaders always recruited their members young from worlds that they saved. Could she have been a recruit that came there to see the Crusade? If that was indeed the case, then the hateful words that she spit it out held perfect merit to them. But the policies by the Crusaders were not my chief concern at that time. I blocked the girl from my mind and proceeded with the plan.

I looked to my left and right and waited to see signs that the others had gotten into their positions. I sat near the back of the store by the exit waiting for the synchronized strike to happen. I was not too far from the enemy forces, and I could count their numbers around fourteen. That was more than I had originally thought, but the nature of the plan would not be affected. I looked back to the left and right and saw the light from the sun reflecting off of their blades. That was the signal. I took a deep breath and sprinted forth from the store and began to crawl through the tall grass like a predator stalking his prey. The thick blades of grass blocked my vision, but I was able to continue toward the enemy due to all of the commotion they were making. As I continued forward parting the grass ahead of me, I suddenly came upon a dead body that had been struck by an arrow. The smell of his decaying flesh almost made me puke but instead I used the cover of his repugnant smell to take out one of my pistols and began to empty out the gunpowder in a long line behind the enemy forces.

I held my breath as I slithered through the grass like a snake doing my best to make the line of gun powder long enough. At first, my nerves were calm, but with every shout from the enemies, my heart stopped as I clenched my fists praying that I had not been discovered as of yet. Sweat dripped from my nose to the soil as I waited and waited, but it looked as though the shouts were only meant for those being held in the church. I exhaled a sigh of relief as I continued onward toward my goal. I had left it up to the two of them to each come up with a way to start a fire, so once my trap had been set up, I waited for the first signs of smoke from the other two until I went to ignite my own trap. My faith had paid off as I saw a thin wisp of smoke emerging from both of their directions behind the enemy. I reacted instantly pulling out my pistol and firing one of the bullets near the tail end of the line of gunpowder. My aim was only to graze the line in order to ignite it. Like magic, the black powder sparked into red flames that began to dance in the fields of the church. Before I was caught on the other side of the flames, I retreated as quickly as I could back toward the store and waited for Christian to take the bait.

Just as I predicted, the flames spread quickly through the fields, which pushed the enemies closer and closer to the front of the church. Christian's forces wasted no time and mowing down anyone unlucky enough to step within the range of the archers. One by one, the enemy forces fell to the soaring arrows being launched from the church until a small platoon of Crusaders burst forth from the church at each side and charged to do battle with the remaining forces near the steps of the church. With the smoke from the flames obscuring my vision, I could only wait for the final part of my plan before I could help Christian.

I looked to the sky and saw the dark clouds I had noticed when I first arrived in that world had now gathered over the whole city. Several drops of rain began to suddenly pour from the heavens splashing on my confiscated uniform and erasing the bloodstains that had seeped into the fabric. The drizzle soon evolved into a full downpour, which calmed down the roaring flames around the church. Once the flames had died down, I drew my blades and rushed into the fray of combat going on. I was surprised to see that the Crusaders forces inside of church were far less than I had predicted. In fact, the two opposing forces were at a stalemate in the battle. From my experience at war with the North, I learned one vital lesson that applied to every battlefield. Take out the general and the rest will crumble as well. I quickly scanned the field of battle until I spotted a man with far more armor than the rest of the men around him. He easily cut through Crusader after Crusader as if he was cutting through paper. The man let out a roar like a savage beast as his blade dug into the skin of each body he cut down. It was then I thought back to Reginald's words about the remnants of the king's forces battling with nothing but grief to carry them on.

I wasted no time as I slipped into the fray of the battle and came up from behind the enemy general. None of the men of that world wore heavy armor, so the only thing that he guarded was his torso and not his back. I picked up my speed as I pointed the tips of my blade toward his back and drove him through as the force of my charge knocked him off of his feet and into the ground. His body twitched for a moment before it fell still, and his men stopped fighting the moment that they saw their commander had fallen. As I crawled off of the general's body, I knew that right before I killed him, he was just about to kill another Crusader. I looked around to see the life that I had saved and froze once I saw the face of the woman I had saved. She was several years my senior, a woman fully grown and blossoming in all the right areas. According to the standards of my world, she was some kind of Asian ethnicity and the dazzling sparkle of his doe-like eyes was enough to make me stop in the midst of a battle.

The spell she had over me was broken the moment I heard a man call her name, "Tai-lee, thank God you're safe. I told you to stay inside the church and—" The man stopped talking as he and I set our eyes upon each other once more. The two months that I had not seen Christian had changed him far more than I would have thought. His hair had grown down to his shoulders and he had even gotten taller than me as well. He possessed some minor lacerations from the battle, but all in all he looked fine. He pushed away the wet strands of his hair to get a better look at me before he embraced me.

"I knew that you'd come to aid me, brother," said Christian as his fingers clutched onto the wet fabric of my uniform.

"Did you really?" I asked.

He stopped hugging me and punched me in the arm and laughed, "Of course I didn't really think that, but saying that made our reunion seem much cooler right?"

I could only laugh at such a stupid statement, but it was the first time I had truly laughed in two months. As the rain continued to pour, I felt that the uniform that I had stolen suddenly had a much tighter fit to it that made me think that I would never be able to take it off. I looked around at all the dead bodies that I had been responsible for killing and thought back to the body of Kita. She was no different from these people that refused to acknowledge the way of the Crusaders, but just as she had they died for that resistance. With the knowledge of Christian's safety firmly placed within my mind, I thought back to the thought that I had locked away earlier. Did those people really deserve to die? That final little skirmish would be known as the finale to the Crusade of Erque, the only world discovered with a 50 percent gay population. And the woman that I happened to save was none other than Tai-lee, the daughter of the head of the Order of Crusaders, Fi-Long. That was my first Crusade.

13
Community

A chill slipped through the window and kissed my bare skin causing me to stir and awake. I tried to crawl out from my bed, but the woman to my left blocked my way and the one to my right did the same as well. Their hands were still laying on my body as I gently moved them to the side. I yawned as I looked back upon the two sleeping women. I grinned congratulating myself for the completion of another fine evening. Even though the festival to honor me into the ranks of Ataxia had passed by a month ago, I still found myself reveling in all the excitements that the festival offered every other night. I walked out to the window and looked at the sun. My injuries I had suffered from Dom had finally healed, so my excuse for not looking for Christian had passed by as well. Searching for Christian huh? The fiery passion behind that idea that had once drove me had all but cooled down over the past month. Grabbing a robe from the chair, I proceeded to the window and looked out at the village I had become a part of.

The view from my window was one of the best in all of Ataxia. Thanks to Lucas, I had been given one of the few newly built homes that were across from the temple. It was a small two-story abode, but it had a cozy feeling to it that I could not deny as I basked in the rays of the sun. Judging from its position, I would have to guess that it was long past midday and thus I had missed another Sunday's worth of church due to my extraneous late-night adventures. I looked at myself in the mirror and could see that my new lifestyle was taking its toll on my body. All the constant nights out had put the first signs of bags under my eyes, and I even had a few scars from the fights that I began to pick.

I ran my fingers along the surface of one nasty cut I received the other night. It was sad but I could no longer remember what he had said to me to make me hate him so much during that instance. Sariah and Rebecca instructed me to forgive him as was one of the mottos of our Creed, but I found that I could not. No matter how many times they urged me on, I knew I could not forgive him not because he committed some unforgivable offence to me, but rather because I just didn't want to. I remembered my days among the Karuks. Days when I could truly do whatever I wished without having a guide book to follow. Those days were so liberating, and that island reminded me of those days. I looked back at the shadows that the sun was casting on the ground and figured I needed to hurry to the arena if I wanted to catch the conclusion of that week's spectacle. I hurried to get dressed and threw on my old uniform. Old uniform…I remember that was exactly how I thought of it after I had been on that isle for the past month. My life as a Crusader was virtually over and I knew that there would be no returning to the Order. As I contemplated my journey to how I even got there, Sariah came into my room unannounced as if she lived there.

"I see that you're enjoying yourself this morning, Your Highness," she said in that snarky tone. As of late, she and Rebecca both had given me hell about the frivolous life that I was living as they called it. I looked at her attire of a modest white dress to symbolize a purity that I knew didn't exist. It was the traditional outfit that all women had to wear when they attended church.

"What is it that you want, Sariah? As you can see, I have company," I said waving her off.

"Oh really now? What are their names then?"

At times I really hated her. I missed her radiant personality she had when we first met, but life as a Crusader had hardened the girl, so the ebullient Sariah I could not take my eyes off of was long gone. In her place was a woman whose life mission seemed to be chiding me at every waking hour.

"Janet and Krystal," I lied. "There, are you happy?"

She could see through my deception, I knew that but I frankly didn't care.

"Terra, whatever happened to finding Christian and the others? It used to be all you could think about, but now you have other activities on your mind constantly it seems."

"Sariah," I said with little patience, "we have been over this before. This island is too large to blindly search for them. In order to find Christian, we'll need help and to do that we must earn the trust of Lucas and the clown."

"It's amazing how you can rationalize any action or inaction that you do in order to make it seem right to you. Admit it, you're simply in love with this lifestyle, a lifestyle that Christian would condemn, so you're afraid of having to give it up if we find him."

I slowly stepped up to her looking down upon her face as our chests were pressed against one another. She could probably feel the tension there because I saw sweat beginning to drip down her face.

"The only thing that I'm afraid of is what I'll do to you if you continue to press me on this issue. Now I suggest you leave before I lose my temper," I said as calmly as I could.

Sariah knew me well enough when to take my threats seriously as she walked out of the room. I noticed that my old temper was returning over the last month. It had often gotten me into trouble when I was a lad, but once I joined the Crusaders I had reined it in check. I was sure it meant nothing, but still I did notice it. I finished getting dressed and left my home only to find a snickering Lucas standing by my door outside.

"So I see that you haven't completely subjugated your subjects yet, Terra," he teased. "Pay it no mind though, friend. Women were meant to be a thorn in our fingers. I've heard though there are worlds out there where women are completely submissive to men in almost every regard."

"Yeah I come from I world like that," I said fairly casually.

"Is that so? It must have been heaven for you down there then. I wish I had hailed from such a promising land."

I took a glance at his light complexion that had been getting tan as of late. I laughed and responded, "Yes you would've fit in there much better than I would have, my friend. My world was essentially made for people like you."

"Oh I imagine that the residents of your world must be the most beautiful people with the most charming personalities?" he jested.

"You could say something like that."

As we walked through the temple grounds, we received a fair share of hellos from everyone as they had quickly become accustomed to my face. Despite what I would have originally assumed about those that were exiled there, the people of the isle were no different than me in any way. We all had our reasons for joining the Crusaders and we all had our reasons for breaking the tenements that they imposed on us. Some people lied to protect their friends; others fell in love; some even killed in order to protect another and were exiled. We all had our own stories for being there, and we all found that it was better to drown our sorrows away in the pleasures of our flesh than face the hard reality that we were being punished for our imperfections. I had often wondered if the Order really expected us to be the perfect human beings because that was how they treated us. We were not allowed to make any mistakes and if we did we faced exile.

"I believe you should treat Sariah kinder, Terra," said Lucas.

He had spoken often of Sariah to me in the past month and most of the time I just shrugged his statements off, but that time in particular I decided to humor him.

"And why is that?"

"Everyone needs a partner on this Isle. Someone that they can depend on when times are hard. Most people just rely on those that were in their group, but sometimes you need more than that,"

"The only thing I need from her is to stop bothering me at every chance she gets," I said. And that was the end of that talk, but his words followed me as if they were my shadow for the rest of the day. Those words plagued me to no end as I thought about how Sariah had indeed helped me through various times over the last five years. I sat in the dark at a table in my kitchen pondering such thoughts. My finger tapped on the table as I recollected my time with her and each memory seemed to have its own rhythm that made the taps of my fingers echo through the house.

The following morning I had all but erased the words that Lucas had planted in my heart as I ventured out into the village. I had not taken more than a couple steps from my house when I was approached by my neighbor Richard and his wife Abby. They were a lovely couple that been one of the first people to greet me and welcome me to the village following my victory. The two of them were what were called Natural Exiles since they were born on the island. They knew nothing of the Crusaders aside from the stories told by the elders of the island and new exiles. They perhaps a few years older than me which showed me how long people must have been on that wretched island. Richard came up to me with his hand outstretched and I took a firm hold of it as I shook it, "Good morning, Richard, Abby, what are you two doing at this hour?" I asked.

"Well the honest truth is that we're looking for you. I saw you leave your house and we rushed outside to greet you," he said.

"Well I'm flattered but why the rush to see me. Wait...if this is about all the noise from the previous night, I can assure you she was a one-time thing," I said.

"Don't worry, Terra, it has nothing to do with that. You should hear us some..." he let out a grunt as Abby slapped the side of his head with a red expression on her face. "Well anyway we came out here to invite you to dinner. It has been far too long since we have spent time together so why don't you bring one of your lady friends to our place tonight."

He left quickly after that without giving me enough time to even say "no," but as I thought about his offer, I wondered who I should bring. Richard was well-liked by many in the village so it was a good idea to get further on his good side for the day I needed to call in a favor. So then the question came to be who to bring and within moments of thinking of that, Lucas's advice came rushing back to me. It was not long after that I found myself knocking upon Sariah's door. I was fully ready to apologize for my previous actions until I saw that a half-naked man opened the door in her place. There was without a doubt an awkward silence we shared as the two of us stood there shocked at the other's appearance. After all that Sariah had said about my "frivolous" activities, she went around and got busy with Sampson over there. I was ready to just slowly walk away until I caught a wicked snicker echoing from behind "muscles" over there. I pushed my way past him and found Sariah in her all-white room putting the finishing touches of a portrait of none other than "Hercules" over there.

"A painting? So that's what that was," I said relieved.

She had a big smirk on her face as she said, "Oh you mean, Chris? Yeah he was just here to help me finish up a painting. It took all night to do wouldn't you believe."

I ignored her childish comment and proceeded on with why I had went to her home in the first place.

"Well I'm glad you had your fun. Because we're about to begin putting in the first steps to find Christian."

"Are you for real?"

"We're having dinner tonight with Richard and Abby. As it turns out, Richard's father happens to be the head hunting force that goes out to the jungle to gather food for the village. So I'm sure having his expertise of the land would be a valuable thing when searching for seven lost people."

"Then why do you need me for something simple like that?" she asked as she continued to brush the outer edges of her portrait. "Take one of your little toys with you for that."

I went over to her bed and flopped down making some of the feathers shoot out from the side. I looked over to her to see; the combination of the sunlight from her window and the feathers floating around her to give off an angelic picture of her as she sat. It was a brief picture but one that made me stop breathing for a moment. I stretched out my arms and yawned as I said, "Well in order to do that I'd have to marry one of them and that's not an idea I'm too keen on.

"What do you mean?"

"I mean it's time that we begin to do what we should've done ages ago and look for Christian, but to do that we need to work as a unit and not as separate powers. We were supposed to be exiled to this island because of the passion I had for you, so we need to show the validity of that story by—"

"Getting married?" she asked. "How would that solve any of our problems?"

"Simple. You seem to truly think that I've done nothing but waste away this past month, but in all truth, I have studied this culture and the truth of the matter is that even if we find Christian, there's no way he'd be accepted into a town such as this. As long as the clown reigns supreme then Christian will always be an outcast. But if we were to, I don't know, pull off the same trick we did on Erque, then we—"

"Would control the village and thus the power to allow Christian to join or not," she finished for me. "Looks like that you've been busy with things other than your little toys. Well if that's truly what you have planned, then you have my support."

"Good. Now go invite as many people has you can to dinner with us tonight as well. Actually, no, try to stay focused around a total of seven or eight couples there with us. If we have that many then everything I have in mind should work out."

Sariah had done well with the little time I had handed to her. Within the next few hours, the whole village was abuzz with news of our dinner party. At first Richard and Abby seemed to be against the idea but after some time the idea of everyone getting together seemed to rub off on them so well they claimed the idea as their own from the start. The dinner had turned into such an event that it was decided that it would take place within the village square as opposed to Richard and Abby's place. I made sure that I was the first one there when the time came. The set up was nothing extravagant, all that was there was a long table that could hold well over twenty people. The courtyard was dead silent as I looked upon the blank table reminiscing about eating with the others in our squad on a daily basis. Right when I began to wonder if I would ever break bread with them again, a hand grasped my shoulder.

I turned around to only stare into the empty void of the woman's hood. I wish I could say that I was shocked to see her there, but she had been overdue on one of her visits with me for quite some time.

"You're looking well for all things considered, Terra," she said as she took a seat at the table.

In somewhat of a panic, I looked around to see if there was anybody else around, but just as usual it was only the two of us when she arrived. I took a seat next to her and said, "And you're still being creepy."

"You wound me, Terra, and here I came to see if I was invited to your little dinner party," she said trying her best to sound like she truly cared.

"I'm sure you must be devastated. So what is it that you want this time from me?"

"In all honesty, nothing really. I just wanted to check up on you."

"Okay, well if that's all, then you best be on your way."

"So cold. I'm shocked that you haven't asked me how I got here and for a way off this world."

"I know you well enough that if you wanted me off of this world then you would've given me the means by now. Besides, last time I used your means of transportation, I almost drowned so I'll past this time around," I said. "However, I do have one question though. Is Christian okay?"

"He is for now. I've kept an eye on him ever since everyone crashed here. He'd be disappointed in how you're behaving though. I'm sure that you know that as well."

"I don't need a lesson from a ghost. This is not some Dickens story."

"Oh so you do bother to read the books I bring you from Earth. I'm touched, really I am," she said with an obvious sarcastic tone in her voice.

"Terra!" called Sariah, "are you over there?"

I looked back toward the woman in the hood to see she was gone. I never would understand her motives, but she was the last thing I needed to focus on. Sariah came forward with around ten others in tow. Each one carried some sort of delicacy brought from their home and placed on the table. The aroma of each item placed there blended together to create a smell that attacked our very tongues and stomachs at the same time. Seeing so much food and people in one location reminded me of Thanksgiving, a holiday I had not celebrated since Christian's father was killed.

One by one we all took our seats, and I sat between Sariah and Lucas as Rebecca sat to the left of Sariah. I looked for the clown but he was not in attendance. Everyone there had worn their uniform to the dinner and made sure that it was in the best condition they could afford. Granted, that meant that some just had less stains and tears than others, but I was not going to complain too much about that. It was the first time that I had seen so many of us in uniform since I was in training. A solemn feeling ran through my body as I truly looked at the image of so many

Crusaders together. The feeling was a fleeting one as I reminded myself that we were all simply exiles and deserved no place at the table of the Lord.

Plates and drinks were distributed to all, and right as I was about to say a prayer over the food, I noticed that nearly half of the people there already began to eat. It was an occurrence that I had seen quite often and even I had become susceptible to as well. It was a small thing that I didn't take too much notice of until that moment. I had often said my prayers before a meal, but as I ate with more and more people of the island, I noticed that my tendency to do so had indeed gone down quite a bit. It was like watching a glass slip from your hands for no reason. You have no idea why it happened but you can only watch as if falls to the ground and before you know what happened it has shattered into so many pieces. It becomes impossible to piece back together.

I looked directly across from me and saw Richard tearing into a chicken leg as if he was a wild animal that had just killed his prey.

"Slow down, Richard," I beckoned to him, "if you eat any faster you'll pass out from a full stomach before we had the pleasure of a drink, my friend."

He continued to ravage the meat before him as Abby spoke in his place, "Pay my husband no mind, Terra. That man's truly a beast when food is placed before him."

"A trait from what I heard runs deep in the blood," said Sariah as she took a sip of wine from the cup in front of her. "I hear that your grandfather was a great Crusader that was famed in several worlds for his voracious appetite. Rumor has it that he was able to purify one world by simply beating the tsar of a land in an eating bout. Though he liberated the world, I hear that it was soon hit by famine and almost was destroyed since your grandfather devoured everything in sight."

A roar of laughter was shared among everyone at our section of the table and Richard nearly choked on all the food that was before him inciting further laughter amongst us.

"And his father inherited that same appetite, but for more than just simply food," snickered Lucas.

"Oh yes we all know about the appetite my father had that got him exiled in the first place."

"Yes never before had I heard of a king that slept with all of the females of his unit. I have to say he was certainly a role model of mine. How many exactly did your old man bone, Richard?" asked Lucas.

"To be perfectly honest, I don't know if there's an exact numerical value for such a number. All I know is that I'm sure I have a couple of siblings out there that would be dying to meet me."

More laughter was exchanged even from Sariah and Rebecca this time around. His joke was not all that funny, but I suspect that the alcohol had quickly begun to take effect. The sad truth though was that Richard was correct. While Lucas and the others praised the legacy of Richard's father, the Order had made sure to make an example of the transgressions that transpired during his time. After he had been exiled, Richard's father was found guilty of being the father of two children from different women. One of which was Richard. As punishment, the Order had the second woman and the child burned at the stake. They did allow Richard's father the courtesy to pick any world of choosing to live a life with Richard and his mother, but before he left it was discovered he had fathered three more children from three different women. That legacy of his that they so admired had destroyed the lives of four different families that he had and gotten the last one exiled to that island. I truly wondered if they would continue to glorify such a man if they knew the truth about him.

I realized such thoughts were a waste of my time and took hold of the wineglass in front of me as I poured the red liquid down my throat. Right when I put the glass back down on the table, I turned to my left and saw that Rebecca had a fluster on her face as she was the recipient of a couple of men's laughter. I said nothing of the matter, but I did lean closer to her in order to hear the commotion. The laughter expressed by Oskey and

Graham, two of the more formidable exiles in the village in terms of power, calmed down as Graham spoke, "Rebecca, truly you jest. The practice of reading the Word has been a long-abandoned art that does nothing aside from waste our precious time. God knows we honor him, so that's enough."

"Graham speaks true," added Oskey, "studying of the Word has been a practiced hyped by the Order for far too long. We should only focus on honoring the Lord through our living of life not from reading an old text most of us have memorized."

I wondered if the elders of the Order had heard that would they have died right there on the spot. The exiles were a truly interesting bunch that held true to their beliefs to preserve their freedom from the shackles that the Order instilled on them. After studying them long enough, I could see that the primary force driving them was a simple one. Abiding by the ways of the Order simply was not exciting. Even I agreed with the notion that the stifling ways of the Order had a way of making those that follow the Creed a tad bit resenting of that same Creed, yet never before had I seen such feelings openly expressed. I found many faults with these people, yet I could not bring myself to condemn them simply for the fact that I knew that I myself was far from perfect, so I found myself seeing a bond between the exiles and my own imperfection warding off any judgmental thoughts that would have had me pull away from their lot.

That strange bond worked two ways though I was sure. Just as I could find no oblivious fault within them to turn me from their side, I was sure that by emphasizing my own faults they would further welcome me with open arms. Amidst all of the festivities going forward, I got up from my seat and rose my hand up as a signal of silence that they all complied with. All of their eyes were fixated on me practically asking the question for what reason did I have to stop their merriment, but I was sure that my reason would become the topic spitting forth from their mouths for quite some time to come. I exhaled and relaxed as best I could before I spoke, "My fellow Crusaders who have found freedom.

I stand before you all to thank you for allowing my unit and I to become a part of the family and community that has been built here. The world that I originally came from would have frowned upon such a congregation as this. People were systematically separated from one another simply because of the difference in skin, but I can see here that people have joined together from the simple desire that we all share in life: freedom. Too long had the Order suppressed my freedom by making be adhere to their creed of suppression but no longer will I abide by that creed, and I owe it to you all for giving me the courage to do so."

    I turned to Sariah and got on one knee with my head looking up to her as if she were my queen and I her loyal subject foaming at the mouth waiting for her to command me. I took her hand within mine and said, "As a king, I asked many to become my vassal and share my will for the worlds, but now I simply wish for one to share my will. My selfish will to be happy and live life without the constraints of the Order and simply as a man of this world. My selfish wish is to be able to claim you as my one and only vassal, Sariah, for all eternity and beyond. Will you accept this selfish wish and be my wife?"

    The silence I had commanded became even stronger as everyone leaned in to hear the answer she would give. I had no clue how often that this happened, but from their faces it must have been a rare enough of an occurrence to make them behave like children awaiting the directions of a teacher. The silence was broken as the piercing echo of Sariah's hand slapping my face reverberated through the air. I simultaneously heard an odd collection of sighs and chuckles, but they too were silenced once more as Sariah wrapped her arms around me and said, "That's what you get for not asking me sooner, you fool."

14

Underground

Terra: 16
Location: Unknown

I had no clue what would happen to me. Just as Zion had warned me, I would not be accepted into the Crusaders with opens arms even if I did save Christian. The rouse that I implemented was over and I had been imprisoned by the very same people that I had just saved. It had only been a week since I saved Christian and my reward for impersonating a Crusader was the fact that I was allowed to keep my head, a reward that they thought was quite generous. My accommodations for the past week have been a cold, wretched cell that always had a chill passing through the air as if it was a ghost roaming back and forth. I had been stripped down to nothing but a loin cloth to cover my private parts, so even the tiniest chill within the cell made every inch of my skin crawl. I lay on the damp floor curled up like a pill bug with my knees touching the tip of my chin. As I rocked back and forth, I could not help but think if that was the same cell that my mother had been imprisoned in for so long. The irony of the situation made me regret the actions that I had taken to save Christian. After all of the sacrifices that my parents had made for me, I ended right back up in the place that they had fought so desperately to escape from. I felt that I had let them down. My parents had both decided that the purpose of their lives was to safeguard a bright future for me, so the fact that I ended up in such a dark, desolate place was like spitting on the lives of both of my parents. I sneezed into the air as the cold touch of the floor made my body tremble. I had lost all sense of day and night, but dreariness had begun to take hold of my body, so I assumed that it was night. Right as I was about to close my eyes, I heard the echoes of footsteps coming toward me.

I opened up one eye and saw a clean, pristine black boot standing right outside my cell, a sign that whoever that person was had not been down there that often. I slowly rose up to my butt and opened up my other eye and was soon greeted by the woman I had saved alongside with Christian. Her name was Tai-lee, daughter of the one of the most prestigious men in the Order, Fi-Long as well as one of the top cadets among upcoming Crusaders. The fact that she was there was certainly a surprise, but at that point there was not too much that caught me off guard. She pulled back the hood to reveal her face and looked around nervously indicating that she was not supposed to be down there. She cut straight to the point and said, "Terra, you're scheduled to be executed for impersonating a Crusader."

The news really wasn't a surprise. I honestly didn't think that they would just lock me up forever. I was disappointed that was all she had to tell me, so I lay back on my side and said, "Well that's nice. Come get me when its time then."

My words no doubt puzzled her to no end. I could hear her fingers wrapping around the bars of my cell as she asked, "You don't fear death? How can one that has not found the grace of God not fear death?"

"The only 'grace' that I've seen from your God is that He saves only those who bow down to him whether they're forced to or not. The God I learned about from my Father may have the same names as yours, but they must be different Gods since the one I learned of would never act the way yours does."

"You speak of the purge then," she assumed. "Yes you're not the only one that has found doubt in the Order for committing such an act for no solid reason," she said. "But you're an outsider though. If you hated the purge so much, then why did you help us near the end?"

"Purge or not, I only went there to save Christian. I did what I needed to do, so I'm content with whatever happens next. I may not agree what with you people are doing, but it's of no real concern to me."

"So you would indeed do anything for Christian then? He has done well to find such a good vassal."

I figured that she would leave after saying that, but I heard the lock of my cell open up and as I looked up I saw the door to the cell swinging wide open. I stood up and saw that she was extending me a bundle of folded clothes along with a pair of rapiers.

"What's this?"

"This, Terra, is your one shot at freedom. I have an important mission for you that you can't refuse."

When she said I could not refuse, she really meant it. Before I could react, a burlap sack had been slipped over my head and I was on the move. I had barely taken a few steps when I began to feel dizzy. The sack over my head had a peculiar smell that seemed to mess with my senses. I stumbled forward and felt my head crash into the bars of my cell and lost all consciousness. By the time that I awoke, I was laying on the reinforced glass floor of one of our airships. I still felt dizzy as I struggled to get my bearings. When I first laid my eyes on the wispy clouds beneath me, I thought that I was tangled within the confines of a dream, but the cold feel of the smooth glass and the serene tone of Tai-lee's voice told me that I was wide awake. All my senses returned to me suddenly like a yo-yo that had been roughly caught. I tried not to move too much since my head was still pounding but I managed to ask Tai-lee, "Where in the world am I?"

Slowly the blurred image that I had of her began to clear up as my eyes began to stabilize. She still had that black cloak obscuring her face which reminded me of Zion. I had grown to distrust anyone that dressed in a similar fashion to that woman. It just wasn't normal. The heels of her shoes tapped against the glass floor as she took a few steps toward me and stopped.

"I'll be blunt, Terra. The Order…no, I, need your help to find the truth about the recent purge."

"The truth? Well I can assure you that the purge was certainly no dream. I still can't shake the smell of rotting flesh from my nose."

"It being a dream or not is hardly my concern. Do you know the reason that we're sent to Erque?"

Before I had been imprisoned, I had some time to speak with Christian over just that issue. Normally, a world of that caliber would not be trifled with. The Crusaders preferred to only meddle in the affairs of class C or lower worlds. Due to the highly sophisticated society that those people apparently possesses, that would have kept them off of the Crusaders' radar, but there was some sort of tip that brought their forces there. According to Christian, the official story was that the new king of Erque and his followers wished to submit to the Christian God and thus called upon the purge themselves, but the one issue with that was that despite their sophisticated society, there was no way they should have been able to contact the Crusaders. Such an occurrence was not so much as rare, but more so unprecedented. The Crusaders preferred to work in the shadows, so the fact that they supported a coup had been troubling to Christian. In confidence, he told me that the only thing that made sense was that someone came to the new king with the proposal of the purge.

"So I see that you're on this idea that the purge was set up by an outside force as well then," I said.

"You know enough about us to know that there are certainly those that would be against what we do," she said.

"Yeah you're looking at one of them now," I said as I thought back to how Captain Stagg killed Kita. I made absolutely sure that I did not forget that man's face. Once I figured out that there would be a chance that I would run into many Crusaders, I promised myself that if I was ever fortunate enough to run into that man again, then he would feel the kiss of my blade for Kita. Any thoughts of that man were enough to send my blood to boil, but I kept on a smile as I continued to talk to Tai-lee.

"It seems that you're not alone then, Terra. After the purge, there are many among our ranks that have come to question the ideals of the Order."

"So what would this have to do with outside forces against you along with me being here instead of in my cozy cell?"

"I don't know Christian all that well, but he and I share the belief that it may have been the scheme of one man or a group to purposely shake the foundation of the Order by instigating a purge."

"So even people that claim to have the answers to all the struggles and mysteries of life can have their conviction tested a bit. Well before you go on any further, I'm going to let you know that I have no intentions of helping your people. I came to that world to assist my brother, and that was all I wished to do for you guys," I said as I stood up and walked to her face. I stood a good several inches taller than her so I tilted my head down so she could see the anger in my eyes as I said, "You and your Crusaders can all die for all I care! So leave me out of your petty little squabbles."

I thought that would have been the end of it, so I turned away from her and took a seat again, fully expecting to be returned to my cell soon, but Tai-lee didn't move. Instead, she took a seat next to me and seemed to sigh a breath of relief. She pulled back her hood and shook out her hair as she just looked down through the glass floor at the last bit of passing clouds. I could see land now down below. Miles and miles of green land along with several large houses occupying it. The setting reminded me of a plantation, a place that I longed to forget entirely.

"I'm surprised that you're not freaked out by the fact that we're flying. I heard you and Christian come from a world where people have not yet discovered the secret to flight," she said amusingly.

She was right though. Despite the fact that it was my first time on one of the airships of the Crusades, I was not shocked in the slightest that I was flying. Granted, there was a moment when I first woke up I thought that I was in some sort of dream but aside from that I remained perfectly calm.

"Not too much seems to faze me these days in all honesty."

"That's troubling to hear. When a man reaches that point then I can only assume that he has nothing to truly live for."

Her sudden show of concern was troubling. Not too long ago she had asked me to help her in some sort of mission that I wanted no part in, but now she seemed to forget all about that and act as if the two of us were good friends. If she hoped to win me over with kindness, she was in for a fun surprise, but I allowed her to continue her charade.

"When you've lived the life that I've lived, you see that there's not much in the world that you need to hold sacred. The world is a cruel place and finding even the smallest bit of light within it can be a trial," I said.

"By light, you must mean Christian. You know when he and I were trapped in that church he spoke often of you. I don't know what you two went through down on your world, but it truly forged a great bond between the two of you. In that regard, you and I are not too different from one another."

"Oh and how's that?"

"When you thought that Christian was gone, did you feel empty and useless like there was nothing else in the world left to live for? And after you saved him, did that empty feeling return and sink into the pit of your stomach?"

I felt as if that woman had been stalking me during my time of despair. It was exactly as she had said. After I allowed Christian to leave on his own, I quickly realized how much I needed him within my life. Ever since Father died, all I had was Christian and once he was gone as well I realized that I truly had nothing of importance within the world. There were certainly moments during the night as I laid in my bed with the chill of the wind making me huddle into a ball that I thought of simply ending all of my suffering once and for all.

"It seems like you, Crusaders, are full of tricks. Have you been stalking me or did you use some sort of magic to figure that out?"

Apparently, there was a good deal of humor in my question as Tai-lee suddenly began to chuckle saying, "No, no, nothing like that. I have simply seen many things as I traveled to so many worlds and it's just that you and I actually have something in common with many people. It's in the nature of humans to try to make meaning of their lives by dedicating it to some sort of goal or system. When a child goes to school, he's oblivious of all the hardships that the world will challenge him with in the future. His whole view on life has been molded from the values that school has presented him with, but once he is free from the boundaries of school, he never knows exactly what to do with himself."

"I thought that was what you Crusaders were for? To guide the lost souls that are helpless without you," I said sarcastically, rolling my eyes as I remembered the haughty attitude of Stagg and his commander when he came to Earth.

"Truth is like clay; it takes whatever form the molder wishes. That's the great motto of the Order. The truth people seek of the world is an ever-changing thing depending on the powers over them. We wish to offer all one solid truth that can't be altered by man. You may be against our methods, but the fact remains that people need some sort of system to invest their lives in. How many people in your own world had pretty much dedicated their lives to the work that they were tasked with? What happens when that source is taken away and they're left with naught but an empty feeling eating away at their soul? People need the Word in order to give them a system that can never crumble away. I'm afraid that system has begun to crack because of the purge that occurred."

"So you're worried about people losing faith in your system. Sounds like it isn't as solid as you guys thought that it was."

"Terra, no system is truly perfect, but before you cast your doubts why don't you help us? I'm not asking for Christian or for the Crusaders, but rather for you. If you feel so empty without Christian, then why don't you see just what we're about?"

I must have been losing my mind because her offer began to wear me down. My steady resolve that once stood erected proudly had diminished to the loose foundation of a sandcastle that a child had made. Or maybe it was the simple fact that I had been looking at her face for far too long. The face of a beautiful woman had a magical way of melting away whatever determination that a man had thought he had. I looked down at the unknown world below me and thought of all the possibilities that may be waiting for me down there. For all that I knew, Father had truly loved Mother, so her passing had ripped away the only thing that he held dear in the world. Even with all of that going on, he did not lose his will to live. All he did was find something else to invest his life within. Perhaps there were still a few lessons that I could learn from my Father even with him no longer being present. I rubbed my fingers along my thighs to feel the thin fabric of my pants. I was not used to having such nice clothes, but I liked the feel on them upon my skin.

"So if I did agree to this, what would you have me do then?" I asked.

I had only intended to crack open the door of possibilities, but that woman took that crack and begun to bust open the whole door. She opened up with the excitement that a child has when given a new toy and grabbed my hand.

"Trust me, Terra, you'll not regret this. I promise you that this decision will change your whole life!"

She was right about that. Sometimes I wish I would have just gone the simple route and elected to stay in prison. I had no idea what particular thing that she said that had changed my mind in regards to the mission, but the only thing I could think about were her words of jubilation as I stepped into one of the pods on the airship for the first time.

I promise that this decision will change your whole life!

I held onto those words as my back rested against the chilling metal of the pod. I began to feel claustrophobic after the door had been sealed. It felt as though my whole world had compressed around me, and I was trapped inside some sort of metal coffin. The idea that pod would be my coffin seemed to become a reality as the casing I was attached to was dropped from the airship. Tai-lee had warned me about the pulling sensation that my body would have to endure as I went through the free fall, but the real thing was gut-wrenching. My eyes were closed as the turbulent vibrations of the fall rocked my whole body. Since I was still a novice when it came to free falls, I didn't have the presence of mind to hold on to anything. The result of my stupidity happened to be that my body was flung all through the pod like a child's plaything. I had no idea when the casing had landed because I had lost consciousness, but by the time that I had awoken, the tip of an arrow was aimed only inches from my face. I traced the arrow back to the shaky hands of the owner as she kept both eyes on me for any sudden movement. She was wearing the uniform of a Crusader, so I was shocked that I would find myself in such a situation upon my awakening.

"State your cadet number and squad unit!" she ordered. Her fingers pulled back a little further on the bowstring to indicate she was ready to shoot me if needed. I was already starting to regret allowing myself to get talked into doing that by Tai-lee. I looked carefully at the girl's fingertips and noticed that there was not a single blister, meaning that she had not fired a bow that often. Was I dealing with an amateur or was the bow just not her weapon of choice? Either way it seemed that it would not be a good idea to try to initiate any sort of conflict with the girl, so I answered her questions, "I have no cadet number any longer since I abandoned my post during the purge on Erque. As for my squad…they're all dead now. I'm a deserter just like you are."

I gauged her reaction closely to see if my story had worked. I knew that if I had failed then I was only a couple seconds away from getting an arrowhead lodged into my skull. She lowered her arrow and offered me her hand to pull me out of the pod. As soon as I tried to stand, I buckled and she caught me in her arms.

"You really must be green if you're still getting hit by the side effects of the fallout," she said.

"You try being crammed into a jail cell for the past two weeks and see how well you function afterward," I said.

With her help, I was able to put pressure on my feet and take a few steps forward unhindered that time. With every step I took, the petals of small flowers were shot up into the air as they rode the air currents all around me. I had often heard how walking through a field of flowers was the most relaxing thing ever and there was certainly some truth to that statement. The aroma of the flowers seemed to bask all around me as I looked upon the endless sea of multicolored flowers. In the distance, I could see the makings of some sort of structure that I assumed was a farm of sorts. I turned back to the woman to ask her, but right as I turned she was in the middle of unbuttoning her uniform. I felt like a child as I turned away, but realized that she was still wearing a white shirt underneath. I turned once more and saw her now in a white shirt and shorts were that short enough to be considered men's groin's clothing. Her back was to me as she placed her uniform in a bag and slung her bow over her shoulder.

When she turned back to me, she seemed surprised that I was still wearing my uniform and said, "I suggest you lose the black garbs unless you want them to find you. Nothing stands out more in a foreign world than the uniform of a Crusader, so I suggest you try your best to blend in, which should not be too hard for you. After all I'm sure you picked this world for that reason alone."

It was just as Tai-lee had said. The parameters of the mission that she gave to me were to investigate a batch of rouge Crusaders that went AWOL during the purge. It was her speculation that suggested that batch of deserters was involved somehow with the conspiracy. It was reported that group of five had vanished in the mist of combat along with their airship. The official report was that the ship was shot down and the bodies were never recovered, but there was some sort of tracking contraption in the ship that signaled the Order that the ship had vanished around the very world that I was standing upon. The class E world Nirvana. In essence, they were similar to my Father, but I had to let those sentiments go as I was on that mission. Tai-lee said she would return in half a year to pick me up, so I had all that time to find out what I could about the purge from them by joining their ranks. Granted all of that was speculation, but apparently that woman had a long track of her hunches being dead on the money.

Just from the first words of interaction with the woman, I could see that the part of them hiding out from the Order was correct at least. I wondered why I needed six months to do a task I had already began to complete within five minutes. Well I knew I had had plenty of time to figure out that question, but for the time being, I followed her direction and took off my coat hesitantly in front of her.

"Hurry up!" she ordered as I struggled to undress in her presence. "Don't tell me you're nervous to be around a girl now?" she asked as she laughed.

In no way was that the case, but despite how faraway from Earth that I was it was still hard to let go of the culture that had been imbedded in me there. The very idea of undressing even the slightest bit in front of a white woman was an offense punishable by death. Even without the constricting boundaries of my society to shackle me, I could feel the pressure of the actions that I was doing. I let out a loud powerful sigh of relief as I dropped my uniform to the ground and stood in just my undergarments in front of her. And just like that, I had spat all over one of the taboos that had restricted my people for quite some time and it was simpler than I thought. *Were all of the norms that governed my people that simple to break through?* As I pondered on such thoughts, she came around while sitting on top of a chestnut-colored horse. She seemed not to care in the slightest that I was nearly naked in front of her. She offered me her hand once more and pulled me onto her horse. It neighed loudly as she spurred it onward in the direction of those houses in the distance. As her hands clutched tightly to the reins of the steed, my arms wrapped tightly around her waist as I held on for dear life while the horse raced onward at full speed.

As the horse galloped through the fields, the woman's blond hair constantly blew into my face, so I had to rest my head on her back just so I could breathe without inhaling a bit of her hair. If I could blush, then I'm certain that I would have as our bodies bounced on the horse making the top of my hands accidentally brush against her bosom. When that happened, I nearly fell off of the horse as the idea that I would be shot any minute ran through my mind. Nothing happened though. She kept riding along as if the incident was nothing to scoff at. My hands had brushed against the pure body of a white woman, and yet there were no repercussions being taken. While I was certainly not looking for any nor was I displeased with the result, but it just struck me as odd how different she was from any other woman of my world. As I rode that horse with her, I felt as though we weren't two different beings separated by an invisible wall erected by the color of our skin, but rather I felt as if we were simply just two human beings riding a horse together.

My assumption from when I was in the airship was correct. As we strolled past a large wooden gate, I could see that we're indeed in a plantation-like area. There were a multitude of large fields fenced off from one other, and each one had a large manor rested near its center. The pace of the horse came to a stall as we both got off of the horse. There was another Negro waiting for us as he approached the woman. He was a scrawny man that wore thick-rimmed glasses and overalls and a straw yet befitting one that lived in such an area. Perhaps that woman was the slave master of this plot of land and her slave was greeting her. I watched fully waiting to shake my head as he bowed to her, but instead my fellow Negro slapped her so hard she fell to her knees. By that point, my mind was ready to burst. Essentially every fabric of the reality that I had come to know had been shattered. Some choice words were said to the woman as she sat on the ground holding her face. A part of me truly wanted to help her since I could see myself in her shoes perfectly, but another part of me enjoyed that whole scene because it was the dream that I had always wanted. My time with Christian had not quelled the anger I had for the opposing white race, but merely showed me that there was an exception to every rule. I truly longed to be in the same position as the man was, but fate had truly shown him a kinder hand than I.

The man soon left us there, but not before shooting me a look, the same look that my old owner would give to his wife after he beat Father or any other slave. It was a look of pity, but not for us. It was a look of pity among them for having to deal with such stupid creatures.

"Are you all right?" I instinctively asked the woman.

The blow had left a noticeable mark on her beautiful face that she seemed not too care too much about. She rubbed her cheek a little and said, "It's a small price for the sake of freedom."

She had a funny idea of what freedom was. Was life with the Crusaders truly that stifling where she considered that kind of treatment a blessing? She motioned for me to follow her to one of the smaller barns. Tai-lee virtually had no clue to the identities of the people that she sent me after. The Crusaders were apparently very bad at keeping in touch with each and every unit that they had. So it was more than a simple impulse that made me ask her, "What's your name?"

She didn't turn back and kept silent as if she was contemplating whether it was worth her time to tell me or not. After a long while, she responded, "Sariah Dent."

My meeting of Sariah was one of the instances in life that, looking back, I could not help but laugh about now because I would have never anticipated upon our meeting that we would have become so close afterward. I followed her into the barn as she opened the door. It was dark for the most part with only a couple of gas lamps illuminating the area. The moment that I was fully into the barn, the door closed quickly behind me. I turned around to see two men wearing the uniform of the Crusaders standing at my back with their hands on the hilt of their blades. I reached for my own blades, but quickly remembered that Sariah had confiscated them a while back. As I blindly reached for my blades, I heard a commanding voice from above me as if God Himself was speaking to me.

"So is this the one that came crashing down, Sariah?" asked the unknown voice.

Sariah held her hand to her heart and bent on one knee and responded, "Yes, Your Highness. He was the one that emerged from the pod."

I looked up to the rafters of the barn and saw a man that looked to fit the picture of royalty that I had seen in various paintings. His hair was buzzed short and he had a rough scruff of a beard. Unlike the others, he had the sheath of his sword on his back and wore the coat of his uniform unbuttoned and loose. He jumped down from the rafters, which wasn't a long fall, and walked right up to my face.

The moment that he came within my striking range, I heard one of the men behind me scream out, "Get back from him, Clay! We have no idea what sort of intentions that he could have!"

Clay held out his hand and said, "Calm yourself, Price. All is fine. Not only is this man unarmed but I doubt that he could pose me any real harm even if he tried."

I decided at that moment I didn't like that guy. The others in the room seemed to gravitate around that man as if he was a walking sun and them being distant planets that could not hope to pull away from him. He was what Tai-lee told me was a king in a Crusader unit. When she first told me of a single man or woman that had complete command over those little squads, I could hardly believe it. From my own time in the military, I knew it was hard enough to follow the orders of a dictator like Hannon alone. I could not image the annoyance of having to bend over backward at a man's beck and call like that. Despite my initial dislike of the guy though, I knew that I had to follow the lead of the others in order to find this truth that Tai-lee had been so adamant about. Six months she said. I would be on that world for six months, so it would be in my best interest to get along with all of them. Still I was sure that they must have had their doubts about me, so I had to play the part of the fool in order to throw off suspicion of me.

"So what are all of you guys doing here? When I picked this world, I knew for a fact that no Crusaders had been stationed here. So judging from the warm welcome that Sariah over there gave me, I'm taking it that we're one in the same. Either you guys are here on exclusive orders, or you're all running away from the Order just as I am. So which is it then? Because if you guys are still with the Order then I'd like to get on with this dance that we'd have to do then," I said as I began to clench my fists.

"It doesn't surprise me that you didn't know of our stay on this world," said Clay.

Yeah because you came here on the run, I thought.

"We're sent here on a secret mission by the Order, but worry not, friend, I have no plans to turn you in. Doing so would call the Order to this world and would jeopardize our cover, an outcome which we can't allow to occur. But with that said, you can't be allowed to roam freely through this world either. Who knows what trouble a rouge Crusader could cause us?"

"I'm not allowed to roam freely?" I questioned. "What makes you think that you can keep me tethered to your little group that you have going on here?"

Right as I said those words, the men behind me acted as f they were waiting for me to say something along those lines. The points of their blades dug slightly into my back enough so I could feel them break my skin.

"Well the fact that I could have you killed at any time helps a good deal, so I believe that is reason enough for you to accept your new leash." There was a moment of silence between us as I decided to simply forgo the mission and take that man down, but then he began to laugh along with everyone else in the barn. "I merely jest, my friend. You're free to come and go as you please in this world, but I do highly suggest you stay with us. We've been investigating whether this world is a good choice for us to plant the roots for a new HQ for the Order. It has taken us some time, but we are just starting to wield some worthwhile results. On that note though, there's much about this world that we simply don't know about, it would be a shame for something to befall you on your little vacation from the Order."

"Vacation? I assure you that this is more of a retirement," I said.

"You say that now, but I assure you, Sir, that the Order has no intention of allowing you to simply run and never hunt you down. I suggest you become comfortable with constantly looking over your shoulder for the rest of your days," said Clay.

The man spoke as if he were no a runway himself. He was no fool. Despite whatever story I told him, he planned to remain cautious of me because there was no telling if I was a spy for the Order or not. His decision was the right one, but it was also the more annoying one as well. I hid my temper as I put forth my hand and shook his. The cold touch of his palm must have reflected the icy sentiments that he had toward me as he feigned a welcoming smile. That was the beginning of my time with that lot. I soon began to understand why they had chosen that world to go to. From what I understood about the Order at that time, they would typically choose only the most decadent worlds to venture to in order to purify it by their standards. On the surface, the world we were stationed at had all the appearances of being a place that the Crusaders would never go to in their lives. The villagers were a good hardworking lot that had epitaphs of God inscribed in literally everything that they did. The hoe to plow had a scripture engraved in the wood; the children wore bracelets imbued with the wisdom of the Bible; the top of every house had a cross on it, and yet all of those things were nothing but a superficial image that they portrayed. During the day, people toiled the fields to bring about a plentiful harvest, but by night the bonfires scattered about the fields were rich with the very same decadence that the Crusaders would have condemned. It only took one night for me to get the overall picture of that world.

Hours after I had made my introduction to the renegade Crusaders I was assigned to watch, I heard a commotion from outside the barn. I had been firmly planted on a bale of hay resting because the shock of my free fall from earlier had essentially drained of energy the same way a desert sun dries up a plant. It was the booming echo of a bongo in the air that stirred my rest. I had heard that same sound many nights when I was a slave so I found it ironic that sound would follow me there. I had a nagging itch on my back most likely from the loose hay still clinging to me like an infant to his mother. As I brushed it aside, I put on the rags that Clay had left me, a white cotton shirt and pair of pants that seemed to be made from the skin of some sort of animal, perhaps a fox. I slipped through the cracked door and proceeded outside to what could only be described as a full-on bazaar.

Tons of tents had been erected only feet from one another and the grounds were littered with people screaming back and forth at one another as I saw various items exchange from one hand to another in such a rapid motion of succession, it was hard for my eyes to follow. The most peculiar sight that I saw though was the fact that the people I had encountered toiling the fields were all white, essentially the polar opposite of my world, but when I came outside, I saw a wide assortment of people of every nationality huddled around every tent screaming out numbers and flinging out money like it was worthless.

The very same people that I had seen being treated like slaves were now wearing plush clothing and essentially running the bazaar that had captured my eyes. As I just stared out at the scene,

I felt the familiar touch of Zion placing her hand on my shoulder from out of nowhere as she said, "Welcome to the underground world Lactia, Terra."

15

Crusade II

"Is there any way I'm supposed to understand what that means?" I asked her.

"Not unless you've gotten a full dissertation from Clay and his group," she said. I waited a moment for her to continue but she said nothing.

Her silence caused me to ask her in an irritated state, "Well exactly what did you mean?"

"I swear, Terra, you have no mind for discovery. Must I spell out everything for you?" she asked, purposely trying to get under my skin.

Right when I went to say something back to her, she cut me off by saying that, "An underground world is one that exists for the purpose of allowing people to freely inundate themselves in their desires without fear of repercussion from the Order. Only on worlds such as this can you deal in foreign substances, purchase people, procure the location of exotic shows, and unleash any other pressed desires. The Crusaders have tried for ages to control the flow of what they call sinful material to other worlds but thanks to worlds like these the business of sin goes right along unhindered."

"And they don't notice a world like this existing?"

"The Crusaders are not God. They can't have eyes everywhere. They'll most likely never find this world unless someone were to tell them. But I don't know anyone on this world that would side with them. Do you?"

It was not like the meaning behind her words were hard to comprehend especially that last part, but when I thought about what she said, it was hard for me to instantly say I would report that world after my six months. The strange part was that I had no reason to think about such a thing. I had no attachment to that world, but there was something about it. I turned to Zion only to see that she had vanished once more. I shook my head and laughed as I went back inside the barn to rest. I wanted nothing to do with whatever was going on out there.

When I awoke the following morning, it was not to the echoing sound of bongos but rather the grunts of two people sparring. I lazily opened one eye and saw Sariah swinging a wooden sword toward an unarmed Clay, who kept dodging the blade with the utmost of ease.

"Don't swing at where I am!" he said. "Swing at where I'll be!"

Sariah let off a passionate scream and swung once more at him, but he quickly disarmed her and tossed her blade to side almost hitting me with it. He pushed her away and said, "Good work. We'll continue tomorrow."

She walked away sweaty and frustrated out of the barn. I watched her walk away and then suddenly turned back to Clay as he stood near me asking, "She has quite the nice backside huh?"

The manner of his question threw me off to the point where I could only respond with an ingenuous "huh?"

"Oh come on. I know that you have to have looked a few times by now," he said.

Well he was not wrong by any stretch of the imagination, but being put on the spot like that caused me enough stress so I couldn't even speak without stuttering, "Well…well I…I don't…"

My embarrassment of his question caused him, along with the other guys in the barn, to erupt in laughter. Clay pointed at me while wiping a tear away from his eyes and said, "You're kidding right. You went AWOL from the Order and you seem just as or even more naïve and innocent as one of the children that they just recruited."

It was hard to tell if Clay meant that he found reason to trust me even less than he already did, or if he just truly found my lack of composure humorous. Either way, I had to quickly quell any further ideas that I could not be trusted. I got up slowly and stepped right into Clay's face. His laughter stopped as I could feel the warmth of his breath against my face. Behind me, I could hear the sound of blades being drawn, but before I gave them time to act, I took off my shirt and turned around to show the scars on my back.

"That's the kind of thing that happens to you if you look at a white woman that kind of way," I said. From that introduction, I proceeded to tell them all the circumstances surrounding life on Earth and my plight as a slave and subsequent freedom. Once I finished telling them my story, there was nothing but silence in the room until Clay said, "Well dang, I suppose I understand why you've been so jumpy around us. It's a rough life that you've lived, and it's no wonder you have such a negative view of the Order after they killed that Kita girl, but no need to fret now, Terra. You're among friends who will look after you."

I was close to asking how they would look after me if they were supposedly not on the run from the Order as well, but I decided to keep such contradictions to myself. From what it looked like, my story had given them the first level of trust in me and I had every intention of not letting that trust slip away. From that day onward, Clay took me under his wing in his little unit and treated me as if I had always held a place amongst them. During my time among them, I learned all the skills as a Crusader that I have at this current point in my life. They taught me of all the different worlds out there and the goal of the Crusades that we were sent on. For the sake of my safety, I was not allowed outside the barn though because I could easily draw attention to myself. Thus for the next three months, I remained cooped up inside the confines of that barn training with Clay and the others.

From my time in the confederate army, I assumed that all little units such as that had all the negative characteristics that my unit had. Because of that thought process, I was very reserved around the lot of them for the first month or so as I waited for them to show their true colors. The longer I waited though the more that they seemed to squash any idea that I had established of them within my mind. I was not naïve enough to base all of my prejudices toward those a part of military groups solely based on my succinct time in Hannon's group, but more so on the stories that I had heard from about the other units in the army. Supposedly, all men in the military were bestial beings that only craved for spilling the blood of their enemies and didn't hold the slightest moral convictions in their life. I don't know why I allowed such hearsay to become the truth in my mind, but after being around Clay in his men for long enough, I could tell that I had simply fallen prey to the same prejudicial mechanisms that my deceased owner had allowed his mind to become trapped by. Just the thought that I could think in the same false context as that man made me shudder.

Even with that realization setting into me, I could not bring myself to warm up to them, a fact that was causing me great distress because I had not learned any new information about their involvement in the purge. Clay continued to stand by the story he gave about them surveying the land to see if a new HQ could be established there after a purge on the land occurred. I knew full well that he was lying, but I had no way of calling him out on it, so I continued to feign ignorance to his true goals. I was well into my third month among their group when the daily routine accustomed to took an abrupt shift. One morning I was training alongside Price, Clay's right hand, when Sariah came into the barn looking like she was ready to pass out. We had not heard any word from her for the past few days after she said she was following an interesting lead one night during the bazaar, so her return was welcomed with all of us crowding her. Clay pushed his way through us and took Sariah in his arms practically shouting, "What happened! What happened?"

Still panting between deep breaths, Sariah told us all that, "Lambo Mandric has procured a Cashern golden idol at the bazaar several nights ago. It's said to contain the very doctrines of the prophet Cashern himself written in several scrolls inside the idol." With that last bit of info, he released her and went toward the back of the barn where we all kept our equipment. The other three followed him and left Sariah there as well and proceeded to arm themselves and put on their uniforms. I stayed near Sariah not knowing what in the world was going on until Price called to me, "Terra, get your uniform and blades! We're getting ready to go on a crusade tonight!"

A crusade, the sacred missions given by the Order to liberate a world from the evils of sin. Even though my excursion to Erque to save Christian was technically a crusade, the one mentioned by Price would be the first legit crusade that I would have to endure. I followed his directives and got dressed. I found a place next to Price as the whole team of Spencer, Price, Harper, and myself stood directly facing Clay. I had been told whenever a crusade was given, the unit would have to file in line in front of their king as they awaited for his directives for the crusade. The atmosphere of the barn was completely different from what I had experienced those last few months. The playful, nonchalant nature of Price and Spencer had vanished as they stood still as marble statues. I felt the tension in the air as Clay walked past each of us exclaiming, "Attention!" We all reacted instantly as we clenched our fists and placed our right hand on our chest. Clay continued, "Thanks to Sariah's intel, it's safe to assume that Lambo Mandric has become a threat to the purity of this world. If he is indeed in possession of material from Cashern, then we must act quickly before his heathnistic teachings have a chance to infect the minds of the people of this world. This may be an underground world, but this is the only one that the Order is secretly aware of. We cannot allow for our influence to be challenged! Our mission thus is to infiltrate his manor in this world and destroy any sort of article linked to Cashern. We move out tonight in two groups. Sariah, Price, and Terra will rummage through his manor while the rest of us find Lambo himself and make him squeal. You're now dismissed!"

Everyone let off a resounding "Yes, Your Majesty" and proceeded back into their own little corners. Before I had a chance to leave, Clay reached out for my shoulder and told me to follow him out into the fields. "I apologize, Terra, for automatically incorporating you within our plans. But if Sariah is right then it's for your best interest as well to help us. The doctrine of Cashern has always conflicted with our own and if their presence is established here then the Order will surely send more Crusaders to investigate. If you truly wish to stay under the radar, then it would be in your best interest to help, but as with anything in life, it's your choice to make. If you don't want to become involved then you can simply leave."

By that point I had seriously begun to doubt the validity of what Tai-lee had thought about Clay and his group. For the last three months, they had not done a thing to incriminate themselves, and as time went on, it began to seem like I was the only one lying about anything. I could see it in Clay's eyes that he was truly worried about that predicament with Cashern, so I felt safe when I agreed to help him. He seemed quite relieved to hear that I would help. He threw his arm around my shoulder and said, "You know, Terra, if all goes well then I'll be able to put in a formal request to have you join my unit. AWOL or not, helping to eradicate any sort of vestige of Cashern will earn you a great deal of leeway with the Order for quite some time."

"Why are you so concerned with my well-being?" I asked. "I'm nothing but a deserter. You should have nothing but shame for me, yet you have welcomed me so openly into your group and trained me as if I belonged here."

"Truth be told, Terra, I too have deserted my post when I was first starting out as a Crusader. It was a quick moment of weakness but a moment of weakness all the same. It's not something that I'm proud of in the slightest. But it was from that weakness that I came to understand everyone in my team. Price, Spencer, Sariah, and Harper have all left their stations for one reason or another, yet we all came back. We understand that people aren't perfect and are prone to make mistakes, but it's the will to minimize those mistakes and pursue the path of the righteous Crusader that made us come back. I specifically picked people that have at one point lost their way to be in my unit, so that each one of us knows that we're not alone in our doubt," he said.

With those parting words, Clay left me alone in the fields as I looked over the workers toiling away in the hot sun the way that I had once upon a time. Clay, I really hated that man. By that point there was no way for me to tell whether or not I could trust him, but I had to continue to assume that he was simply lying to me still. My doubts on the man continued well into the night into the time of our crusade. I met up with Sariah, who looked much better than she did earlier, and Price out in the fields near Lambo Mandric's manor. Like the rest of the manors on the wide acres of land, Lambo's was only guarded by a white picket fence that could hardly keep out the hares that ravaged his crops. We met on the outskirts of the north side of his manor and crept through the tall cornfields that concealed our movement. We moved in complete silence like lions stalking their prey as we weaved through the stalks moving closer and closer to the manor. As Clay's right hand, Price was the leader of our squad and commanded us with just as much authority as Clay would have. He held up his hand and motioned for us to stop as we were nearing the end of the cornfields and approaching the stretch of open land that stood between us and the manor. I peered out through the stalks and saw that the vast landscape was empty aside from a scarecrow or two here and there. It looked like it would be a simple run to the manor, yet despite that I could tell that Sariah and Price were both much tenser than usual. If Lambo Mandric were at the manor then I could understand their fear, but according to Clay,

Lambo had taken the majority of his guards with him as he went to the bazaar that night since safety was a must when dealing in such a chaotic environment. We had the simple job of sneaking through an abandoned house. Finally, Price seemed to calm down for a moment and gave the silent signal to charge into the manor just as we had planned.

We all took off into a dead sprint toward the manor. I took the lead among our group but as I passed by each of them, I saw the fear of death in their eyes. It was a look that I had seen tons of times when charging out into the fray of battle in the war with the North. I don't know why, but my instincts told me to look up and right; when I did, my heart stopped. Great balls of fire hailed down from the sky just as they had when the Crusaders came to Earth and took Christian. I quickly looked over to the other two and understood what their cause for distress was. They knew that would happen, but the next question was who was attacking us? I threw that thought from my mind as I put every ounce of power into making sure that I would not get caught underneath that barrage of fire. My surroundings began to compress around me as my focus zeroed in on the manor ahead of us. I did not know if the other two were okay by that point because I all I thought about was getting to safety. I could feel the heat of the flames from the impact of the first explosion as it crashed near me which only made me pick up even more speed as I pressed onward. The next one landed a few feet from me and the force of it knocked me to the ground. An intense pain ran through my body as the smell of charred flesh floated around my nose. I didn't want to know where I got burnt. I just back to my feet and continued to run. The intensity of the flames made it harder and harder to breath. Another explosion occurred near me but I managed to stay on my feet that time around.

I could hear an agonizing yell from behind me, but instead of turning to see the source it only made me move faster. One explosion after another continued to rain down from the sky until I finally managed to burst through the door into the manor.

As I lay on the floor, the sudden change of setting threw me off as I went from escaping from the fiery depths of hell outside to the dimly lighted entrance to Lambo's manor. The fires from outside had not scathed the manor, so I could only assume that the intention of that attack was meant for us.

I finally looked to my right arm and saw that my shoulder down to my biceps had been severely burned to the point where I could see too much pink for my liking. Aside from that I was fine, or so I thought. Perhaps it was a delayed effect because sudden the pain from receiving such an intense burn shot through my body and I began to roll around on the floor trying my best not to scream in agony. I could feel myself beginning to black out, but I returned to my senses as Sariah came running through the entrance calling my name. She immediately tore off a good deal of fabric from her shirt and wrapped my arm in it tightly. It didn't help the pain but at least I didn't have to look at it any longer. Somehow I regained control over myself and looked past the entrance to see the flames still burning outside the manor. Suddenly I remembered the look her and Price had before hell was dropped on our faces and pushed her away while drawing one of my blades. My right hand shook intensely as I tried my best to hold my blade but it was apparent I could not do much with it.

"What the hell is all this, Sariah?" I shouted at her. "I know you and Price…" The mention of Price made me think back to the person who I heard scream. It was obvious that was the painful scream of a man, so I had to assume that Price had died in the attack. The realization of his death quelled my anger for Sariah. Outside of Clay, Price had been very accepting of me and acted as my mentor when it came to furthering my training. The fact that I had allowed him to die was certainly a discouraging one that caused me to lower my blade.

"There's no time to lament of Price," Sariah said. "If we want to finish our mission, then we have to keep moving and find that relic of Cashern."

Her words gave me the strength to raise my blade once more and give her a defiant look as I said, "You're a fool if you think I'm going to continue this mission without getting some sort of answer to what happened!" The excoriating pain in my shoulder only made me more irritable with her, so I lashed out with no restrictions, "Dang it, Sariah, I know you two were holding out on me. Did you two hope I would be the one to die? Dang it!"

"If you're thinking that attack was a part of our plan then you're sadly mistaken. How could Price dying be a part of the plan? It's true that we knew that there would be an airship patrolling the manor in the absence of the guards, but we hoped that it would not rain fire down like."

"So you're telling me that airship that fired on us belongs to Lambo?"

"He has powerful connections and, remember, this is an underground world, so the presence of one is expected, but it being armed like that was certainly a surprise. Now if you're finished being a little girl I suggest that we get to moving before more trouble finds us."

I still wasn't on the best terms with Sariah, but I saw her point so I lowered my blade and proceeded down the nearest flight of stairs into the basement. I found it humorous that all manors on plantations seemed to be built the same. Even on a completely different world, I knew the layout of the manor fairly because of my time working in my deceased owner's manor. We proceeded down a case of winding stairs into the dark abyss of the basement. With nothing but the light of candles along the side of the walls to guide our way, I was only able to see what was in front of us. The echoes of our footsteps as we went down had me on edge as I feared another random attack at any time. Sariah must have been able to feel my nervousness as she said, "Don't worry not every crusade is like this."

The suddenness of her statement threw me off. "What do you mean?"

"For the most part, a crusade consists of traveling to some backwater world where we find the people worshipping sticks as Gods or something silly like that. Only in more extreme cases do we need to resort to violence."

"Is that what they told you?" I asked still with obvious content for her in my voice because I was not informed of the possible attack. "From my own experience with the crusades you guys go on, you seem to be willing to resort to violence fairly quickly and enjoy every second of it."

She completely ignored my statement as she caught my mistake, "What do you mean, you people? Surely you have not broken away from the Order so completely that you don't consider yourself a member, or is that you never really were a member?"

I went for the hilt of my blade as I felt thankful that we were just a desolate place where I could dispose of her but before I acted she said, "Relax, Terra. Stay your hand and relax. Clay is no fool. He had you pegged as a spy for quite some time. We could see it as we worked during your training. You're far too old to be that unpolished with a blade yet have the look of a killer in your eyes. His guess was that they recruited you from so lower world precisely to check on our progress with the mission. We don't know what sort of trouble that got you on the leash of the Order, but fret not you're safe here. We've seen the last of surprises for this crusade by my guess. All we have to do now is..." she stopped midsentence as we reached the bottom of the stairs and entered into an area that resembled an old wine cellar. It was not the cellar though that raised our guard. It was the ominous echo of people chanting that alarmed us.

We crept through the decrepit halls of that underground cellar. We came into a small opening where we saw a ground of half-naked men and women bowing down before a silver statue of an eagle with a dusty piece of rolled parchment in its talons. There was a young boy there as well, bound and gagged before the lot but still trying his best to get free. By the time we came in, I saw one of the men cut the boy's arm and began to suck the blood from the wound as if he were some sort of vampire. Sariah motioned me to pull back as we ducked around a corner.

"That's the relic for sure and that paper must be the teachings of Cashern," she said. "But I didn't expect for there to be followers already. Depending on how much they have been converted, they may be willing to die for that relic. It will be hard to get it without causing trouble…Terra, where are you going?"

I didn't need to hear any more of her concerns before I decided to proceed. The moment I saw the distressed boy, I had made my decision. Perhaps it was the sight of a young boy in a plantation manor against his will that evoked such strong emotions within me, but I could not stand idle to such barbaric treatment. The pain in my shoulder vanished as I drew both of my blades and stepped into the room with Sariah running close behind me. Now that I was in the room, I was able to get a complete look of the scene. Blue flames burned on four torches in the corners of the room giving off a mystical glow to the room. A circle of blood had been drawn around the boy as he had been literally chained to the floor. Even with the light, it was too dark to get a good look at the faces of everyone in the room, but even if I could see them, the image of what they looked like in my mind would not have changed.

Through my eyes the whole lot of them had the face of my owner as he showed off his wicked grin. Through some sort of unconscious action, I remembered the words of Stagg's commander when they first came to Earth and repeated them word for word, "Once again, I shall beseech you all to forgo your worship of these pagan gods and come and acknowledge the one true God of all worlds. There's still time for you all to accept his wondrous mercy and grace."

They were the same words I heard Captain Morgan use, but I said with a hollow tone that lacked any real emotion to them. I thought of Kita and my rage after she died. I thought of Father, Christian's father, and Hannon. I thought all the fires still burning outside and finally I thought of that poor boy bound to be nothing but a toy for those you captured him. I saw myself in that boy and acted accordingly as I lashed out at every soul in the room cutting them down like an unleashed animal. By the time I came to my senses, everyone in the room was dead and their blood was all over my body. Only the boy was alive. I removed the solid rod that was in his mouth to ensure he didn't bite off his tongue when he clenched his teeth in pain, and he spit on my face. The boy cried out, "Why did you do that, you heathen! They were in the middle of sucking all the evil poison from my body that a blasted snake gave in the fields today!"

"A snakebite…" I said as I looked back toward Sariah who had a horrified expression on her face.

"The teachings of Cashern specialize in ways to remove evil impurities from the body. That was just a simple ritual to suck the poison from the blood, not some evil ritual." she said.

16

Union

The union of Sariah and I came as a surprise to none aside from the two of us. When I had first proposed the plan to wed her, I thought she would have no other reaction than taking my own blade and running it through my chest due to our previous history. To my surprise, her reaction was nothing but a simple nod and a hint of a smile that I thought my eyes had misread for a moment. In truth, I had not planned what would occur after my proposal. My idea was simple. Ever since my bout to the death with Dom, I became well aware of the fact that Christian would not be able to belong in that village. Since then, I wished for nothing else than to create a place for him within the village. I saw the kind of power and respect that the clown had over the place and wished for nothing more than to wield that same power myself.

It was to that end that I found myself cuddled next to Sariah that morning. I woke up spitting out the strands of Sariah's hair that found its way into my mouth. I picked the strands from my mouth and tossed them to the side of our bed as was my normal morning ritual. As I pulled off the cover to get up from the bed, I caught a glimpse of the smooth white skin of her slender legs stretched out on the bed. I turned toward her sleeping body wanting to do nothing more but slide my fingers along her skin and embrace, but right as I was on the verge of grasping my fantasy, reality came crashing back to me as she began to stir and awake. By the time she had opened her eyes, I had withdrawn my hand and threw on my pants. She snuck up from behind me and wrapped her arms around my waist, a gesture she had no idea that how much pain it caused me, and told me "good morning." I pulled away from her before the heat of my body escalated into higher levels.

Though I had only stepped a few paces further, I could feel that there was a great rift between the two of us. Her voice called out to me trying to bridge the gap between us, but her words held the weight of paper and could not withhold the weight of my desires.

"Terra," she called, "It wouldn't be too bad of an idea if we went out to the beach today. I can ask Rebecca if she's interested in coming as well."

Now she wished to further torture me by having me go out to the beach with her as well. That woman's cruelty knew no bounds. I could not stand the idea of having to watch her prance around the beach in some sort of revealing clothing and me unable to do anything. We had been married for two months at that point, and I had yet to take advantage of the benefits that were supposed to come with being married. Of course, I had gone longer without being able to fulfill my primal desires, but never before had I had the opportunity to do so literally laying in front of me the whole time. The last few months the two of us had part of the married couple flawlessly. In fact it was too flawless. From constantly being around each other's company, I indeed had become somewhat infatuated with her and the feeling was mutual for her as well. I know not whether these feelings were lingering emotions we had from years ago when we shared a bed, or if we just had truly obtained a greater appreciation for one another there. It was those feelings that the two of us developed which made my drought so tough to endure.

It became increasingly difficult to be around her as the days went along until we reached a point where I tried my best to avoid her entirely until I retired to our bed. Her request to go to the beach must have reflected her awareness of my prolonged absences of late. She was a conniving one for sure, and I knew that she truly didn't care for the beach but rather wanted to see if I would continue to avoid her. I knew that was her game, but I was a poor player within it.

"The beach?" I questioned, "I'm sorry, dear, but I have plans set with Lucas and the others for the day, so I'm afraid that I'll be unable to."

My back was still turned to her, so I did not have to see the condemning look that was without a doubt in her eyes. I took another step forward intending to end the discussion there, but she had other plans.

"So I take it that you don't care about making this place for Christian that you were once so adamant about. You killed Dom to do so after all, so I thought that you're committed to the idea."

Despite my dislike of Dom's betrayal, I still held fond memories of the kid as he was a fellow vassal of our king, so throwing his name around so callously was something I would not stand for.

"How long must you plague me with this question, woman?" I asked. "It takes time for such things to occur and I've been doing the best that I'm capable of, but of course that's not good enough for you!"

"The best you can? So I assume that you going off to drink the night away with Lucas and the others means you're trying your hardest. Why you poor thing! I can't imagine how stressed you must be picking between ale and rum every night!" she yelled. "I swore my loyalty to Christian as did you, yet you avoid me for some childish reasons, which is impeding us helping him. For all we truly know he may not even be alive."

Despite how much I wanted to assure her of his safety, I did not exactly know what condition he was in. All I knew was that he was alive. Zion had made occasional visits to me when I was alone and eased my own worries by saying that Christian was alive and for me to continue whatever plans I had. I did not know the fate of the others, but I could hope that they were with him as well. I wanted to argue with her further, but in truth she had me. The fact that we had not been seen tighter in quite some time was not helping us arise through the ranks in the village so that we could secure a place for Christian to make sure he didn't meet a similar fate to Dom, but I had hit a wall. I truly did not think that it was possible to get any further in the village without resorting to underhanded tactics.

I had no desire to continue this fight between the two of us and just walk out of the house while drowning out nagging words she threw my way. Waiting outside of my house was Lucas and Ramsey, a new exile that had been in the village for a couple weeks or so.

"I see that you two truly enjoy being at each other's throats at times. What was that about?" asked Lucas.

I knew I could not very well tell him of my plans for Christian, but I could not risk the chance of Lucas discovering that I was hiding something from him as well. So a half-truth seemed to be the most appropriate action in play.

"While it shames me to no end to admit this, my friend. Sariah and I have yet to break in our marriage bed together and…"

Apparently that was all he needed to hear because he reacted instantly by lightly slapping me across my face. Doing such actions had become a norm for Lucas and me over the months, so I knew he meant no ill will, but I wish he would have allowed me to at least finish my sentence.

"What's wrong with the two of you? It's been months, has it not? My poor friend, how could you go through such an ordeal while living on this island of all places?" he dramatically asked. "And I thought she was the one that you were exiled because of, so why would she withhold her body from you now?"

"It's her sister. She was Dom's lover and since his passing by my hand, Rebecca has decided to become celibate and Sariah is supporting her by doing the same. Sariah has always regretted the fact that she abandoned her sister to join the Order when she was younger, so now she takes whatever opportunity that she can to act as a pillar for her," I explained to him.

"What a load of crap you've been given there, Terra. A woman forbidding you to have her body is like a tree refusing to change the color of its leaves. It's all a part of the natural order of the world. She should be ashamed for denying you life's greatest pleasure," said Ramsey.

Ramsey's presence was an interesting one simply because that man had many eerie similarities to Lucas. It was like the two of them were just clones of each other, and the fact that the two of them each wore their Crusader uniform that day made the likeness between them escalate into a creepy level.

"Ramsey's right, Terra. We can't allow you to be barred off from the fruit that Eden bears. It has been far too long since you've had the chance then to sink your teeth into that glorious fruit," said Lucas.

"Your care is well noted, but I'm afraid that I have no power over the matter," I admitted.

"You have no power with her, but there are others in the village, Terra, who highly regard you," said Lucas. "There's a certain ritual that all men here in Ataxia go through at some point in their marriage if they so wish, and I believe that now is the perfect time for you to partake in such a ritual. Go fetch your uniform and meet us at the temple."

Those were the only words he left for me as the two of them left. I wondered what he meant by some sort of ritual, but I had become much closer to Lucas to the point that I didn't second guess whatever he had planned. I crept back into the house, trying my best to avoid drawing Sariah's attention. As I slipped back into our bedroom, I saw that she was conversing with Rebecca at the kitchen table. I could not hear the manner of their conversation, but I was able to glance that her eyes had a red tint to them now. Though the original intention of our marriage was as a means to protect Christian and the others, I still wished not to cause her any unnecessary pain. Especially now so because I found myself becoming quite fond of the girl. The guilt of whatever I said to cause her pain hung around me like shackles weighing me down as I reached into the closet grabbing my uniform. I had kept it in pristine condition lately because of my new position as the warden of the village. Even within a world of exiles, there were still laws in place and I had been given the task to capture and execute those that broke those laws.

 I was able to slip out of the house just as quickly as I came and then proceeded to the temple. I caught myself clutching at the sides of my arms as the cold of the wind kissed my body. Several months or so had gone by and the weather of the island was making a slight change. It was because of the weather that I made notice that the women of the isle were not wearing the same scanty clothing I had become accustomed to them seeing. Once that thought passed through my mind, I suddenly became enraged with Sariah as when I realized that I was right and the idea of going to the beach was in fact nothing but a ploy. There's no way anyone would want to go to the beach in that weather. I hated how she tried to do that. Well I respected her when she did that kind of trickery when it was employed for my side, but aside from those instances she could be a real pain.

 With those thoughts of her trying to make a fool of me still lingering in my mind, I came to the steps proceeding into the temple and squeezed through the crack of the slightly opened wooden door. That was my first time inside the interior of the temple. For the most part, it was only allowed for members of the clown's counsel of Fallen, aka his most trusted aides in the villages, to have access to the temple. From the hearsay that I heard from the other villagers, all of the most important decisions that would impact the village originated from these halls. From the outside, the temple had the visage of a worn-down architectural wonder from an age-long past. So I assumed that the interior would be lavish and have the visage of an old Victorian church. To my surprise, the interior was just as bad as the outside. While the inside showed that it once held the magnificent splendor of a highly respected temple, that splendor had long since faded just as the smooth exterior of a grape does before it shrivels into a raisin. Vines from the outside had made their dominion inside the temple as well as they stretched along the side of the walls and onto the ceiling as well.

The stone slabs that had once considered seats had all but crumbled leaving nothing but broken rocks scattered along the floor of the temple. The only thing of note was the long table that held twelve seats located at the top of the pulpit where the minister would have preached from. Seated at that table were the clown, Lucas, and several others that I had only seen acting as a long shadow of the clown.

I was motioned over by Lucas to sit next to him as the others were still in the midst of their conversation. As I took a seat next to him, I asked, "So this is the infamous counsel of the village that I heard so much about?" In all honesty I was a tad bit disappointed. Aside from Lucas, the whole lot were made up of drunken louts that could only repeat whatever the clown wished for. There was an awkward silence between me and the rest of the men there as I didn't know quite what to say, nor did I know exactly why I was there. Finally after a good fifteen minutes or so, the clown shifted his attention to me saying, "So, Terra, I see you've come to that point in your marriage where you need to undertake the ritual of bliss."

"The ritual of bliss? Exactly what would that be?" I asked.

"The act of taking your happiness into your own hands, my friend," said Lucas. "Married or not, you can never trust one woman to be able to give you all the happiness that you deserve."

I could start to see where he was beginning to go with this whole ritual he spoke of.

"You're speaking of cheating on Sariah are you not?" I asked.

"Cheating is such a negative word. We prefer to call it pursuing other ways to express your manhood. After all, she's practically holding out on you. You owe it to yourself to find other means to pleasure yourself. A marriage is not meant to last without sex in any form," said Lucas.

"Lucas speaks the truth, Terra," said the clown. "What I find peculiar is the fact of why did you marry someone that would do such a distasteful act as hold her body out from you?" asked the clown.

"Well it wasn't as if we have no feelings for one another. Sariah was my first many years ago and she was the one that opened up to the idea of not allowing the Order to suppress my manhood as they did to others," I said.

"So you do in fact share strong feelings for one another?" asked Lucas.

"That is indeed the case," I responded.

"Worry not about those feelings of yours, Terra," said the clown, "The only thing that you have to think about is what you can do in order to make yourself happy, and we're here to help you with that."

In all honesty, I wasn't too keen on the idea of cheating on Sariah again, no matter whatever excuses that they planted into my mind, but the fact did remain that I was now sitting at the same table that held all of the power in that village. It was from that table that it was decided that I would have to kill Dom in order to be accepted. The whole idea to marry Sariah originated with the sole purpose of finding a way to get to that table, and now that I had reached there I knew I had to do whatever was necessary to make sure I would be invited back.

"Okay, so tell me more about this ritual of bliss then," I said.

"Lucas, would you be so kind and tell him of the ritual," said the clown.

"While we call it a ritual, it's in fact akin to a game between your wife and you. We will host a grand party and during it you're responsible for finding another woman who meets your fancy and thus seducing her all the while without your wife's knowledge of the incident."

Only those that had been exiled from the Order would come up with such a trial and call it a game. Their insensitive nature didn't surprise me, but their overall lack of morals when it came to the sanction of marriage was a tad bit appalling. Though the Order forbids casual relationships, they still considered marriage a sacred union that we should never meddle in. The main reason that it was avoided in the Order was simply to keep us focused on the task of liberating other worlds without getting distracted or placing concepts such as family before duty. Despite my relationship with the Order, even I could respect that rule. I saw firsthand what a lingering loyalty for family do to you when you had other goals in mind. The need to go back for my own father had cost me several years of freedom with Christian.

"Doesn't sound too hard. It's been a while since I got to release the beast because of Sariah lacks of duty to me as her husband, so might as well release it on someone else who wants it," I said realizing how much I sounded like them.

"I'm glad you see the truth of it, my friend," said Lucas. "If you keep this up, who knows where you may find yourself when it comes to the village."

I looked around the table and saw a nod of approval from the others and realized that it may be as simple as if I cheated on Sariah then I would finally be accepted into the little society that they created at that table. I left not too long after with Lucas as we continued to speak of the ritual of bliss.

"So do you have any idea what kind of meat you plan to thoroughly tenderize?" he asked while barely managing to keep a straight face on.

"Oh so now we're resorting to code words now? What are we, five?" I asked as I gave him a slight push.

"Oh excuse me for not walking around shouting out, *Hey, Terra, which of these sluts do you plan to bone later tonight.*"

"Trust me, where I come from, you can say that kind of stuff whenever and wherever you want. Also you would not have to go through so much trouble to conduct a ritual of bliss there. If you wanted to cheat on your wife in America, all you had to do was do it and not care about how she felt about it,"

"It's a shame that the Order never allowed us to talk about our own worlds," said Lucas.

"Why's that?"

"Imagine how well people could bond if they weren't forced to reconstruct themselves into one uniform being."

"You mean how the Crusaders have us try our best to forget where we came from and only remember our new lives?"

"Yes, it's a sick way of reprogramming us into one solitary being. All they want is a perfect person that adheres to all of their religious and social norms, which is why they recruit us when we're young. That's the reason I left. I could never forget the people I care about in my world. I left to help them, so why would I forget about them?"

Lucas was right. The Order did always seem to have an ideal model that it wanted us all to follow and if we couldn't we were regarded as less than the others around us. My reeducation following the incident on Lactia served as a prime example of that attempt. Even with that experience firmly etched into my memory though, I never paid the idea too much mind because unlike Lucas, there was nothing on Earth that I wanted to remember. The only good thing about my life was Christian, and I joined the Crusaders because of him, so I was simple for them to reprogram in that sense I suppose.

"So when should this little game go down then?"

One of the villagers named Becky walked by and I could see Lucas's eyes shift from me to her behind as she walked past.

"I'm sorry what did you say?" he asked while still stalking Becky with his eyes.

"When are we trying to do the whole bliss thing?" I asked once more.

"Oh that. Well I suppose we can do it whenever you like. Now if you excuse me I have to run my rounds around the village and make sure everything's in order."

"All right then. Tell Becky I said 'hello' then," I said as I walked away.

By the time I came back into the house, Sariah and Rebecca had left to do whatever they do. I wanted to do this thing as soon as possible, so that I could help Christian but knowing Lucas, he would be far too preoccupied that night to help me. The rest of the day went by quickly as I found myself just napping the day away. Despite my position, unless a criminal was apprehended or something then I had no use. I fell asleep in the chair at the kitchen table and woke in the middle of the night with a blanket draping over me. I knew it had to have been Sariah. She had a cute habit of doing those sorts of things while I slept. As I got up from my seat, I turned to my window as I heard a sound of something hitting it. Not to my surprise did I find Lucas outside the window with a handful of pebbles in hand. He had a white mask sitting on top of his head with another one in his free hand. I left the house as quietly as I could to not wake Sariah who I assumed was fast asleep.

"Good, you're still in uniform," said Lucas as he handed me the expressionless white mask. The sight of the mask brought me back to my turbulent years as an executioner, but I was able to quickly break free from the barrage of painful images in my mind.

"What's this for?"

"For the ritual of course. We're holding a grand festival in the square as we speak. You could say it's like a costume ball, but without all the elegance," he said.

When mentioned the lack of elegance, he was speaking true because as we arrived at the village square, I did not hear the soothing music that could rock a baby to sleep, but instead the pounding drums and hollers of people that seemed to be trying to keep some evil spirit away. Everyone that was there was in uniform and sporting the same bland mask that we were which concealed our identities. Lucas and I stood on the outskirts of the party so that we could still hear one another speak clearly before we joined in on the fun.

"So all of this is for me?" I asked.

"Of course not. Don't be so vain, my friend. All of this is for me as I plan to bring the one hundredth girl to my bed tonight," said Lucas rubbing his hands together like he was concocting a plan of some sort. "I jest though truly. While I do plan to get my one hundredth tonight, tonight is a celebration of the Isle of the Fallen granting us freedom from the Crusaders. We are truly grateful for the freedom given to us to express our base desires and still honor or Lord, so we hold this festival every now and again. The masks act as a way to say that we had no individuality while we were in the Order and serve as a reminder of the gift that exile has brought with us. So I suggest you take advantage of that mask and go do that ritual, my friend, as I conduct several of my own."

With those words in parting, Lucas left to go find his one hundredth, a gaudy number that I have no idea how he achieved it. I placed the mask over my own face and saw peripherals of the world vanish as I could only manage to see straight ahead at that point. I slipped into the party with the full plan to go just as wild as the lot of them in my attempt to find my blissful partner for the ritual, but the harder I tried, the more disinterested I became. Unlike them, I had not been raised on the Word and the Creed of the Order when I was a child, so this new freedom meant more to them. I had experienced true slavery to another being and the exuberant freedom that followed from it. With knowing the true taste of freedom after having it taken away, I found their celebration to be a tad bit shallow for my taste. Just as quickly as I had entered the festivities, I left them and was sitting against the cool bark of a tree looking in the dancing lights of the party from afar.

"Not a fan of the party either?" said a voice emanating from the woods behind me.

I turned around and saw a dark-haired woman in a casual white dress come forth with a basket of mushroom around her arm. I had never seen her before, and even in the darkness I could see the radiance of her beauty shine forth.

"Yeah I've taken in my fill for the night," I said, planning to start making my way home soon.

"If that's the case, I take it you're not too keen on the whole idea of this celebration at all then. Are you not grateful for being here on the island instead of the Order?"

"Of course I prefer it here. The Order was like a plastic bag that had been placed over my head. It was suffocating there."

The woman looked at me for a second before finally saying that, "There's no need to lie or poke out or chest with me. If you don't believe in the way the island does things then there's no harm saying it and being honest with yourself. After all it would be a shame if those lies in your mind turned into the truth all around you."

It was with those words that she truly grabbed my attention. For months I had gone along as one of the villagers and preached exactly what they would have wanted to hear. While there were certainly many times I did believe in the words that I spoke of my affection for that village and the island, I had told just as many lies about it as well. Despite what I said though she was the first one that I had encountered that could call my bluff. In all truth, I had no idea which I preferred more between the Order and the island.

"They each have their pros and cons," I said. "It's hard for me to ultimately cast one place aside and say that the other was better."

"I envy the fact that you had a chance to choose which that you liked better. I'm a natural exile born to this land and plan to die here as well without having the chance to see these other worlds that I've heard others speak of."

"Oh you're not missing out on too much there. Each world has nothing special about it in itself, but rather it's the people that make up those worlds that make it better. The world of my birth for example was a place where I saw only the worst sides of humanity on many occasions. But I've also been to worlds where I saw the true benevolence that people can offer one another. It was a shame that it was those worlds that we're the most violent with."

"Surely you must be mistaken. I was always told that the Order mainly tried to focus its efforts on the worlds that they deemed to be pervaded with evil and perversion."

"And that's the problem with the Order. They didn't lie to you about that. We did indeed go and spend the most times at worlds that *they* deemed to be pervaded with evil. Too often did the Order look at the lifestyle and judge the people living it as evil as well."

"So you're saying that the whole notion that good and evil is simply a matter of perception applies to those people you speak of?"

"In a way that's indeed what I mean. If a man has never been taught that the sky was blue, then is he stupid or if he claims the sky is green?" I said while thinking what a kick Lucas would get if he heard me using a similar metaphor to the one he used when we first spoke. "In my world, I was nothing but a simple man enslaved by Christian men that believed what they were doing was not wrong in any way."

"So do you not hate or blame them for their actions then?"

I caught myself laughing a bit as I thought back to how I had killed my owner and his family with a smile on my face. I answered her by saying, "No, I do hate them and I even killed some for their actions against me, but I did that as a man seeking vengeance not as someone offering down righteous judgment. They're the kind of people that I hate. Ones that were raised one the principles of the Lord and how they should treat others equally, yet I was treated as an animal or just as some kind of tool to fulfill their desires. The people are as well as myself simply are just living a different way than they're taught. As long as we don't hurt anyone, then I don't see an issue with it."

The last words I said trailed off toward the end as I realized just how much I had been talking to her.

"You certainly are a talkative one aren't you?" she said, laughing.

"I apologize. I did speak way more than was accustomed to me," I said getting up from my seat about to go home.

"No it's okay," she said as she grabbed my hand, but quickly pulled it away when she realized what she had done. "I mean I enjoyed talking to you, so there's no need to go unless you have someone that you need to go back to?" she said, while looking away from me seemingly out of embarrassment as her finger stroked the exterior of my wedding ring.

My hand grazed my face to make sure my mask had not been on during my time with her. As my fingertips slid across my cheeks, I asked, "Do you know who I am?"

"Sadly I don't. Those are the words that describe my life entirely," she said, placing the basket down and sitting next to me. "Sickness has plagued me since I was a girl so I never had the chance to go out and participate with the other villagers. The main reason though that I hardly ever got the chance to converse with the villagers myself because of how my father restricted my movement for my *well-being* he says. Being the sickly daughter of the *Father* of this village forces me to stay within the closed confines of our house. I truth I'm sure he'd be quite furious with me for sneaking out this late."

The daughter of the Father? It took me a moment before I realized that she was the daughter of none other than the clown. Suddenly as if my mind has been struck by a tidal wave, I remembered how important the ritual of bliss was for me and how I had just been handed the perfect partner for it. While she did seem like an enjoyable girl, I did not feel anything close to the same attraction for her that I had for Sariah. She was gorgeous without a doubt and her mind was sharp, but she wasn't Sariah. If it weren't for her position with her father, I would have disregarded her as a candidate. I had no emotional attachment to her, so she was the perfect tool for me to get what I wanted.

I reached for her hand and smiled, "Nope, I've nowhere or no one else that I could possibly go to."

She smiled and I could see from the look in her eye that this was what she had wanted all along from the beginning. As I led her into the jungle to complete the ritual, I thought about asking her name but quickly realized that it didn't matter.

17
Duty

The torn fabric of my clothes hung loosely off my body as I stepped back to look over the conquest I had just achieved. As I looked upon the clown's daughter's bare body, a smile came across my face; not from the deed but from the fact that I had spit on the honor of that man. My hatred for the clown was not due to the fight between Dom and I, but something far deeper. Just looking at his attire: that white-powered face and flamboyant robes coupled with his teachings make me think of the Order along with the lingering resentment I would always have for them. Even though I was well aware of the fact that the clown was an exile just like me, I took pleasure in the fact that I had completed the ritual of bliss with his own kin. I was sure that my funny sense of irony would be lost to him but all the same my smile still remained. There were no more words spoken between his daughter and me. I soon departed from the small meadow we found in the woods and proceeded back toward the sound of music from afar. A cool wind slipped through the woods making me rub my hands together to generate some sort of warmth, but when I touched my hand, I felt only the warmth of my body leaving me. I frantically took a look at my hand and saw that my wedding ring was no longer there. It was obvious that I must have lost it during my little tussle with that woman, but there was no telling where such a small thing could be in those woods.

My preoccupation with the ring dulled my senses slightly enough that I did not notice I was not alone in those woods until it was too late. A dark figure with a blade in hand emerged from the thicket of the woods and charged at me. I went to grab my blade but realized that I had left it at home, so all I could do was evade the attacks of the figure. I found it difficult to get a clear grasp of his movements because of the darkness of night hanging around, but in a brief instant when the light of moon made the blade of my attacker shine, I reached out and grabbed his wrist and quickly broke it, a trick that I had learned while with Clay and his group years ago. Finally, my attacker made a sound as he let off a grueling yell while holding his wrist. I wasted no time in picking up his blade to finish him off, but the passing clouds that had obscured the light of the moon opened up and allowed me to use the moonlight to see his face. The truth revealed by the light of the moon made me stay my hand and take a step back.

"Reginald? Is that really you, my friend?" I asked. The months on the island had really allowed for his uncouth appearance to thrive as he looked like a true wild man with his beard now grown to legendary proportions. I went to my knee and quickly snapped the bone I had dislocated in his wrist back in place.

With tears starting to stream down his face, Reginald embraced me and said, "I'm sorry, my friend, for attacking you. I couldn't tell that was you in the darkness."

I grabbed the back of his head as I embraced him as well, "It's all right, friend. It's all right I'm just glad to see you well and about. I feared the worst!"

"As did we for you," said Reginald as his words were muffled with his sniffles. "Tell me, Terra, do you know of the whereabouts of Sariah and Rebecca?"

"Yes, they're with me. They're safe. What of Christian? Is he with you?"

"Yes, we all met up not too long after the crash and found refuge in an abandoned village. We waited for you guys to find us, but after a while we assumed the worst. After all, we all know that no one in the unit loves Christian as much as you," he said with a chuckle.

They waited for me. They waited for someone that was never coming to them. Hearing the happiness in Reginald's voice made me loosen my grip around his neck as my guilt set in.

"So what are you doing around this region of the jungle then?"

"It's been hard but we've been going village to village liberating the people that we've come across. You wouldn't believe how crazy the people of this island are, Terra. This has turned out to be one hell of a final test!"

I couldn't help but laugh at his story. Christian and the others had been going all along this past month still being the dogs of the Order. They had no idea that they were exiles as well and that the Order didn't care about them. It was a waste of time. An utter waste of time.

"Reginald, do you have any idea where we are? This is the Isle of the Fallen! We're not sent here to liberate the people. We're exiled here by the Order!" I screamed at him.

I had unconsciously grabbed him by the collar while I screamed at him, which made him push me away as he said, "Exiled? Terra, what are you talking about. Wait…if you think we've been exiled…then what have you been doing these past few months?"

I tensed at the sound of his question but played the part of the innocent fool as I responded, "What do you mean, Reginald?"

Reginald had put some more distance between us as he spoke cautiously, "We've come across a wide array of people, and all of them believe that they're exiled by the Order and thus have resorted to a life of debauchery. Forgive me questioning you, Terra, but if you thought we'd been exiled then what have you been doing till now?"

With the most annoyingly perfect timing, the daughter of the clown came from nowhere and caught Reginald's attention. With just one movement, he drew a dagger he kept hidden at his side and charged the girl, but I quickly stepped between the two of them as I caught his arm.

"Reginald, what are you doing?" I asked as he tried to force his way past me.

He pulled back and yelled at me. "Terra, she's most likely a member of the village of Ataxia. Through of liberation, we've heard nothing but tales of how that village is the worst of all. Christian sent me on ahead as a scout to see what I could find. She has seen the two of us, Terra. She has to die!"

Just then as I struggled with Reginald's request, the daughter of the clown wrapped her arms around me and said, "Oh yes, I've seen quite a lot of Terra here," as she bit my ear seductively. I looked at Reginald with wide eyes full of fear of what he may think as I pushed her away from me.

"Terra," Reginald began, "I found this in the woods not too long ago before I happened upon you," he said as he held up the glimmering metal of my wedding ring.

I already knew what he was thinking because I would have come to the same conclusion myself. "Reginald, I promise you that I have not wed that woman."

"But it's clear that you have lain with her. She's a heathen, Terra! How am I supposed to let believe you if you've been amongst the enemy. God have you, Dom, and the sisters all just been among those heathens?" he asked grief-stricken.

"Dom…is that not the boy you killed in the arena, my love?" said the daughter of the clown as she leaned against the bark of a nearby tree.

I wanted to kill her. I didn't know what game she was playing at, but I wanted to kill her. If I could I would have teamed up with Reginald to silence her forever, but I got the feeling that the time for an alliance had passed. I looked over to him and saw that he had his dagger drawn.

I took a step closer to him and said, "Reginald, relax this is all one big misunderstanding, my friend."

He took a swipe at my hand, which made me step back, and said, "The only misunderstanding that we had was when we thought that the four of you were on your own liberating other villages. Jon and I suggested that we look for you, but Christian was adamant that you were fine and taking care of the others then. He placed so much faith in you and here you were literally sleeping with the enemy! Christian can't be allowed to see this! It would crush him. I'm sorry, Terra…"

"Wait, Reginald! Are you seriously taking the word of this harlot over mine? Me? Kill Dom," I said, sounding as offended as possible. "You need to get your story together, Reginald! I found his body near the crash sight of his pod. He must have died upon the impact of the landing. I carried his body back to the village and…"

"So this is the darkness of the Island that Christian spoke of. Even with being called out, you find a way to lie about it. You may have never been a fan of the Order, Terra, but you were never one to blatantly lie and ignore one of our Creeds."

He came at me with his dagger in hand as I still held onto his blade. Unlike my fight with Dom, I reacted without a single thought as I dodged his initial slash and then thrust his blade through his chest and watched him fall to the ground. As he lay there bleeding in the grass, he laughed, "I suppose that title, the Executioner, is certainly appropriate for you."

Those were the last words of Reginald before he passed from this world. I stood over his body without knowing what to do. Suddenly a wave of rage came over me as I began to continually stab his body cursing him for not believing my lies. As I went through my rage, I felt the hand of the clown's daughter on my back. I pushed her down with the intent of doing her harm, but calmed down once I realized I needed her to live. I pointed Reginald's blade at her throat as I warned, "Your little game cost me a dear friend. If you ever tell anyone what happened here, then I'll kill you."

She pushed away my blade and smiled as she said, "You only have yourself to blame for this, Terra. If you didn't cheat on your wife, then he'd still be alive."

She left me in the jungle to ponder on those words. I wanted to blame her, but she was right. As I looked upon Reginald's body, I realized that he was the sacrifice for my ritual of bliss. My indiscretions had a cost and Reginald paid it for me. The thought of Christian's anger once he found out about both Reginald and Dom frightened me for a moment but then subsided.

Christian didn't have it in him to cut ties with people so easily. That was one of his flaws. All you had to do was believe in him and he would consider you a friend for life. I could do whatever I wanted and still not have him resent me in the slightest. That's what I kept telling myself as I washed off Reginald's blood in a nearby stream. All during this little incident, the music from the festival had dissipated and all I could hear were the accusations that the clown's daughter had threw at me playing through my mind over and over again.

I don't know how long I stayed at that stream, but I emerged from the woods around the break of dawn and walked sluggishly through the village as I ignored the whispers of everyone around me. Right before I reached the door to my house, Lucas came from behind me and stopped me.

"Terra, stop, are you all right?" he asked. He looked over my body and saw the weird combination of scratch marks and blade lacerations on my back and chest. As I turned to face him, I saw the worry in his face vanish as his eyes noticed the bloodstains near the crouch of my pants. He laughed and said, "Wow, I'm impressed, Terra. Looks like you had quite the vigorous bliss ritual and with a virgin no doubt. I'm almost inclined to bow to you."

It took me a moment to catch his meaning and then realized he had mistaken the blood of Reginald for the blood of a virgin.

I quickly thought of telling him the truth, but then there was no way they would ever allow Christian in the village if he was considered a threat.

"Yeah it was one wild night for sure, my friend," I said. It pained me to use those words, as I thought back to how I had called Reginald and Dom both friends and now look where that had gotten them. "Well I need to get some sleep, Lucas. I'll see you later."

"Sleep will have to wait. I'm sorry. Your duties to the village come first," he said.

My duty. There were several wardens of the village whose purpose was the execution of criminals in the arena. Even among exiles, there seems to be some sort of loose moral code that prevents them from allowing complete anarchy to take over. If Lucas was speaking of my duty, then there must have been somebody fool enough to get sent to the arena. As Lucas began walking toward the arena, I stayed on the porch of my home. After a moment, he turned around and asked, "What's your problem, Terra? Let's go."

The events of last night had shaken me too much to show Lucas the same amount of respect he was accustomed to with me. I gave him a dirty look as I walked inside my home and said, "I'll be your butcher another day, Lucas, but not today."

I slammed the door behind me as I dragged myself into the bedroom where I saw Sariah getting ready in her vanity. Without a word said, I flopped to onto our bed and closed my eyes as I tried my best not to think of Reginald. I don't know how much time went by as I slept, but I awoke to Sariah shaking me as she asked, "What are you doing with this sword?"

I slowly opened one eye and saw that Rebecca was in the room as well examining Reginald's blade. Lucas had been so preoccupied with my duty that he failed to notice I had a different sword than usual, but leave it to Sariah and her sister to pick up on such a thing. I rolled over and yawned as I shamefully responded to their inquiries, "Its Reginald's sword. I killed him last night."

The tone of my voice was about as dry as one could get, yet I still looked up at Sariah and Rebecca with tears streaming down my face as I repeated, "I killed Reginald!"

I grabbed Sariah by the waist and pulled her close to me as I sat on the edge of the bed and muffled my cries on her shirt. She said nothing as she stroked the top of my head and let me pour out all of the sadness that I had built up to that point.

Rebecca went to her knees and held my hand tenderly as she asked, "What happened, Terra?"

It was difficult, but between my moans I managed to tell them what happened between Reginald and I while leaving out the details of how I slept with the clown's daughter. I simply said that she happened upon us and proceeded from there. Once my tale was complete, we could only sit there in silence as we all pondered what to do next.

Sariah broke the silence as she said, "We need to warn the Father and Lucas."

Rebecca snapped her head toward her sister as she struggled with a look of disbelief at her suggestion, "What are you saying? What Terra did was in self-defense, but you're talking about blatantly betraying our king!"

Rebecca's voice had unintentionally raised as she spoke to her sister and thus Sariah responded with a firm tone saying, "On this island our only king is Terra. Christian doesn't exist. We've all been exiled from the Order, but he wished to continue this foolish crusade. We have to think of ourselves here and act in our best interest."

While Rebecca couldn't believe what she was hearing from her sister, I understood what she meant. This Sariah was the woman that I had spent so many years with as a dog of the Order. This version of her knew exactly what it would take to survive, and it was a side of her that only I had seen. Sariah of all people hated the idea of being an exile. She always had wished she could return to the pure life of a Crusader, but the fact that I had killed Reginald changed our options.

"So you have realized that this is a lose situation all around then?" I asked.

"Yeah, if we assist Christian, then there's no guarantee that he would accept us back into the ranks after what we've done. For them, what we've done may be akin to treason, and even if he did take us back, we may have jeopardized our position of security on the island. As for helping Lucas and the clown, if we do that then we're officially betraying our king. Either way we're screwed," she said.

I could see the color draining from Rebecca's face as the reality of our situation hit her. "The best course of action would be to get the clown to safety and then…"

"Or we could let Christian and the others kill him," interrupted Rebecca.

We both turned our heads toward her and listened as she continued, "If the clown were dead, then it would be a good chance for us to try to gain a higher seat of power for security in the village and making a spot for Christian and the others. Maybe we should just stay here and do nothing and wait for it to play out. That way we're safe from both sides."

It amazed me to see how quickly Rebecca caught on to the situation, but still despite how much I wanted to do her plan my conscience would not allow it. Maybe it was because of how fresh Reginald's death was in my mind, but I could not live with the idea of allowing another person that trusted me to die in that same day.

"I shall go to the arena and warn the clown after the matches of the danger he faces. Reginald was only a scout so knowing Christian we have a couple days before he tries to make a move on the village. If we're lucky, we may even be able to find him and convince him to hold off any action," I said.

The girls reluctantly agreed with my plan and began to walk with me to the arena. I thought back to Reginald's words about how Ataxia is viewed to be the worst village in their minds. If that was the case, why did I not feel the same about the village?

Sure there were times when I condemned the land and the people, but never to the extent where I was willing to do a crusade. They were a filthy lot, but they had some good qualities as well. As I looked around the village during my walk with Sariah and Rebecca, I was reminded of why I never took the place too seriously. I had been to several other worlds by that point in my life, and the construction of the village was the most primitive of all the worlds that I had seen. Most of the homes had been constructed from broken stone rubble that was once a part of the foundation of the temple that resided there. So in essence, that whole town was nothing but a land of scavengers. Seeing such truths day after day had dulled my apprehension for the area and considered no one there a real threat.

After a little bit of time, Lucas called over and joined our group. He didn't seem too pleased about me shirking my duties, but he didn't mention anything about my earlier rudeness as he said, "Perfect timing, Terra, we just got word of a special prisoner that you need to execute today. I trust you'll be up for the task?"

Sariah reached for my head, but her touch reminded me of how I had betrayed our union and how that betrayal killed Reginald. I pulled my hand away from her as I answered Lucas, "It would be my pleasure to end the life of a plague to the village, my friend."

"That's good to hear. It seems as of late you and I are the only ones that can be relied upon to get things done in the village. Well I suppose I'm the main one, but you help every now and then," he said.

"Lucas," Sariah began, "why is it that of all the jobs given to Terra, you made him a warden of the arena."

I had no idea where she was going with this. It could have been some sort of ploy to help us down the line with our plan, or she may have just been simply curious. Either way I didn't know.

Sariah had a point though. If anything, with so many exiled Crusaders on the island any one of them should have been able to have the skill to be a warden. My abilities were nothing of note in the Order. In fact, her question brought to mind a feeling that had been plaguing me as of late. According to the stories, the Isle of the Fallen was supposed to be a place of exile for only Crusaders that had spit upon the tenements of the Creed. With that myth firmly etched into my mind, I found that the majority of the citizens were civilians without a shred of Crusader training after going through careful thought. The thought had never crossed my mind to look into why there seemed to be so many simple civilians in the village until that day.

"In truth, over the last few decades, our numbers have dwindled when it came to actual trained Crusaders," he said.

"What do you mean?" asked Rebecca.

"The Isle of the Fallen has been a prison for Crusaders for ages, but yes the majority of people are not Crusaders but the descendants of some like how Richard is. After being exiled to the isle, the first batch of exiles mated and mated and mated some more until the isle was bursting with children and so it is those children's descendants that occupy the isle now. In all truth, it is rare to get more than a couple legit Crusaders come to the isle in a single month. In fact, it's only been you all and I that have been exiled here with our entire team. Most others come alone," he said.

"That's right, you said before that you were once a king of a unit. Are any of them here in the village now?" I asked.

Lucas stopped walking and sighed for a moment. "My king, Fister, in order to spread the Word he thought it would be a wise idea to seduce a heathen and use her affection for him to teach her of the Word. He was executed by the Order for his decision and our whole team was exiled here and I had to take control. But the freedom of the isle made many of them challenge my rule. One by one I silenced them in order to solidify my rule and do what I thought Fister would have wanted, but before I knew it I was all alone with nothing but blood on my hands."

His story made me think of how Dom and Reginald alike seemed so eager to kill me.

"I failed Fister and my men when I became their king, and that's a sin that not even this Isle can alleviate," said Lucas.

His words of regret seemed so sincere. Though I was saddened by the fact that I had to kill my own teammates, I felt no regret toward it. Sure it was an unfortunate occurrence, but it was something that I would do over if I could. Maybe that was why I could never be a king in my own right. The compassion that Lucas had for his fallen men far exceed my own. I could see why he was a king in his own right even though the title was forced onto him. Every king was different and every king had a quality that made others follow him. While everyone just naturally loved Christian and wished to die for him, Lucas had a charisma to him that made you want to be around him, yet I could see that it was that same charisma that made his team hates him. Ever since I met him, he just seemed too cool, too perfect. Ever woman in the village loved him and he was the friend of every guy as well. It was easy enough to be jealous of the guy.

As we continued to walk, we passed the temple and I saw that there were hardly any people there for worship that morning. It took a second for me to remember, but I recalled that it was Sunday and was quite shocked to see such a poor number of people in attendance. I asked Lucas for the reason, "So where is everyone? Not only does that village seem dead but even the temple grounds seem devoid of life."

"Do you not recall the grand festival we had last night?" he asked. "Well half of them I suspect are in bed nursing their headaches and the rest are like us and heading to the arena."

I thought of how the Creed explicitly punished any that dared to miss a Sunday service in the Order. They always told us that without the fear of missing a service, then people would skip all the time, a habit that was certainly the case on the isle. Not much time passed till we all arrived the arena. The morning fights had gone by without much cause for commotion but it was the afternoon fights and Lucas's special prisoner that had the whole settlement a buzz.

The arena had a completely different vibe as I strolled through the corridors to find seat in the pulpit where Lucas always sat with the clown. Sariah and Rebecca had gone their own separate ways to find a seat in the crowd. While there was certainly a good deal of excitement in the air, I could sense a level of tension that was normally absent from the arena. I decided not to pay too much attention to it though and pushed the thin veil that acted as a doorway into the clown's pulpit. As the clown sat off his fat butt getting fanned by two beautiful women, I saw that sitting in a cushioned chair to his right was his daughter. She looked back our way, and gave Lucas and I an innocent wave. I wondered if she had told her father what went down between us.

Just seeing her face made me want to kill her, but I reined in my rage as I entered the pulpit. Lucas and I approached the clown as he was sipping wine from his jeweled goblet and stood on opposing sides of him with me standing closer to his daughter fighting my urge to do her harm.

"Father, it brings us joy to see you this morning," said Lucas as he bowed his head. I mimicked the gesture and looked down to the dry field of combat where I saw another warden doing battle with a ragged man that already lost an arm during the fight. As the crowd went crazy calling for more blood, I turned to the clown as he said, "The masses are always such an amusing bunch of simpletons. Look at them losing their minds over a sport of death simply because the person next to them is doing the same thing. I find it ironic that we all are barred from the Order because we could not conform to their standards, yet we stand here conforming to principle of blood and slaughter. I love it."

It was a strange sight to actually hear words of sagacity come from the bloodred lips of the clown. As I was about to comment on his words, I heard the crowd erupt and looked over to see that the criminal had been killed. As I watched the blood flow from the body of the nameless man, the anxiety that once filled my bones as I stood in that dry field of death waiting for Dom to attack had now been replaced with a jubilant excitement. The entire arena suddenly seemed to be a marvel in my eyes.

I leaned over to Lucas and asked, "Do people normally skip sermons often to watch these fights?"

"You mean do people skip these fights for sermons?" said the clown's daughter. "If anything, watching the bouts every Sunday has become more of an actual religion than going to the sermons to pray. I don't know when it happened, but suddenly Sundays became more about these fights than prayer," she said.

I gave a look of disapproval her way. Despite my own absence from services the last few weeks, I had my own legitimate reasons, but those people should have been ashamed of themselves forsaking God for blood and carnage on a weekly basis.

"Don't give her that look, Terra," said Lucas. "It's not like we've forgotten our faith. We just chose different times to display our love for God is all. That's the wonder of being free from the Order. They're the ones that tell us to worship on Sunday. Why can't we choose another day to do so? Worship is worship. The day doesn't change the meaning behind it at all."

Lucas's words certainly had some merit to them that I could not help but agree with. Between him and the clown, I found myself warming up to the idea of trying to save them. I turned from him to look down to the ensuing fight when my heart skipped a beat. I rubbed my eyes again to ensure I was not delirious, but being dragged out there in the arena that day was Captain Stagg. So that was what he meant by special prisoner. I did not know what Lucas knew about him, so I had to keep a stoic look on my face as I looked on at one of my mentors. Stagg had been one of the men that killed Kita, so I did not know whether I was happy or sad that he was trapped down in there. Stagg stumbled forward with a bloodstained sword in hand that still dripped fresh blood from one of his recent matches. Small lacerations were all over his body as he dragged one foot through the dirt. He was tired and weak. Most likely he had been fighting consecutive matches all day up till that point.

As he came forward, the crowd reacted harshly throwing out all manner of insults and jests toward him. Whatever he had done was widely spread through the people and he was highly disliked. As the intensity of their shrieks of anger grew, the faster my heart beats. I looked around nervously to make sure that no gazes had fallen upon me as well. As for my true identity, only Lucas and the girls knew that I was no king, so I feared the outcome of the people if they discovered I had lied. Even among exiles, they valued the title of a king very highly and me masquerading as one would certainly not help my case to win them over.

I had to know though how much in danger I was, so I leaned over to Lucas and asked, "What exactly did that man do to deserve this kind of scorn?"

"Why ask me? You're the one that knows him best."

The moment that Lucas said those words, the clown and his daughter turned my way. I had the foresight to bring both of my blades with me to the arena that day, and my hand immediately reached for them, but as Lucas continued to speak, he calmed my worries.

"Don't worry, Terra. I've already told the Father that man was the one that discovered of your relationship with Sariah in the Order. I'm sure it must come as a shock to see him here. Lucky for you, we shot down the ship that brought you here as well and captured him among the wreckage. Think of this as a final-welcome-to-the-isle gift."

So Lucas and them had shot down our casing and the airship. It worried me that there was a weapon capable of that kind of destruction that had remained hidden from me for so long until that point. Regardless, his story did not add up. If Dom had told Lucas everything there was to know about me and coupled with whatever information he got out of Stagg, then there was no way he didn't know about Christian and the others. If he knew all of that, why was he covering for me still?

"While I thank you for the gift, he's no king nor is he a criminal for what he did to me, so why is he in the arena? Or did you simply put him there to appease me?"

"Not a criminal? Terra, you poor, innocent sap. All those affiliated with the Order are guilty of the highest crime of Ataxia. That man openly supported the ridged philosophies of the Crusaders that stripped away our individuality. He's a cog in that corrupt machine that banished us to this existence on the island,"

I looked into his eyes and could see the flames of hatred that were burning within his pupils. He had the same passion toward the Order that I had toward white people for all those years. Any time that a powerful group excludes you because of simple differences like race or ideology, then you become bitter toward that group no matter their reasoning. You will start to find flaws in that group no matter how small and make those your solid reasons for hating them.

The Order…they were masters at excluding people that didn't fall into their niche. They preferred to recruit their members when we were young, so they can mold our minds to see what they want us to see, but when someone strays from that path, they treat us as if we aren't worth their time. There was a time when I felt that the Order actually cared for my well-being, but over time as more and more of the little quirks of my personality came out, they slowly began to distance themselves from me and just treat me as if I was only one of them in name only. Thus when I felt that they turned their backs on me, I in turn turned my back on them. It's hard to believe in a system that mocks your very existence in the world and treats you like some sort of plague that needs to vanish. I understood his hatred for them. I understood all of their hatred for the Order.

When I had first arrived at the Order as a captive, Stagg made sure to never make my life within the Order ease by any means. From the very beginning, he had me pegged as some sort of scum that didn't belong in their righteous ranks. He treated me differently from all of the others on every occasion he got, but what really stuck with me all of those years was the fact of how in one lesson he went on about how great the Crusaders were because we were the only people in all of the worlds that actively sought to forgive the transgressions of those ignorant of the Word. He went on and on about this forgiving idealism that had been embedded within the Order and how we should all be honored to be a part of something so great dedicated to helping the ignorant ones find the truth. That lecture always stuck in my mind because I believe that was the first time outside of Kita's death that I found myself actually resenting the Order. Maybe I was jealous that they coddled these primitives for their sins but shunned me for mine. Either way, I knew that day that I would never belong with those people. I was nothing but a black sheep to all of them.

As the lingering resentment I had for the Order resurfaced, the vibrant shouts of the crowd that once seemed to possess a chaotic nature seemed to soothe my soul. The shame I once had for them behaving like ranting monkeys melted away as I found my own hand thrusting forward screaming for Stagg to meet a bloody end. It was like I had strings moving my limbs as I continued to cheer for blood. I didn't feel like I was in my right mind, yet I didn't care. I was enjoying letting my hatred…no, my passion for the arena take over.

"I love what I'm seeing here, my friend!" said Lucas. "Now go into the arena and claim your vengeance."

The thought of finally getting my vengeance on Stagg for Kita's death made a wicked smile emerge on my face. Right before I leapt from the pulpit into the arena though, the clown stopped me.

"Wait, Terra," he said. "Take these and leave those dull blades of yours behind. A king should go into battle with the weapons of a king."

I looked to him and saw him holding out two Lionheart blades, the prestigious weapon for all those anointed king within the Order. Christian always kept his close by his side and a small part of me had always wanted it. It was a masterpiece of craftsmanship, but the ones that the clown handed to me were different. The normal mold of the blade was a dual-edged longsword that had a silver blade protruding from the roaring mouth of a lion's head that acted as the hilt. But the ones handed to me were singled-edged katanas crafted with ebony steel. I took them in hand and wrapped my fingers tightly around the hilts. I took the blades and then leapt into the arena and raised my hands in acknowledgment as the crowd went wild for me.

As I soaked in the cheers of the crowd, Stagg limped over to me and began to say something, but I punched him so hard in the face that I knocked him to the ground. Seeing Stagg there should have reminded me of Christian's impending arrival, but I was lost within the depths of my own anger. The crowd loved my hateful actions and as I looked around the arena at all of them cheering my name, I saw the image of Sariah and Rebecca with looks of disgust on their faces. I turned away from them and drew my new blades. Coughing up blood, Stagg said, "Terra! What are you doing working with these heathens!"

I walked over to him and delivered a kick to his jaw that knocked him on his back. I cared nothing for his words because I had told myself long ago I would gladly kill him for Kita when I got the chance. Whether he was working with Christian or not mattered very little to me. I knew Christian would understand and would not condemn me for my actions since he was such the forgiving type. As I went over to Stagg to deal him more punishment, I thought of the regret that Lucas had over killing his entire team for power and laughed at the thought. I had already killed Dom and Reginald, so I figured one more wouldn't hurt my conscience too much. A loud whistle from Lucas caused me to stop moving as that meant that I had jumped the gun and attacked before the clown wished to address the crowd and begin the match.

The cheers only intensified as we saw the clown rise to his feet to speak. The feet of the crowd began stomping the bleachers, causing a resounding echo to fill the air. We all waited for his hand to come down to signal the start of the match, but it never did. Instead we heard the thump of his body hit the floor of the arena as he fell from his pulpit bleeding to death on the ground. I looked over and saw that standing in the place of the clown was Christian with his Lionheart blade raised high in the air causing the crowd to come to an abrupt silence as all of our eyes keyed in on him. Standing with Christian were two other members of our unit, Jon and Tennaz, as they each held a blade to the throats of Lucas and the clown's daughter.

"Attention, people of Ataxia. I am Christian T. Black the king of the 186th cadet unit sent to this island to purify all of the poisonous thoughts that have taken hold of your mind. You all know the process of crusading from firsthand experience or stories from your parents. But this is no crusade. This is a purge of evil that has festered in this land for far too long. Long ago you turned your back on God's way and now it's judgment day for those actions. Repent, my fallen brothers and sisters of the Order, or you shall meet the same fate as your leader," he warned.

Christian looked directly at Stagg and I and leapt from the pulpit and began to run toward us. My initial reaction was to look for anyone wishing to harm Christian for his actions but I didn't move an inch. I didn't know what to do. Everything that I had done to secure us a spot in the village had been ruined and now even my cover was in danger of being blown. I barely heard the hollow yells of Lucas as he broke free from Jon and ordered everyone able to fight to stop Christian.

Everything seemed to evaporate around me as I only focused on Christian's stride as he sprinted for our mentor. I took an oath to help Christian in every way imaginable, but still I found that I could not move. Had my time among the people of Ataxia really meant that much to me where I was willing to stand there and do nothing? Lucas and a few of the guards stormed the arena and erected a wall of men between Christian and Stagg as I stood behind them all unable to move or speak, but I couldn't bear it any longer. I snapped out of it and took a step forward. The moment I did though, Christian looked my way with eyes full of sadness. I froze once our eyes met and then I turned the other direction and left the arena as quickly as humanly possible.

The commotion of the arena had spread throughout the village as a stampede of people ran toward the arena as I put more and more distance between it and me. I looked over my shoulder occasionally and watched as the stone structure grew smaller and smaller in the distance. I didn't know where I was going, but my feet carried me into the very depths of the jungle. Nothing stopped me from running. I thrashed through overgrown plants impeding my path. I trudged through mud that crawled up to my shins. I endured the sting of thorns and tree bark as my clothes were cut along the path I created. Finally my feet stopped as I found myself standing in a graveyard on a cliff overlooking the sea. The graves had been marked only by a single large stone and an assortment of flowers was strewn along between all of the graves honoring the memory of the fallen. I walked past each grave and wondered if the men and women sleeping in the soil I traversed upon had shown the same cowardice as I did ever in their lives.

Why? Why did I stay my blade and not rush into the fray to assist Christian? I was fully aware of the fact that I had been gone for quite some time and thus the altercation with Christian must have long passed. Was he alive? Did he rescue Stagg? Or did my cowardice cost my brother his life? So many questions jumped around in my mind that I wished to never find the answer to. The only question I knew the answer to was that in the heat of the moment. The words Sariah said a while back proved to be true.

We should have left a long time ago to search for the others. I could have easily given some sort of false pretense to go out into the jungle, but I was afraid of losing the peace that I had just found. The Order, the words that they spoke and the values they possessed. I found them all to be right after my incident with Tai-lee. I believed in every lesson that they taught and wished to abide by those laws, but it was just too difficult. Stagg had indeed been right to be wary of Christian and me since we joined the Order at the nearly impossible age to mold of sixteen. Our view of the world had already been cemented in our minds and their ridged ways just showed me a truth that I could not follow. Being a Crusader, an embodiment of the Lord's will, was liken to chasing a star that no matter how bad I wanted, it was impossible for the realm of men to accomplish. Living under such suffocating circumstances day in and out, fighting a hopeless battle that I could never win quickly felt like a never-ending struggle for a redemption that didn't exist.

The few months among the exiles liberated me from those anxieties that had taken root in my life. Living life with them felt like it was as easy as breathing. No more doubts of myself and no more lies I had to tell my reflection to get me through the day. Life among them was truly a freedom where I could honor the Lord in my own way. Once I saw Christian though, I knew that peace couldn't coexist with him. I always knew that. That's why I delayed my search for him for as long as possible. I was a coward truly afraid of being locked back up again in the prison that the Order forced me into.

I sat on one of the graves for a long while until I heard someone thrashing about in the bushes behind. I drew both my blades right as Stagg emerged from the depths of the jungle and into the graveyard with me. A dagger was protruding from his leg allowing a trail of blood to drip behind him as he hobbled toward me. I kept my blades pointed his way as he sat down on one of the graves as well.

He shot me an angry look as he waved his hand ordering me, "Get that blade out of my face, boy. Even if I'm creeping toward death's door, I don't intend to get there any sooner by your hand."

I took note of his casual demeanor and subsequently threw a punch right at his face knocking him to the ground.

"Stagg! What was that in there? And what of Christian? Is he alive?" I demanded.

Stagg coughed up a wad of blood as he chuckled, "Oh so now you care about him eh? Well yes, the boy is still alive no thanks to you and your new friends. The two of us just barely managed to escape. He returned to where his hovel is, and he told me to find you to tell you the truth of your arrival here."

"The truth? You mean about how we have been exiled to this place. Sorry but I kind of figured that part out already," I said.

"Exiled? No, no, boy. You all were sent here for the sole purpose of liberating this island since, as you can tell, it really needs the guidance. The original mission that you all had has never changed one bit," he said.

18

Splinter Cell

Terra: 17
Location: Lactia

The world around me looked completely different after I had slaughtered those people. At that time, I had no idea what was happening to me, but after talking about it with Sariah much later, it is safe to say that I had a complete mental breakdown. My body was paralyzed as I fell to my knees and just sat in all the blood that I had just spilled. I could feel the thumping of the boy's fists striking my chest, but it was a hollow feeling. Despite the immense guilt I felt because of the boy, I just looked right through him. I practically just looked right through everything as if it weren't there. My senses had dulled to such a low point that I barely felt a thing when I saw Sariah kill the boy in front of me. Even in death, the boy still had those piercing eyes that hated me. Sariah picked me up and leaned me on her shoulder. As she did so, I could barely hear her muffled words. To me, she sounded as if she were trying to talk while underwater, but when I asked later on, she told me she said, "I had to kill the boy, so he didn't tell anyone of what you did to those innocents."

Killing in order to protect the holy image of the Crusaders. It was a cruel irony for anyone that was caught in the crossfires of such a dangerous doctrine. I'm sure Kita could attest to how troublesome such thinking was. I continued to hear the muddled words of Sariah as she struggled under the burden of my weight and limped through the cellar back to the stairs. My vision became blurred as I kept thinking back to how I mowed those people down. Why did they have to die, I kept asking myself. Why did they have to die? A misunderstanding, it was a simple misunderstanding that killed those people. It was the mistake of a fool in all honesty. I had no knowledge of this Cashern following, yet I acted with such strong convictions toward it based off one superficial glance of a ritual of theirs. I acted so superior when I saw those people. As if I knew that I was better than them just because I didn't understand what they were doing and in my own eyes it seemed barbaric. I didn't even try to understand that culture either. I just took what I saw at face value and then allowed for that small glance to influence my whole entire perception of them. Why didn't I ask Sariah? It was clear that she knew much more about them than I did, yet I did nothing of the sort. The truth would have been simple to procure as long as I had shown the will to find it instead of relying on my own foolish ignorance as the base for my beliefs.

Sariah had managed to carry me out of the manor and into the burning fields once more. I could hardly feel the heat of the flames even as they burned right alongside me. Those people I killed…they were trying to save a life and I repaid that honor by killing them. What was so evil about the Cashern doctrine? I didn't ask myself that question one time as I prepped for the mission. I was akin to a child never questioning the words of his parents and blindly following their guidance whether it was right or wrong. How was it that I managed to defy the wise orders of my own father and venture out into the woods yet obediently adhered to the story that they gave me of those that followed Cashern? Was my lack of naiveté as I got older replaced with willful obedience to some sort of higher power over me?

Sariah's progression stopped and she laid me down on the ground. With half my face buried in the soil, I could barely see what was going on with Sariah. From my one good eye though, I spotted her being surrounded by half a dozen other Crusaders. A wave of relief came over me as I realized that we were now safe, but that fleeting feeling of safety slipped away as I saw Sariah draw her blade as they all drew theirs. Perhaps it was due to the sight of a new threat that my senses came back to me a little bit. My hearing greatly improved as I heard Sariah scream out, "Why are you all doing this! We've followed all our orders. For Christ's sake, Price died carrying them out!"

The other Crusaders were stone-cold silent as they continued to creep toward Sariah.

"Fine," she said, "if you all don't intend to talk, then I'll make you! I have no plans on dying tonight!"

All I could do is lay there and watch as she struggled to stay alive. I wanted to move to help her, but I couldn't. It was as if I was in a dream of some sort. I felt a tear roll down my cheek as I saw the blurred image of Sariah being disarmed and with a blade to her neck. My voice screamed in my mind for me to get up and save her, but nothing happened. The strain of trying to forcefully recover from my breakdown was too much and caused me to pass out with the last things I heard the being distant shouts approaching us.

By the time I awoke again, I was laying comfortably in the bed, and it was well into the morning and the nauseating smell of herbal medicines filled the air. I turned my head to see Sariah next to me grinding some sort of plant into a fine powder in a bowl. The rays of the sun crept through the blinds next to me making horizontal lines of light stack up against Sariah's thigh. I rose up and leaned my head against the bed post and allowed for my blanket to fall off of me. My movement caught Sariah's gaze as she stopped her grinding and turned her chair toward me.

I took a good look at her and didn't see any semblance of the injuries she must have occurred. Was it all a dream? Had we even raided that manor? With the pleasant thought that my last painful memories were nothing but an illusion, I placed my hand on my forehead and smiled until I saw that my right arm had been heavily bandaged. The memory of the severe burn I received came back to me along with the other events of that night. I turned to Sariah and asked, "What happened to us?"

She walked over to my bed and slowly began to unwrap my arm. The burnt skin had been removed leaving only a long patch of pink skin.

"It's good to see that you healed well," said Sariah.

"Yep good as new I suppose," I replied.

"I only wish the same could be said for me," said Sariah as she was suddenly covered with blood. Her body fell in my lap and I was suddenly jolted back to my cruel reality. The two of us were still running. From what exactly I couldn't say. My head was too foggy for me to tell what the real threat was anymore. I tried to speak but I found that I couldn't. This sensation was different from before. Instead of feeling numb, I felt disconnected from my body as if I was some sort of specter looking at the events around me from afar.

"Just a little further now, Terra, and then we can rest. I know this night has been hard on you. Trust me, this was not what I had anticipated either when the crusade first began, but what can you do right? God, I must look crazy right now talking to semi-conscious fool, but I need to I suppose. I need to talk to you so I don't think too much of my own pains right now."

Ever since we left the manor there had been a slight drizzle that did nothing but make the light texture of Sariah's hair darker under the moonlight. By that time though, the rain had severely intensified to the point where even in my mental daze I could tell the added weight of our soggy clothes was slowing her down some. My feet had rebelled against my mind as well as they dragged along through the mud leaving a visible trail for anyone to follow.

"You know I find the timing of all this truly funny," she said. "Not too long before you arrived Clay had begun to tell us tales of a world that he had happened upon by chance. He called it the

Isle of the Fallen. Throughout our training, we had often heard of the isle as a terrible place that the worst of us were sent to for a fate worse than death. The details varied greatly from teacher to teacher, but in the end we all thought that we must do our best to strive toward the holy teachings in order to avoid such a dreaded place. Clay though offered us a different perspective on the matter. He told us of a world filled with Crusaders that were free from the restrictions of the Order and could do what they wished with their lives. The details of his version were sometimes akin to some sort of erotic utopia with no social controls, but we always chalked his stories as nothing but tales for the campfire. It is only now that I wish his stories were true. Seeing the poor state that you're in right now only makes me question the way we do things. Many Crusaders have no idea what are the customs of those that follow Cashern, so they would have reacted in the same way that you did. I wonder how many Crusaders have acted in such a way and felt the same level of guilt you feel right now. Ha, I bet you're wondering why I said you and we. After all, I should feel just as bad after I killed that kid, but I don't. I didn't feel anything too overwhelming when Price died, and I felt even less for that child. We Crusaders are taught only to think of our cause and little else. We should not care about ourselves. We should only care about the mission of the Order. But here we are. I don't even want to know what's going on in your head at this moment and then there me dragging you through the mud and for all I know you may never snap out of this little funk you're in."

Sariah began to laugh while the little bit of consciousness that I did have began to fade away once more. I awoke once more because of a roar of thunder nearby followed by a crack of lightning that lit up the sky. When I came too, I saw that my senses were much stronger than they were before. I raised my hand and was pleased to see that I had control over my body once more. As I peered around my settings, I saw that Sariah had managed to find us shelter in a cave and had the makings of a fire well underway. I watched as she struck two pieces of flint together time and time again until the first embers of fire began to start. With the light of the fire now illuminating the cave, I could see that Sariah was practically covered in mud, a sign that she must have fallen a time or two while she carried me. I looked down at myself and saw that I too was a muddy mess and began to laugh.

Sariah looked up seemingly astonished that I was conscious at that moment and asked, "What are you so happy about?"

"Oh nothing. I was just marveling at what poor a job you did taking care of me. I mean these were some really expensive clothes after all."

"You're such an jerk," she said smiling.

"Aren't we all?"

"I suppose. Well if anything it's good to see that you're awake now. Even though it makes things a little more awkward for me," she said while her face began to blush.

At first I was perplexed by her words until I realized how damp my clothes were. During my time in the army, our campaigns took us all over the confederacy so there were many days when we had to deal with the fallbacks of marching through the rain. I sadly can remember many nights when I was forced to cuddle with Christian by the warmth of a fire while stripped down to just our loins and a blanket to keep us warm. The memories were ones that I wished to dispel as soon as possible, but the similar scenario with Sariah made them all come back grudgingly. On the other hand, the thought that I may be forced to undergo the same kind of situation with Sariah soon was not an idea that bothered me in the slightest. Through the thin veil of smoke from the fire, I was able to see her take off her Crusader jacket, an action that did make my heart pick up its pace a little more. Out of courtesy, I turned my head away from her but still tried my best to catch a small glimpse by looking as far to my left as I could without turning my head. Once I was sure that she had finished, I turned back to the pleasure of being able to gaze upon her fair skin without any sort of condemnation.

"Well if you plan to get sick because you refuse to undress be my guest then, Terra," said Sariah as she caught my eyes scanning her body.

"Oh yes of course just give me a moment to…" I froze as I realized that I still did not have full control over my body. I was trying to simply move my hand to unbutton my jacket but my hands still shook too profusely for me to attempt anything action such as that. "What exactly happened to me?"

"From the look of things, I'd say that you suffered from a complete mental breakdown. I've heard of new Crusaders going through episodes such as that when they're introduced to the concept of a purge or something similar, but I never knew a person could just completely shut down like that."

"It's not like I wanted to. Seeing all of that blood and the words of that child as well. I don't know how to describe it. It just felt as if a large boulder had just been dropped onto me and I was crushed beneath its weight."

"Well no one said being a Crusader would be an easy task. That's why there are few like myself that actually volunteer for the job."

Hearing her say that she volunteered for the job reminded me of how Christian practically threw himself at Stagg in order to join.

"Why would anyone want to join the Crusaders so badly?" I asked without really anticipating an answer.

"To ensure that there are no other little girls that don't have their parents because they believed in something different from what another group of people did," she suddenly said coldly. I was not quite well-versed with her enough yet to completely read the undertones of her words, but I got the gist of it.

"I'm sorry for your loss. I can understand how painful it is to lose a parent based on a stupid difference of beliefs between people."

"That's right you used to be a slave. I heard it all from Clay," she said. She got up from her seat and approached me while beginning to unfasten the buttons of my jacket. "I'll be danged if I allow you to get sick and die after all the trouble I went through dragging you here. We've been forced by the weather to spend the night here until morning and then we can head back to the barn."

As she continued to slowly undress me, I asked her, "How did your parents die? If you don't mind me asking."

Her delicate fingers ceased their movements and slowly began to grip the fabric of my sleeve tightly as if she were reliving the very moment of their passing. "On my world," she began, "there are all sorts of scientific communities that believe in different theories of why there are so many vast worlds out there. Essentially, their logic is another kind of religion in itself, and, well, my parents came up with this radical new idea that went against the current thought process of their lab and were killed in order to supplant any disorder within the group. The same people who killed them professed to be their friend only a couple days prior. It was then after much crying that I realized that if everyone did not think so differently and just believed in one thing then my parents would still be alive."

"That's why you joined. The Crusaders try their best to spread one set of teaching across the worlds. But you know they kill as well. I'm a perfect example of that," I pointed out trying my best not to blatantly call her hypocrite.

"I know. I'm not naïve enough to believe that such a utopia comes without a price, but it's one I'm willing to pay for the future generations. I can never forget the wailings of my younger sister once she found out about our parents. Those screams still slightly haunt me at night. Don't you wish that your own world all just adhered to one train of thought so that your father would not have had to die?" she asked.

I thought of how silly such thoughts were, but I could not stop myself from smiling at the notion of Father still being alive and well. It was a fool's dream but that didn't mean it was a bad one.

I suddenly noticed that while we had been talking, she had managed to get my jacket and pants off. Her hands traced along the path from one of my scars on my back that reached out to the side of my arm. Her hands grazed across my skin slowly as our eyes met and then it's difficult for me to put into words what occurred next. It was like there was some sort of great magnetic force that pulled us closer to one another as our eyes stayed focused on the other's eyes and then we found ourselves sharing a kiss. Strangely, the numbness that had once possessed most of my body vanished as I moved my hands along the side of her body and our kiss became much more passionate. Right when I was getting into to it though, she broke away from me with a frightened look in her eye as if I had just attacked her.

"I'm sorry. That was wrong of me. The Creed. We cannot violate the Creed," she said.

I had learned about the frustrating Creed that bonded a Crusader to a pledge of abstinence from Price and Spencer, so I knew exactly what she was talking about. A wave of shame came over me partly for being rejected like that and partly for kissing the lips of a white woman. A taboo that had not completely worked its way out of my system.

"Let's just get some rest," I said just wanting to forget that the whole thing happened.

Despite the shunning that she gave me, we still ended up having to cuddle next to one another beside the warmth of the fire. It was weird at first not trying to get excited about the fact that a beautiful woman was within the grip of my arms, but the events from the day had taken their toll and it did not take me long to fall asleep.

The following morning, I can say for certain that I was completely back to normal. I awoke to see that Sariah was no longer by my side, but that was the least of my concerns as I clenched my fists and realized that I had complete control over my body without the slightest indication of shaking. My clothes were still damp but it was not nearly as bad as the previous night. I quickly got dressed and saw Sariah stretching outside. I shielded my eyes from the sun the moment I stepped outside the cave and from a distance I could see the small image of the manor we had raided last night. As I looked on at the place of my transgression, Sariah handed me my blades. The steel had been wiped of any trace of the murders that I had committed, but I still felt as if I could just see the slightest tint of a crimson stain when the sun hit the blades the right way.

"So shall we head back to the barn now?" I asked.

Before Sariah could respond to my question, another voice did saying, "Oh there will be no need for that, Terra. Your mission's done here."

I looked behind me to the top of the hill where the cave was under and saw Tai-lee along with several other Crusaders standing in a single file above us as if they were a firing squad. I was really getting tired of all the unexpected surprises that had been following me around lately, but Tai-lee's presence was even more confusing than the others. Had she found the evidence to convict Clay and the others without my help? And if so, did that mean that I was now expendable? Despite how much it pained me to admit it, in those last few months I had lost the grizzled edge that made me not fear death. I had gotten too attached to the joys of life and so seeing Tai-lee so far ahead of schedule caused a feeling of dread to stir within my very bowels.

"Tai-lee," I began, "what are you doing here?"

She tossed her hair back and said, "Well I had hoped that the firestorm from last night would have done you in, but you managed to show that same resilience that Christian spoke so highly of. So I came down to clean up this mess myself."

The firestorm that killed Price and nearly us along with him was her attack? Even though it calmly came from her own lips, I had trouble believing it to be true. It made no sense why she would do such a thing. Before I could even ask why, Sariah took my place and fiercely posed the question herself while drawing her blade, "It was you that did it! Price said that the airship hovering above the manor looked to be of Crusader grade, but it was too dark to confirm. You would slander the covenants of the

Creed and kill your own! I demand answers! Or are you secretly some sort of Cashern spy?"

Her accusation of Tai-lee only made her laugh, "A Cashern spy? My, I wish they were clever enough to pull something like that off. It would give us an excuse to wipe them out. Speaking of which, I have to commend you on a job well done, Terra. You left a fine message for everyone on this world to not challenge the way of the Order. For that I thank you, but sadly this is the end of our little partnership."

Sariah came from behind me and put her blade to my neck, "So you're working with them huh? I should have put that arrow through your skull months ago."

I tried to break free from her grip, but for her small size she was mighty powerful.

"Sariah, you need to relax. I have no idea what's going on right now either!" I pleaded.

"Oh yes, Sariah, you really should relax. Terra has no idea what's going on. Cut the poor boy some slack. He's just some heathen from a low-class world that got dragged into a world that is far too big for him to handle," said Tai-lee amusingly.

"I swear if you don't tell me what's going on right now I'll kill this piece of garbage!" screamed Sariah as she pressed the blade closer to my neck. Personally, it did sting a little bit being called a piece of garbage from someone I kissed the previous night, but the sting of her blade made me not think of it too much.

I saw the look in Tai-lee's eyes at that moment that laughed off Sariah's little threat. I meant nothing to her, so she cared very little if I died or not. I could hear the panic in Sariah's voice. She must have known that her blackmail attempt was a weak one. Tai-lee had just said she wanted to kill us, so I doubt she would budge at such a miniscule threat. There was only one explanation that I could think of for all of this. Clay and them must have been responsible for the purge. The truth of the matter stung because I did in fact develop a soft spot for a lot of them especially Sariah.

I wanted my mission to be a waste of time, but I guess Tai-lee was spot on.

"Sariah, please just give up and surrender. Tai-lee and the Order know about your involvement in the purge in Erque. It's over," I said.

This time around Tai-lee really burst into a fit of laughter as she said, "Oh wow I completely forgot that I told you that bogus story. Sorry to make you even more confused, Terra, but there was not even a shred of truth to that. Well I suppose that wouldn't be true either I suppose. Clay and his squad had nothing to do with the purge. In fact, their mission of surveying this land was a legit one handed to them from the Order."

"But what about that traitor that convinced the new ruler of Erque to go through with the purge?" I asked.

"Oh well that was us as well. The Order really wanted Erque for long and boring strategic purposes along with the obvious fact we really wanted to exterminate that inbred gay population growing there, so we did the purge. It's that simple. But this is where you come in, Terra. We needed someone to take all the backlash from the purge and well the fact that you were spotted by several of our men masquerading in Crusader clothing helped a bunch. So as of now you're that traitor and Clay and his men are your accomplices."

With all of this new information being thrown at us, Sariah released her grip of me and backed away. I took a step forward and had my blades drawn as I said, "You used me for your own goals even after I saved your worthless life. You, Crusaders, never cease to amaze me. I can't believe you would use innocent members of your group as scapegoats for your wrongs!"

"Innocent? Oh don't misunderstand me, Terra, we specifically chose them because of the problem that Clay was quickly becoming. You've been among them for a while now. I'm sure that you've heard of his grandiose tales of this Isle of the Fallen. Simply put, he knows far too much about it and we needed to silence him anyway. Him and his entire little team of misfits. Anyway, I've spent far too much time talking. I need to take you back with us so you can confess your crimes before the high council of the Order and receive your punishment."

"Terra," Sariah began, "we'll have to spend some time to sort out how you know this woman, but until then I hope you have no qualms with me cutting off that annoying grin of hers."

"Don't fret. We're not particularly close. In fact, she kind of got on my nerves quite a bit during the ride over to this world. I'll leave her to you while I handle her friends."

"Oh well aren't you just brimming with confidence," she said. "Last time I checked, you could hardly walk without any help."

"I'm surprised you noticed. I thought you were too occupied shoving your tongue down my throat," I said without thinking. It was a simple comeback and by far not one of my best especially when it came to her, but that was the first little snippet of banter between the two of us. It was a moment that for some reason has stayed with me all of this time. Tai-lee had brought a total of four guards along with her. By normal standards that would have been much more than enough to handle two Crusaders that were already fatigued, but it was rare that I fell underneath any sort of normal generalization. Tai-lee motioned for her men to charge and all four drew their blades in creepy synchronization and came at us. I sheathed one of my blades and took a step forward and in one fluid motion I pulled out my flintlock pistol and fired a bullet right at one of the men. Sufficed to say he dropped instantly as the shot pierced his chest. The rolling winds of the plains which we stood on made the odor of the gunpowder swirl all around me reminding me of smell of the battlefield.

I dropped the pistol and drew my other blade and as I charged the men, I thought back to the lessons that Clay had given me. I kept my eyes on the shoulders of the closest man in front of me and to predict his moves. The moment he went in for a simple slash, I parried his move with one blade and delivered a swift thrust with my right through his gut. As I pulled out my blade,

I kicked his body forward into another guy which freed me up for another one on one confrontation for a brief time. I waited for him to make a move just as I had been instructed to. The best offense was a good defense as they say. In the war, I learned that the best time to charge was while the other side was reloading their guns. The same sort of mindset applied to a dance of blades between men. When my opponent finally attacked, I parried his attack while slipping behind him and quickly slitting his throat. The last one I did not even give any time to gather himself after he pushed off the body that fell upon him. The moment he had freed himself from the body, I stabbed him with both my blades before he could get up. The instant I heard the man exhale his last breath of life, I fell to my knees, exhausted still from the other night and just exerting myself so much in such a short time.

I turned my head to see how Sariah was doing, but Tai-lee's hand wrapped around the base of my neck and her blade rested right underneath my chin.

"Well, I have to say that was unexpected, but it does paint the picture of you two being radical traitors even more. Just look at all the blood you spilled, Terra. Tsk tsk…what would Christian think?" asked Tai-lee.

I focused in on how her hands felt. They were completely dry. Meaning that she had not even broken a sweat with Sariah. If that was the case, then I knew I had no chance against a seasoned Crusader such as her.

"So what now?" I asked.

"Congrats, Terra. You're the first man I would've ever taken home to meet my father," said Tai-lee.

"Gosh, I feel so honored," I said dryly.

"Don't worry. It'll be a fun trip. After all not everyone gets to die in the holy land of the Order, Olympus," said Tai-lee.

19

Indoctrination

Sariah: Age Unknown
Location: Olympus

Indoctrination: by definition it is called teaching or inculcating a doctrine, principle, or ideology, especially one with a specific point of view. Indoctrination can be done through simple teaching or by excessive force. In the Order, we call such a thing reeducation for lost lambs. It always sounded like such a pleasant term in the past: *reducatiOOON!*

The crack of the whip against my pale skin felt worse then the carving of any blade ever had. My breath panted heavier than a dog's as I struggled to breathe and keep my head up as my body dangled by chains in the reeducation cell of the Order. Every time the word reeducation came through my mind I laughed…well I tried to but my cracked jaw and swollen face made all my laughs come out as apelike grunts.

"The Order is a vassal of the God and giver of the Word to the primitives of the world," said my gentle torturer as he continued to whip me. It's by the grace of the Order that people in all the worlds can live safely!"

He had gone on and on saying the same kinds of things for several months now. The Order was this and the Word was that.

I thought my hatred for the Order after betraying Clay and the rest us would have acted as a barrier to such indoctrination, but I could go without food and water for only so long. In the beginning, I figured I would lie to them and act as though I was being reformed, so I could eat but my hatred for the Order soon turned into a hatred of my pride for not just giving them what they wanted so the beatings would end.

I sang. I sang loudly for days how I loved the Order and wanted to bask in its golden aura of righteousness, but if lying had a scent, it must have went right through their noses because the more I professed my love for the Word the more I was beat. Fingers were broken, skin was burned, lacerations were made, and bruises developed bruises on them. For half a year, I went through this treatment and sadly I could not remember why I was being treated that way. Was I a criminal or a sinner of some sort? The question always danced through my head, but every time I screamed for an answer all that was said was, "Kill Clay."

Clay…it seemed like such a warm familiar name that brought me a smile every time upon hearing it until every mention of his name brought about the sting of a whip or my head being doused in a tank of chilling water. Whatever this Clay had done, it made the Order hate him more than they me and I had done…well that thing that they seemed to be upset about.

The purge. They were upset about a purge of some sort, I learned as my face was being beaten repeatedly by my guard. God did deliver me from this suffering though just as the guard said he would. One morning in the stead of my earlier-morning reeducation about how Paul went from debt collector to apostle coupled with my daily whipping, I awoke to the screaming of a crowd all around in a stadium. Despite my relief of not being beaten, I found that I was still chained to the floor of the stage I was on (I guess you had to take what you can get). My chains were long enough to allow for a full range of motions though as my hand reached for my face only to feel the hard exterior of some sort of mask on me. While I wished that I could say the sight of that jeering crowd around me made me think I was some sort of star, the reality of me being chained like an animal told me that day was my execution perhaps. Looking around the rest of the platform at least relieved me of the loneness of dying alone. Chained next to me was another man, who I assumed was the person I denoted Maestro simply because when they reeducated him, his screams almost sounded like he was singing a tune. Due to this, I always assumed he was of slighter frame like a girl's but I was pleasantly surprised to see defined tone of his muscles nearly jumping out from his ebony skin. Ahead of the two of us chained to the stage as well were…Clay. Underneath his swollen and bruised face, I could still recognize the face that had taken me under his wing and taught me how to be a Crusader. I could feel the tricking of tears cascading down my face like a waterfall as I realized the horrid condition he was in. The memories that I had suppressed the last half year came back to me as I suddenly recalled why all of us were in that position. I screamed out his name, but underneath the clatter of the crowd, my words did not reach him.

    The words that did reach him were the sagacious tones of the High Seven of the Order. Around the outer edge of stadium, residing in pulpits looking down on the rest of the stadium, were the High Seven, the leaders of the Order. I had never seen them before and even then their pulpits were emanating such brilliant light that I could barely even make out their glowing figures. Despite the seven heavenly figures, it seemed as if when one spoke that all of them spoke as well. As their holy authority resonated all around us, I lowered my head to the ground as one or they all spoke (it's hard to tell), "Children of the Order, you have all been questioned the legitimacy of the Order in the wake of the purge of Erque nearly a year prior. In order to assuage your disquieting minds, we have brought before you all the perpetrators of the purge, Clay Carroll and Tai-lee Xin."

    If the mention and sight of Clay brought my heart happiness and sadness mixed into one sorrowful batter, then the mention of

Tai-lee and the realization that she was chained to the stage with me made me foam at the mouth like a rabid dog. I lunged toward her but my chains restricted me from wringing my hand around her neck, a thought that I immediately had to repent for just as the Order dictated. As my eyes glared at her like she was a prey, I waited eagerly to pounce on, the High Seven continued to speak, "Thus in the wake of these crimes against our Order, children, we have deemed that the perpetrators suffer death by the hands of those they lead astray."

Once the word astray rang through the stadium, filled with all the Crusader recruits of the Order, my chains were unlocked and I was given a steel blade to carry out the commands of the Seven. I didn't know what sort of game that was, but there was no way I could kill Clay…

Kill Clay
Kill Clay
Kill Clay
Kill Clay
Kill Clay

My head snapped back as if I caught myself from falling into a deep sleep. The stadium was silent aside from a subtle drip I heard next to me as if it were raining. I looked down and nearly screamed as I saw the remains of Clay's freshly executed body underneath my bloodstained hands alongside the body of Tai-lee as well. What had I done? What had I done? What had I done!

I almost let off a soul-rending scream, but my soul quieted when I felt the warm sticky touch of another's hands around my own. Suddenly my arm was jerked into the air erected proudly as if I were celebrating the victory over a slain warrior. Amidst my confusion, Maestro said, "In front of them we're puppets of the Order doomed to live our lives under a lie to survive but," he squeezed my hand tighter as he held our bloody, intertwined hands in the air, "when you're with me you can be yourself and cry all you need to."

He was not crying, but I could just feel underneath his hard exterior he displayed for me and the crowd of recruits he was a broken man, maybe even more than I.

"Children of the Order, you have just bore witness to the slaying of these vile criminals of the Word. While such an act is barbaric and reserved for the primitive worlds we enlighten, we have also shown you the Grace of the Order as we have allowed these two blasphemers of the Word redeem themselves through blood just as Christ has redeemed us. The masks they wear symbolize that before their salvation and rededication to the Word, they were simple voids of emptiness, but now through our guidance they can step forward as your peers once again. They can…"

The holy voice cracked as Maestro removed his mask and tossed the image of a blank face. I went to follow his lead, but his grip around my hand tightened. "No," he said. "Only me."

I wondered what he saw as he looked out at the burning eyes of the recruits that now that they knew his face would always associate him with the purge, a crime he didn't commit.

Once the voice of the Seven had recollected itself, it continued saying, "Behold, your born-again brother and sister of the Order. Your new Executioners of the Word, Terra and Sariah!"

There was a moment of silence and then a single round of applause from one man that seemed to draw Terra's gaze for a moment before he turned his head away in shame. Never before did the sound of my name sound so foreign to me.

20

Executioners

Sariah: Age Unknown
Location: Ozma

It was a new term for us at the Order. These Executioners, as we were called, were supposed to act as moral martyrs for any Crusader unit. After the purge, many things within the Order had supposedly changed. With the lack of trust among the recruits after many of them were subjected to such a brutal slaughter of innocents, the Order proposed that it may be better to have the dirty tasks of a mission conducted by those that could handle the guilt of completing the mission. For this reason, the Order decided to use Terra and I as the first lab rats one would say for the this theory. Was it possible for a person to stay loyal to the Order while still having to use the tactics of the unrighteous to benefit the Order? Hypocrites we were called among some circles. We were nothing but ghosts for many people, specters that haunted the halls of the Order yet whom did not belong among the ranks of the pure.

It was during that time when Terra and I became so close, closer than we could ever become.

Ozma, it was a small world blanketed by the eternal cover of the night sky. There were several worlds such as that one where darkness was a perpetual part of life. It was our first mission together as a team. It was the first time that we came to acknowledge our roles of phantoms.

"It looks like the talks are going well," I said to Terra as we peered through our binoculars at Christian and his unit as they spoke to the denizens of Ozma about the Word.

"Of course it is. Christian has always had a natural way of making people feel comfortable around him, but the problem lies not in whether they like him, but if they'll accept our Creeds," said Terra.

"Creeds. You say that as if you actually believe in the Order after what they did to us," I said as my voice reached a higher pitch than I would have liked.

"I do believe in the Creed," he said as he continued to watch Christian and ignore my irritated glare his way. "The Creed and the Word are our guides to salvation. Despite the fact we were told those words under the pain of a whip doesn't make them true. The Word is pure, but it is people that corrupt it. Our reeducation was nothing new to me. It was just another example of the depravity of man. If it weren't for the Word, then who knows how bad things would have gotten left in the hands of people with no guidance."

All this he said in a stoic tone, devoid of emotion. Terra was different from when I had first met him. He was never one to display excessive bouts of emotion, but he was never so cold. But I understood his pain. In spite of Christian, the man he called his brother and who he was closer with than any other being, being so close by he could never feel at home in the Order, a place where he was always aware of how different he was from everyone else. I knew that's how he felt because I felt that loneness too now after being branded an Executioner. Though we were supposed brothers and sisters of the Order, we were treated as outcasts by the other recruits. Without even knowing us, we were touted as sinners that would rather live by the ways of the world than by the way of the Word. Rumors amassed like wildfire that Terra and I monsters that reveled in breaking the commands of Moses. Because of this cruelty and shunning, I had yet to take off the mask that was handed to me, and I had yet to see my sister Rebecca who was among Christian's unit as well. To be so close by, yet feel so distant was a punishment worse than the reeducation I received.

Finally, Terra put down his binoculars and walked away from the edge of the cliff overlooking the plains where Christian and the Ozman met after the meeting was finished. The two of us had found refuge in a cave similar to the one we stayed in so long ago. I wondered if Terra remembered our time in that cave. It was not so long ago that he could forget, could he? The idea of being forgotten had haunted my thoughts greatly as of late. Had they told Rebecca that her sister Sariah was the Executioner, it was a common name, Sariah, so I figured she wouldn't think it was me right off the bat. I left her years ago to join the Crusaders and during my time with Clay's group, I heard she had joined as well, so I had yet to see her since I left home.

"Sariah," Terra began, "You're too easily distracted by miniscule concerns. We're on a mission to assure that Christian and his group succeeds in establishing the presence of the Word. We don't have time for you to lament over your sister."

How was he so calm about this? Did he not understand that we had been beaten to the point of death in order to essentially reprogram us? Now we were the handlers of some horrible task that we would have to do. Did he truly not care? What happened to the Terra that had a breakdown after he killed those people? Did the Terra I met die in that reeducation?

"Leave me alone," I said with my head buried in my knees. "Unlike you, I have no intention in becoming a pawn of the Order after what they did to us."

"I'm sure Clay would've loved to hear you say that before you killed him," he responded without an ounce of remorse in his voice.

Upon hearing those words, I ripped off my mask and threw it his way. I reached for my blade until I realized that Terra was the first person to see my face since the reeducation.

"Your face has healed nicely," he said. "Take pride in the fact that you didn't kill him of your own free will."

He was right about that at least. Soon after the execution I found out from Terra that we had been heavily drugged to the point where my actions on that stage were akin to a puppet being controlled. As my head continued to look toward the fire in the cave, Terra walked over to me and placed the palm of his hand on my face. My cheeks reddened at his touch and I could feel my chest tighten as his forehead pressed against my own.

"Terra, what are you—" I asked before being cut off.

"The Order gave us a chance to save the ones we love from the burden of sin from being a Crusader. I'll never forget the burden of death that has stained my head, and I want to save Christian and even your sister from going through that for the Order. The Order is supposed to be a perfect body that gives hope to others. I can't allow for the sins of those in control to stain the hearts of those who believe in it. I left my world solely to protect my brother in any way I could. But I'm willing to do the same for you if you can't handle that burden once more," he said.

I was overwhelmed by the kind of coyness and flutter that one feels when among those who speaks a tongue foreign to your own, a sense of loss and displacement. His words were so kind, so warm that I clammed up afraid…no more so ashamed of my selfishness and that any word I would say would ruin that beautiful moment. That was the true face of Terra, a face that no amount of reeducation could erase. I reached out for his hand by instinct but grabbed nothing but air as he pulled away from me, unconscious to the effort I had just made. He returned to his side of the cave and put on his mask, the sign it was time for us to work. He has every intention of saving me from the burden of being an Executioner. Just as he had saved me from the shame of showing my face to the recruits that day. Terra intended to shoulder the burden of protecting his brother on his own. Such a lonely burden. I ran to where I had thrown my mask and picked it up quickly placing it over my face. Surprisingly, I turned out to be a faster runner than Terra, a fact he seemed to care little. Without a word said between us, we dashed through the plains of the night as we headed to the settlement of the Ozman people Christian had spoken to.

Ozma was a class F world that exuded a primitive existence. The settlement we infiltrated was a small town hidden in a small valley not too faraway from our own campsite. As we made our way through the night taking cover behind trees, boulders, and tall grass, we found the majority of the townspeople to be enjoying a festival to a pagan god. From the look of things, the talks with Christian and his group had broken down from the sight of them burning Christian's gifts of a Bible and a wooden cross. As their merriment continued, we waited in a patch of tall grass as still as a lion stalking its prey until they finally wore themselves out. As the pagans slept, we quickly made our way through the site of the festivities and sprinkled a black powder on the skin of as many as we could.

The rest went without a hitch. By morning half the settlement awoke to burning rashes. None of their natural cures had any effect, but when Christian came to the settlement to speak to them once more, the advanced medical items he had on hand cured all ailments in no time at all. The people of Ozma, like ignorant children, praised Christian and his God that saved them and pledged their loyalty to Christ. As we returned to the Order, there were rumors of our involvement, but not even Christian knew or not if we had been there. I envied Terra for his strength as he roamed the corridors of the Order without his mask, but I could not do that. That time though it was not out of fear of rejection or shame, but I just wanted to keep it, the fact that only Terra was the one to see my true face.

21

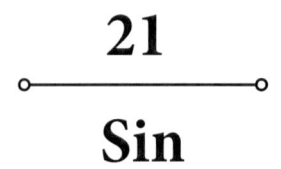

Sin

Sariah: Age Unknown
Location: Fiore

"I implore you to reconsider! The Word of the one true God is a force that can negate every ill that the people of your land suffer!" screamed out Rebecca with tears of shame spilling down her face. She continued pleading with General Borthose with nothing to cover her fair yet no longer innocent body but a thin sheet. As she continued to protest against his threats of telling the prince, their words became silent for me. My single eye was fixated on the whole scene as I peered at them through the slight crack of the door. My nails dug into the paint of the wall as I looked upon the stains of my sister's lost innocence on the sheet she clutched to. Next to her laid that vagabond Dom with a smug of pride despite the turbulent circumstances around them.

"You, Crusaders, come to our land and preach of the holiness of your Order and the righteous ways of your people who follow your God, and yet here you are children in my eyes defiling each other in such a way. You ask our proud people to forsake our traditions and gods that have been with us since I was a child, but you cannot live by the same creeds you wish us to accept. No! I refuse to allow my people to be mocked by mere children," proclaimed the general.

"Sariah," said Terra as he placed his hand softly on my shoulder. "I didn't show you this so you could mourn over the loss of her innocence. I showed you this because—"

"Because we now have a job to do after all then," I said with my voice slightly choked up.

"Are you able to handle this—" I did not allow for Terra to finish his question as I cracked open the door just wide enough to allow me to slip into the room. The eerie creak of the door alerted them all to my presence as I stood in the darkness only allowing the light of the flickering candle to illuminate my image.

"An Executioner?" said Rebecca with a startled face that soon turned to one of horror. The realization that I may had been there to take her out must had went through her mind. Though I could never blame her for thinking such a thing. It hurt deeply that my little sister conceived the notion that I would do her harm. I mean, sure, the whole wearing a mask thing would throw anyone off, but it was still my sister. Did she not feel my maternal-like love emanating from my body? Just what were we Executioners to the recruits of the Order? I knew that Terra and I were looked down upon as some sort of vile filth that were too attached to the worldly ways of sin, but did the mere presence of one of us create such a fearful tension in a room? As I took a step forward toward her, she took a step immediately back. While it was only a slight step, I felt as if she had jumped across an entire ravine in order to get away from me. Executioner or not, I was a Crusader same as her and yet, yet… my rage suddenly exploded as I turned toward the general.

General Isaac Stain, he was the leading military force of world of Fiore, a small city state, on the world of Acadios, a class C world similar to Earth from what I heard from Terra. It had been on the Order's radar for quite some time, and due to the extensive size many units had been sent across its numerous regions to covert as many as we could. Christian's unit had been assigned the task of converting Fiore, an impossible task that became plausible in the wake of a new prince ascending to the throne marrying a devoted Christian woman from a successfully converted village not too far off. While on paper, the union was a simple matter as the prince was fully for converting the city to the ways of the Word, there was an opposition forming that wished to retain the gods of their fathers and fathers before them. General Isaac was the face for that opposition. He had insisted that we Crusaders were devils that only cared for furthering our own interests through the conversion of Fiore and was hell-bent on finding a way to prove we were not as holy as we seemed. Sadly, my little sister and that piece of trash Dom she seemed infatuated with were the evidence he needed. I don't know how he found out about them, a secret that not even I was privy to, but now that he knew we were not only in danger of losing our standing in Fiore, but our lives could be in danger as well.

Delicacy I was sure that was how Terra wanted us to handle such a dangerous situation that could result in another purge if played wrong.

"An Executioner," said the general, "It doesn't take a clever one to see that you must be here to clean up the mess of your filthy little teammates have gotten into."

Delicacy was exactly what Terra would have wanted in that situation, but I was different than Terra when it came to my sister. Before he could open his mouth to say another word about Rebecca, I closed the distance between us with a powerful dash and ran him through with my blade. As if our minds were in perfect sync, Terra had already thrown two daggers toward the other two men stationed in the room with the general. I was sure I was going to get reprimanded for my action in the future, but at that moment the only thing on my mind was protecting the remaining innocence of my sister. The image of the general's blood upon my blade sent an image of Clay's body back through my mind. I could no longer rely on the fact that I had been drugged into killing a man to settle my conscience. That time I acted entirely on my own will. A feeling that felt surprisingly good. It was just as the Order stated: there was no need to pity the heathens of the world. Due to our moral righteousness, we were on a higher plane than them. I had always thought the plane they spoke of to be a manifestation of the ego of the Order, but I could feel myself standing upon it as I reveled in the fact I had protected the honor of a servant of God.

As I continued to soak in my victory, Terra took command of the room as he said, "Were there any others that saw you two?"

In a brash tone that I had come to expect of someone their tender age of fourteen, Dom replied, "Who do you think you are, Executioner? Don't speak to us as if you're our leader. There was no need for you to kill them anyway after all it would have worked out if we had faith right?" His little bit of sagacious wisdom made me sick yet made Rebecca nod her head in total agreement saying, "This is why you two have been removed from the title of being a Crusader. God looks down upon all those that slay the lives of His children."

"If you little brats knew anything about the Word then you'd know that he looks at all sin as equal to one another, so if He's looking down on us for saving your ungrateful lives, then I wonder how he thinks of you two little adulterous brats whose selfishness is compromising His holy mission." I said with a stern voice resembling that of our mother.

"Sariah, that's enough," said Terra. "You've said too much."

The mention of my name almost made me jump back as I thought he had just revealed me to Rebecca, but then my senses returned. Sariah was a common name for girls of the Order just as Ester, Ruth, and Mary were. The fact that I shared the same name of her sister would hardly make Rebecca blink or even think for an instant that there was a correlation. It was the times such as that when I hated the mask that obscured my true face. I was nothing but a tool of the Order in the eyes of my sister and who knows what in the world Terra thought of me.

"Anyway," continued Dom in the same smugness from earlier, "could you clean this mess you caused up and allow us to finish what we had started." He rolled over to Rebecca and slightly slapped her cheek. "This time don't be so loud, so your intense desire for me won't make us get caught again, you stupid girl."

"You're an idiotic kid," said Terra before he took a step back.

As all of Dom's attention was focused on Terra, I dragged his scrawny butt from the bed and threw him against the wall. Without holding back, I went to punch his face, but he managed to slip under me and crawl away right as my fist put a hole through the wall. Was I slowly becoming the monster that Rebecca feared so much? Perhaps so, but all I cared about was making sure that kid would never be able to use his tongue to say such words to my sister or touch her again. For a brief moment, I drew my blade.

"Terra, we may not be able to cover this up. Perhaps a dead body from our side as well will make whatever story we create more convincing," I said making direct eye contact with Dom.

"That would be unnecessary, but do what you want with the boy. Just make it quick," he said.

Dom turned once more to Terra as if pleading for his help would stop me, but I had leapt on top of his petite frame and began to bash his cocky face in with my fists. With every blow, I became angrier until I felt I was about to kill the kid. Just as I expected, I could feel a force pulling me off the boy, but it was not Terra as I had anticipated. I smiled as I was able to land one final hit, a small gash across his face that came from my nail raking into his skin. Once I had hit the floor, I saw that Rebecca was the one that pulled me off the punk. Before I could even complain, I saw the horrid sight of my sister coddling the bruised body of Dom in her arm. I could not even form proper thoughts that could express my torrent of emotions. Why was she protecting someone that regarded her so lowly? Before I could even react, another voice was introduced to the room.

"What in God's name is this?" asked Christian as he entered the room. I could only imagine how ridiculous the sight looked.

Three dead bodies on the ground along with two naked teenagers and Terra and I mixed into the scene as well. I stood up to say something but when I heard a shriek from Rebecca I stopped. I looked toward her direction and saw her clasping her mouth with both hands trying her best to muffle her sobs. I thought I had injured her at first, but once I heard Terra softly say my name I knew. My hand reached for the hard exterior of my mask but only felt the bare skin of my face. I was exposed. All of us had been exposed.

22

Inequity

Christian was truly better than the rest of us. Terra had always said as much, but it was not until then that I understood his meaning. Any other man with the knowledge of the ramifications of Rebecca and Dom's sin would have known not only could we be killed, but the Order would lose an important world and Christian could be exiled if he lived. With all of that a firm possibility, Christian approached the prince and apologized profusely for the incident and recounted every detail that Terra and I told him. I expected death for killing a general, but the prince was so moved by Christian's condemning honesty that in the first sign of his conversion to the Word, he "forgave us of our trespasses just as God forgives us for our sins." He meant to quote scripture there, but he was still new to everything.

The Order was not so forgiving.

Because the mission had still been completed, we were spared exile, but Terra and I had been sentenced to a labor camp on a distant world for a full month in order to make up for out lack of moral judgment and the murder of men of Acadios. The word that was spread through the Order was that Terra and I had been the ones to commit the act of adultery that nearly jeopardized the mission. The High Seven all agreed that for the sake of the image of the Order, we should be honored to pay such a price just as we should be honored we still have our lives…unlike Clay and Tai-lee.

Not much can be said for our stay at the labor camp. Simply put it sucked, and I was glad to have returned to the Order. That was what Terra said and what he told me to say, but that camp changed how we thought of one another.

Terra once told me that bonds between people were much stronger for those that had experienced hardships with one another. The realization and comfort that there was another soul out there that felt the same pain that you did had a much more potent effect on one's soul as opposed to the invisible bonds of those that share blood. His words were proven true as we labored together in those mines. Day after day we toiled in the dank tunnels of darkness with our only light being that of a flickering candle. For me the work was grueling, but Terra strove through it all with little difficulty. It amazed me watching the muscles of his body twitching as he bore his pickaxe down upon a rock with all his might. My own weakness when it came to the mines only made me envy him even more. Blisters had made a permanent home upon my hands and the grim of the caverns seemed to become a daily, unintentional makeup upon my face.

"If you keep that up, you'll end up being darker than me one day," said Terra as he bit into the daily piece of stale bread we were allotted to have.

"Perhaps, but I'd make a much better black person than you ever would. Come on teach me what does it mean to be black," I asked with more energy than I had intended to. I was still exhausted from the day's work, so even speaking had a way of wearing me out. I looked over to Terra whose smile had vanished after I proposed my question.

"Being black is simple. All you have to do is believe what others tell you it means. If someone tells you that you're worthless then that's blackness, if someone tells you're stupid then that's blackness, if someone tells you your existence is solely to enrich the lives of your white counters then that's what it is. There are a plethora of meanings to blackness all depending on what the power in charge of you says, so I'm sure it won't be too difficult to figure it out," he said resting his head on the gravel.

Terra had begun to tell me bits and pieces of his past during our time in the mines, a privilege that only Christian had experienced before me. I felt horrible that my playful statement had drudged up the memories of his painful past. His whole life seemed to always be full of some sort of pain. I could hardly see a time aside from Christian's time with him that he had a reason to enjoy his life. If I had to live through an ounce of what he endured, it was so that I would have broken down long before he did. But as I looked upon the peaceful face that seemed to exude no amount of anger at his lot I was overcome with a need to just comfort him in any way that I knew how. I leaned over to his still body and grazed his cheek for a moment before I lay down beside him.

"Sariah, what are you?"

I wrapped my arms around his waist as I could feel the continuing vibrations of other workers through the walls around us. The feel of his body pressed against mine was the first time I could have a genuine smile that I didn't have to force since we arrived there.

"Can we just stay for a while? I don't want to move till we have to work tomorrow," I asked as I buried my face in his chest. I could tell how tense he was as the rate of his heart had increased to a humorous level. Was a woman's embrace that foreign to him? It made me happy that the stoic demeanor of Terra had some cracks within his armor that I had nestled my way into. Unexpectedly, he wrapped his arms away me and said, "Please don't leave me, Sariah."

By that point I believe that we understood what we meant to one another. It was not the same kind of romantic puppy love that my sister had for the piece of filth, but rather it was an affection for one another out of survival in a way. To have to live the life of an Executioner alone was too daunting of a task. We needed one another to lean on in order to get through it, and if those needs correlated to our desires as a man and woman, I was fine with that as well. I was fine with anything that Terra wanted back then.

Our growing comfort around one another was the lone bright spot amidst our pain in that labor camp. It had become commonplace for the two of us to lay together night after night, a crime that I did not mind breaking. Simply put, I had grown tired of being the tool of the Order, and I wished to experience the same happiness and reckless abandon that Rebecca felt. Terra and I had done exactly what had been asked of us as Executioners, but our loyalty was repaid with this vacation to the labor camp. My frustration of the betrayal ignited my growing passion for Terra, and as the days went on, my mind was filled with more and more thoughts of him. Ending his pain became an obsession of mine as if he were a lost world in an abyss of darkness that I had to liberate. My obsession could give him no peace, and all it did was cause me further pain. Unlike the dramatic stories where I heard of such treacherous heartbreak, mine had seemed so casual that I look back upon it a tad disappointed. Perhaps I had achieved my goal and reached such a deep understanding of that man that when I saw him sharing his mat with another woman in the camp I felt no rage as I had with Dom. I felt not even the slightest bit of anger as I witnessed the next woman and the following ones afterward he brought to his mat. If anything, I felt pity for them and Terra. Whatever he was looking for, he would not be able to find it with those women and the comfort and companionship they sought was not something that Terra could give. I didn't know if I thought I could give Terra what he sought.

There was a time when I wished I could, and perhaps he wished for that as well. But our time together showed me that he was a broken man underneath all that rough exterior. He never had to say such a thing to me, but I could just tell that aside from the Order he was empty inside. They had given him a life away from the cruelty of his own world, so that was why no matter what they did he did not fault them. He faulted people for sin. He had always faulted people.

Aside from Christian, I truly wondered if there was any sort of love left in his body that he could give out. There were times, many times where he showed a softer side to me that he didn't show around others, and I was grateful for that, but it felt like I received nothing but the consolation prize when compared to his love for Christian. It was weird this competitive feeling I had toward Christian, a person I had yet to have an actual conversation with, but while I didn't care about the distance that had occurred between us, I still wished for us to share that deep bond he once spoke of.

The day did arrive when I felt that the emptiness that had consumed his soul began to finally recede. After several months at the labor camps, our punishment finally came to an end as Christian arrived with his unit to pick us up as we were released. The nature of his appearance there startled the two of us, but it was a surprise that meant the world to Terra even though he would not dare show it. As the two of us stood on the rocky terrain outside the entrance to the mines, Christian handed us our old masks. Behind him, I could see Rebecca standing close to Dom still watching with that same painful face I had burned into my mind on Fiore. Terra and I had made our resolution as Executioners long ago, so placing the burden of the mask back on was not something that was difficult, but for a split second we hesitated to grab the masks before us. Our hesitation was indeed brief, but as we went for them again Christian tossed the masks over into the current of a nearby stream.

"Christian, what are you doing?" asked Terra.

"While it pains me greatly to admit this, I lost two of my team the previous mission. They were staunch believers in the word and thus elected to stay on a recently liberated world to continue to guide the people. With their departure, it seems as though I have two open spots that are in need of recruits with some experience in them. I do hope that you'd consider the offer," he said with a smile that warmed my soul.

I looked over to Terra and saw his radiant smile plastered on his face as he laughed off Christian's offer saying, "I've seen the kind of king you are, so I think I'd like to pass on the offer. There's no telling what kind of trouble you'd get me into."

"Well I'm sorry. I thought you were a man of Earth, one that didn't mind a little danger in the job description. Sufficient to say, you would have to go through some additional training so you can learn how to interact with natives without killing them, but I'm sure you could get used to it…eventually," said Christian.

"Danger for you equates to babysitting for me, and my time in those mines showed me that I'm getting too old to deal with people like you," said Terra.

The two of them continued this banter back and forth until they were simply laughing hysterically for no good reason. I thought I had seen Terra's true face, but perhaps such a thing was only possible with Christian around. Curiosity began to reignite my obsession with him for a moment. If anyone ever asked me, I would tell them I joined Christian's unit as a way to look over my darling little sister but that was half the reason. Everyone in our unit had a reason for joining Christian. I, for one, wanted to see just what was so magical about this man that commanded not only Terra's loyalty, but gave him the key to the happiness I realized I could never give. Even with the title as his wife now hanging around my heart, I could still not find the answer to why only Christian seemed to make him truly smile. But that was the Terra that I once knew. The Terra that had succumbed to the beauties of the isle didn't need Christian or the Word to give him meaning. He looked toward the darkness of the world to guide his actions, and such faith in that darkness could only lead him into despair. No matter what actions he took, I knew I could not abandon him to his blind trust in the isle. Just as I had shouldered burden of carrying him to safety once, I would be ready to save him from himself.

23

Truth

Terra: 21
Location: The Isle of the Fallen

The original purpose of our mission had never changed? That couldn't be! My whole world had been rattled by those words. If that were the case, then the life of indulgence that I had been living was nothing more than a betrayal to Christian. Even when I had originally discovered that we had been sent to the Isle of the Fallen, it took some time for me to think that we had been exiled by the Order. I know that the Order and I had gotten off to a shaky start after the incident on Lactia with Tai-lee, but after that whole idea I had not done anything too wrong to deserve exile in my opinion. Still, once I had been told by Lucas and the others that my deepest fears had been realized, I didn't even try to resist the truth. It was like deep down I wanted to get exiled. Had all of my past feelings of resent and doubt of the Order resurfaced the moment that I landed? I had thought that my altercation with Tai-lee had eased those worries, but it seemed as though I was the same as I was when I was younger. The first chance that I had to run away from the life that I was trapped in I took it. Just as I had run away from home and from Christian, I ran from the Order.

The news that Stagg had brought was enough to rattle me to the core. As I tried to question him, my voice shook and broke on numerous occasions as I asked, "Explain yourself! What do you mean we had not been exiled? Talk now, Stagg!"

The man didn't have much time left in him. Even I could see that. His eyes were glazed as if he was already looking upon the gates of heaven for his judgment as he said, "Only Christian and I had been given all of the details of the mission. This, Terra…is another purge crusade just like Erque five years ago. I don't know the details, but something here had the higher ups spooked enough to call for a purge. After we made our fallout, we were to sow enough chaos on the island by killing their leaders and then make our way to the peak of Mt. Amerigo and send the signal for the other airships to come in, and well you know how a typical purge goes."

He was right. I did know how a typical purge went down. I could still remember the flames that had encircled the city as we killed the people of Erque, and my part had been nothing compared to the rest of the battle. I could not image doing something on that level to another world and without a definite reason at that. But even with that information, I was still confused why only Christian had been told this aside from Stagg. I understood the nature of that mission was not something we liked to brag about, but I was far more suited for that sort of thing than Christian.

"Stagg, why did you all keep this from me and the others? If we had known, we may have been more prepared for that attack."

"This was not just a purge," he said. "This was still a graduation test for you all. The Order wanted to test Christian's ability as a king. It was well-known your group was not the most righteous of our Order considering that both you and Sariah were once slated for execution, so the Order wanted to see if Christian could keep you all from falling into the darkness of the isle. It's the duty of a king to guide those to the safety of the Word. How could we ever trust him to save others, if he could not even save his friends?"

A test? Despite how much I hated the idea that we had all been blindly tested, the Order was right. If we had passed, then we would be full-fledged Crusaders with the responsibility of saving others from the darkness of the world. If we could not resist that darkness ourselves, then how could we ever save others? I thought back to all of my actions since I came to the isle, and in just a couple of months, I had broken nearly every commandment of our Creed. I had lusted, lied, killed, and even put other things before the Word. I was the very definition of an exile of the Order, and I had even enjoyed doing all of those things. Any other Crusader would have dedicated all of his time in finding and serving his king after he crash-landed, yet I spent the last couple of months coming up with excuses to put it off in order to enjoy the new life that I had found. I was nothing but a coward. Christian was all alone trying to carry the heavy burden of the mission on his shoulders while I gave into the darkness just as the Order would have predicted.

But just as with any primitive that we are sent to save, once the truth had been given to me, then I knew I had to make a change for the better of my life. I had to find Christian and help him…no, the idea of committing another purge made me lose all of my nerve. I had to talk to Christian in order to find out everything. Stagg was notorious for not telling me every detail I needed, so I had no clue of what to make with his information.

"Stagg, I'm sorry for making your mission harder on you. Do you know where Christian is? I have Rebecca and Sariah with me, so if we could all come together we could figure this out."

"Figure out?" He spit toward my feet. "There's nothing to figure out. You have your orders and so now it's time to act on them. The king of that last village was the last one on the isle, so they're leaderless and with your talent for blood, you could finish up the rest of the mission before nightfall."

"I'll be the one to decide what orders I follow here! Now tell me where's Christian's hovel!"

Stagg fell from the boulder to the ground and began to breathe heavily. He struggled to get back to his feet and leaned against the side of the boulder with his legs shaking. He only had a little while longer to live.

"I don't know. Christian said that it would be better if only he knew. I'm sure once you purge the rest of the town, then he'll come out of hiding. You still have a chance to redeem the name that both you and your father sullied within the Order. I suggest you take this information and make good use of it."

"You're right," I said. "I better make good use of the information that you know nothing else to help me, and your tight lips made me kill Dom and Reginald!" The fact that he couldn't tell me where Christian was had brought up memories that were unrelated but dangerous. I pictured Kita's throat being slashed again…and again…and again. I took a look at the wound that Stagg had once more and it reaffirmed that there was little he could do to live at that point. Once I realized that, I acted upon the impulse that had consumed my soul five years ago and drew my blade. With one quick strike, I slit his throat just as he had slit Kita's and watched as his body fall to the ground one last time.

Whether I was exiled or not, I had wanted to do that for the longest time. Besides, I had a feeling that I would need his head in order to get back on good graces with Lucas and the others since I did run away when they asked for my help. I unbuttoned my shirt and wrapped Stagg's head within the fabric. I looked upward to the sky so I didn't have to look at the severed head, but just the wet feel of it on my hands was almost enough to make me puke. I proceeded back toward Ataxia slowly. As I traversed back through the jungle, I thought back to Stagg's story about the purge. The purge that occurred at Erque had been called for by an "anonymous" source within the Crusaders claiming that there was a faction of people there that wished to convert to Christianity and be rid of the majority of the populace which was gay. The plan was simple. The Crusaders would bring in a large number of their forces and carry out a coup over the reigning king of that world. The new king happened to be a strong supporter of the Word and wanted nothing more than for his family to be wiped out. Well that was the official story. From what I heard after the battle, the new king had practically no chance in the previous line of succession to the throne, so he employed underhanded tactics to get the throne. The Crusaders were a well-known force among some people, and the fact that we had an army that could compete with any other world was a widely known fact as well. We promised that new king the throne in exchange for him submitting to the Word. It didn't matter if he truly believed in it or not, we just wanted him to publicly acknowledge it in order to get his subjects to get onboard as well.

By the time I came into the battle at the capital city, they had already killed the former king and placed the new one in charge. I had been lucky according to Christian. The purge had gone on for about two weeks or so. The initial phase was brutal as we had dropped in several hundred casings into the inner part of the city, and slaughtered everyone in sight as we made our way to the capital building. While that went on, all those unlucky enough to live by the pier had artillery shells and fire from the airships rained down upon them. At practically every turn, there was death and destruction. The outer part of the city was the only one that avoided the carnage of the purge. I looked up to the starless black sky and imagined hundreds of casings being dropped into Ataxia and the slaughter of everyone there that I had come to know over the last few months. I wondered if that happened, would I be spared, or would I fall in with the rest of the lambs waiting for their slaughter. Thoughts of going through a full-on purge raced through my mind as I finally returned back to Ataxia. Upon my return, I saw that several people were being attended to medically by both Sariah and Rebecca. It seemed as though Christian had left his mark on the village as he escaped. I wondered if they knew that Christian had done those injuries and that they were helping our enemies. *But why were they our enemies?* I wondered. Was it so wrong to go against the Creed of the Order? Hadn't exile been bad enough already? Why in the world would the Order call for a Purge against people that had already been punished?

Before I could take another step inside of the village, I was rushed by several exiled Crusaders all in uniform. They had their blades drawn and pointed toward me. It was no surprise. After their leader had just been assassinated, I was expecting some new security measures put in place. I had never really seen any of the villagers in their uniform outside of special occasions since I got there aside from Lucas, but I suppose I should have remembered that everyone in that village either used to be a recruit or was related to one in some fashion. The men that had their blades pointed at me must have been natural exiles because their form was pathetic. If I had wanted to then, I could have disarmed the majority of them but it seemed that I was already on bad enough terms with them so it was best not to provoke them any further.

I allowed for them to take my swords and when they went to take Stagg's head I allowed them to unwrap it as I said that it was a gift for Lucas. The men led me to the entrance of the temple. There was a cold chill blowing through the temple entrance which indicated that the amount of passageways built into the interior of the mountain must have been quite numerous indeed. I had always found it peculiar why there was a temple built into the interior of a mountain, but had decided not to delve any further into the issue before hand. In fact, due to the tremendous size of the mountain, I figured that at least half of the island was blocked off from normal passage by foot. I wondered if by passing through those caverns could I reach the other side of the island? The majority of the guards left once we entered the hollows of the temple leaving only the guard, Jared, with me. He was regarded as the most able of the Crusaders in the village since he had only been exiled recently as well thus his skills were still intact. The lighting within the caverns was a problem as there were only a couple of torches placed alongside the walls in order to illuminate the way in front of us. I followed close behind Jared who, despite the darkness before him, maneuvered through the dark halls without a second thought or doubt in his mind about where to go.

Our steps echoed through the cavern as we both proceeded onward without making a sound aside from the occasional dripping of blood from Stagg's head in my hands. I wondered who I would be meeting as we continued onward. Lucas didn't seem like the type to take over for the clown, so it would have to have been a person I had not yet noticed. The deeper we went into the depths of the cavern, the less likely it seemed that I had been lured inside to be killed. They could have done that at any time, so there was no need to drag me all the way in there. The thing that was eating away at me though was the fact I had to solely trust Jared to get me wherever I was going. I never particularly liked the idea of once more being dragged along by the whims of another individual, but I had no choice in the matter. The situation was made to be a further annoyance because of all of the obstacles that kept finding their way in my path.

The path we took was riddled with nothing but scattered bones and spiderwebs that seemed to gravitate toward me. While these distractions were mild, they certainly played their part in aggravating me. I became so distracted by my surroundings that I didn't even notice the fact that Jared was suddenly gone and I was standing in nothing but absolute darkness on my own. Before I could panic though, several lights came on and I saw that I was in crypt. From the decorum of the room I was in, I would have guessed that I was in the central portion of the crypt. Each of the shelves holding a body had been laced with golden fabric and fine jewels and the main coffin had been gilded with gold and imbedded with a fine assortment of jewels. Standing in front of that coffin was Lucas hunched over it like he had just finished saying his good-byes to whoever was inside.

"You came earlier than I had expected, Terra," said Lucas as he turned around to face me. "I see that you have brought me a gift. I suppose that's your olive branch for running away."

I unwrapped my olive branch and rolled it at his feet as I said, "Running away is such a crass term. I prefer to think that I was cleaning up the mess you all had made."

"You dare to insult us while the body of our leader is still warm in this tomb? With an attitude like that, I can see why you were exiled," scoffed Lucas.

The word "exile" had a bitter sting to it after I had learned the truth, but Lucas was right. The friendly atmosphere that we had once shared between us was gone as neither of us knew whether the other was a friend or foe. The gut-wrenching feeling that perhaps I had been brought there to die returned as I noticed a vacant shelf. Lucas did seem like the type that would rather deal with those he deemed as a traitor himself, but I could not see past the guile that he wore that day. Trying to see the true intentions in his heart was akin to trying to peek through a brick wall. No matter how much I stared at him, I could not see a glimmer of anything.

"So why did you return here, Terra?" asked Lucas. "I would've assumed that after your true king returned to the forefront that you would've followed him into the depths of hell just as any good Crusader would do."

"Well we both know that I'm not that great of a Crusader or I wouldn't have been exiled in the first place," I said as I walked up to the coffin holding the clown. I kicked up a small cloud of dust with every step I took. I looked upon the paleness that had taken hold of his face and continued, "I want the truth of everything. Christian was not the type to carry out an assassination on his own. We're sent here under the presence of liberating the island, not taking the head of one of its leaders. As you can very well imagine, such tasks would more so fall into my skillset."

Lucas drew his blade, a black Lionheart blade like mine, and pointed the tip at my throat. It looked like the idea to kill me had indeed been on his mind quite often as of late. With the tip of the blade prickling the skin of my neck, Lucas asked, "How am I supposed to believe that you had nothing to do with the Father's death? You could have easily slipped Christian information to aid him."

"Hey, I was looking forward to that fight with Stagg, so there's no way that I would've told Christian to kill him then and there and end my fun," I jested.

"I'm not playing games with you, Terra! With Father dead, every last king on the island is dead now!" exclaimed Lucas.

Now that was news to me. Every king was dead now? Despite how much I didn't want to admit it, it seemed that Lucas's statement aligned with the story that Stagg told me. If that was the case, then Christian was indeed acting on the premise that there would soon be a purge. I could see the panic in Lucas's eyes as he realized there was some sort of meaning to the madness of these executions, which might have explained why he hesitated in killing me. It would only be natural to assume that I was in on Christian's plan as one of his vassals, so I was either a valuable source of information or just a pawn that had been thrown away by my old king that Lucas could now use. Either way, it seemed as though I would be able to keep my head for a bit longer.

Another factor that I had going in my favor was the fact that I had returned to the village. The fact that I had returned is what must have addled his mind to whether I was a friend or foe. Not just me though, both Sariah and Rebecca were acting as though we knew nothing of Christian's actions which we indeed had no prior knowledge of, but Lucas didn't know that. I was wrong in my initial assumption that Lucas would not be the next one in charge, so it seemed as though he had taken the task of figuring out what would be Christian's next move upon himself. If the news of the clown being Christian's final execution were true, then it would only be natural to assume that Christian's goal was to break down to stability of the isle just as Stagg said. In order to commit a purge, the reigning power structure would have to be thrown into chaos which was exactly what he was doing.

 The fear that was in Lucas's eyes would soon be in the eyes of everyone in Ataxia if I allowed for this purge to occur. I remember the hatred that one girl I found in the general store had for me simply because I wore the uniform of the crusaders. I could only imagine the hatred that Lucas and the others would have for me if I actual helped orchestrate a purge. There was no way that I would sell out Christian by telling Lucas what I had learned from Stagg, but I knew the moment I saw how anxious Lucas was that I never wanted a purge to befall the people of this island. If things had been different, then perhaps my father could have run away here with me as a child and this place could have been my home. I had to find Christian in order to get him to stop his mission. I didn't know what reason why the Order instructed Christian to commit this purge, but I knew that if I had just the chance to talk with him then perhaps we could come to an agreement. There was no way that someone with Christian's meek nature would have ever condoned such measures.

 I knew that I had to choose my words carefully as I told Lucas, "If all the kings have already been killed, then it's safe to say that Christian will soon try to preach to the people to repent from their ways. It may be hard to find him, but as long as we have an idea of what his goal is then we can stop him."

 "We? You make seem as though I need you in order to hunt this man down. So tell me, Terra, what need could I possibly have of you?" Lucas stepped away from me and from the veins that were popping in his neck I could see that his anger toward me was real. His anger was understandable though. Enduring the rigorous training of becoming a Crusader was nothing to scoff at. It was during those brutal moments when not a single one of us thought that we could persevere onward toward our goals that the bond between brothers was formed. I was no stranger to such bonds. During my time with Christian and his family, I learned an important lesson: it was not the blood between people that strengthened our relationships, but rather it was the misfortunes that we endured together that really brought us closer together. My time among the Crusaders was no different. It was through the turmoil in hardships that were suffered together that the bond between us was able to grow to such an extent where we are able to die for one another in the field of battle, in order to strive toward such a ludicrous goal as liberating of people. Such sentiments were not mine alone. They were shared among many Crusaders alike. With that truth in mind, I could only imagine the rage that Lucas had toward me for I had abandoned the kindness that he offered me upon my arrival to the isle. Whether these people were exiles or not, they still strongly believed in several of the Creeds that made the union between Crusaders stronger among us. But it was that bond among us Crusaders which would allow me to get back in on the good graces of Lucas.

"Your trust is not something that should easily return to me. One of the key principles among us Crusaders is coming to the aid of one of our brothers when needed to. And honestly I had forgotten about that, but now seeing the body of the clown fresh before me caused by no hands other than my own king, I see that there is indeed a difference between his actions taken against the leader of this village in the actions that we would take toward liberating people."

"Oh and what actions would that be exactly?"

"As Crusaders, we've always taken a haughty stance above others, but such pride is absurd when it comes to each other. The people of this village are not simply barbarians that need to be herded like sheep and we their shepherds. They're individuals that we should respect due to the suffering that they've endured along with us as Crusaders and thus I desire to talk to Christian in order to find out what reasons does he have for aiming his blade against one of our own whether they be exiled or not."

Lucas seemed to examine me carefully searching for the smallest glimmer of falsehood within my words. I knew that no matter how pretty my words were that I could never dispel the notion that I may be secretly working with Christian away from him, but I could at least tell that his intense urge to kill me had now faded away.

"The Isle of the Fallen has a very delicate balance among it. And it seems as though your king is well aware of that fact and is systematically sowing chaos among the different regions. I am no fool, Terra. I can see the initial stages of a purge when they're in the making."

"Well if you already know this information about the purge then you already know where Christian's going to go next. It doesn't seem like he has signaled for it as of yet. In order to find him, you're going to need a team that can track him fairly quickly and that possesses the power to take him down."

"I know," he said. "Just like I know that no matter what I say or what threats I throw at you that you'll try to tag along to find him. I'd much rather lock you in a cell, but if you're to escape, then I would've another unforeseen element thrown into my plan so I'm done fighting you about this. If you really want a chance to uncover the truth of his actions, then I suppose that you and I will have to uncover the truth together."

"Well and a little help from the rest of my team. If you think that I was stubborn, then I should lock you in a room with those two girls and you'll really understand what stubbornness is all about."

"Locking me away in a room with two beautiful women. I think I can handle that kind of torture," said Lucas. "Terra, you're a two-faced prick that would betray anyone close to you as long you had a reason to justify it. I'm going to need that where we're going."

"And just where is that?"

"Have you ever wondered why the Order only initiates crusades from primitive worlds and never more sophisticate ones? I can assure you that these class A worlds are just as sinful or even more so than the primitive ones. The reason relies solely on the fact that the Order is simply one large church with an elite fighting force of orphans and volunteers. They have nowhere near the necessary numbers to take out a full-fledged world. But they're aiming to fix all of that with a conference on their home world of Olympus with all the other nations of that world. If the conference goes well, then the Order will have the manpower and resources to force the Word down anyone's throats. I don't know how much longer my people have until the purge, but I won't sit by and do nothing as they burn!"

"So what, do you plan to go to Olympus and simply kill the High Counsel of the Order in order to prevent the purge?" I asked. The moment I said the words though, I already knew the answer that he would give me. In somewhat of a panic over the idea of him trying to wage a one-man war with the Order, I said, "Lucas, even if you wanted to there's no way you could get to Olympus. You'd need an airship for that."

"That would be true if Olympus was indeed located on another world other than this one. As you already know, Olympus is a class A world that incorporates several other nations in its boundaries. It would not be far-fetched to say that a certain little island is also within those same boundaries," said Lucas.

As he said this, he pulled out a map from inside the tomb of the clown and laid it out on top of the coffin after he closed it again. I had seen that map before as it was a world map of Olympus, the location where the Order was located. There was only a slight difference in the map that I noticed as I saw the tip of Lucas's finger point to a small island in the corner of the map that I had never seen before. I looked at Lucas and instantly guessed at what he was trying to imply. The Isle of the Fallen, the island that had served as a ghost story for many years was in fact a small island thousands of miles of the coast of Holy Land of the Order.

"Did you really think that the Order would allow people they viewed as dangerous to have their own world? This island has served as none other than a prison that was in their arm's reach for ages," said Lucas.

"So this conference then…we have the means to actually get off this island and go to it."

"If the Order truly plans to purge us, then I plan to pay those guys a visit. If you plan to discover the truth, then the Holy Land is where we'll need to go. We leave in the morning. The Father and I always had a ship in the lagoon of the island that can take us to the mainland. I'll inform my men to get Sariah and Rebecca to pack their things as well."

"What of Christian?" I asked. "Aren't you concerned about him?"

"By my guess he's already fulfilled his mission, so I'm not going to worry about him until I get back. Our main focus will be forcing the Order to end the purge."

"And what do you plan to do if they refuse to end the purge?"

"They'll end the purge one way or another, Terra. I can assure you of that much at least."

24

Reformation

I woke to the gentle touch of Sariah's fingers caressing the rugged beard that was slowing growing on my face. I reached for her hand and found our fingers interlocking with each others as the rays of the sun made her hair glisten. She nestled her body closer to mine as she said, "So this is the day, huh? I never would've imagined that we'd be leaving the island like this."

I had told both her and Rebecca the plans of the purge, and Christian's involvement with it. At first, the two of them would not believe me but as I continued to persist, they gradually began to accept the truth. After speaking to them, I knew that I was not alone in my struggles with essentially siding with Lucas in this endeavor. We were all sworn to give our lives for Christian and the Order, but we all could not forsake those that we had come to call friend over the last few months. I pulled Sariah closer to me and kissed her on the forehead. The touch of her skin reminded me of how I betrayed our union with the daughter of the clown for essentially nothing now that the purge was upon us. As I thought back to my indiscretion, her skin became cold as if my betrayal had frozen all of the warmth in her soul. I felt guilty not because of the action, but rather because I did not regret what I had done. That night in the woods with the clown's daughter was one of passion I would not soon forget, yet there I was holding the only woman that had truly ever mattered to me in my arms and yet she felt cold. I tried my best to forget these haunting feelings as I asked her, "You remember the last time the two of us had to go to Olympus?"

She answered my question with a chuckle, "Do I ever. I still have the scars from the lashings that Tai-lee's men gave us on our way over there. In that way, the two of us are legends kind of. No other Crusader has ever been brought before the High Order and then allowed to continue service as a Crusader. As such we became the first Executioners for the Order."

"Continue service you say? It was more like that they forced one suicide mission after another in order to punish us. Their goal was to have us die like dogs in the line of duty, but we survived. It was hard but we survived mission after mission together and—"

"We fell in love because of it," she said, cutting me off.

I was startled when she said those words to me.

"Excuse me," I muttered out in shock.

"Let us not be coy with one another, Terra," she said. "While this marriage was one of convenience to further our standing on the isle, it was not one absentee of any sort of affection for one another. We've been through hell with one another and that has made us trust each other to a fault. Besides, I was stuck on an island and you were passably cute so…"

"Shut up," I said as I kissed her and got out of bed. It was a queer feeling of having someone say that she loved you. My own father had used those words seldomly. Now my guilt was even worse. Did I love her? I did not know. If I did then I would have gone through with the ritual of bliss so easily. Zion had said that my father loved my mother, yet he left her to burn in order to save his own skin. Were my actions some sort of hereditary curse or were the two of us just that selfish? I could not find the answer to that as well.

"I know you don't like to think things this far ahead, but do you have a plan, Terra? By going off with Lucas to this thing, we're really putting ourselves in deep water with the Order. We got by last time just barely with the Lactia incident by the skin of our teeth, but this is a whole new game. We could be branded as heretics and killed or cast into an even deeper exile than we are now," said Sariah with concern.

I was putting the finishing touches to getting my uniform on as I said, "Then what do you propose that we do then? Run away?"

"Is that such a bad idea," said Sariah. "In all truth, being on this isle reminded me of how tired I am of the Order. I volunteered when I was younger because I truly thought I would be helping prevent tragedies such as mine from spreading, but the Order's sole concern of power and warring against other factions that oppose us has only made me spill more blood than I care to admit. Life here on this island, away from the world of the Order, has been a true blessing. Even if we can't return here, once we reach Olympus, we don't have to stay with Lucas, we can use that chance to start over."

I buttoned the last part of my jacket and looked at myself in the mirror. My fingers played with the buttons as I thought back to the first time I wore that jacket as an official recruit. The Order had told me that my purpose was to help others and spread the kindness of the Word to every known world, but instead I found myself judging people based on merits that didn't coincide with those of the Order. As I continued to look into the mirror, I saw the thin pink scar that ran from my collarbone to my chest. I called Sariah and said, "Do you remember when the Order tortured us after we were captured by Tai-lee? For weeks, they drilled the tenements of the Word and the Creed into my mind as they pressed blazing rods of steel against my skin. Whether I wished to know it or not, the Word was etched into my body and I followed it obediently as well as I could. Is it strange that I didn't hate them? Of course I had my resentment for them, but I never hated them."

Sariah had gotten fully dressed herself by that time and answered me as she wrapped her arms around me, "The Order gives us only one way of looking at things, Terra. But you did hate them. You always have, but those worlds we're sent to with Christian as a part of our reformation…we saw things that made us believe in what the Order was trying to do. You said it yourself that humans were filthy selfish creatures that needed to be policed in order to exude kindness and mercy."

The memories of those dark times made me suddenly break away from her, "I'll meet you on the ship," I said as I walked out of the house. Although it was only a Monday, everyone in the village had gathered at the temple for a special service. Even Rebecca had decided to go in order to pay her respects to the memory of the clown. As I thought of dropping by there myself for a moment, I heard a whistle behind me and saw Zion motioning me to come over toward the jungle.

"I'm a married man now. We can't keep meeting like this you know," I jested as I leaned against a nearby tree. "So what's it that you want this time?"

"I hear that you plan to go back to Olympus of your own volition despite all the sacrifices that your parents made."

"I'm sure that you know why I must do this, so there's no need to judge."

"Do I? I don't even think you know exactly why you're doing what you're doing anymore. Without guidance, Terra, all you know how to do is follow the desires of your flesh, and I'm sure you must have quite a few desires by now."

I wanted to give her a retort of some sort, but I realized that she was right. I had never lived my own life until I came to the island. When I was a boy, I simply followed Christian around, and from there I took directions from Zion and Tai-lee on what to do in order to find myself. After that, I became the dog of the Order and did exactly as they bid me to in order to live a free life that I had truly never known. Even my actions on the island were guided for either Lucas's or Christian's benefits. I felt like I had just noticed the strings that were attached to my arm by my puppeteer. I thought of asking Zion what she thought I should do, but I had grown tiresome of not making my own decisions.

Even this whole business with the conference and the purge was by the whims of Lucas. Was I destined to be nothing but a cog in the machinations of the plans of others? As I lamented on these truths, I suddenly noticed that Zion had vanished. I took a few steps forward looking for her until I passed through some underbrush and walked into an open clearing. Within the clearing, I could only chuckle at the fact that in the place of Zion I found Christian standing there as if waiting for me.

Before my very own eyes stood Christian, my brother, friend, rival, and enemy. Looking into his eyes, I instantly knew that a peaceful solution for the purge would not be possible. He stood there with his blade drawn and his eyes keenly focused in on me. Though it was a surreal feeling to see Christian glaring at me in such a way, I could not blame him. Twice now I had decided to side with Lucas over his ways after coming to the island. The fact that he had his sword drawn when he saw me, the same man that killed two of our sworn brothers, was comforting in a way. It showed he had not gone soft. I would have lost some respect for him if he had backed down so easily to me. I ignored the possible threat of his blade and walked right in his face then I gave him a cold, ridged hug. I believe that we didn't even need to communicate at all from that point on. I could feel the disappointment that was overflowing from his heart at that time, and I'm sure that he could feel all of the anger I had built up for the Order over the years. It was strange to think back on all of the years of happiness and joy we had shared reduced to this. I was not able to pinpoint an exact moment when I decided to break away from him. It was a gradual rift that being on the island had created.

"Christian, why have you come here?"

"I came to get my brother so we could finish the mission assigned to us," he said. "We're tasked with liberating this island and—"

"Let's be honest with one another, Christian, by liberating you mean setting this people here up for a purge! I can't believe that you'd condone such means once again."

"Even if I didn't condone the means, why would I care for a sorry lot of people such as the ones on this godforsaken land? These are the same people that cheered for the death of Dom and who somehow warped your mind to thinking that it's okay to kill Reginald and treat it as though nothing has happened. With that said though, I still trust you and the fact that you have not returned to my side means that there may be some merit to these people."

His open mind to the present circumstances were a recurring trait that Christian seemed to solely possess a part from the Order. I was always aware of this little quirk of his, but it caught me off guard to hear him say what he said at that time.

"So does that mean you're not going to go through with the purge?" I asked.

"I have my orders and they're to eliminate the elements that would prevent the people of this island from accepting any sort of reform," said Christian in a cold tone that caused me some concern.

My hands drifted to the hilts of my blades as I asked, "So have all of those elements been eliminated?"

"They have…aside from Lucas that is," said Christian in a very curt manner as he seemed to wait for what I would do next.

"Brother, Lucas is simply looking out for people that he considers family. I beseech you to reconsider the actions that you're about to take," I pleaded as my hands slowly began to wrap around the hilts.

"And Lucas has taken something from me that I've considered family for quite some time. Terra, you'll always be my brother and I'll forcibly cut the hold this man has over you by force if I have to, but that man is a threat to the Order and to my team as you of all people should know by now."

That must have been why Zion spoke to me of following my own desires as opposed to those of others. I never would have thought that Christian would come for Lucas's head as well. I knew that if I allowed Christian to do as he pleased, I would be welcomed back into his graces, but that would essentially be the end of any chance to end the purge.

"Lucas has taken nothing from you, my brother. Everything that I've done has been of my own accord," I said with my hand still on my hilt as I began to pace back and forth.

"Despite the shaky relationship you have with the Order, you believed in the principles of the Word and most of our Creed correct?"

"It took some time, but yes you know that I came to respect the Word of the Order and the Creeds associated with it. While there were several times I did indeed break those Creeds, I did so with a regretful heart afterward. But you know all of this, Christian."

"I do. I know that you're not perfect, nor did I care for your misgivings at times because you always were sorrowful and understood your wrongs, but ever since coming here you've embraced the evils of your life as if it were a normal part of it."

"My brother, can't you see what this island has truly done for us or rather what it can do for us? It…it allows us to see things clearly for a change. The Word and the Order are not one in the same!" I began. I had no idea what I was in fact saying. The thought that the Order and the Word were in fact different entities from one another seemed like a foreign concept to me that I did not truly grasp, and yet there I was spitting it out like I had spent many hours meditating over such thoughts.

"This island has truly poisoned your mind, Terra," said Christian. "The Order is what gives us the Word. They're the ones that originally wrote the Word and thus they're the ones that know what to do with it."

"You know that's a lie! The Word is supposed to be the divine words of God chronicled by men, yet it's not the Word of God we act upon, but rather the interpretation and edicts of the Order that control the Word. Let's be real, Christian, this is the same Word that was prevalent on Earth and you saw how the whites there said that enslaving me and my people were justified by the

Word. That's the truth of all the worlds. The Word merely acts as a tool that the powerful can use to control people at their leisure. The pure Word of God has been tainted by the hands of man and altered for our own uses," I cried out.

My hands had let go of my blades as I flung them around frantically enforcing my points. Christian maintained a stoic look on his face with his own blade drawn, but I could see the level of frustration in his eyes as he spoke trying to withhold the anger in his voice, "You speak as if you have transcended and spoken to God himself about the hypocrisy of the worlds. You know nothing of being righteous! You've always looked to blame the world for the cruelties in your life and have always taken the first opportunity to pay back your treatment with blood. You saw yourself as a victim that lived above the Creed because of what had happened to you. Even when the Order gave you a second chance, your arrogance and ego clouded your mind and you continued to live as a hollow shell of a man blindly following the Creed of the Order yet never putting faith in it. That was your problem, brother. All you could faith in was me and without that you wavered in some sort of purgatory between good and evil. Those that are lukewarm for the Word will never find salvation. The Word is not a tool that you can pick up and use at your easiest convenience"

I lashed out and punched a nearby tree with enough force that the bark of the tree left multiple splinters in my hands and the red smear of my blood stained the tree. As I plucked the pieces of bark from my knuckles I said, "The more you say, the more that you remind me why I could not leave this village. You've been tethered to the corrupt notions spewed by the Order for far too long. The people of this island are a living testimony to the hypocrisy of the Order! The Order preaches on and on of accepting others and showing kindness, yet we ostracize our own for not believing as strongly as some do and throw punishments and scorn toward those that break the Creed, instead of love and forgiveness. How can you expect these exiles to follow the Order, if the Order continues to show a face that's only concerned with power, control, and conformity to the likings of the few powerful that control it?"

"I have failed you, brother. I was supposed to be a guiding light, but I have allowed the darkness of this world you taint your heart," said Christian as he raised his blade.

I drew my two blades as well as I said scornfully, "That's the issue with you, Crusaders. You all think that you're the light of the world and try to force others to be like you! Have you ever once listened or asked what I thought of this all? You've always just told me what's right and wrong without giving me the option to think for myself and when I did, I was branded as an exile. Lucas though, no, everyone in Ataxia allowed me to think for myself, and now you want to take that away from me. I don't want to hurt you, brother, but I'll not have you and the Order take away this peace that I've found here!"

"Peace?!" exclaimed Christian, "This place is nothing but a cesspool of sin where you can let the desires of your flesh run wild without fear of consequence. If you call this peace, then you are truly lost, brother."

"So I suppose that we've reached an impasse then, because I intend to make sure Lucas has a chance to stop this purge."

"Do you truly intend to fight your king that you've sworn loyalty toward?"

"I've already spilled the blood of my father, commander, and two comrades. I doubt giving you a few cuts would ruin my conscience," I said coldly.

I charged at full force, but I was fully aware of who I was up against. I weaved side to side to make my movements less predictable...not that I thought they were, but I wanted to be safe. My goal was not to kill him, but I knew how determined he would be to kill Lucas, so I had made up my mind that I had to incapacitate him. And in order to do that, I had to come at him like I planned to truly kill him. As I charged, I kept my left blade horizontally in front of my body while my right blade trailed down around my legs. When I was near enough to see his face clearly, I saw a tear roll down his face. I never hesitated, and I slashed my left blade at him. He jumped back and using the inhuman agility and grace that only training in the Order could teach.

I looked into the very core of Christian's eyes and saw that he possessed no wavering fear of our battle at hand. He possessed not a single doubt in his mind of his victory, and I hated it. I wondered how he dared look down upon my skills in such a manner. I knew that he viewed me as nothing but a roadblock toward his goal of Lucas's head, and thus I became dead set on shattering any belief of victory that he had.

With the rage of an animal, I lifted up my other blade and struck down upon his, but he continued to stand his ground. I then repeatedly hammered his defensive stance with both blades hoping to break through his defenses. Such a process though short was of very fatiguing to execute and endure. I was such a fool to blindly rush into battle with him. Not only was it a horrible choice because of my betrayal, but Christian seemed to have been made to beat me. The defensive way he fought was the perfect tactic against my strengths.

He patiently endured the rapid attacks I continually pressed upon him as he waited for just the right moment to counter. After a little while, I assume that he had gotten a feel for the timing of my blows. Unfortunately, there was a small window when neither of my blades was attacking him. The time period was ever so small, so I never imagined that he could hit it, but that's exactly what he did. I suppose that doing the impossible just fell into one of Christian's numerous skillsets.

During one of my brief retractions of both blades, he countered. He attacked so suddenly that I was frozen with shock. He quickly slashed his blade right as I jumped back to put some sort of separation between us, but it didn't work out as well as I anticipated. Without any wasted time, he followed suit and leapt after me. With his blade raised behind his head, he executed a full downward swing once in range. All I was able to do was halt his impeding attack by catching his strike with my blades by crossing them. The shear strength that he possessed surpassed any initial premonitions I had. My arms shook and trembled as I used every ounce of strength I had to hold him off from cutting me in two. When I knew that I could no longer hold him at bay, I had to rely on one of my classic tricks that Clay had taught me long ago. I simply jumped back while simultaneously releasing my blades' grip against his blade. He fell for it, and his weapon slammed into the soil.

With this being the first chance I had to inflict serious damage, I hesitated and allowed him to pull back away from me. He had always been a defensive fighter and didn't want to attack unless it was self-defense, but this was the first time I ever saw him take the lead, perhaps as an indication of the threat I was. He suddenly sped up and closed in on me faster than I expected. He raised his sword and slashed downward, but I pivoted my leading foot and spun right around him. I could tell this had caught him off guard. I took this chance to attack while his back was turned. I attempted to cleave him right in half, but he swiftly placed his blade behind him and blocked my attack. Because of the power I had led in for the attack, I staggered back a bit, which gave him the time to spin around and follow up his block with another attack. Fortunately for me, I knew that this was coming. As I regained some semblance of balance, I pivoted my foot once more and spun around to meet his attack with one of my own. Our blades echoed and rang throughout the jungle as they met.

After that, we thus began in a series of swift slashes and swings at one another. Only one with the keenest of eyes was able to see the amazing detail in our movements that kept both of us from getting carved by the other. The slightest foot movement after a swing, the simplest twist of the wrist, and even a seemingly pointless wink of the eye managed to keep us alive. If you weren't quick on your feet after you attacked, you would leave yourself wide open for a counter.

After what seemed like an eternity though, he made a mistake. He suddenly tried to thrust his blade through me right after he had blocked one of my attacks. Because of the sudden change in movements, his aim wasn't precise. He thrust his blade toward the outer edge of my torso. I leaned to the side so that his blade went under my armpit, which allowed me to apprehend the blade. While this move had caused me minor injury, I was now in control.

With him momentarily stopped as I still clung to his blade, I quickly dropped one blade and used my free hand to slam down on his arm with enough force to fracture something. I saw him wince in pain, so I knew I had succeeded. Because he was distracted with the pain, I followed up by hitting him with the bottom of my palm right in his jaw. That attack made him release his blade. I then tried to do a roundhouse kick, but he wasn't dazed enough to allow himself to be hit by that, too. He caught my leg in midswing and then began to twirl me around. I was helpless to stop him from spinning me, so I had to wait and just counter when I could. He let go of my leg and sent me sliding through the air into a nearby tree.

After the impact, my vision was blurred from the constant spinning and the ringing in my ear made me so incoherent I could hardly stand. As time went on, the images around me were becoming more coherent. I slowly got up and wasted no time and charging at him once more. With the idea of freedom from the Order still hanging in my mind, I let off a scream as I closed in on him. Despite the injury I gave him, he still picked up his blade and swung it as I swung mine as well with all the power we could. The impact made every bone in my arm vibrate thus was his immense power even weakened.

We thus began another flurry of swings and swipes at each other. This sequence was much different, though. Our blows were focused more on power than speed. Our aim ceased being to cut each other to ribbons but to rather make just a single killing blow connect. Such tactics were nothing but brute and far beneath us, but the injuries that we suffered had started to affect our movements. During our flurry, he caught me off guard and knocked away my blade. He took another slash for my head, but I ducked and then tripped him.

It was then that I noticed that my goal had ceased from just injuring him. Whether it was the adrenaline of actual combat, or it was my resentment for the Order being directed toward him, I resulted to being nothing less than a barbarian and picked up a large stone nearby and tried to use it and smash in his head while he was down. He flipped over his blade and struck me with the blunt end right in my gut. I gasped for air as he suddenly kneed me in the face right after that. I dropped to my knees and struggled to regain myself.

I slowly looked up and saw his mighty blade coming down upon me, but its course slightly changed during its descent. Instead of a surefire kill, all his attack did was cut me diagonally, starting from above my left eye and cutting underneath my right eye. This was how I would obtain my scar, the testament of my betrayal to Christian.

Blood dripped down from my face, but it never reached the ground. Every drop of my blood fell from my face and landed upon my necklace. As I looked up at him once more, I could see the same pitying eyes he had for me earlier. Nothing had changed; here I was nearly exhausted of all of my strength and completely at his mercy. He dropped his sword and slowly walked over to me. He picked me up by my collar and threw me down.

"Why!" cried Christian. "Why do you fight so vehemently for this sinful land? After all we've been through you would throw it away for this land!"

By this point, tears began to stream down his face as he dropped his blade. His back turned to me as he began to walk away, "Killing Lucas would serve no purpose for me now. Your soul has been captured by this land of inequity and his death would only further sow your soul into this soil. Cling to your evils if they grant you so much happiness then. I shall not stop you, brother. If you desire freedom so badly, go to Olympus and see the tyranny of the world without the Order or the Word. See the truth with your own eyes and once you do…you'll know what's right."

    Christian vanished into the thick of the woods not soon after leaving me to ponder over his words and the reasons why I had chosen to betray him and thus the Order. The pleasures of the isle were certainly sweet, but were they truly worth the rift that was created between my brother and I? As the blood from my wound continued to drip down my face, this question haunted me. A little while ago, I had fought so passionately for the freedom that the island gave to me, but now that the passion had passed and I was left with a hollow feeling of yearning. My hand wiped what little blood it could from my face and as I went to clean my hand in the grass I saw my bloodstained cross necklace laying in the grass. As I went to grab it, the sound of a horn bellowing in the direction of the village resonated through the jungle. That was the signal that the ship was readying to leave. I quickly got up and hurried through the thicket of the jungle toward the direction of the horn without giving the necklace a second thought.